Praise for David Angsten's

DARK GOLD

"A page-turner . . . for grown-up boys who lust for swashbuckling literary adventure . . . will take readers back to the days when a good book meant you stayed up all night under the covers with a flashlight."

—*Publishers Weekly*

"[A] pastiche of Crichton, Lovecraft, Jules Verne, and *Robinson Crusoe*."

—*Entertainment Weekly*

"I sat down with Angsten's thriller this afternoon, and I was still reading at two A.M. *Dark Gold* builds to a frantic and explosive climax."

—Royce Buckingham, author of *Demonkeeper*

"Taut and well-crafted. I couldn't put it down."
—John Scott Shepherd, author of *Henry's List of Wrongs* and *The Dead Father's Guide to Sex & Marriage*, and screenwriter for *Joe Somebody* and *Life or Something Like It*

"Thrills and chills . . . sunken gold, black magic, sea monsters, a beautiful Brazilian in a bikini—what more could you want from a summer thriller?"

—*Kirkus Reviews*

"A first-class roller-coaster ride of a novel."
—Nick Redfern, author of *Three Men Seeking Monsters*

"Like Benchley's *Jaws*, David Angsten's debut will once again chase swimmers out of the water. Fraught with shivering suspense and a hauntingly eerie atmosphere, *Dark Gold* grips with feverish intensity. As literate as it is frightening. Read it with both a silver cross and a speargun at your side."
—James Rollins, the *New York Times* bestselling author of *Map of Bones* and *Black Order*

DARK GOLD

David Angsten

St. Martin's Paperbacks

DARK GOLD

Copyright © 2006 by David Angsten.

Cover photo © Gary Bell/Zefa/Corbis

Library of Congress Catalog Card Number: 2006041714

ISBN: 0-312-93793-8
EAN: 978-0-312-93793-5

Printed in the United States of America

St. Martin's Press hardcover edition / July 2006
St. Martin's Paperbacks edition / August 2007

St. Martin's Paperbacks are published by St. Martin's Press, 175 Fifth Avenue, New York, NY 10010.

10 9 8 7 6 5 4 3 2 1

To my father—
simply the best man I ever knew

AUTHOR'S NOTE AND ACKNOWLEDGMENTS

To clear up in advance a potential confusion, let me state up front that I am *not* Jack Duran. Although we share a superficial physical resemblance, the fellow who told me the story that follows is no relation of mine, nor was he a friend or even a passing acquaintance. As is true of all of us at one time or another, the two of us were perfect strangers, brought together by circumstances only partly under our control. The shady nature of those circumstances is better off left in the dappled dark, but the result of our collusion is herein set out in sunlit detail.

Whether Jack's story is deemed worthy of retelling is now entirely up to you, the curious reader who has happened on this book. That collision of curiosity and happenstance has now brought another perfect stranger into collusion. I will take a positive view and declare in advance our triangular encounter a triumph of "serendipity." That triple-tailed term of the happy-go-lucky was derived from an antique fairytale, *The Three Princes of Serendip,* concerning three callow youths who in their travels discovered things they had not been in search of. Their story is a distant echo of our own and returns with something Jack now echoes to me, quoting a typically oracular pronouncement of his balmy brother Dan: "The fault line linking a coincidence of consequence may not in itself be a consequence of coincidence."

A wisecrack easier said than seen.

Now, with your permission—that is, with the continued

indulgence of your colluding curiosity—I would like to thank a number of people, all of whom were strangers once, hard as that is for me now to believe.

First, the uniquely self-made media mogul, Ken Atchity, a divine literary manager and devilish tennis opponent: Your prodding set me to this task, your enthusiasm kept me at it, but it was, more than anything, your friendship that sustained me.

Thomas Dunne and Peter Wolverton, the best of the few gamblers left in publishing: Thank you for offering me a seat at the table at such a wee hour of the night.

My friends at AEI and Writer's Lifeline: Chi-Li Wong, long-time collaborator and favorite femme fatale; Andrea McKeown, whose fresh insights as always were perceptive and pragmatic; Margaret O'Connor, my tender and tenacious ally; Michael Kuciak, youngest of the old-time Hollywood raconteurs; and the always helpful and reliable Brenna Lui, without whom we would all be in a whole lot of serious trouble.

This book owes much to its remarkably thoughtful and thorough copy editor, India Cooper. Also thanks to Captain Rick, who runs the best sailboat charter in Los Angeles and helped me to navigate treacherous waters; the sharp-eyed writer David Freeman, who guided me over equally treacherous terrain; my patient Spanish translators: Sylvia Resendiz and "Jilly Bean" Beronio; my dear friends Roy Freirich and Debrah Neal, two of the finest screenwriters in Los Angeles, whose opinions and support I prize above all; the writer, filmmaker, and photographer Dirk Wales, who taught me with his towering example what it means to be a man; and my wise and resilient mother, Ruth, who kept her faith in spite of the devil and thereby set another eloquent example.

One more person must be mentioned, a woman who, on our first meeting, my heart recognized as not a stranger at all. Without the seemingly limitless and enduring love I found in her, I could not have written this book; I could not in all likelihood have become a writer at all. You are my treasure, Joanna; you always stir my heart.

Lastly, I would like to speak for the late Captain Bellocheque, who, if he were alive today, would undoubtedly want to thank the brilliant Carl Sagan for his provocative book, *The Dragons of Eden*, which Leo literally stumbled upon while hiding in the stacks of the Hooke Library at his twenty-year college reunion in Oxford in 1978. Reaching even further back, I am sure he would also want to express his gratitude to the esteemed psychologist Marie-Louise von Franz, whose remarkable lecture he happened upon as a young man in Zurich during the fairytale winter of 1957.

—On second thought (Jack again), given that all three of these royals of Serendip have returned to the stardust from which they were sprung, surely the dear Captain is in a better position than I to offer his thanks in person.

the Author(s)

DARK
GOLD

Though in many of its aspects this visible world seems formed in love, the invisible spheres were formed in fright.

—HERMAN MELVILLE

Part One

VAGABOND

THE PROMISE

The last we heard from my brother Dan was a postcard he sent from Puerto Vallarta. He'd been traveling for three years without coming home, and a card in the mail was the most we'd ever get from him. Every now and then he'd drop a line or two, enough to let us know where he was—and that he wasn't dead. My mother always had that worry in the back of her mind. She thought he'd get killed out there, looking for whatever it was he was looking for.

He had trekked through South America, nearly every country on the continent, mailing local postcards from cities we'd never heard of: Guayaquil, Nazca, Porto Alegre, Belém. We'd check the stamp and postmark, then find it on a map. A year after he left he crossed the Strait of Magellan to Tierra del Fuego and sent a postcard depicting the town of Ushuaia, the southernmost city in the world. He spent one Christmas in the Amazon jungle with a tribe of Kayapo Indians. We only found out about it with a card from Barranquilla that arrived in early spring. For a time he worked with an "exporter" in Caracas, bombing around town on a Moto Guzzi and dining like a king at the Restaurant Lasserre. When the military clamped down on the Venezuelan drug trade, he moved into the mountains of Colombia to grow cocaine with a peasant rebel named Carlos Marx. My mother was uneasy, kept waiting for "the call." It never came, though she found out later he'd been jailed in Bogotá; they sent her a belated notice through the U.S. consulate.

After that he kicked around Central America, then worked his way up slowly through Mexico, starting with the Mayan pyramids in the Yucatán, up along the western spine of the Sierra Madres, and over to the resort towns strung along the coast. It was easy to pick up a temporary job: translator, tour guide, tennis pro, scuba instructor. He was just what the hotel managers wanted, a bright, friendly, athletic American, fluent in Spanish, and willing to work for Mexican wages—but Dan would get bored, wouldn't last long. He'd screw the help, sell some dope, collect his "tips," and skip out of town.

Postcards were sent home to my mother in Hinsdale, or occasionally to me at Grinnell. My brother had a talent for finding odd little photo-cards illustrating his eclectic array of stone-brained enthusiasms: bizarre insects and animals, ancient nature gods, local aphrodisiacs, and the favorite obsession—legendary lost treasures. Dan was a sucker for the dream of buried fortune. He imagined himself a latter-day Lumholtz, leading mule caravans through the Sonoran desert, sipping corn beer with the Tarahumara, hacking up the jungle in search of lost tribes and ancient artifacts. For a while he fancied Mayan relics and actually did join an archaeological dig, but shoveling shit out of pack-horse stalls and grinding coffee for grad students failed to fulfill his Victorian vision of the Grand Expedition. He eventually got himself arrested for trying to unload thousand-year-old Casas Grandes pots to a German collector in Mexico City. He had forged the certificates of provenance; the pots turned out to be terra-cotta knockoffs from Tijuana, aged in an acid bath. He mentioned this in a postcard he sent from Guadalajara. It pictured a dazzling glass-bead jaguar, a god of the Huichol Indians—the ones that do the peyote. No doubt Dan had spent a lot of time with them.

The card from Puerto Vallarta was addressed to my mother. She kept it in a drawer in my father's rolltop desk, the storage place for everything of importance to her life: mortgage papers, old photographs, stock and bond certificates, long-forgotten love letters, a brass monkey paperweight that had belonged to my grandfather, and all the post-cards ever sent by her errant eldest son. Her bony fingers tip-toed through the dog-eared stack of cards, picked out the one from Puerto Vallarta, and offered it up like an article of evidence. I glanced at the picture, a reproduced daguerreo-type of a two-masted clipper ship, then flipped it over and checked the printed logo: CAPTAIN SALTY'S PRETZEL STICKS. How this little promo card from a snack company in Terre Haute, Indiana, ended up in Mexico, I had no idea. Dan had scribbled a typical line, one that prompted more questions than answers: *"I've found the mother lode—we're going to be rich!"* He signed it as he always did, *D.J.*, for Daniel James. Dan Duran, the vagabond man.

"It doesn't mean anything," I told her. I could see she wasn't sleeping well and feared it was her dreams, the "mes-sages" she said were delivered in her sleep. These were in-variably dark and disturbing, full of things you didn't want to hear at five in the morning as you were heading off to work. My mother was a sweetheart, sensitive and kind, but her psychic intuitions I often found unnerving. She could see shadowy things in me I didn't know were there. "You're always running off, John. What are you running from?"

This morning I felt her very presence was invasive. She was wearing the same frilly-necked robe she had worn for as long as I could remember. It gave off the scent of a stale per-fume that reminded me of something I couldn't quite recall—or didn't want to. Why was she always floating in a cloud of that perfume, an aging widow alone in her house?

She pointed to the date on the postmark. "That's nearly four months now, and not a single word."

"It's happened before," I told her, though it wasn't really true. The longest we had ever gone without a postcard was the three months he was locked up in the Bogotá jail.

"Something's wrong, John. I can feel it."

My mother always had feelings about things. Unfortu-nately the feelings were usually right. "Don't worry," I said. "He's probably up in the mountains with the Indians again. They don't sell postcards."

She took back the card, stared at the ship. "He's not in the mountains."

I didn't think so either, but I didn't want to admit that anything was wrong, not even to myself. I was always favoring the brighter side of things. "We'll find out soon enough," I said. "What do you bet we get a card within a week?"

My mother didn't answer. She wouldn't bet on anything, especially on Dan. "When are *you* leaving?" she asked. One vagabond son seemed torture enough.

"End of the month. When we finish Mr. Madigan's." My friends and I had at least ten days' work left, painting the humongous house of my ex-girlfriend's just-divorced uncle. We'd been painting houses in the western suburbs of Chicago every summer during the last three years of college. Now we had graduated and were at it again, rising every morning at the crack of dawn with dried paint under our fingernails and dull headaches from polyurethane fumes. Faced with an eighty-foot-long, three-story wall of cracked and curling paint, we'd guzzle the Starbucks, suck on a joint, crank up the Goo Goo Dolls, grab our razor scrapers, and go to work. If we had learned anything at school during the course of the year, it was undone by the stupor of those mind-numbing days. I could feel my feeble brain cells slowly burning off.

The monotony of mindless work fed a growing wanderlust. We envied my brother's nomadic freedom and his talent for avoiding manual labor. We began to talk about traveling ourselves, saving up our hard-earned cash and taking off for a month or two. Hawaii, maybe. Or Tahiti. Or Thailand. Or Tibet. None of us was ready to get on with our lives. Duff was putting off law school. Rock had broken up with his girlfriend at Brown and was fully occupied licking his wounds. I was debating graduate school and didn't want to commit, not yet. What was the hurry? What was the point? The world was hardly clamoring for another grad in English lit.

In the dog days of August, dripping with paint-flecked sweat on the second-floor scaffolding of that blazing south wall, an idea swept over us like a blast of arctic air. Why not go all the way? A big trip, the biggest—all the way around the world. Southeast Asia, India, Istanbul, Prague. Start with a month in Hawaii and end with a week in Spain. Four months total, maybe six. What the hell, maybe a year—who could say how long we'd last? We'd trek the globe until we ran out of money or ran out of luck. This could be our great adventure, a swan song to swift-passing youth, a final stab at freedom, a last hurrah before the curtain fell and the church bells rang and the baby and the bills and the mortgage came due.

We began at once to plan and prepare. We bought hiking boots and backpacks, studied maps and guidebooks, scoured airfares on the Web. I sold my trashed-out VW van and traded the cash for traveler's checks. Rock borrowed his hang-gliding brother's GPS handset, bought a shortwave radio aptly named the Global Explorer, and ordered a used videocam for a hundred bucks on eBay. With his mind as usual on food and fornication, Duff limited his purchases to a Zebco collapsible fishing rod and a carton of lambskin rubbers. By the time we had finished off the Madigan job, we were ready to pick up the old man's check, buy our tickets to Honolulu, and kiss the suburbs good-bye.

But another two weeks had passed without a word from Dan. My mother awaited the mail in vain. Troubling nightmares ruined her sleep and left her pale and anxious. I found her at dawn on my last day of work, fallen asleep at the rolltop desk. The look in her eyes when I woke her up stuck in my head like a voodoo curse.

I had seen that look three years before, on a snowy night in December. My mother had been frightened out of her sleep by a terrible premonition. A few hours later we learned that my father had been killed in an auto crash. An SUV with a drunk at the wheel had slid through an icy intersection and slammed into his passenger door. My dad was riding shotgun and never saw it coming. He was busy talking to the guy at the wheel. The guy at the wheel was my brother Dan.

Dan was in his final year at the University of Chicago, an honors student in anthropology, minoring in Spanish. My father had picked him up from campus to bring him home for

Christmas. Miraculously, Dan emerged from the mangled Ford without so much as a scratch. A week after the funeral he went back to school. I thought he was doing all right, but halfway through the semester he quit and moved back in with my mom. He let his hair grow, stopped shaving, and ended up wandering the house in his pajamas.

The arrangement didn't last long. Seeing the look in my mother's eyes made me understand why. My mother had powerful feelings, and if you were her son, the feelings eventually migrated to you. Her love for my father had gone that way, into us and through us, wrapping itself around us like a flowering vine. When he died, the vine died, leaving around our broken hearts a brittle bark of grief. It hung in the air like the wilted scent of her perfume, reminding you that when someone was lost he was lost forever, that nothing you could say or do could ever bring him back, no matter how hard you tried or how far you went looking.

Of course, that didn't stop you—the feelings were too strong. They grew and festered and overwhelmed. They haunted you and sent you to the corners of the earth.

That's what had happened to my brother Dan. Now I could see it was happening to me.

I made my mother a promise that we'd find her other son.

SAND FLIES

It must be the heat that gets them going. They started the moment I felt sunlight on my cheek. By the time the shadows had crawled off the beach, I was ready for murder.

"Motherfu—!" I started to shout, and quickly stopped myself. I'd been trying to curb my swearing habit. I yanked the sleeping bag over my head and grumbled to myself.

A shriek shattered the air beside me. Duff tore loose from his nylon cocoon to rant and rave and wreak revenge. I peered out the hole at the top of my bag as he staggered past, flailing his arms like a lunatic. He was wearing only his underwear, revealing an ugly scar on his belly that looked like an old war wound. Some hack surgeon had pulled out his appendix when Duff was a little kid. From the look of the scar, the guy must have opened the flesh with his bare hands. Watching Duff go spastic now, I began to wonder if the surgeon had stuck something else back in—a leaky battery maybe, or a time bomb with a ticking clock.

A pair of troll-like feet appeared. They belonged to the Rock, a gap-toothed giant, standing bare-chested against the sky. He lifted the video camera in his fat little fingers to make a record of my suffering. Duff joined him, taking hold of a driftwood microphone the size of a baseball bat. "The body of an American refugee, identified as the illiterate house painter John 'Jack-off' Duran, was found on a beach in Puerto Vallarta this morning. After a shameless night of drinking and debauchery, it appears he was eaten alive by a ravenous swarm of Mexican sand flies, known to have a taste for alcohol in the blood."

"Illiterate. That's a low blow, Duff."

"The dead speak!"

"Go away," I said, retreating like a turtle. My head was splitting, and the light hurt my eyes. "And turn off those fucking waves." The surf had been blasting the shore all night. It sounded like the bombing of Baghdad.

Duff took the camera from Rock and aimed it at him as they headed for the water. "The bloated body of a second American was found washed up on shore late this afternoon. Authorities stated that Brown University football dropout Roland 'the Rock' Redick had apparently gained too much weight after getting dumped by his lesbian girlfriend—"

Rock grabbed the driftwood out of Duff's hand. "And Alfred U. flunky Bobby McDuff got the living shit beat out of him—"

I stuck my head out to watch the loping giant with the caveman club chase the diapered cameraman halfway down the beach. I was committing this precious moment to memory when the two of them came to a sand-spewing halt.

Crossing our otherwise empty beach was a long-limbed, deeply tanned, exotic-looking young woman. She wore a Popsicle pink tank top and a curving white thong. Her black hair was wrapped up in a baby blue bandanna, and half a dozen silver bracelets rattled on her wrist.

Duff and Rock stood gaping like the dumber two of the Three Stooges. Rock, nonchalantly twirling his club, glanced back to see if the third Stooge was watching. I acknowledged with a wave. Blithely unaware that he had on only Jockey briefs, Duff lifted the video camera to capture the passing female as she sauntered toward the shore. She seemed completely indifferent to them, as though the scarbelly camcording her and the sunburned fullback swinging his club were of no more consequence than the pesky little sand flies flitting about her beach.

A wave crashed down with a foam-filled splash that crept up over her feet. The cold of it made her legs go straight and her ass primp up like a Vargas girl's. Rock whispered something to Duff as he filmed, and Duff slowly nodded his head. Shielding his eyes from the sun, Rock looked back again and gave me a thumbs-up. Apparently Lucky Duffy had immortalized the moment.

I decided, headache or not, it was time to get out of bed.

The girl pulled off her tank top and tossed it onto the sand. This left her in a white bikini top with a string tied behind her back and another behind her neck. She slipped off the bandanna, dropped it on top of her shirt, and shook her head, sending to her shoulders a tumble of midnight curls. Then she looped her fingers into the bikini cups, tugging them up snugly beneath her breasts. This seemed to do more for me than it did for her. Apparently unsatisfied, she began to retie the string around her neck.

At least, that's what I thought she was doing. In fact it was quite the opposite.

First she untied the neck string, then she reached for the back. It wasn't easy finding the end dangling down her spine. I slowly rose to my feet, as if I were thinking I should offer to help—but she found the end soon enough all by herself and, with a sharp tug, untied the knot, slipped off the top, and tossed it onto the pile.

My headache vanished. Duff lowered his camera and plopped down on the sand. He had suddenly become aware of his Jockey shorts.

She went into the water then, diving bare-breasted straight through a towering wave. In no time she was beyond the surf and swimming out to sea. Was she doing this for exercise, or was this some form of torment designed especially for us? The guys watched her for a while, then crouched beside the abandoned tank top, the white bikini, and the blue bandanna, poking at them in a way that reminded me of the apes in *2001*.

"You missed it," Rock said when they had drifted back to me. "Should've seen 'em up close."

"Guess I'll have to catch the video."

Duff searched through Rock's duffel bag, pulled out a

pair of binoculars, and scanned the jungle covering the hills. "You think there's more where she came from?"

"Give me those," Rock said, grabbing his binoculars out of Duff's hands. He aimed them out to sea. "Broads like that don't grow on trees."

I had known the Rock since we went to kindergarten together. He talked like Edward G. Robinson even as a five-year-old. Looked like him, too.

"Can you see her?" I asked.

"Yeah, baby, and she's doing the backstroke."

Duff stood beside him, searching the waves. "Give me 'em, Rock."

"Fuck you, get your own."

I reached for them. "Rocky, let me see." He held on with an iron grip. "C'mon, Rocko."

Continued badgering forced him to relent. I looked through the glasses and spotted the girl. She was swimming steadily away from shore. "You lied about the backstroke," I said.

Duff was getting impatient. "Let me see, Jack."

"Keep your shorts on," I said. "She left her clothes down there. She'll be back soon enough."

"Maybe not," Rock said. "Look where she's going."

I panned the binocs out ahead of her, and the view filled with a sleek white hull. I lowered the glasses and squinted at the sailboat out in the bay. The long, magnificent schooner had been quietly anchored there all night.

Duff grabbed the binoculars from me. He looked through them without saying a word. Rock and I peered at the deck of the boat, where a dark figure appeared with a dog at his side. The girl was barely visible in the water nearby.

"Who's that?" I asked. "Is it a guy?"

"Oh my God," Duff said.

"What's the matter?"

"You're not going to believe who it is."

"Give me those," Rock said, but Duff pulled away. "Who's the guy?" Rock demanded.

Duff continued staring through the glasses. "Idi Fuckin' Amin, that's who."

"He's a black guy?" I asked.

Rock jerked the binoculars away from Duff. He took a bead on the guy. "Idi Amin my ass."

"He's sailing around the globe," Duff said. "Free as a bird." Duff had a thing about Idi Amin. He had taken some course in African history, and the former Ugandan dictator had become a favorite villain of his. "Pig murdered half a million people," he said. "Now he's wearing a smoking jacket and lounging around on a yacht."

"It's a caftan he's wearing," Rock said. "And he's not more than sixty years old. Idi's got to be ninety."

"It looks like he's eating something," Duff said.

"Yeah, he's eating," Rock said. "He's like, slurping."

"He's probably eating oysters," Duff said. "Idi likes oysters."

"It's not Idi Amin," Rock said. "It's just some rich black asshole." Rock handed me the binoculars without my even asking. Apparently the sight of this opulent rival had diminished his interest in the girl. He started packing up his sleeping bag.

I watched the bald-headed dictator eat his oysters while the black dog sat at his feet, then I spotted the girl climbing up the ladder at the stern. She stepped onto the deck, tilted her head back, and took her hair in her hands. As she wrung out the water, I got a beautiful view of her upturned breasts.

"What's going on?" Duff asked.

"Nothing," I said.

Another woman emerged on deck with a towel around her neck.

"Who's that?" Duff asked. "Is that another chick?"

The woman was thonged and topless and, from what I could tell, even hotter-looking than the first. She had auburn hair and wore big black sunglasses. She was tall and slender, almost skinny, but her breasts were so large and perfectly formed I wondered if they were fake. I was trying to make

up my mind about this as I watched her dry off the girl from
the beach.

"I think . . . Yeah . . . I think maybe . . . I think it might
be another ch—"

Rock reappeared in a flash, tearing the glasses out of my
hands. He trained them on the girl. "Jesus," he said
solemnly.

This had a predictable effect on Duff. He pleaded and
begged Rock for a look, but Rock would have none of it. The
horny monster fullback who had been dumped for an
African American lesbian social worker from Greenville,
Mississippi, was busy sailing off on a magic ship staffed
with half-naked Victoria's Secret models who toweled you
off, brought you oysters, and took you below for pleasures of
the flesh that were probably illegal on land. In this seagoing
fantasy world, values like friendship and sharing carried little weight. Duff got pissed off and started making threats,
but Rock knew the threats were empty. Rock was bigger and
stronger than Duff and me put together, he owned all the important gear, and he always seemed to know what to do and
what not to do in any given situation. Usually two steps
ahead of us, he always kept his priorities straight, and beautiful young women with bare breasts were right up there on
top. So he took his time watching the threesome on board
and waited until Duff had exhausted himself before finally
releasing the specs.

"Where's Red?" Duff asked as he scanned the deck.
"Where's Idi?"

I couldn't see anyone at all on the boat.

Rock was stuffing his bag in his pack and jerking at
straps. He seemed a little upset, though it was hard to tell
whether it was the overflowing backpack that aggravated
him or the scene he had just been privy to. "They went down
below," he said. "The other one's sunning herself on deck.
She's lying on her tanned little tummy now, so there's nothing more to see. So let's get the fuck out of here."

He hefted his backpack and walked away.

"What's with him?" Duff asked, still peering through the binocs.

I thought it might be envy, or suspicion, or maybe nothing more than frustrated lust. "Who knows?" I said. "With Rock it's always something."

Rock stopped at the spot where the beach girl had discarded her clothes. He picked them up and stuffed the bikini top into his bag. Then he carried the tank top and the bandanna back over to us.

"What are you doing?" I asked.

He tossed the tiny pink tank top to Duff and the baby blue bandanna to me. "Souvenirs," he said.

We couldn't have the girls, but at least we'd have our memories.

Duff held the teensy-weensy tank top to his chest, utterly baffled. "How is it possible? Somebody tell me how."

I started to pack the bandanna, then stopped and pressed it to my nose. The soft scent of it tickled my spine like a feathery tumble of curls. I rolled it up and tied it around my head. When I looked up, I saw the Rock watching me.

"Ready, Geronimo?"

I hoisted my backpack. "Ready, Rocko."

"Let's go find your goddamn brother."

SKULLHEAD

W e'd been looking for Dan for a week and a half, scouring the town during the day and crashing on the beach at night. Bars, hotels, restaurants, resorts—we tried every spot he might have stopped into or worked at or stayed in or run from. Some days we'd split up, fan out over the city; some days we'd go together, hit the big resorts. We each carried one of the photographs I had brought along from home: Dan, age nineteen, posing like Brando on his junkyard Harley; Dan, age twenty-one, lolling on the Ferris wheel out on Navy Pier; Dan, age twenty-two, his Charlie Manson phase, wild hair and Taliban beard, donning dive gear on a skiff off Key Largo. We'd show the photograph to the guy at the front desk or the waitress in the café, asking in butchered Anglo-Spanish if they had seen this gringo sniffing around the hotel or stopping in for a drink. If they spoke English, we might get an answer; none of us spoke Spanish. Most often we'd get the sympathetic head shake or the curt, indifferent no. Several times we got a *sí*—one quite enthusiastic—but all of them were mistaken IDs, dead ends more disheartening than a day full of nos. We started at the top resorts and worked our way down, eventually hitting every two-star hotel and taco joint in town. In Puerto Vallarta, that's a lot of legwork; the guys were losing interest. Nine days in, they were ready to quit. I was getting desperate.

"You're obsessed," Duff said. "You got a one-track mind. You're like that monster with only one eye."

"He's right," Rock said. "We gotta move on. I'm sick of this fucking place." Rock had hated Puerto Vallarta from the very first day. Somebody had stolen his carry-on bag and made off with his brother's GPS handset and the shortwave he had never even had a chance to use. I couldn't help feeling that he blamed it on me.

"Just give it a couple more days," I said. "Nothing turns up, I promise we'll go."

None of us wanted to blow his wad in Mexico when we had a world of traveling to do, but it was the off-season; the weather was hot and the resorts half empty. It was easy to freeload and live on the cheap. We'd pick a hotel in the morning after sleeping on the beach all night, pay the concierge a few pesos to stash our stuff, and chill out at the pool or the beach as if we were registered guests. At night we'd join in the flow of people strolling down the Malecón, the promenade that ran along the edge of the water where the heart of the city met the moonlit bay. It was always crowded with tourists and locals, young and old, gay and straight, eyeing one another the way people do in a town built for pleasure, where everyone's a stranger yet familiar all the same.

For us it became a prowling ground. The Mexican tourists and the local girls wouldn't give us the time of day, so we'd hit on the Americans: California college girls on their end-of-summer binge, or wayward teenaged daughters with hotel wristbands, girls who had slipped off into the city while their resort-prison parents sucked their "free" margaritas and stared in a stupor at the mariachi band.

"The one with the hair looks like Daffy Duck," I said. "The other one must have left her Prozac back in Prettyville."

"Good," Rock said. "Chicks on Prozac never get horny."

We were tailing two teenaged blondes, maybe seventeen or eighteen, a pretty one with a grumpy sneer and a bright-eyed one with cornrowed hair and lips that puckered out like

a duck's. We followed them across the street into one of the
neon bars that tourist girls seemed attracted to like buzzing
bees to honey, a campus bar airlifted into Mexico from some
Nebraska football town, blasting American rock tunes and
mimicking big-city sexual hype with mirrors and glass and
flashing lights. It all felt tired and strained to me, but I followed along as we crowded in beside the girls at a grubby
table littered with overflowing ashtrays and spilled beer.

Duff hit on Grumpy the moment we sat down. He pulled
out a photograph and gave her the spiel—only he told her it
was *his* brother we were looking for.

When Grumpy didn't respond, Daffy spoke up. "That is
so sad," she said.

She had an accent. Turned out the girls were French
Canadians from Montreal, staying at one of the cheaper hotels that catered to the Québecois.

I asked them if they'd like margaritas.

Grumpy looked offended. "What makes you think we
want margaritas?"

I shrugged. "I don't know. You look thirsty?"

Daffy smiled brightly. "You must be *psychic*. I'm *dying*
for a margarita."

I told Daffy my mother used to make her living as a psychic. It sounded like a line, but it happened to be true.

"Why did she stop?"

"I guess she didn't like what she saw. Divorce. Poverty.
Cancer. Death. She said she could never tell people the
truth."

This, it turned out, was not the sort of thing to tell a
bubble-headed teenager intent on an evening of light flirta-
tion. She never said another word to me that night. By the
time the waitress appeared with our drinks, her attention
had turned completely to Rock, who was telling her that
with all his high-placed connections, he could—without *too*
much trouble—help put her admission form into the right
hands at Brown.

Meanwhile, Duff had launched into high gear with the
beautiful Grumpy. He had taken some French classes at Al-

fred and had finagled his way into a study abroad program in Montpellier for a semester. French was probably the only thing he had ever learned at college, and I suspect it was only for use on occasions like this, but as he sputtered on to Grumpy in a tortured version of her native tongue, her scowl remained firmly in place. Daffy explained: The girl was the casualty of an exploded nuclear family; her philandering father thought a vacation with his daughter might help expunge his guilt. Daffy was her friend, brought along to help Grumpy have a good time.

She wasn't. It was clear that nothing would make this girl smile, yet Duff, with his inimitable logic, believed the recent upheaval in her family made her all the more susceptible to his garbled efforts at seduction. He would use her anger and resentment to kindle the fires of passion. His latent mastery of French would incite an insurrection, condemning Monsieur Grumpy to the guillotine while winning his sullen daughter over to the swashbuckling American who lived only for romance and slept out under the stars.

By this time Rock had grown enamored of Daffy's lips. I watched him offer to share with her his gigantic, bowl-sized strawberry-guava margarita, which he told her was so much better than the boring one I had bought her. She seemed so delighted, I thought at any second she'd start waddling around in it.

I polished off my shot of tequila. Realizing I had no place in the unfolding scheme of things, I bid my friends adieu, saying I'd meet up with them later on Sand Fly Beach.

The air outside was humid and smelled of fajitas and rotten fish. Car lights streaked past, and the pedestrian parade on the Malecón seemed to be moving in slow motion. The only single girl of note was a short, boxy mestiza in a hotel uniform, shuffling through bus fumes after a day spent scouring bathrooms. I noticed a tiny silver cross at her neck—another long-suffering Mexican saint. She looked up as we passed one another, and the brief glance from her warm brown eyes gave rise to an unexpected shiver. It may have only been a flare of desire brought on by the buzz of the tequila, but it seemed that her eyes had revealed something darker—something like the mystery of Mexico itself.

Dan had written about this more than once in the time he'd been traveling the country. I remember in particular a postcard he sent showing the monstrous, massive stone carving of Coatlicue, the Aztec earth goddess of fertility and death. He said the statue was a perfect example of his unjustly ignored anthropological thesis, "A Freudian Geography of the North American Mind." In this dubious disquisition, the USA took the role of the ego, the lone pioneer on the Great Plains, the central, controlling, conscious will that dreamed and schemed and acted on the world. Canada was the superego, the hunter on the harsh, intolerant tundra, the high and mighty conscience of the Great White North. Lowly Mexico was the id, the crazed Nahuatl priest in the lush mountain jungle, the deep subconscious, teeming with untamed instincts and arcane imagery, ruled by a primitive nightmare logic. This was the ancient land of the Olmec, the Maya, the Toltec, and the Aztec. Of bloody human sacrifice, pyramids, and treasure. Of conquistadores and missionaries and zealous revolutionaries. A nation of greed and grief, of cruelty and corruption, of grinding poverty and religious fervor. A country that prayed to saints and danced with the devil. A country that celebrated death and the dead.

Had I seen all of that in the poor girl's eyes?

I turned my back on the Malecón and headed into the drearier streets, away from the tourists and the lights and the traffic, into the darker heart of the city. This was the real Mexico, or as real as it gets in a town that sprouted from a Hollywood movie. The cobblestone streets were largely deserted, just a few taverns and shops were open, and soon the clamor of oceanfront traffic faded to a distant rumble. I trudged up a steep, curving street studded with closed courtyard doors and high, unshuttered windows. Behind a wall of jasmine, a fountain trickled noisily. A filthy white cat crossed my path. From a high balcony draped with laundry, a Latina TV soap opera star berated her unfaithful lover.

Surely if Dan was still in the city, this was where he would have come, I thought. He'd be looking for dirt-cheap rents, drinking twenty-peso shots in neighborhood cantinas, and buying his meals from the smoky sidewalk grills that tourists avoided but locals were drawn to like flies to shit. We'd been looking on the wrong side of the tracks. Dan was a proud Third World wanderer. He spoke fluent Spanish and liked to mingle with the masses. He wouldn't be sipping tea in the lounge at the Four Seasons, and he wouldn't be chasing after French-Canadian teenagers along with every other American college-boy tourist.

The street grew quieter, and as it did, my thinking seemed to grow clearer. I'd been working on the assumption that Dan had come to Puerto Vallarta to pick up a job at one of the hotels. I had figured that he had grown tired of scratching out a life with the Indians in the mountains, that he had probably depleted his cash and come to the city for his routine dip into the capitalist trough. Now I thought that might not be why he had come here at all. Maybe he had come for something else entirely, something bigger, some American ego dream or scheme that took hold of his imagination and wouldn't let go. What had that postcard meant, anyway, its cryptic message promising a fortune? Whatever it was, it wasn't about earning tips as a cabana boy at the Holiday Inn.

I stopped in front of a *farmacia,* a tiny little slot of fluorescent light with a single narrow aisle. Inside, an old man, so small and thin he was barely visible behind the counter, sat watching a soccer match on a flickering black-and-white television set. His wrinkled face looked like a crumpled paper bag.

"Por favor?" I said. I held out the photograph of Dan on the Harley. "Ever seen this guy?"

The old man looked at the photo, shook his head, and went back to the game. I wasn't sure he understood my question, so I repeated it, slower, pointing to Dan on the bike.

The old man's eyelids were half shut; he looked weary and utterly uninterested. He mumbled something in Spanish.

"I'm sorry?" I said.

He mumbled again, *"Los Vagos,"* gesturing toward the door.

It sounded like "Las Vegas." Maybe some kind of casino. "Which way?" I asked.

He pointed vaguely up the street, then turned away, quickly slipping back into his soccer trance.

I walked outside and looked up the street. A dilapidated pickup from the 1950s was slowly bouncing down the cobblestones. Tethered in the back of the truck was a goat, somehow looking utterly placid while struggling to maintain its balance. The streetlight above gave off a feeble light, not enough for me to see the face of the driver. I wanted to stop him and ask about *Los Vagos,* whether it lay up ahead like the old man had said, and if it did, I wanted to ask him what the hell it was.

The truck rolled away into darkness. No one else was on the street. All the doors were shut, and all the stores were closed for the night. I had no idea what time it was—I had left my watch in my pack at the hotel. Was this going to be another wild goose chase? As I trudged up the street, I began to wonder just how badly the tequila had affected my judgment.

Vagos. Vámonos. Old man gets rid of annoying *gringo.* What was I doing?

An erratic growling sound emerged up ahead. A Mexican kid on a moped was coasting down the hill. Every few yards he'd drop it into gear, trying to get the engine started. It didn't work. As he skidded toward me, I recognized his face. Duff had bought a quarter ounce of reefer from the kid. We had seen him nearly every day since on the beach, and sometimes in the evening on the Malecón. With his marijuana connections, we always hoped he might turn up something about Dan.

I waved for him to stop.

"You hear anything?" I asked.

"*Nada*," he said.

I had never heard him speak a single word of English, but he always seemed to understand everything we said. I didn't know his name. Duff had taken to calling him Skullhead. He had close-cropped hair with a bare spot around a jagged white scar on the top of his head. He had a nearly identical scar on the other side of his scalp. There are gangs and knife fights in any city, but this boy couldn't have been more than twelve years old.

"Do you know anything about *Los Vagos*?" I asked.

He nodded. "*Sí, Vagos.*" Then he said something else in Spanish that I couldn't understand. He pushed off and continued coasting down the hill. Half a block down, the engine sputtered into life. He turned the bike around and drove back up to me.

"*Señor*," he said, patting the seat behind him.

"You give me a ride to *Los Vagos*?"

Again he said something I couldn't understand. I climbed onto the back of his bike and noticed immediately that the slot for the ignition key was empty. Suddenly I was imagining bunking with this kid in a Mexican lockup over Christmas. While I was still trying to figure out what to hold on to, he took off. Reflexively, I grabbed his waist. He was nothing but skin and bone.

The ride over the cobblestones was so bumpy it made me wonder if I'd have been better off walking. I held tight to my emaciated driver. The shaved little jagged scars on his scalp jiggled frantically in front of me, looking like tiny white faces with teeth, or a pair of eyes sewn shut.

We crested the hill and descended, riding another four blocks. I began to worry. Where was this place? Maybe the kid had misunderstood. When he turned onto a two-lane highway flowing with traffic, I wondered if I had fallen victim to a kidnapping scheme.

"Where are we going?" I shouted into the wind.

"*Sí, sí,*" was all I could hear.

We drove for several miles. *This is insane,* I thought. "Could you please *stop*?"

Incomprehensible Spanish blurred past my ears. The boy kept on driving. I thought about jumping off. We were only doing twenty-five or thirty, but there was traffic, and trucks, and a bus one car behind us. I decided to stay put.

At an intersection with a broken stoplight dangling useless in the air, he pulled off the road into a dirt parking lot beside an abandoned taco stand and an auto mechanic's garage shuttered for the night. In front of us was a long wooden shack with a Tecate beer sign in the window and Mexican music rumbling inside. The lot around us was filled with half a dozen beat-up cars, a few muddy pickups, and a whole lot of motorcycles.

"*Los Vagos,*" the boy said, nodding toward the shack. I climbed off the moped and looked the place over. Except for the Tecate sign glowing in the window, there was nothing to indicate what was inside. But seeing the motorcycles parked all around us, I realized in an instant not only what the place was but why the old man in the pharmacy had sent me here.

The picture of Dan on his Harley. This was a Mexican biker bar.

The kid sat straddling his idling moped, waiting to see what I would do. I started to climb back onto the bike. "Take me back," I said. "*Por favor.*"

Just then a potbellied Mexican wrestler pushed his way out the door, followed by a lanky, gray-bearded pirate with a ring in his ear, his long hair held back by a black scarf wrapped tight across his forehead. The fat man popped a lighter and lit up a hand-rolled cigarette, and when he spotted us standing there with our pathetic little moped, he began to laugh, making cracks to the pirate in Spanish. As they stumbled off, still laughing, to find their motorcycles, I saw an emblem sewn across the back of the fat man's leather jacket. It had skulls and flames, and a wheel with a wing, and emblazoned across the top in ornate green letters was the single word VAGOS.

Vagos was the name of a motorcycle gang.

"Let's get out of here," I said.

The kid started to turn his moped around. That's when the odor of the reefer hit me.

"Wait," I said.

The two guys were standing over a big hog Harley, sharing the fat man's bright-glowing joint. I thought of Dan on his Moto Guzzi with his smuggler friends in Caracas. The cocaine in Colombia and the time he had spent in jail.

Motorcycle gangs had to buy their dope from someone. That someone, I imagined, might very well be Dan.

I glanced again at the bar. "What do you think?" I asked the kid. "Want to go inside?" I felt like I could use little Skullhead's company, even if he was only twelve years old.

He looked at the bar, then looked at me. He shook his head no.

"Okay, *amigo*," I told him. "Will you wait for me, then?"

He kept staring at me until I reached into my wallet and pulled out some pesos. Without counting them, he stuffed them into his pocket and nodded in assent.

"Keep the engine running," I told him. "I won't be long."

CYCLOPS

The music pouring out of the bar was not the usual ranchero or mariachi you hear everywhere you go in Mexico. It sounded like Mexican surf-rock, with a ripping beat and Spanglo lyrics—Beach Boys gone Latino on speed. When I stepped through the door the sound was so loud I couldn't hear anything else, not even the burly guy inside shouting at me in Spanish and gesturing with a sloshing glass of liquor in his hand. He had a messy beard and tousled hair, eyelashes long as a woman's, and a wide open shirt with a loop of fat gold chain dangling from his neck. Except for the jailhouse tattoos on his arms, he looked like Tennessee Williams on a bender. He downed the shot and grabbed my shirt in his fist and then let it go as a little *señorita* half his size slid between us, ran her hands up through his chest hair, pulled his gold chain like a leash, and kissed him on the mouth. He grabbed her hair and tugged her head back to get a better look at her face. "Rosita?" She smiled and gripped his beard in her hands and yanked him back toward her open mouth. As intrigued as I was with this charming romance, I took the opportunity to slowly slip away. I wormed off through the noisy crowd as inconspicuously as I could, given that I was the only lily-white *gringo* in the room.

To order a drink, which I thought the only sensible thing to do under the circumstances, I had to weave my way through an entire regiment of bruising bikers and their attendant hookers, each bruiser bigger than the one before him, and each hooker uglier. Heretofore I had not seen many obese people among the Mexicans I had encountered, apparently because they spent their entire waking lives drinking in dives like this.

The bartender, a squat, round-shouldered woman with pigtails and a constant grimace, ignored me for at least ten minutes after I had squeezed my way up to the bar. I suppose she figured if she waited long enough I'd eventually climb back aboard the booze cruise I had fallen off of. Either that or I'd go deaf from the music, something I was certain had already happened to her. I was about ready to give up when she came over at last and set a dirty glass of clear liquid down on the bar in front of me.

She answered my puzzled look with a nod toward a Mexican cowboy sitting by himself at the far end of the bar. The cowboy had on dark shades and wore a buttoned black shirt and a bolero with a silver cow-skull clasp. His tanned, clean-shaven face was topped off by a black felt cowboy hat with turquoise beads strung around the brim. He looked like a handsome country-western star who had just collected his third Grammy up in L.A. Wondering what he was doing here and why he had just bought me a drink, I raised my glass and nodded in acknowledgment. With his thumb and forefinger, he tipped his hat, slow and subtle, exactly like a country-western cowboy ought to do.

I took a sip of the mysterious drink and immediately knew what it was. My brother had mentioned raicilla in one of his dispatches, praising its hallucinatory power and brain-obliterating intensity, so I had dutifully bought the guys a round on our first night in Puerto Vallarta. We were so pleased with the results of the first round that we went through three more before calling it quits and reverting to beer. By then it was too late. Raicilla takes no prisoners. A form of mescal distilled from the maguey cactus, the drink gave birth to a common barroom expression: Its effect on the human brain is exactly that of a hammer on the head of a nail. After consuming our three short rounds that night, we staggered out of town in a delirious haze and collapsed unconscious on a garbage-strewn beach. We finally awoke, under a blazing sun and a blizzard of bugs, nearly twelve hours later.

Some lessons, however, are only learned through repetition. There is something transcendent in a glass of raicilla, a mystical quality that imbues the drinker with a profound sense of eternal well-being and a godlike feeling of omnipotence. At the same time, it charges the mundane world with a heightened intensity bordering on the psychotic. One minute, the smashed butt in a foul-smelling ashtray can appear to be a smoldering toadstool in hell; the next, a glorious golden throne in Utopia. As I sipped this precious but perilous potion, the hard-rockin' surfer music pounded through my head, a column of cigarette smoke reached up to curl around an invisible limb, and the linoleum bar top with the squiggly lines began to flow like an animated river in a Disney movie.

I was back once again on the bright side of things.

This one glass of raicilla was all that I'd need. In a minute I'd be ready to pull out my picture of Dan on his Harley and find out if any of these fat, happy people had happened to make his acquaintance of late. I began to feel that I belonged in this biker bar, that the universe had conspired to bring me here, that all my questions were about to be answered, that all I had to do was hang on a little longer and I'd see my brother Dan come gliding across the crowded floor with a Mexican hooker under his arm and a bottle of raicilla in his hand.

I could almost hear his voice now, shouting in my ear. *"Amigo!"*

I turned to see the Mexican cowboy with the black hat and sunglasses, only for a second I didn't recognize him because he had taken off the shades and removed his hat, and because he wasn't as pretty when you saw him up close. The dime store toupee didn't help much, either. *"Señor,"* I said. "Thanks for the drink." I held it up as I said this, and he saw the glass was empty.

"Sylvia!" he shouted to the bartender. In an instant she poured out two more shots of raicilla. "Welcome to Mexico," he said, raising his glass.

"Nice to be here," I said. We clinked and sipped.

His eyes were black and veined in red. I could see every pore on his face. He had a soft, raspy voice and had to shout over the music. "Tell me, *amigo,* what bring you to Puerto Vallarta?"

"I'm looking for someone," I said, and fumbled for the photograph in my wallet. "I'm looking for my brother." I handed him the picture.

He glanced at it barely a second before handing it back to me. "Why you looking here?"

I set the photo down on the bar and pointed to the Harley. "He liked motorcycles. I don't know. Seems like I've looked everywhere else. I can't find him."

"Maybe your brother, he no want to be found," he said.

I took another sip of my drink. "Why wouldn't he want to be found?"

He shrugged, answering my question with another of his own. "Why you think your brother came to Puerto Vallarta?"

It was a good question, I suppose, but it seemed like he was asking too many good questions. "Have you seen him?" I asked.

"No," he said. "I no see him." He put on his sunglasses and turned to gaze at the crowded room. "Maybe your brother is dead."

He snapped his fingers at Sylvia, and she instantly refilled our glasses again. I was so preoccupied with what he had said that I failed to notice this was shot number three. I downed it like a thimble of water.

"Did you say my brother might be dead?"

"Your brother, he ever talk about Punta Perdida?"

"Poonta-what?"

He silently sipped his drink.

"What are you talking about?" I asked.

"*Nada,*" he said. I had answered his question.

"Why do you think my brother is dead?"

He shrugged. "You look for him but no find. He no here. So I say is possible he is dead."

Sylvia refilled my glass.

"But you don't know anything about my brother." His face went out of focus a moment, then grew sharp and clear. I tried to see his eyes behind the shades, but all I could see was my own reflection. It felt like I was talking to myself in a mirror, or talking to Dan in a black hole. I completely forgot where I was.

"No, I don't know nothing," he said. He sipped his drink and watched the crowd. Tennessee Williams was dancing with a man. The *Vagos* whooped it up.

I noticed the glass in my hand was empty. When had I downed the shot? Why was this stranger buying me drinks? "Who are you?" I asked. His face came sharply into focus again. His skin was a minefield of pores, each one sprouting a little black wick. "What do you know about my brother?"

He turned to me, slowly, and lowered his glasses. His eyeballs looked like a pair of evil planets, with black polar caps bleeding rivers of blood. He leaned in close to whisper, "I know he like to play my piñata."

I squinted at his cratered face. It went out of focus again. *"What did you say?"*

He called out to Sylvia and asked for something. She reached down low, behind the bar, and pulled out a baseball bat. She handed the bat to the cowboy.

I felt a sudden flutter in my gut, a limpness in my legs.

The cowboy turned to the crowded room and raised the bat in the air. He whirled it menacingly over his head. *"Vagos!"* he shouted. *"Vagos!"*

In no time he had everybody's attention. Tennessee stopped dancing, and the drinkers grew still. The cowboy called out to them in his raspy Spanish, all the while waving the bat over his head. I caught only a few of his words: *Yanqui, amigos,* and *porko* or *puerco.* This last brought a huge cry from the crowd. Their faces lit up with anticipation as they turned their gazes on me.

I backed slowly away from the bar. I didn't want to be strung up and beaten. I thought about making a run for the door, but the cowboy pointed the bat at me, exhorting the *Vagos* to join in the fun. They eagerly closed around me, a tightening circle of bursting beer guts, studded leather, and scraggly beards. Even the women joined in. Peering out from fleshy mugs plugged with rotten teeth, half-bashed boozers and blue-veined dopers eyed me with a feverish intensity. One of them dragged a bar stool into the center of the room. The cowboy pushed me toward it, using the bat like a prod.

He was going to show me what had happened to Dan. He was going to bash my brains in.

Just then, from the kitchen, a massive Mexican momma emerged, holding aloft a pig on a platter. The pig was made out of bright pink paper.

The crowd roared. I breathed in relief.

Somebody put on a mariachi song. Trumpet blares pummeled the air. The song must have been a *Vagos* favorite; it drove the bikers giddy. They laughed and wailed and waved their drinks, while the lady with the massive, quaking tits climbed atop the rickety stool and strung the pig to the rafters.

The cowboy, resting the bat on his shoulder, glared at me over the rim of his shades. "I teach you the *catequismo*, amigo."

I squinted at him. Catechism? My throat was clamped too tight to speak.

"La Fe! La Esperanza! La Caridad!"

Chalk it up to the raicilla. Or years of Catholic grammar school. I knew hardly a word of Spanish, but somehow I had understood what he said.

"Faith, Hope, and Charity?"

"Sí!" the cowboy exclaimed, once again raising his bat in the air. The bikers roared their approval.

The cowboy pointed his bat toward the pig, dangling freely above me. *"El puerco*—he fat with the Charity, no?"

This brought a raucous cheer from the crowd.

I nodded nervously. *"Sí. Mucho."*

The bikers guffawed. I was a comic. The cowboy held the bat out to me, offering me the handle. *"Esto es la Esperanza."*

The baseball bat was Hope? Whatever you say, *hombre.* I took the bat in my trembling hands as the *Vagos* raised their drinks and shouted, *"Esperanza!"*

The cowboy removed his dark sunglasses. His ghoulish eyes sent shivers through me. *"La Fe,"* he said, moving closer. "They say the Faith is blind, no?"

I stared back and didn't answer. What was he going to do, exactly? What did he want me to say?

From behind me, Big Momma lowered a blindfold over my eyes and tied it tight around my head. I felt her bosom against my back and smelled her boozy breath. I didn't know what to do or say, or whether to try to resist her. I was woozy from the raicilla, so sloshed I could hardly stand, and all I could see through the black blindfold was tiny pinholes of light. Could I fight off these gangbangers using the bat? Could I make it outside and escape on the bike?

Big Momma spun my body around. I stumbled as others grabbed and pushed me, passing me roughly from one to the next. Blaring trumpets split my ears. Women screamed and laughed. I choked on smoke blown in my face. Fingernails scraped my neck. Someone grabbed my balls. A pair of lips locked on mine. A bottle smacked my jaw. Whirling blindly around their circle, reeling from the raicilla, I soon lost any sense of where I was, of even who I was—of what was me and what was not, and what was just the darkness.

Finally they shoved me out onto the floor. I staggered forward and bumped the pig.

The crowd called out to smash it. Dizzy and disoriented, I swung at it and missed. The bikers howled with laughter. I took another swing and missed again. Someone pushed me forward. Clawing the air like a bear at a circus, I fell face-first into spongy flesh. Immediately I recognized the boozy breath. The Mexican momma shoved me back. I stumbled, dropped the bat, caught a heel, and crashed to the floor. The room resounded with laughter.

A rage arose like a wave in me, an angry surge that

cleared my head. I stood up slowly and gripped the bat. Blindly probing the darkness around me, I searched for the dangling pig. This time when I found it, I took careful aim and swung. The bat slugged the pig with a papery thud—enough to send it into a spin but not enough to break it. I swung again and missed, then swung and struck it hard. The crowd whooped and hollered, but the pig was still intact. The bikers clamored for murder. This time I reached out and stilled the swinging swine, cementing my attention on the unseen spot. I reached back with the weighty club, loading it with power, then launched it through the air in a sweeping upward stroke.

It proved a fatal blow.

The pig exploded. The crowd went wild. The bar descended into chaos.

Before I knew it I was fighting for my life. The *Vagos* were barreling over one another, scrambling for a share of the prize. Hollering, cursing, they shoved and grappled past me like a stampede of linebackers rushing a fumble. An elbow thwacked my ear. I stumbled over the fallen stool. Finally I managed to tear off my blindfold and saw what the devils were after: tiny Ziploc bags of powder, scattered all over the floor. The air was suffused with a cloud of cocaine. It covered my hands and arms.

Bikers blundered into me, battling one another. Head down, eyes hooded, I tunneled through them, clutching the bat—and ran straight into the cowboy. His hat was gone, and he was covered with powder, black eyes glaring from a ghost-white face. He tried to wrest the bat from me. I yanked it and lost my grip, and the butt of the bat rammed into his eye.

The cowboy grabbed his face and wailed like a Cyclops.

I picked up the bat and fled through the fracas. When I finally reached the exit door, a hand with frosted fingers took hold of my snow-covered arm. I turned to see a man with a fat gold chain and a crazy smile on his face. Tennessee Williams was feeling no pain. His cheeks and beard were covered with powder, his long eyelashes dusted white. I shrugged him off, then suddenly froze: He was pointing a pistol at me.

My heart stopped. "What do you want?"

"What you want, *amigo*."

"I just want to get out of here," I said.

The cowboy emerged from the cocaine cloud. His eye was a slit, he had lost his toupee, and his hairless head looked white as an egg. Tennessee called out to him, for a second taking his eyes off me. I swung the bat up and clipped his hand, knocking the gun away. Tennessee cringed, cradling his fingers. The pistol rattled to the floor at our feet. I grabbed it and raced through the door.

The kid was waiting across the lot, straddling the idle moped. Seeing me running with a bat and a gun, he started to push off away toward the street. I caught up and jumped on behind him.

"Go—go—go—!"

But the bike was dead. Skullhead had turned the engine off. The keyless moped was going nowhere.

We turned to see the cowboy striding toward us, *Vagos* pouring out behind him.

I climbed off the bike. Amazingly, Skullhead appeared undaunted. I handed him the bat.

Then I turned the pistol on the cowboy.

"Stay back," I said. I had never held a gun in my life. My hands were trembling. I fought a surge of dizziness. My eyes went out of focus.

The cowboy stopped. Tennessee and the others gathered behind him, all of them covered in cocaine dust. The cowboy's swollen eye squinted at me.

"I'm just looking for my brother," I said. "I don't want any trouble."

"You looking for your brother," the cowboy said, "you looking for trouble."

He moved slowly toward me. He knew I wouldn't shoot.

I turned to glance at the kid behind me. He was holding the bat ready in his hands.

I turned back to the cowboy. "Please don't hurt the boy," I said. "He only gave me a ride."

The cowboy stopped in front of me. "You *no comprende, gringo*," he said. "The boy, he working for me."

I turned as the bat came swinging to my head.

GODS

I awoke in pain and darkness. Little of the dream I'd been having remained—something about blindness and water and death. It reminded me of my mother's nightmares of Dan. If I was getting closer to him, I wasn't sure I liked it. All I felt was paranoia and a sickening sense of dread. I closed my eyes again.

When I opened them, hours later, a girl was standing over me in the feeble light of dawn. The girl was maybe five or six. She wore a filthy little dress, and her face was nearly as dirty as her feet. She reached into the empty pockets of my jeans and pulled them out one at a time, leaving them to stick out in the open like rag puppets. Then she picked up my discarded Hawaiian shirt. It had only one pocket, and that was empty, too. This was not her lucky day.

I woke up again later when the sun was high. The girl was gone, and the sky was an unmarred ocean of blue. The heat brought out the stench around me, and for a moment I thought I was lying in a dumping ground of corpses, a Mexican version of the killing fields. The flies concentrated their efforts on my back, where a fiery pain was raging. When I tried to move, my headache surged. I felt the lump atop my scalp: The bat had merely grazed me.

Something was wrapped around my neck. The baby blue bandanna? No. I had left that in my pack. This was my white T-shirt. Pulling it off over my head, I saw that it was stained with blood, as if someone had used it to wipe off his hands, or to clean the blade of a knife.

I turned at the sound of laughter. It came from the pile of garbage behind me. Two of the skinniest buzzards in Mexico were arguing over the remains of a restaurant fish. I watched them tear the bones to shreds.

Reaching over my shoulder, I felt the tender skin of my back. It was scarred with cuts and crusted with blood. What did the son of a bitch do, whip me?

I threw away my undershirt and pulled on my Hawaiian shirt. This I did slowly, because every move I made stretched the skin of my back and made me dizzy with pain. I left the shirt unbuttoned, hanging loosely from my shoulders. It had been lying on empty cans and smelled of refried beans. My socks were still on my feet, but my Nikes were nowhere to be seen. Maybe the girl hadn't left empty-handed.

The dump covered many acres of ground, a mountainous landscape of endless garbage. A few Mexican Indian women and children were scavenging near the access road, where trucks were whiningly dumping their loads. The women paid no attention as I minced past them in my stockinged feet, but the children ran up to me to beg for coins. I looked for the girl who had taken my shoes but didn't see her among them.

I hitched a ride back into town on a garbage truck driven by a Mexican who looked like he'd have been better fed if he had scavenged with the women and children at the dump. When he dropped me off in a blighted neighborhood in the northwest corner of the city, I wanted to give him something in thanks, but they had taken my wallet and money. All I could offer was a feeble *"Gracias, muchas gracias."* It seemed to be enough for him; he probably lived on less.

The sun was just setting when I finally reached Sand Fly Beach. I'd been walking for several hours, and the cuts on my back were bleeding again. I took off my shirt and waded into the ocean to wash off the blood. The water cooled my feet but stung the broken blisters and seared my back, so after wringing out the shirt, I waded back to shore and stretched out on my stomach in the warm sand.

In less than a minute, I was sound asleep.

J ack. Wake up." Rock crouched down beside me in the sand, the moon staring over his shoulder like a ghostly second face.

"What time is it?" I asked.

"After eleven. We've been looking for you all day." He called for Duff, who was searching farther up the beach with his flashlight. Duff ran up and shone the light in my face. When I turned away, he saw the blood on my back and was horrified. "What the hell happened to you?"

"Forty lashes. Punishment for drinking too much raicilla."

I started to pull on my shirt, but Rock stopped me and took a closer look. "Wait a minute," he said. "It's words. You got words cut in your back."

"What's it say?" Duff asked.

"Hold the light still," Rock told him. He moved his face closer and wiped the dried blood with his hand.

"Easy!" I said. "It hurts like hell."

Rock began spelling out the first word: "Y,A,N,Q—*Yanqui.*"

Standing behind him, Duff could read the whole thing. "*Yanqui* Go Home."

"Not very original," I said.

"Who did this to you?" Rock demanded.

"Some yokel I met in a bar. I think he knew Dan."

I told them what happened—Skullhead, the cowboy, the piñata, the brawl.

"We ought to go back there," Duff said. "We ought to go back there tonight and beat the shit out of the guy. Make him tell us what the fuck is going on."

"I don't think so," Rock said. He seemed to sense a deeper danger. "Let's wait and decide what to do in the morning. Meantime, better put something on those cuts." He took Duff's flashlight and went to his backpack to look for his medical kit.

Duff sat down beside me in the sand. "We could go to the cops," he said. "Have the guys arrested."

"How? I couldn't prove anything. All they'd have to do is deny they ever saw me."

Duff was quiet for a long moment. The sense of helplessness made him depressed. He pulled out his Baggie of dope and stared at it. "That little bastard Skullhead," he said.

He began to roll a joint.

Rock came back with a bottle of iodine and applied it to my back with a cotton swab. Duff lit up a humongous raft, and before long we had forgotten all about the *Vagos* and the cowboy, and my missing brother who might be dead. Even the raw pain of my back seemed like a relic of the distant past. A few tokes of Acapulco gold and we were off and rolling, riding the wave, the ever-changing Present that knows nothing but itself and lives in the center of the cosmos like a beating heart. We were young and free and high as kites, taking a trip around the world in the greatest adventure of our lives. We were back where I liked it, on the bright side of things. The ocean beckoned; the warm sea breeze blew through our hair. We felt completely at home in the universe. We felt like gods.

But even gods have to sleep. And dream.

That night I dreamed a white worm crawled into my ear, turning my brain into a tequila distillery. A woman who worked there broke a bottle over my head, leaving a scar that looked like teeth. The teeth chattered, forming words in garbled Spanish, words I could not understand. The cowboy grabbed me by the collar and stuck his ugly face in mine. I could see my scar in his black sunglasses. The teeth chattered, sputtering Spanish. I listened as hard as I could.

"Poonta-*what?*"

PUNTA PERDIDA

Rock kept the map in the side pocket of his backpack. Swatting away the morning sand flies, I unfolded it and scanned the area around Puerto Vallarta, starting with the coastline just to the south. Yelapa, Chimo, Aquiles Serdán, Punta Tehualmixtle, Punta las Peñitas. It didn't take me long to find it. Punta Perdida looked to be a fishing village about fifty miles down the coast. I knew there were no roads there; the coastal villages south of Puerto Vallarta were separated from the highway by ten or twelve miles of mountainous jungle. This lent a town like Yelapa the kind of quaint isolation that appealed to lazy, hard-drinking tourists bored with the regular beach routine; they could take an Epcot voyage to "real" Mexico while getting bombed en route. We had watched the ferryboats load up every morning with sleepy-eyed tourists and return in the evening with a cargo of drunks.

Punta Perdida was not one of the advertised destinations. Probably too small and squalid, and too far down the coast for the standard day trip. It looked to me like just the kind of place that would have appealed to my brother Dan. I knew at once we had to go there.

"Forget it," Rock said when I woke him up and told him. "We have to get out of here. Today."

"What are you talking about?"

"Sleep well? I'm talking about the e-mail on your back."

Duff stuck his head out of his bag, waved aside the flies. "What's going on?"

"Jack wants to get us all killed in some little town down the coast."

"Killed?" I said.

"Don't be an idiot," Rock said. "Your brother dealt dope and smuggled fake pottery. I'm sure he made a lot of friends, but he probably made a lot more enemies. It's likely that cowboy's the tip of the iceberg."

"I can't believe you just want to pack up and leave," I said. "We're finally on to something. How do we know Dan isn't down there right now?"

"Doing what? Working on his suntan?"

"Look," Duff said. "We give up now, it's exactly what they want us to do."

"Gee," Rock said, "how did you get that impression? *Of course* it's what they want us to do. They don't want us to find him!"

"And why wouldn't they want us to find him?" I asked.

Rock glanced impatiently at Duff, then looked at me without bothering to answer.

"Are you saying Dan is dead? Is that what you're saying?"

"It's a clear possibility, Jack. And don't tell me you haven't considered it."

I looked at him a moment. Then I looked at Duff. Both had arrived at the same conclusion. They didn't like it any more than I did; they were just more willing to believe it.

"There's only one way to find out," I said.

Rock cursed and turned away from us. He bent down to pick up a stone and chucked it into the ocean. He walked off and stood at the edge of the water.

"He'll go," Duff said to me.

I wasn't so sure. Despite his youth and physical power, Rock was surprisingly circumspect and generally heeded his own advice. I walked down and joined him at the edge of the water, letting the surf roll over my feet. Last night we had taken a blissful swim and I hadn't even noticed my blisters. Now they hurt like hell.

I plucked an inky stone out of the sea-soaked sand. It shone like polished ebony. "If you guys want to leave,

Rock . . . it's all right with me. Maybe I can catch up with you later in Hawaii."

Rock looked at me incredulously. "You actually believe you can get along without us?"

Another wave submerged our feet. We watched them sink in the sand. "What are you going to do if you don't find him?" Rock asked.

"I'll find him," I said. "At the least, I'll find out what happened to him."

Rock persisted. "What if you find out he's been killed? What if you find the guy who killed him?" He was squinting over at me, staring sharply into my eyes. He wanted to know how far I would push it, what I'd be willing to do.

I peered at the jet-black stone in my hand. It reminded me of the cowboy's eyes, and the stinging pain I felt in my back. "I'm really not sure what I'd do." I pitched the stone as far as I could out over the water. It disappeared without a splash. "What would you do, Rock?"

He squinted at the horizon. "It's like you say. There's only one way to find out."

According to the chief cabana boy at the Casa del Mar Hotel, the best way to reach the isolated villages down the coast was to hire a boat out of Boca de Tomatlán, the southernmost fishing village off the main road. To get there, we had to take a bus. So after a trickling shower at the pool, we checked our bags out of hotel storage, made a stop at a neighborhood bank, and continued up the road to the nearest bus stop. I pulled the blue bandanna out of my pack and tied it around my neck for good luck. With fresh clothes and my spare leather sandals, I felt like a whole new man. Fortunately, most of the money I had lost had been in traveler's checks. The call the bank clerk made to American Express, which required her to summarize my peculiar misadventure, would have made a memorable television spot. I left there with a thick roll of cash in my pocket—not that it was necessary. I might have lost my bank card, but I still had my passport and a credit card, which was all you really needed to make your way around the world.

To get to Boca, all you needed was three and a half pesos. The bus was filled with Mexican workers—bricklayers and carpenters and cooks and cleaning ladies. Puerto Vallarta is a city of hotels, with more being built every day of the week. These were the Mexicans who did the hard labor, just as they did in Los Angeles and Dallas and Chicago and Denver, only in Mexico everything always broke down, nothing ever seemed to get finished, and the proletariat in their dusty clothes always looked tired and worn and beaten. I turned my eyes away, gazing out over the green cliff at the vast ocean below. Mexico is a stunningly beautiful country—as long as you're sitting on the right side of the bus.

In less than half an hour, we were off the bus and strolling into the seaside village of Boca. Fishing boats were anchored offshore, and the little cove had a lovely sand beach and plenty of thatched *palapas* offering picturesque shade. We made our way along the shore and over the footbridge that spanned the shallow mouth—the *boca*—of the Tomatlán River. It was a relief to find fewer beach vendors here, not the usual onslaught we'd encountered back in town. For weeks we'd been waving off hucksters hawking silver-plated jewelry, sombreroed string puppets, gaudy Indian blankets, demonic wooden masks, pink flamingo cocktail stirrers, Spider-Man parachute dolls, iguanas, parrots, gourd wind chimes, heaps of bead necklaces, and a host of other tourist trinkets whose inevitable end lay in a place not unlike the one I had found myself half naked in the day before.

Here they seemed to take us for wandering drunks. At tables under grass huts, eager barmen beckoned. *"Cerveza, amigo? Margarita, señor?"*

"No, gracias. No, gracias." It was nine o'clock in the morning, and we had a job to do.

"We're looking for a boat to go down the coast," I said.

"Water taxi, *señor*?" Half a dozen desperate-looking men gathered around us, each offering his boat and a colorful destination.

"Yelapa, four hundred pesos! Each."

"I take you now, *amigos. Panga grande.* Three hundred fifty pesos!"

"You want Quimixto? Very beautiful. Two hundred pesos."

"I take you to Chimo. Especial place, especial price. One hundred fifty pesos. Is nothing."

Rock interrupted them. "We want to go to Punta . . ."

"Punta Perdida," I said.

They looked at me as if I had just named the deepest region of hell. *"Punta Perdida?"*

"Sí," I said. "Punta Perdida."

"You no want Punta Perdida, *señor.*"

"Yes, we do."

"No, *señor.*"

"Is not for you, *amigo.* Is a bad place."

"Why is it a bad place?" Rock asked.

The men frowned, shrugged their shoulders. The oldest of them wore a tattered straw hat that barely shaded his eyes. One of his legs was shorter than the other; his hips were cockeyed and his shoulders bent. "There is no beach," he said. "No *restaurante.* No *cerveza.* No the *palapa.*"

"We don't want that stuff," I said.

Duff shot me a look of uncertainty. "No *cerveza?*" he asked the man. "What kind of a town doesn't have *cerveza?*"

"You no like this place, *señor.* This place is not for you."

"It's okay," I said. "It's where we want to go." A tiny, gnomelike Indian woman approached, buried under looped armloads of bead necklaces. *"No, gracias,"* I said, turning back to the men. "Who will take us to Punta Perdida?"

They glanced at each other and looked at the ground. None of them answered.

"C'mon," I said. "Four hundred pesos. Round trip to Punta Perdida."

One of them mumbled something in Spanish, then walked away. The others looked apprehensive.

"Okay," I said. "Five hundred pesos."

The short-legged old man spoke up. *"Señor.* I take you to Quimixto. Is very nice. You will like it very much."

"We don't want to go to Quimixto," I said.

The men looked at me without speaking.

I said, "I'll give you a thousand pesos to take us to Punta Perdida."

The men shifted uneasily. Another one of them walked away. Then they all began to leave.

"Wait a minute," I said. "I'll give you three hundred dollars American to take us to Punta Perdida."

The men kept walking. Only Straw Hat turned around to speak. His voice was tinged with melancholy. "You no understand, *señor*. We no take you to Punta Perdida. Not for any kind of money." He turned and walked away.

"Do you fucking believe that?" Duff asked.

We watched the old man hobble down the beach. None of us spoke for a moment.

"Señor?"

We turned around. The Indian dwarf was standing behind us, holding her burden of beads. *"No, gracias,"* I said.

She held up a leather necklace with a heavy silver cross. *"Para Punta Perdida,"* she said. *"Hueso colorado."*

"What?"

"Hueso colorado." She held up the necklace and thrust out the cross, speaking an odd-sounding Spanish. All I understood was the last word she said: *diablo*. It gave me a chill.

"How much?" I asked, and reached for my cash.

She shook her head. "No," she said.

"You, too, huh?" I peeled off three hundred pesos and held them out for her. "How about this?"

She shook her head no again. Then she took my other hand, placed the silver cross into my palm, and folded my fingers over it, saying, *"Para el Diablo Blanco."*

"What she say?" Duff asked.

"Something about the devil," I said. "A white devil, I think."

"She mean you?" Rock asked.

"I don't know," I said.

The woman ignored my offer of cash. She turned and looked at Duff. Staring him in the eye, she made the sign of the cross. Duff expelled a nervous laugh. The woman's steady dark brown eyes never seemed to blink. She turned and stared up at Rock.

Never had I seen him look so thoroughly disconcerted. He glanced nervously at my silver cross necklace. "Got one of those for me?" he asked.

She didn't answer; she barely shook her head. No cross for Rock. Just the holy gesture: forehead, heart, shoulder, shoulder. She broke off her stare and slowly shuffled down the beach.

We stood watching her for a moment before any of us spoke.

Finally, Duff said, "I don't care what time it is—I need a margarita."

THE COIN

If Mexico hadn't already turned us into dipsomaniacs, we were certainly on our way. By late morning, we had fallen into a drunken sleep on Boca's crescent beach. Lying on my stomach to avoid the pain in my back, I opened my eyes to a sideways view of a black Labrador retriever, its panting pink tongue flopping out of its mouth. The beast leapt over me, scattering sand, and charged out into the water to catch a Frisbee in its teeth. I turned to see who threw the Frisbee and for a moment was caught in a time warp. What beach was this? What day was this? What was that woman doing here?

"Hey, check it out."

Rock rolled onto his side like a beached whale and spotted the girl and the dog. "It's her," he said.

Duff came to, spongy-faced, pie-eyed. "Who?"

"Pinky," I said. It was the name we had used for her whenever we had reminisced, only this time she wasn't wearing the pink tank top because Duff had stuffed it with his dirty clothes to use as a pillow at night. No, this time she was wearing a white cotton spaghetti-strap top with nothing on underneath, and instead of the thong, she had on white shorts with the bottoms rolled up to the tops of her thighs. She held her sandals up in one hand and the dog-gnawed Frisbee in her other, and as she twirled and frolicked, the Labrador circled her, leaping to reach the disk. She stopped her taunt and threw it again, winging it down the shore. The dog ran off to fetch it.

"Will wonders never cease," Duff murmured.

Before I even had a chance to think about it, calculating Rock had already scanned the beach and spotted Pinky's companions.

"There's Red," he said. "And Idi Amin."

They were drinking umbrella drinks in lounge chairs under the generous shade of an oversized *palapa* a short way down the beach. Mr. Amin's ample bulk was draped in a green and gold bamboo-theme Hawaiian shirt that looked like a sheet of wallpaper. His head was bald and shiny, he wore a pair of streamlined sunglasses, and he sucked on a cigar as thick as his wrist. Red wore a pair of white capri pants and a navy blue sleeveless blouse tied in a knot above her navel. She looked like a daydream fantasy of the American flag, one any red-blooded American boy would be willing to march off to war for.

"And there's their boat," Rock said. It was anchored out in the cove just beyond the fishing boats and water taxis, its sails rolled tight, its white hull glistening in the noonday sun.

Duff had already found the binoculars and trained them on the *palapa.* Idi Amin was waving off a trinket vendor, and Red was brushing her hair. "If a girl has red hair like that," Duff said, "it means she's got a red bush, too."

"How would you know, Frenchie?" Rock grabbed the binocs from him.

"I speak from experience."

"Right. Like Miss April?"

"It was March."

"April."

"March."

"April."

I had to make my move before these dingbats blew our chance.

"I love Frisbee," I said, and headed up the shore toward Pinky.

The closer I came to her, the taller and more dauntingly

beautiful she appeared. She stood in ankle-deep water, watching the Lab swim out for the Fris, and as she lowered the hand that was shading her eyes, the silver bracelets tinkled down her slender wrist, and a strap fell, baring a shoulder that peeked out through the black silk of her hair. She turned as I approached, flashing green eyes lined with black kohl, and for a moment I thought she might be Middle Eastern, a harem girl who had shed her veil and didn't know when to stop. She looked at me as if sizing me up, then turned back to the sea.

"That scarf you're wearing looks familiar," she said. Her voice was silvery and aristocratic, with an accent I couldn't place.

Immediately I untied the bandanna from my neck. "You left it on the beach the other day," I said. "When you went for your swim. I've been trying to find you so I could return it." I held it out to her.

She looked at the bandanna and then looked at me. "Why don't you keep it?" she said. "You can wear it with my swimsuit." She watched the dog grab the Frisbee off the water.

"I think I look better without the suit," I said. "And I'd have to say the same for you."

It might have been the trace of a smile on her lips. Hard to say; it vanished before I could figure it out. She slipped her strap back over her shoulder and bent to the dog as it bounded toward her with the Frisbee in its mouth.

She took the Fris and ran off, splashing through the water, the dog at her heels. I stood watching her black curls bounce away from me like a Clairol commercial in reverse, wondering if I'd ever have another chance after clearly blowing this one. Then she stopped and twirled around with the Fris held high, taunting the dog to grab it again. I was starting to think this might be a metaphor for the way she handled the men in her life when, to my delight, she stopped and flung the Frisbee over the surf in a perfect horizontal arc to me.

Well, not quite perfect. I leapt for the falling saucer like a shortstop, nabbing it out of the air and landing on my belly in the shallow water, knocking the wind from my pipes and burying my face in the sandy bottom. Did I mention I was wearing my clothes? A wave rolled me onto my butchered back, and the dog came hurdling over the surf to pounce on me and grab the disk. I tried to hang on to it, but when the sharp-clawed dog bared its frothy teeth and growled like a rabid wolf, I decided there had to be a better way to impress Pinky with my manhood.

"Well trained," I shouted to her as the dog bounded back to its master.

She took the Frisbee and waded toward me with a now clearly recognizable smile on her face. "You all right?" she asked.

I sat up in the water and wiped the sand from my eyes. "Fine," I said. "Water's warm. You ought to come in."

"You know what they say. If you're not in over your head, you're not swimming." She held out her hand.

I took it, pulled myself up, and stood there in my dripping clothes. Stunningly gorgeous beachwear model helps idiot college boy back to his feet. I might not have been swimming, but I was definitely in over my head.

"Jack Duran. Glad to meet you."

I continued holding her hand, waiting for her to offer her name.

"Eva Yerbabuena."

It was a beautiful name, at least the way she said it, blowing it out through her lips like a kiss. For a moment I conflated the sound of it with the emerald gleam of her eyes. Eyes so green and gorgeous they seemed to embody the very music from which poetry is born.

Eva Yerbabuena.

"Something wrong?" she asked.

I was staring at her with my mouth open. Blushing, I released her hand. "No, nothing," I said. I had tried to ignore Idi and Red sipping their drinks on shore, but I knew we had an audience—and not only them, of course.

"Are those your friends?" Eva asked. Rock was peering at us through the binoculars while Duff tried vainly to wrest them away.

"I'm afraid so," I said.

"I hope they don't expect me to take my clothes off again."

I wasn't sure how to answer that. "They're just . . . curious, I think."

"Then why not join us for a drink?" she said, nodding toward her companions. "Perhaps we can find another way to satisfy their curiosity."

"I doubt it," I said. "But you can certainly try."

An hour later our curiosity, while far from being satisfied, at least had found purchase on sounder ground. Idi Amin, it turned out, wasn't the brutal ex-dictator of a war-torn, diamond-rich African kingdom but a gentle, middle-aged Bahamian businessman with a welcoming smile, a gracious manner, and the princely but vaguely sinister name of Leopold Bellocheque. He introduced Red as Eleanor Tuohy, but she told us, please, to call her Candy. Happily we obliged. Candy said she worked for Bellocheque in Miami Beach, though none of us had the nerve to ask exactly what she did. Who knows, maybe it was the same thing Eva claimed she did: financial management in his banking business. She told us she worked out of Bellocheque's office in Rio de Janeiro. Eva was Brazilian, Rio her hometown.

"You ought to come down for Mardi Gras," she said when she found out we were traveling around the world.

"Always wanted to go," Duff said. He leered at Candy. "Biggest party on the planet."

The tantalizing proximity of these stunning women had gotten the better of Duff. After half a dozen margaritas, his normally genial demeanor had gone manic. "We ought to do it, you guys!"

I shrugged. Rock gave a noncommittal nod. "If we ever get our asses out of Mexico," he said.

"By all means go," Bellocheque suggested. Any word this big man uttered commanded your total attention. His resonant voice, deep and dramatic, seemed to carry with it the full weight of Caribbean colonial history: the melodic lamentation of the African slave and the crisp enunciation of the English ruling class. He spoke like a baritone British admiral in a Gilbert and Sullivan operetta, savoring every scrumptious syllable and chewing the air around it. "But I warn you," he intoned, "once you arrive there, you may not want to leave."

"Why's that?" I asked.

He glanced at Eva and puffed his cigar. "You look at her and you have to ask?"

I followed his suggestion and smiled at Eva. Brazilian siren indeed. I turned to my friends. "Better pass on Rio. We'll never make it out of port."

Bellocheque's laugh was a volcanic eruption: His belly shook, and smoke came out of his mouth. It took a full minute for the man to settle down.

Duff ordered everyone another round of drinks. Not all that magnanimous a gesture, it turned out. He had spent all his pesos, and the bare-bones beach cantina couldn't handle plastic.

Rock and I reached for our wads, but Bellocheque quickly intervened. "Not to worry, gentlemen. The drinks are on me." He pulled out a fat roll of Mexican cash and peeled off some bills for the waiter. The waiter thanked him, and they exchanged some words in Spanish.

We sipped our margaritas. "Do you know what 'hueso colorado' means?" I asked.

Bellocheque licked the salt from his lips. "I believe it means 'blood of the bone.' They use it when they speak of the depth of their faith." He gazed at me with his big brown eyes. The look made me uneasy.

"This really ought to be our last round," I said. "We have to be moving on."

He continued peering at me, his sharp eyes glistening. "Always restless, this one. Always the mind is working away."

There was truth in what he said. Nobody seemed in a hurry but me. Least of all Mr. Bellocheque. He and his crew were on a monthlong vacation: a "sailing holiday," as he cheerily put it. They had traveled through the Panama Canal to sail up the Mexican coast. Having ventured as far north as Cabo San Lucas, they were heading back down now to Acapulco, stopping at various points on the way. My mind was working overtime, all right. I knew they'd be going by Punta Perdida. I had already explained that we hoped to find Dan there and complained of our failure to enlist the help of the local boatmen. If what he needed was another hint, I was more than willing to give it.

"We've got to find a way down the coast," I said.

Rock had been hoping that I had finally given up. I'm not sure what had worried him more, the reluctant boatmen or the pygmy with the cross. "What we've got to do is get on with our trip," he said. "Punta Perdida is a wild goose chase."

Bellocheque's eyebrows lifted. "Sounds as though there's disagreement in the ranks."

Duff licked the limy mustache left from his margarita. "I can go either way," he said. "Mexico's fine with me."

Bellocheque exhaled a blue cloud of smoke. "This town," he inquired. "Punta Perdida. What do you know about it?"

"Nothing," I said. "Just that my brother might be there."

He picked up one of the photographs I had laid out on the table. "The long-lost brother."

"It's really only been about four months," I said.

"A lot can happen in four months." He tossed the picture back on the table. Long-haired, bearded Diver Dan on the boat in the Florida Keys. "A lot can happen in four seconds."

This was starting to sound familiar. "What do you mean?" I asked.

"Life is lived in the moment," he said. He stretched out his huge black hand, palm down, and one by one gathered his fingers into a fist. "One, after another, after another, after another." Slowly, he turned the fist over. "One's destiny can change—for better or worse—like that!" He opened his fingers. In the hollow of his hand was a large, thick, gleaming gold coin.

I reached out and took it without thinking, as if some pri-

mal synaptic wiring had been triggered, short-circuiting the
higher functions of my brain. Consideration, politeness, social inhibition—all were swept away as I lifted the gold
piece and turned it in my fingers. It was old and worn and
scratched, beaten and dented and bent—and it was the most
beautiful coin I had ever set eyes on. Its age seemed to add a
kind of gravity and weight that couldn't be measured in
ounces, and its peculiar luster under the shade of the *palapa*
appeared to gather its light from the shadow itself, commin-
gling the light and the shade and the yellow of the gold in a
luminous cauldron of color.

It might have been all the drinking I had done, but I don't
think so. Bellocheque was a conjurer, and this coin of his
held a special allure, a kind of magic I couldn't put my finger
on. I could barely make out a trace of stars and a woman's
crowned head on one side; the other imparted the impression
of an eagle. Any words engraved on it had long ago been
worn away. All I could read was the year, faintly: *1850*.

"Where's it from?" I asked.

Bellocheque bared his big white teeth, apparently pleased
at the keenness of my interest.

Rock grabbed the coin from me and took a careful look.
"Eighteen fifty," he said. He looked to Bellocheque. "It's a
gold rush coin."

"From a private San Francisco mint," said Bellocheque.
"The gold in that particular coin came from Hector Bellocheque's mine in Dowling's Ravine. Hector Bellocheque
was my great-great-grandfather. One moment, he was just a
dirt-poor nigger chipping away in a mine; the next, he was
the wealthiest black man in America."

Duff took the coin from Rock, looked it over, then
handed it back to Bellocheque. "What's it worth?" he asked.

"It's worth a trip to Punta Perdida."

"How's that?" I asked.

"Are you a betting man, Jack?"

"Depends on the bet."

"Well, how about this: I'm going to spin the coin on this

table. If it lands heads, I'll take you all down to Punta Perdida in my boat, and you can have a look for your brother."

"And if it's tails?"

"You do what your friend here wants: Forget Punta Perdida and get on with your trip."

I stared at him a moment and realized that this was the only offer he was going to be willing to make. I glanced at my friends.

Duff shrugged. Rock looked at me. "Do it," he said.

I wasn't sure what they wanted more: to sail off with the girls or to give up our search and get on with our trip. I knew what I wanted. As far as I could see, nothing would keep me from getting it but my word—and I knew how easily that could be broken.

"Okay," I said. "You're on."

"Splendid."

He cocked the coin between his thumb and middle finger and held it out just over the tabletop. All eyes focused on the man's poised hand. With a sudden, expert snap, the coin dropped spinning hard onto the table, whirling in a balled blur.

We all sat up and watched it—Duff, Rock, Candy, Eva, and I—watched it spin around the table in slow orbit, a ghostly gold planet circling a long vanished sun. As it slowed to a wobble, I could feel Bellocheque's eyes moving over us, one to another, taking pleasure in the power of his manufactured moment, each of us a question mark, our fates flung out into space on the wheel of the earth, all of us watching, waiting to see what this tottering cauldron of gold had in store for us, what destiny it held.

OBI-MAN

W hat does it mean?" I asked.

Eva cast her eyes far out over the water. "You'll have to ask Leo."

"You never asked him about the name of his boat?"

"I asked him."

"What did he say?"

"It's an island thing. African myth."

"You mean like voodoo?"

"Black magic, spirits of the dead, that sort of thing."

"So he's an obi-man?"

She finally deigned to look at me. "I'm afraid I really don't know. Like I said—ask Leo."

She turned back to the wheel. The Lab was curled at her feet, sleeping in the sun.

I could watch her sail this boat all day, I thought. Eva Yerbabuena. Emerald eyes like a jungle cat. Legs that never quit. Shimmering black hair wild in the wind.

I pulled the bandanna from my pocket, held it out for her. "Please," I said.

She considered it a moment. "Hold the wheel."

I did what she told me. Then I watched her put the bandanna on her head.

If you're falling in love with a woman like Eva, you take an interest in how she does this sort of thing. First, she held the corners and folded it in half. Given the stiff wind whipping our sails, this was a more difficult task than one might imagine, but she carried it off gracefully, and soon enough a baby blue triangle flapped between her hands. She threw back her hair, shook the black blowing strands from her face, then swiftly lifted the fluttering triangle over her head, capturing beneath it the feral flow of locks. Unlike before, when she had worn her hair up, with the bandanna tied under it at the nape of her neck, this time she tied down the corners of the cloth in a natty little knot beneath her upturned chin. I've seen nineteenth-century French paintings of plump peasant women bent over bales of wheat, their heads wrapped in babushkas very much as Eva's head was wrapped in this bandanna, but somehow Eva turned this simple, age-old hat trick into a glamorous fashion statement, a look destined for the pages of *Vogue* and the runways of Milan and Paris. As a final touch, she slipped on a pair of impenetrable black sunglasses. Then she smiled at me tightly and took over the wheel.

I stood there trembling as I watched her—though more from the cold than from my fascination. My clothes were still damp, and with the stiff breeze blowing across the deck, even the sight of her sexy babushka couldn't warm my chill.

"I'm going to change my clothes," I told her.

"You said that an hour ago."

Had it really been that long? "Guess I got distracted. It's so beautiful out here." I pretended to peruse the passing coastline. "Think anybody lives in those mountains?"

"No idea," she said.

It looked like no human had ever lived there; the jungle was pristine and forbidding. "I guess this town really is isolated," I said.

Eva didn't respond. Our conversation—what little there had been of it—had turned pathetically one-sided. Fearing I was boring the woman to death, I left her and headed below.

Bellocheque's boat was everything money could buy. Sixty-two feet long, according to Eva, with three staterooms and a bunk in the bow. Lots of inlaid teak and polished brass, all the trimmings and all the latest technology—even the sails lifted with the push of a button. Bellocheque told us he could sail the yacht single-handed, but I never saw him lift a finger; the girls did all the work. Back in Boca, they had lashed up the dinghy, raised the anchor, set the sails, and skippered the boat out of the bay. Eva had the air of an experienced pilot, and Candy seemed to know a thing or two herself; I had seen her down below, charting the course and checking the weather on the shortwave.

Shortly after we had set sail, Bellocheque and Candy had retired into the master suite at the back of the boat. Stepping down into the airy, windowed dining area they called the "saloon," I glanced back down the corridor past the chart table to peek at their door. Still closed. A male singer's smooth voice—who was it, Perry Como?—softly crooned over the speaker system. I turned toward the bow and made my way down a mahogany-paneled corridor past the two front cabins on either side of the boat. Like the master, each of these had its own bathroom. Apparently one of these suites was Eva's and the other one belonged to Candy.

We had been told to use the cabin in the bow if we wanted some privacy or shut-eye. I opened the door and found Duff sprawled on his back on the V-shaped bunk, fast asleep. His mouth hung open, and his breath rasped in and out like a poisoned drunk in the throes of death. Rock sat beside him and didn't seem to notice. He glanced up at me and immediately went back to the book he was reading, a travel guide to Mexico's Pacific coast. He had found it in a shelf of books on board.

"What are you doing, Rock? You're on a million-dollar yacht with two beautiful women, and you're hiding down here like a rat in steerage."

"I don't feel so hot."

"Seasick?"

"Maybe."

"Then definitely you should come out on deck. Trying to read down here will only make it worse." I opened my backpack and started changing into dry clothes.

Rock rifled through page after page. "Every little town and village on the Mexican coast has a blurb in this book, but there's no mention of Punta Perdida. Nothing at all."

"So? It's not a tourist town. In fact it's probably a hell-hole." As I tugged a clean T-shirt out of my backpack, the silver cross necklace tumbled out onto the mattress.

Rock picked it up and looked at it.

"I guess she thought it wouldn't suit your attire," I said, and pulled on my shirt.

He tossed it to me. "That little witch gave me the creeps."

I lowered the necklace over my head. The silver cross was huge. I struck a rapper pose. "'S' up, bro?"

Rock, unamused, glanced at the closed door, leaned toward me, and spoke in a near whisper. "There's something weird going on here, Jack."

"Bellocheque?"

"Bellocheque. The girls. The whole fucking thing."

I knew he was right. I had felt a creeping uneasiness but had forced it out of my mind. "Relax," I said. "We're just hitching a ride."

"Million-dollar yachts don't pick up hitchhikers."

"Don't worry about it. Look on the bright side. An hour from now we'll find Dan on the beach with a native girl rubbing oil on his back. Everything's going to be fine."

He looked at me and didn't say anything.

"You need a little Adashek," I said. David Adashek had been our high school football coach freshman year, the only year I played the game. Our team had the unique distinction of providing his otherwise outstanding career with its one and only losing season. Mr. Adashek had a favorite expression, one he used to describe the fundamental essence of football—the act of throwing yourself headlong into an on-rushing opponent.

"What happened to your 'reckless abandonment,' Rock?" I glanced at the wheezing walrus splayed out over the mattress beside us. "It's obvious Duff's still got his."

Rock shrugged wearily. "All it did for me was ruin my knees."

◆ ◆ ◆

By the time we came within reach of our destination, Duff had convinced Candy that all the money she had put into her fabulous boob job was nothing but a big mistake, that all it did was bring unwanted attention from worthless young men with one thing on their minds and one thing only. He convinced her of this, not through any reasoned argument he put forth, but by the simple fact of his behavior, his absolute inability to see or do anything else until the main issue had been resolved, that being the exact size, shape, color, and feel of those costly balloons that so captured his attention. When he saw something he wanted—especially something female and just beyond his reach—Duff could be unrelenting. He'd been working on Candy now for over an hour. At the present moment, in the middle of relating a long and involved story about his Irish great-grandmother and her possible proximity to the Tuohy family in the city of Cork during the period between the first and second world wars, Candy looked up from the chart she was studying to say that somehow she had missed the rocks.

"What rocks?" I asked.

"It's high tide," she said, rising from the table with the charts in her hand. "They may be under the surface, and they may not be marked."

"So that's, like, important?" Duff asked.

"I have to warn Eva," she said, and started up the stairs.

"Wait!" Duff called after her. "I'm just getting—"

Candy was gone.

"Go ahead, Duff. I love hearing about your grandmother Ethel and the work she did scrubbing floors in Cork."

"Five more minutes, she'd have been eating out of my hand."

Rock's red face suddenly appeared in the skylight overhead, calling through the glass. We couldn't understand what he was saying, and for a second I feared we were about to hit those nasty rocks on Candy's chart.

"What's with him?" Duff asked.

I was starting for the deck when Bellocheque emerged

from the master suite. He had changed into an immaculate white linen suit with a gold satin neckerchief, and he held a brass-handled walking stick and a black-banded Panama hat in his hand. He glanced over at us and noticed Rock babbling in the skylight.

"Land ho, gentlemen!" he declared in his rich baritone. "It seems we have arrived." With that he placed the hat on his head and clambered up the steps.

GHOST TOWN

It didn't look like a hellhole at all—at least not from a distance. The village lay crowded along the low foothills between the narrow strand of sand beach and the jungle-covered mountains. The late afternoon sun broke between the bright-rimmed clouds, sending down beams of light onto the hillsides like spotlights onto a stage set, illuminating one stuccoed ramble of bungalows after another. It looked like the cue for a singer to appear—Carmen wailing with blood on her hands, or a guy named Rodrigo plucking his guitar—but in fact no one appeared at all. The village looked abandoned, and the beach was empty. Idle gray fishing boats rocked at their moorings, waves splashed the vacant dock, and the sole sound we could hear from the dinghy was the forlorn howl of a dog.

I gazed back at the *Obi-man,* anchored out in the bay. Eva had stayed behind with the boat, and I watched her on deck now wrapping the sails, loyal Lab wagging beside her, until a brilliant shaft of sunlight set the water on fire and burned away my view. Bellocheque sat facing the shore, his hands propped on his walking stick, an unlit cigar clasped in his teeth. Candy sat behind him, throttling the outboard against the wind, aiming us doggedly in toward the dock.

"Doesn't look too promising, Jack." Rock lowered his binoculars and glanced back at the yacht. "Maybe I should have stayed behind with Pinky."

Duff leaned back against the bow, stretching out his arms

on the polished wooden rim. "She's all meat and no potatoes, Rock. And we all know how much you like your potatoes."

"You should've seen Margaret before she left," Rock said. "Lost so much weight you wouldn't have recognized her."

"The things they do for love."

"Fuck you."

"Hey," I muttered. "Chill." Even with the sputter of the outboard I thought they might be overheard. Not that Bellocheque had any grand notions about us, but I figured the longer we concealed our true juvenile selves, the longer he might tolerate our presence and lend his support to our cause. What I couldn't understand was why he had decided to accompany us to shore. Had he himself grown curious about the fate of my vagabond brother? Perhaps we brought out some paternal instinct, or maybe it was simply his sense of adventure. Whatever it was, it made me uneasy; but when his gaze fell on my inquisitive eyes, I grinned back reassuringly.

Candy cut the engine, coasting the tender into the pier. Rock reached out from the bow to buffer the impact, sliding the boat up alongside the rail. I jumped out and fastened the bow rope to a post, but Candy quickly intervened, undid my tangled square knot, and expertly retied the line in a humbling display of nautical know-how. *Watch and learn,* I thought, but the knot was so quick and complicated, and her sumptuous cleavage so delightfully distracting, that I shortly abandoned the effort.

Bellocheque was the last to disembark. Given his ponderous bulk, the process required a team effort. Two people, four helping hands, one cigar lost in the drink. Firmly installed on solid dock, he shot his cuffs, straightened his jacket, and planted his hat on his head. Then he plunked his cane to the planks and led our parade off onto the beach.

There was no welcoming party. Just a half-starved mutt with a raw wound on his foreleg and the saddest eyes I had ever seen. It followed us across the boulder-strewn beach with its head bowed low to the ground, an obsequious emissary sent out from the town to inquire about our intentions. We're looking for my brother, I wanted to say. Have you seen him? Has he fed you any crumbs or blown any dope smoke up that battered nose of yours? Surely he wouldn't let a dog like you starve to death for the want of a bone. Why don't you take us to him instead of groveling after us like the sorry bearer of bad news?

We passed through a chicken yard between rain-rotted stucco houses with shuttered windows and closed doors, emerging onto a narrow street. Paved with fitted, smooth-worn rocks, the street snaked up a steep hill through a rambling jumble of houses and shacks. The homes were all closed up, all shuttered and curtained off and bolted—but they were not abandoned. Sheets fluttered on clotheslines, brooms rested beside doorways, pigs and chickens rooted about, and there was the definite sense of a presence in the air, of eyes in the shadowy cracks of the shutters, of murmuring voices and unseen movement. We knew they were here; they just weren't coming out.

Why?

Bellocheque rapped on a door with the brass handle of his cane. *"Hola!"* he declared in a loud voice, then inquired in Spanish if anyone was home.

Apparently not anyone who wanted to admit it. Though the house was rather upscale given its neighbors, it exhibited the same state of general decay: rotting, rust-stained stucco walls, a roof of broken tiles, and a little open square of flaking pavers around an ancient oak tree, its withered leaves rustling dryly in the breeze. Dust swirled up from the ground, and as Bellocheque turned away from the door, sunlight flared from a gap in the clouds, igniting the big man's incandescent suit in a dazzling spectral glow. Bellocheque pulled a cigar from his pocket and cast his eyes at the sky.

"I dare say we'll have rain before the sun goes down. Doesn't afford us a great deal of time." He stuck the cigar in his mouth and lit it with a match cupped in his hands. His puffing cheeks stoked the flaming tip, and billowing smoke soon swallowed his hat, as if he had set his head on fire. Emerging unscathed from the conflagration, he marched on briskly up the street.

Duff looked at me and shrugged. Rock stood with his hands on his hips, watching Candy as she followed Bellocheque up the hill. The swing of her hips had a mesmerizing motion, and before we knew it we had fallen in behind her like a trio of sailors under a mermaid's spell. The dog was still with us, slow and lethargic, yet somehow always right behind, its sad eyes gazing up at me whenever I turned around. I wasn't looking for the dog; I was looking to see if, after we passed, anybody poked a head out a window or stepped outside a door. There wasn't a hint, not a visible or audible peep. It was as if the town had fallen into a slumber and our odd little parade was nothing more than a passing figment of their collective dream.

Farther up the hill, we came to a stop where the stone road forked off in three directions. One way switched back left across the hillside of houses before looping over the crest into the gully beyond. The right fork meandered through a tangle of bungalows in a slow descent toward the southern shore. The third way led straight ahead up the hill through brush and trees and scattered houses, bending gently toward the mountains beyond. There was nothing to indicate which way to go or why one route might be better than the next. As we stood there looking off in all directions, I began to wonder if Bellocheque ought to give his coin another toss. Instead, he made a suggestion.

"Let's split up, shall we? We're sure to cover more ground. Certainly we'll come across someone in this town who's willing to talk—or at least to reveal his face."

"Sounds good to me," I said.

Bellocheque nodded down the lane that descended toward the shore. "Candy and I will continue this route. I've had enough uphill for one day."

"Fine," I said. "Rock, why don't you and Duff take the left fork? I'll continue up the road."

They nodded in consent.

Bellocheque started off with Candy on his arm. "Meet back at the boat before dark," he said.

We watched them for a moment as they strolled off down

the road, the tall, ravishing redhead glancing back with a sultry smile, and the heavy, white-suited obi-man jauntily swinging his cane. Don't ask me how, but the two of them seemed to belong together.

I turned to my friends. "See you back at the dock," I said.

Rock warned me not to get lost; Duff wished me good luck. Then they turned and walked away.

The dog stood staring up at me, mouth open, panting.

"You could save me a lot of trouble, Pancho. You know where he is. Take me to him."

The dog kept staring up sadly. I crouched down, scratched its head, and chased a fly off its foreleg wound. When I patted the dog's side, all I felt was bony ribs. "You need something to eat," I said. Then I stood up, and as I did, the dog began trudging slowly up the road.

My turn to follow.

B y the time I reached the top of the hill, I could clearly see the sailboat waiting out in the bay. Sullen clouds blotted out the sky and muted the late light of the sun, turning the ocean gray and the village the drab sepia monotone of an antique photograph. A patchwork of rust-red rooftops spread out below me, cut by the empty curve of Bellocheque's road, but I couldn't see the street that was taken by my friends, and the shore and the dock were obscured by a line of sagging trees. I stood there for a long moment taking in the view. There was something about it that bothered me. Something that seemed to be missing. It took me a full minute to realize what it was.

The twentieth century.

Forget about the twenty-first—these people had never made it out of the nineteenth. There were no TV antennas, no satellite dishes, no cables strung from house to house. Not even a single telephone pole or power line. There were no hoses, no pipes, no running water. There were no automobiles. Not even a motorbike or a lawn mower. Now that I thought of it, even the fishing boats had been motorless. I cast my gaze out over the bay and contemplated Bellocheque's push-button yacht. The man was a magician after all: He had sailed us here in a time machine.

I wanted more than ever to talk to the citizens of Punta Perdida, but there was still no sign of life in the houses around me. More of the same up ahead on the road as it worked its way along the crest of the hill, but farther on, the white cross of a church stood out starkly against the leaden sky. A common enough sight in a country of Catholics, but somehow, here in this sepia dream of a ghost town, it shone like a glowing neon sign, a familiar connection to the wider waking world.

Pancho turned his head back to me, as if asking what I was waiting for. Then he turned and sauntered on, and I followed after him up the road. Drops of rain began to fall, spotting the dusty pavement stones and wetting my face and shoulders. By the time I reached the churchyard with its high wrought-iron fence, the downpour was coming hard and the dog and I were drenched. I pushed through the creaking gate, hurried to the shelter of the church's thickly arched entry, and stood with my back against the studded wooden door. Pancho strolled up, gave me a second shower, and sat down beside me on the stone-step threshold. We waited there for a while, watching the rain pound down on the churchyard. Water gushed off the red-tiled roof, danced on the sober tombstones, and coursed down the rocky slope of the road, its roar and spatter a welcome slap of life.

The torrent didn't stop. I began to wonder about the others, whether they had been caught out in the rain. Bellocheque in his natty suit. Candy in her cotton blouse. Had she been wearing a bra?

Not a thought to contemplate on the doorstep of a church. Pancho whined and scratched at the door. I opened it and followed him inside.

The walls of the church were thick and the windows high and narrow. With the storm heaving down outside, only a faint light penetrated the gloom. Rain thundered on the roof and leaked through the ceiling, dripping into puddles on the rough stone floor. The dog went directly to one and began lapping up a drink.

As my eyes adjusted to the darkness, I saw we were not alone. A black figure was standing off to the side of the altar, bent over what looked in the shadows like a gleaming casket. An array of votive candles burned nervously on a ledge above him, and the faint, unworldly ding of a bell echoed around him eerily.

I ventured closer up the aisle. It was not a casket the black-cloaked figure was working on but a long, rectangular glass case. He was wiping water from the top of the case, water that had leaked down from the ceiling and that now fell into a tin bowl he had set atop the glass. Each drop landed with a bright metal ping, the source of the numinous sound.

"*Hola,*" I said, but the figure didn't turn. I moved closer, trying to get a look inside the strange translucent box. Its glass panels were sealed in a crudely soldered metal frame, and the flickering light of the candles played across its mirrored surface with a hellish glow.

"Excuse me," I said.

Still no response.

I stepped closer. "Sir?" I reached to touch the inky figure's moving shoulder, then gasped when I saw the body in the box. "*Oh my God!*"

The body was Dan's.

The dark figure whipped around in surprise, hands flung in the air. The young padre wore a Roman collar and a black frock; his skin was dark, and he had the onyx eyes and flat features of a Mexican Indian. His lips moved to speak, but the sounds he uttered were completely unintelligible, like the jabbering of a madman.

The dog began to bark at the case.

"Why is he in there?" I shouted. "What have you done to him?"

He continued to babble in his imbecilic tongue, his hands gesturing wildly, flapping his sopping rag in the air. Seeing his fear seemed to dissipate mine. Emboldened, I moved closer to the case, peering at the body through the fiery glass. It was wrapped in a sheet. "Oh, no," I said, recognizing my brother's longish hair, the gentle beard and soft mustache. I moved closer to examine the face.

What I saw made my heart skip a beat. The face was made of polished plaster. "Oh," I said. "Oh."

It was Jesus. In a tunic. The most lifelike version I had ever seen.

I was smiling now. So was the padre, even as he blubbered on. "It's Je-sus," I said, enunciating each syllable. "Je-sus."

The padre nodded enthusiastically. "Hey-shu! Hey-shu!"

I had broken through the language barrier—or so I thought. It took another minute of labored conversation to realize it wasn't my lack of Spanish that made it so hard to communicate. The padre, it turned out, was deaf.

SPEAK NO EVIL

The rain continued falling hard, and the priest had his hands full keeping off the flood. He was a paranoid little fellow, glancing at me at every chance to see what I might do. To set his mind at ease, I knelt at the communion rail and pretended to pray. On the wall above the altar, a giant white plaster Christ floated up toward heaven, which apparently lay just beyond the shadowy rafters of the leaky ceiling. A lack of windows in the front of the church left the altar in relative darkness and rendered the chalky Redeemer a ghostly shade of gray. His upraised hand pointed a finger to heaven, but his gaze fell down upon the high wooden pulpit, which rose like a staircase from the flooded floor below. My eyes alighted on a painted sculpture carved into the front of the pulpit: the strange and fearsome figure of an ancient god of the sea.

I rose to my feet and moved closer until the figure loomed above me. It had the hoary, bearded head of an Old Testament patriarch, his mouth stretched open in fury, his fierce eyes blue as the sea. The powerful, bare-chested body tapered into the scaly tail and fanlike fin of a fish. I quickly realized that the creature wasn't actually carved into the pulpit but was attached to it. The realization quickened my pulse and sent my mind racing back to Dan's mysterious postcard.

I was staring at the antique figurehead of a ship.

The padre was mopping up a puddle on his hands and

knees. As I approached, he looked up at me like sad-eyed Pancho, who now lay resting under a nearby pew.

"*That*," I said, pointing to the pulpit. "Is that from a ship?"

He couldn't hear me, of course, but he saw what I was pointing to. "Ship," I said. "Boat." I moved my hand in a floaty motion over a wavy sea. He looked confused and more than a little frightened, and he shook his head no. I wasn't sure whether it was in answer to my question or whether he had simply not understood me. Didn't Mexicans play charades?

I crouched down in front of him and pulled out the photograph of bearded, long-haired Diver Dan on his skiff. A picture is worth a thousand words, especially when you're deaf. The moment I held the photo in front of him, I had the answer to my question. Dan had been to Punta Perdida, and this priest had seen him. Judging from the terror that filled his face, it had been a memorable experience. The priest rose to his feet and slowly backed away.

"What's wrong?" I asked. "What is it?"

The padre eyed the doors as if he expected an entrance from the devil himself. Then he turned and started to flee but slipped in a puddle, falling hard on his hip.

"Padre—"

He scrambled to his feet, limped through the gate in the communion rail, and crossed in front of the altar without so much as a nod. Then he disappeared through a door to the side, hidden from the gaze of the floating Redeemer.

I jumped over the rail and hurried after him. The door led into a narrow passage that followed the curved wall of the church around to another door. I opened it and entered a small room with a single high window secured with an iron grate. A faint cobweb of light fell across a dusty clutter of candles and chalices and a half-empty crate of wine. The padre was not in the room. To the side was another door with a heavy iron bolt—unlocked. Passing through it, I found myself outside in the churchyard, the rain pouring down on my head. Across a muddy slope littered with tombstones, I could see the padre entering another structure, a small, windowless stone cabin with a slanted roof, built into the granite side of the hill. He closed the door behind him.

I raced across the cemetery through the slanting rain and knocked on the door.

"Padre!" I shouted. "Open up!"

I tried the handle and pushed on the door, but it was bolted shut. A rusted metal cross was nailed over a rectangular peephole, shut from the inside. I turned away from it and faced the gravestones, the rain soaking my hair and clothes. Pancho trotted up and stood before me, that damned annoying look in his eyes. I turned back to the door and banged on it with my fist.

"Where is he?" I demanded. "Open the door!"

The door remained shut. I turned my back to it again and slid down onto the step. Let the rain fall. I could wait. The sun was probably down by now, and my friends were at the dock, but I wasn't going to leave until I had gotten an answer.

The dog started barking again, this time at the tombstones. Staring into the rain, I thought I detected a shadowy movement at the far corner of the church. The dog kept barking, and I rose to my feet. I sensed a presence somewhere nearby, concealed in the curtains of rain. After a long minute of watching and waiting, I turned with a start as a door slammed shut through the wrought-iron fence to my right. The fence was covered in morning glories, their pelted leaves randomly twitching, and I peered through the intermittent gaps in the green for some glimpse of the doorway beyond. It failed to be revealed. I saw nothing but the pallid cheek of a stucco wall and the shuttered eye of a window.

The dog stopped barking. I heard a creak behind me and turned as the peephole snapped shut. I raised my fist to strike the door, but just then the bolt lifted, the door cracked open, and the padre hurriedly motioned for me to enter. When I did, the dog tried to follow me inside, but the padre closed the door on its nose and quickly bolted the lock.

The room was spare and tidy, dimly lit with a kerosene

lamp and a candle above the fireplace. Against the wall was a simple bed with a neatly folded blanket, and the meager plank table in the center of the room had a single ladderback wooden chair, draped with a black-bead rosary. The padre took the lantern from the table and held it up to study my face. He had the anxious look of a man who felt his life was on the line.

"Where's my brother?" I asked, pulling out the photograph. "Where is he?"

He glanced again at the picture, then quickly shuffled to the door and opened the peephole, maneuvering his head to take in the view. Satisfied the coast was clear, he crossed the room to a stack of logs by the fireplace, set down his lamp, and began to move the logs one at a time, setting them down nearby. When he had cleared the space, he used a poker from the fireplace to pry loose a square stone in the floor. Beneath it lay a small chamber, out of which he lifted a scruffy old leather and canvas rucksack.

He picked up the lantern and brought the bag over, offering it up like a gift. When I took it from him, he went back to the door and checked the peephole again, then hurried over to replace the stone in the floor and cover it up with the logs.

I set the rucksack down on the table. It was soiled and worn, the leather had been damaged by water, and one of the shoulder straps had torn loose at the seam. I opened the bag and looked inside. It contained a few nautical books in Spanish, another book in German, a dog-eared copy of a Uto-Aztecan–Spanish dictionary, a tattered, coverless Wilhelm/Baynes *I Ching,* and a leather-bound notebook stuffed with loose map pages and wrapped shut with a thick rubber band. Without removing the rubber band, I stretched it open and scanned the pages, quickly recognizing Dan's nearly illegible handwriting, notes scribbled in Spanish and English. Along with the books was a sooty brass hash pipe, a box of wooden matches, three antique Chinese coins with square holes, turquoise and silver Indian trinkets, a moldy paper bag with a few shriveled mushrooms, and a handmade cloth packet hung on a braided necklace. I opened the packet and found Dan's passport.

The padre, finished with the log pile, stood waiting anxiously in front of me as if he had done all he possibly could and was wanting me to leave. I held up the passport and pointed to Dan's picture. "Where is he?" I asked.

The priest tried to speak, but the word he uttered was incomprehensible. I shook my head to say I didn't understand.

He glanced around the room until his eyes seized upon the candle burning on the mantel. He picked it up and held it between us, the yellow flame flickering in his glassy black eyes. He lifted his free hand, licked the pads of his thumb and forefinger, and with a dramatic little flourish pinched out the flame. A tiny sizzle, a whiff of smoke, and the light went out of his eyes.

Again he uttered the word.

This time I understood. Some words you know from any language, whether you speak it or not. They're the vital words, the curse words, the words that deal with the primal things of life. Love. Fuck. Shit. Death. I knew how to say them in German. I knew how to say them in French. And I knew what *muerto* meant in Spanish, even when mangled in the mouth of a mute.

I didn't want to believe it, and he could see it in my face. So he started to say the word again.

I cut him off. "How?"

He knew what I was asking—I could tell from the fear that came into his eyes. He shook his head and stepped back.

"What happened to him? Why is he dead?"

The padre shook his head again. I grabbed two fistfuls of his black cloak and thrust him up against the wall. His frightened face went blurry; my eyes were full of tears.

"Why?" I shouted. "Why?"

He opened his mouth wide and stuck out his tongue. It was nothing but a scarred little stump. He made his fingers into a scissors and "cut" them in front of his face.

It didn't take a lot of imagination to understand what had happened to him. Maybe the Mexicans did play charades.

I let him go, but the game wasn't over. He pointed the "scissors" into his ear and made a jabbing motion.

Speak no evil. Hear no evil.

Now I knew why he needed me to leave: The man was afraid of losing his eyes.

THE GREAT MYSTERIES

Ablind man is a burden. A deaf mute merely a nuisance." Pearls of wisdom from the mouth of King Leopold.

I heard him speaking as I made my way up the gangway steps into the salty night, where the lick of the humid air on my face felt like the tongue of the old man's dog. For the past several hours, tearless and numb, I'd been huddled in fetal seclusion on my bed, reading through Dan's vestigial notebook, listening to the lap of water on the hull and the sound of muffled voices. Now the voices pierced me like shards of glass, the sandpaper deck stung the soles of my feet, and everything around me seemed vibrant and threatening, as if I'd been suddenly ripped from the womb, as red and raw as a newborn.

Denial is a kind of placental protection: It safeguards the soul from life's brutal facts. Like the fact that my brother was dead and had probably even been murdered. That fact appeared as plain to me now as the stars in the sky overhead, like bright pinholes of light piercing the black band of a blindfold. Only now that seeping starlight was blinding me as well, and I shut my eyes as I stood there at the precarious top of the stairs, trying for a moment to bring into balance the brightness amid all the blackness.

How can Dan be dead, I thought, *and be so alive in my head?* Obsessively stroking his beard. Biting his dirty fingernails. Lifting weights in the basement. He has a horrid scar on his hip from the time he flipped his Harley. His whistling is pathetic; he cannot carry a tune. Perusing his beloved comic books, he's lost in concentration. Studying some obscure research text, he appears relaxed and amused. No matter what you're talking about, his eyes narrow intently as he listens to you speak. He has an annoying tendency to oppose your point of view, but he doesn't like to argue; he'd rather just get high. He sucks like a blowfish on his Persian hookah pipe. He carries the hubbly-bubbly on a climb of the Grand Teton, in order to smoke some primo hash at fourteen thousand feet. How did he ever make it down from there alive?

Dan is an oddball, eccentric in his tastes and obsessive in his enthusiasms. A brainy body builder, he has a brilliant if often puzzling mind. I watched him once talk circles around his preening classics professor, without a single word of it making any sense. Yet the world always seems to somehow *vibrate* in his presence. He has a rare capacity to breathe life into things. He can find endlessly fascinating what most of us consider profoundly mundane. Ants. Lizards. Imported cigarettes. The patterns of ocean wave formations. He once wrote a ninety-page dissertation on the pharmacology of catnip. In my admittedly limited world, I haven't met anyone who is anything like him. I know I'll never find anyone who is anything like him again.

So what do you do when someone is dead and your heart is unable to admit it?

I thought of my mother, alone in our house. How could I possibly tell her?

"Come join us, Jack. The air will do you good." Bellocheque had spotted me standing in the dark, teetering at the top of the stairwell. "Did the girls give you something to eat?"

"Maybe later," I said.

"You should eat," he insisted. "It'll keep your spirits up. Did you find anything more in the notebook?"

"Yeah," I said. "Apparently there's a patch of psilocybin mushrooms at the base of a waterfall in the mountains east of town."

Duff laughed. Rock said, "Some things never change."

Rock and Duff and Bellocheque had retired from the saloon after a dinner of boiled lobster and icy champagne and were now lounging in the open-air cockpit, smoking fat stogies under the brilliant dome of stars. Eva had caught the lobsters in a set of traps she had thrown over shortly after the rest of us had left that afternoon. Candy had prepared the dinner, and now the two of them were cleaning up. I'm sure that Rock and Duff would have been delighted to assist them, but Bellocheque had asked the boys to join him on the deck.

The night was still and the ocean extraordinarily calm. From where we were anchored, occasional sounds made their way out across the water from the distant shore—the clanging bell of a goat, the bray of a donkey, a human voice briefly calling—but the town itself was lost in dimness, its pale silhouette barely visible against the darkly looming jungle. Aside from the yellow firefly of a lantern crawling down a crooked street, there was little else to let you know the place even existed.

I sat down next to Rock. "You all right?" he asked.

"Yeah," I said.

"Drinky-winky?" He poured me a glass of Dom Perignon.

"Sure."

Duff held out a box of Hugo Cassars. "Cigar?"

I picked one out. Rock clipped and lit it for me. We all settled back in our seats.

"You guys talking about the priest?" I asked.

"Yeah," Rock said. He tapped an inch of ash into the water and turned to Bellocheque. "Why didn't they just kill him?" he asked. "No burden, no nuisance, no nothing."

"It seems that whoever maimed the poor man must have wanted to keep him around."

Rock persisted. "What good is a deaf-mute priest? He can't deliver a sermon, and he can't hear confession."

"Might bring me back to the Church," Duff said. He looked as if he'd had a good deal of champagne. He was contemplating the bubbles in his glass.

A shooting star blazed across the sky above his head. "Another one," Rock said, pointing, but by the time Duff turned around it was gone.

"It's a warning," said Bellocheque.

"The meteor?" Duff asked.

"The maiming of the priest. His muted tongue speaks louder than any sermon."

Rock exhaled a plume of smoke the size of Manhattan. "Like, if you say the wrong thing to the wrong person, you might lose your tongue?"

"Your tongue . . . Or perhaps your very soul." Bellocheque stroked the blue-black dog sitting like a statue beside him. "You see . . . now when a villager commits a sin, there's no one to listen who can offer God's forgiveness."

We chewed that one over in silence, staring into the starlit haze of cigar smoke like Ottomans at an opium banquet. My stomach growled. The champagne was having a salubrious effect, despite the conversation. I refilled my glass.

Duff looked at me with his eyes out of focus. "*Yanqui* go home," he said dreamily.

"What did you say?" Bellocheque asked.

"Nothing," I said.

"*Yanqui* go home," Rock repeated. "A 'warning' Jack got in PV."

Bellocheque narrowed his eyes at me. "Tell me about it."

"I'd rather not."

Rock and Duff were less disinclined. Whatever concern they might have had for me at the moment, they were not about to let it stand in the way of a good story. Nor were they entirely merciless, however; they delivered a slightly sanitized version of the tale.

When they finished, Bellocheque eyed me in amazement. "This fellow cut the words *into your back?*" he asked.

I suddenly realized I had never seen the words myself. "That's what I'm told," I said.

"And you didn't go to the police?"

"No."

"Do you think this man might know you're here?"

"I don't think so," I said. "I mean . . . I don't see how."

Bellocheque continued looking at me, as if trying to decide for himself whether this was true.

It made me nervous. The scars on my back started itching. I pictured the poor priest losing his tongue, and a frightening idea occurred to me. "Is it possible the cowboy is the guy who did the priest?"

Bellocheque leaned back, took a drag on his cigar, and released a round, silvery cloud that hung above his head like a nimbus. "Difficult to say . . ."

"We know he likes to give his warnings with a knife," Rock offered.

"Indelibly," Bellocheque added.

"He knew something about Punta Perdida," I said.

"Evidently, yes."

Duff chimed in. "And he knew that Dan was—" He stopped before he said it.

"He knew that Dan was dead," I said.

Bellocheque nodded somberly. "It would appear so."

Appear so, yes. Definitely so. I might have disbelieved the cowboy, but why would a priest with his tongue cut out lie about a thing like that? I no longer felt any need to deny it. We all knew it was true, even if we didn't know by whom or why or how, or what they had done with his body. All we had to go on was his notebook, and though it had yielded intriguing secrets, nothing it contained gave a clue to his demise.

A pall fell over the conversation. It felt as if the shadow of Dan's death had crept right out of the black water into the crypt of our boat, leaving a vapor trail of smoke that encircled us all like a funeral wreath. There's nothing the living can do in the presence of death except to turn away, not look at it or think about it too hard or too long. Otherwise you might end up wandering the house in your pajamas, talking to yourself and forgetting to shave. Trouble was, I couldn't let go of all the questions I had, the who and how and why of it all. I wanted the answers but knew we couldn't find them until the night was over and we could pull up anchor and check out the point Dan had circled on his map. Until then,

I'd lug around this riddle of death like an unmarked tombstone on my back, its polished face an inky mystery mirroring all those stars up there in the big eternal unknowable Nothing, their brilliant light so beautiful it brought a teardrop to my eye.

Beauty and Death, those are the great mysteries. I suppose somebody said that once, or if nobody did, I was saying it now:

Beauty and Death. The great mysteries.

Why else study English if not to serve these eternal twins?

So lost was I in this celestial meditation that I didn't even notice the music at first. It was Sinatra, standing at a gate somewhere, and sure enough the song that he sang was of moonlight, with the breeze kissing the trees, that sort of thing, though I really didn't hear the words until Eva removed the glass from my hand and set it down gently on the moon-washed teak. She took the cigar out from between my teeth and flung it over the side of the boat. Fine with me; I was sick of the damned thing, and besides, her eyes were just what Frank proclaimed they were: stars brightly beaming.

She held out her hand. Believe it or not, Eva wanted to dance with me. She took my hand and led me onto the forward deck, where she stopped and turned around to face me, resting her silver-bangled wrist on my shoulder. I slipped an arm around her waist and placed my hand on the small of her back. She had tied up her blouse, so the small of her back was bare and her skin felt warm and taut to my touch. That's when I knew for sure it wasn't a dream, when I touched her back and felt the exquisite warmth of her skin. No matter how much Dom Perignon you drink, you'll never dream anything quite like that, quite that bracingly, vibrantly erotic. It can only happen if it's real, and this was so real it felt like a dream, if you know what I mean.

I led her in a close little slow dance under the stars. Right there beside us was my old friend Duff, dancing with Candy, whispering in her ear, making her laugh. Probably the punch line to the Ethel story, which really was kind of funny if he ever could get to it. Bellocheque had taken the dog and disappeared down below deck. Rock was smoking and watching us, not envious or jealous or lonely or sad, just watching us dance there and letting it be. There was time enough; other opportunities were bound to arise. It was a small boat, after all, and it was clear to us now we'd be on it for a while.

Part Two

DESCENT

SAUSAGES

2/12. *Arrive Punta Perdida [illegible]. Astonished beach hag flees. Villagers [illegible] and freak. Visit to Punta's church reveals why: resemblance to reliquary Jesus uncanny. Have encountered these all over Mexico and down in [illegible] but none so unnerving. Good omen? Bad omen? Padre treats me like visiting deity. Unable to dissuade him. Hopes stoked by lectern figurehead—exactly as described by Sebastián and Wirikuta peyoteros!*

2/13. *Shave off beard & mustache. Feel naked, renewed. From saint to sinner a razor's edge. [illegible] and explore town. Salem, 1692. Inhabitants wary, fearful, insular. Beyond your standard xenophobia. Most Huichol descent, with dark complexions similar to Sebastián's. Padre only one who'll talk. Admits no knowledge of Argonaut. [illegible] beach has a cheery name: Playa de los Muertos.*

2/14. *Old black crone Obuela, bold but circumspect. Picks through my hair like she's looking for lice. Sells me delicious fried eel, 50p. Religion bizarre Huichol-Yoruba-Christian mix. Bottles hung round her house, full [illegible]. Swim & sleep, then snorkel outer rocks. Nothing.*

2/15. *Padre remains enthralled. Use it to my advantage, wheedle info. Catholic-Spanish name Ramón Ochera, Huichol name Kukuru. Claims grandfather big-shot mara'akame in*

Sierra tribe; maybe shaman-priest talent hereditary.
[illegible] *C. Levi-Strauss.*

2/16. *Padre opening up. My knowledge of Huichol reassuring, but his fear is palpable.* [illegible] *afraid of?*

2/17. *Dive, snorkel all day, but getting nowhere.*

2/18. *Fishermen won't talk, avert their eyes. Net mender mumbles curses. Throw I Ching. No. 36—Darkening of the Light. "One should not needlessly awaken overwhelming enmity by inconsiderate behavior." OK—veil it, under a bushel. 6/top: "Not light but darkness. First he climbed up to heaven, Then he plunged into the depths of the earth." Lovely. Sleep plagued by visions of fire & brimstone.* [illegible]

[Handwritten notes, in pencil, on folded page of lined yellow paper, inserted here:]
Argonaut departs San Francisco March 20th, 4:00 P.M. March 23rd, 2:00 A.M., exchanged signals with steamer Sonora bound northward; March 27th at 8:30 A.M, arrived at San Lucas; received supplies and left at 11:30 A.M. [illegible] Weather clear. No mention of trouble. But log of steamer Diamant notes approaching gale W. of PV ca. 2:00 P.M. [illegible] Arg. ran along Mexican coast generally two miles from shore. Was steering an offshore course most likely. Direction and trending of the beach was W.N.W. half W., and E.S.E. half E.

2/19. *Review notes from maritime log* [illegible]. *Storm may have driven* [illegible]. *North shore obvious choice. Decide to start on outer reach, first thing A.M.*

2/20. *Dive short rocks. Snorkel grid patterns. Nothing.* [illegible] *Fried eel lunch. Surly witch Obuela never walks a straight line. Rants on "el Diablo Blanco." Assume Yoruba spirit, maybe Shango cult. Language*

*blend unclear. She picks through my hair like a
monkey, pours out putrid bottle in a circle. Sickened,
I bolt, fall asleep in church. [illegible] Rain all night.
Padre amazed by my Hot Shot lighter, christens it
"Light of Christ." I make it a gift. Ecstatic, he lights
every candle in church.*

2/21. *Breakthrough! Padre hints of wreck off north shore's "lost
point." But refuses to accompany me. Forbids me to speak
of it. [illegible] Snorkel all aft. to no avail. Resign myself
to go deeper.*

2/22. *3rd tank. Still no luck. Obuela shows toothless smile, cooks
me octopus lunch—50p. Delicious, but pungent ochre herb
leaves me nauseous. No more diving today.*

2/24. *[illegible]*

2/25. *Hallucinations unrelenting. [illegible]*

2/27. *Padre admin.'s last rites. Halfway through, vomiting begins.
[illegible] recover. Just another miracle, according to P. Fine
[illegible] don't end in glass box. Marks on skin. Suspect
Obuela a bloodsucking sukuyan.*

3/1. *While sick, someone stole my liter raicilla. [illegible] Move
pack, peyote stash to padre's lair for safekeeping. Trust local
gods.*

3/3. *Storm churns water, heaving waves. Visibility 6 feet.
[illegible] sharks and great whites in these waters. One hour,
call it quits. Unrelenting headache.*

3/4. *Storm cont., heavy rain. [illegible] inside church. Derrumbe
mushrooms far superior to mountain hongos. Padre sings
weird, ethereal icaro, sends me soaring. [illegible] audible
imagery, towering wave of crystalline information utterly
sublime.*

3/6.   Storm finally relents. Vis. zero. [illegible] *Padre claims
         virgin patch of derrumbe near base of falls. Hike through
         jungle: 4 hrs.; climb to falls: 2 hrs. Falls stunning;
         mushrooms gone. Padre blames Obuela. Pick up new
         Huichol curses.*

3/9.   Snorkel & dive, all day. Nada. Two tanks remaining.
         [illegible] *Recall merchant ship* Rapid *sunk off Western
         Australia. Capt. set her afire to hide location. Could same
         have happened to* Arg. *after treasure & figurehead recovered?*

[More handwritten notes, blue ink, on torn scrap of manila
paper, inserted here:]
    Argonaut built of wood, 1834, Smith & Dimon shipyard,
    New York. Dimensions: 100' 4" on load waterline; 23'
    extreme beam; 22' 6½" moulded beam; 8' 8" moulded
    depth; draft, 6' 9" forward, 9' 7½" aft, at 153–3 tons
    displacement. *[illegible]* Rigged as fore-topsail schooner,
    carrying *[illegible]* to her fore-and-aft foresail a course and
    two fore-topsails. Hull painted black with contrasting
    sheerline strip at deck. Orig. owner: R. W. Freirich. Sold
    [illegible] James Pierson Cliburn, Charleston.

*3/11.   More than 2,000 transport galleons lost in Western
         Hemisphere. Fewer than 100 found. Paralyzing thought
         deepens despair.* [illegible] *more nausea, headaches. Delve
         into Hidalgo's mushrooms, throw* I Ching, *pass out on
         beach. Sukuyan witch Obuela swims into my nightmare,
         hoary head, tail of fish—Diablo Negro. Awake ar.
         midnight, wet from rising tide.* I Ching *open to No. 5—
         Waiting. "Fate comes when it will." 9/2nd place: "Waiting
         on the sand . . . water means danger . . . The danger
         gradually comes closer." Any wonder I drag this tome with
         me?* [illegible]*!*

3/15.   One tank left. Snorkel south of Whale Rock. [illegible]
         *Find barnacled scrap of iron. Once bright work? My heart
         races. Back tomorrow.* [illegible]

3/16. *More buried scraps. Circular metal bands. Recall on outbound voyage, Braga reputedly smuggled coffee into California in biscuit barrels.*

3/20. *Wake again with headaches. 3:00 A.M. Strange cry, like animal slaughtered.*

4/1. *Late aft., last tank—uncover wrought-iron anchor! Overburden removed by hand-fanning sediments, severely clouding water. Move deeper to escape clouds—enter into a dream. Utterly magnificent! Upended [illegible] preserved! [illegible] found before dark. What I wouldn't give for another tank of air! Must return to PV [illegible]. Try to tell padre of my find, but he won't hear of it. Suddenly realize I am April's Fool. Recall steam paddler Central America sank in hurricane off Carolinas in 1857. 420 people lost. Salvors used ROV to retrieve [illegible] and gold bars, but they had hardly begun before lawsuits ended their work.*

LESSON: *Silence is golden. This will be my last entry; I must bury this book.*

> *I bless you for the sausages*
> *that lasted me so long—*
> *Tho' I'm thankful they are gone, Mary,*
> *For they smelt a little strong.*

TWIST OF FATE

No, I didn't sleep with Eva, not that first night. What could I expect? I had known her for all of twelve hours, this woman who was probably still a mystery to her own mother. I was nothing more to her than an unemployed house painter who had filched her bandanna. The lady was totally out of my league. Venus on the half shell. The face that launched a thousand stiffs. She'd pick the who and when and where. All I could do was wait and hope. Like Dan's *I Ching* said: *Fate comes when it will.*

For the passengers and crew of the wandering *Obi-man*, fate came in the form of a spiking needle on a marine proton precession magnetometer. According to Candy, a magnetometer measures and records the earth's magnetic field. Neatly packed in a small, foam-filled metal case, the instrument was connected by a long, thin coil of insulated electric cable to a little rocketlike sensor with fins. Candy had tossed the sensor over the transom into the water, while Bellocheque steered us over the area circled on Dan's tattered chart of the bay. Towed through the water, the rocket sensor would detect anomalies in the local magnetic field that might be caused by ferrous material—like, say, the cast-iron anchor of an old shipwreck. It seemed like a long shot to me, but it certainly beat groping around the bottom for months while a batty old witch tried to poison you to death.

I stood with Eva and the dog at the bow of the boat, watching for hidden rocks at the surface. The weather could not have been better, and as I peered out over the sparkling water, feeling the warmth of the sun on my face and the pleasant draft of the ocean air, the sorrow that had weighed on me from the previous day began to lift, and I started to favor again the brighter side of things, to believe that whatever had happened to Dan had happened for a simple reason: He had brought it upon himself. His demise had occurred, if not in another place, at least at another time, or as Bellocheque might put it, another fateful *moment,* the culminating moment of Dan's heedless history, and was therefore unlikely to repeat itself with us, certainly not under the aegis of this magnificent boat, with these extraordinary people guiding our way.

The three of them had quite naturally assumed authority over us incompetent landlubbers, an authority to which we willingly submitted. How could we have done otherwise? Standing like a Titan against the oncoming wind, with his great bald pate shining in the sun and his massive hands on the pilot's wheel, Bellocheque was every inch the man in command, a black Caribbean Captain Courageous. Candy, despite her obvious physical attributes, had taken on the decidedly male role of chief petty officer, snapping orders and reprimands to the two befuddled crewmen at the rear. Eva, standing beside me at the bow, her dazzling eyes cast out to sea, could easily have taken on any role she pleased. Mermaid? Nile queen? Whip hand of the deck? She wielded a more mysterious power than that of Candy or Bellocheque, a power that seemed to emanate from some hidden place inside her, that found unforced expression in her beauty and her grace. Both alluring and intimidating, she inspired a desire in me bordering on awe. It seemed to flow out freely from some crack in my inner core, carrying away with it the sense of containment that until that point had held my life together. Although a little frightening, the experience was exhilarating; the simple act of standing beside her gave me an unforgettable thrill.

"You see it now, Jack?"

"Huh?"

"The rock—over there."

"Oh. Yeah. I see it."

Although we were nearly a mile out from shore, the Whale Rock that Dan had mentioned hunched out of the water less than a hundred yards away. It was the one visible vertebra of a sunken spine of land that stretched from the north end of the bay far out into the ocean. Whoever had named this place Punta Perdida—"Lost Point"—probably hadn't been happy to find it. I wondered aloud just how many ships might be lying in the water below.

"Perhaps not as many as you might think," Eva said. She was looking out through a pair of binoculars. "This coast has been charted for over four hundred years. In all likelihood, these rocks were marked on charts as far back as Sir Francis Drake."

"No kidding. My patron saint."

Eva lowered the binoculars and looked at me uncertainly.

"Wasn't he the first guy to go around the world?" I asked.

"First Englishman," she corrected. "It was a twist of fate, really."

"How's that?"

"He was afraid to go home the same way he came."

"Why?"

"It's a long story."

"It's a long day."

Eva looked at me, then cast her eyes back out on the water. "Drake set out from England with five ships to raid Spanish settlements along the Pacific coast."

I interrupted her. "Why would he do a thing like that?"

"Rivalry of superpowers. Not enough gold and silver to go around, I suppose. Besides, a few years earlier, he had commanded a ship in a slave-trading expedition that was attacked by the Spanish. His was one of only three English ships to survive."

"So it was personal."

"The word he'd have used would be 'honorable.' "

"Good word." I noticed—not for the first time—the dark

of her nipples beneath her blouse. Thank God one of us was watching for rocks. "So what happened?"

"He crossed the Atlantic, headed down the coast of South America. Two of his ships were abandoned in the Rio de la Plata—"

"—Buenos Aires?"

"Yes," she said, visibly impressed.

Postcard trivia from Dan. Was I getting points for this?

"He took the remaining three through the Strait of Magellan. One ship was lost in a storm. Another was separated and headed back to England."

"So just his ship was left?"

She turned to me. "Three minus two equals one, yes."

Debit point.

"The ship was called the *Golden Hind*. He sailed it up the western coast, plundered Valparaiso, destroyed the ships at Callao, and captured a Spanish treasure ship. That's how he got hold of the charts—"

"—and missed the rocks at Punta Perdida."

Was that a grin—or just a twinkle? Two points either way. Eva continued: "Having lost his ships in the strait and having stirred up the Spanish all along the coast, Drake decided it would be unwise to return the way he had come. So he continued north, searching for a passage back to the Atlantic. He went as far as the bay of San Francisco, and then went even farther. Of course, he found no passage."

"So he decided to cross the Pacific."

"The Moluccas, the Celebes, Java, and around the Cape of Good Hope. He arrived back in England nearly three years after he had departed."

"How is it you know so much about Drake?"

"I studied maritime history at the university. It has always been a particular interest of mine."

For a second I considered changing the course of my life. Forget English lit. Maritime history sounded so much more exotic. "Why is that?" I asked.

She shrugged a shoulder. "I've been on boats since I was

a child." She looked at me. "My father is an admiral in the *Marinha do Brasil*."

"The Brazilian navy?"

She smiled. *"Sim."*

Candy shouted from the back of the boat. "I've got something!"

Bellocheque spun the wheel, and the boat began a sharp U-turn. Eva handed the binoculars off to me and headed toward the stern, ambling lithely along the rail. With the sails wrapped, I could see Rock and Duff in the cockpit rise from their seats and move to peer over Candy's shoulder at the magnetometer. Bellocheque throttled the engine and headed back over the wake he had made. I hung the binoculars over my neck and made my way to the back of the boat, nearly tripping over the dog on the way.

Candy was wearing a hooded, half-zipped terry cloth jacket over a coral-colored floral bikini, a combination that added to her influence over my friends. She had Rock hauling in cable on the transom deck and Duff wrapping it into a coil on the floor of the cockpit. As I slipped down into the pit beside him, Eva passed me the instrument's printout and disappeared into the cabin below. I studied the lines and figures on the paper. It resembled a miniature cardiogram with line tracings and endless columns of meaningless numbers. I felt like the patient pretending to be the surgeon.

"Right there," Candy said, pointing a red fingernail at a particularly jagged peak.

"Think that's it?" I asked.

"Could be," she said. "It's in the right area."

Bellocheque pulled a lever that seemed to disengage the engine, and the boat coasted lightly into the chop. He called to Candy over his shoulder. "Ellie, dear, what do you say?"

"Maybe another twenty yards, Skipper."

Bellocheque eased the prop into reverse. The engine whined until the boat gradually pulled to a stop. Then he pushed a button and we heard the anchor drop. The line rolled out for half a minute before it finally stopped.

"Sounds deep," I said.

"Only about fifty feet," said Bellocheque. "We're on the edge of the point, I think."

A scuba tank was handed up to Candy from below, then another, followed by regulators, buoyancy compensator vests, weight belts, two pairs of fins, masks, and snorkels. As Candy stood upright and peeled off her terry cloth jacket, her minions froze at attention. Eva emerged wearing a stunning black high-neck Speedo with a huge rubber-handled bowie knife strapped to her calf. She looked like a navy SEAL's wet dream. With her breasts pulled tight under spandex and her lovely midriff hidden from view, for the first time I noticed how finely muscled she was, her long, shapely arms and legs lissome but strong. This woman could be a formidable wrestler or an Olympian swimmer; she probably liked to run a marathon before breakfast and was undoubtedly a strenuous lover in bed. Watching her strap into her gear on the deck of the *Obi-man*, I could hardly stand steady on my own two feet. Suddenly I had a thought: If Aphrodite was going into the water, shouldn't her bandanna bearer be going in with her?

Drake had given a twist to Fate; why on earth shouldn't I?

The guys were helping the girls on with their equipment. "Can I go?" I asked bluntly. All of them stopped what they were doing and stared at me. "I mean, I'd like to, if I can."

Candy, who had just attached her regulator to one of the tanks, lifted the assemblage and set it at my feet. "Be my guest," she said.

I looked to Bellocheque.

"Why not?" he said. "It was your brother who found the wreck."

NETHERWORLD

The thing that always strikes you is how cold the water is. Doesn't matter where you're diving or what the actual temperature is, when you first enter into that underwater world, it's a shock to the system. If it's Lake Michigan, you're wearing a wet suit, but there's still those first few moments when the icy water seeps into the suit and makes you want to scream. That's where Rock and Duff and I had learned how to dive—in the turbid waters of Lake Michigan, and in a brilliant blue quarry just outside of Rockford. It was cold in the quarry when you first went in; then down about thirty feet you hit the thermocline, and it got even colder. The temperature dropped off a dozen degrees, and visibility fell to near nothing. We used to swim down into that frigid, murky netherworld, forcing ourselves to linger down there as long as we could stand it, just so we could feel that much better when we floated back up into the luxurious warmth of the shallower "tropics."

Down here off the central coast of Mexico, we were on the edge of the real tropics, and the water was warm enough for us to wear only our swimsuits. Even so, as I plunged into the bay sporting Candy's diving gear, the cold took an icy grip on me, and I regretted having put on my skimpy Speedo instead of my long-legged surfer trunks. Wearing a T-shirt seemed to help a little bit, if only psychologically. I hadn't wanted to advertise the writing on my back, and the shirt offered some protection from the uncomfortable rub of the tank on my scars.

As the bubbles dispersed and I took my bearings, Eva Yerbabuena drifted into view. She hung weightless before me in the shimmering water, strapped into her gruesome mask and regulator like a floating angel on a respirator. The silky tentacles of her long black hair seemed to reach out to feed on the life of the water, and her hands moved in a gentle wading motion, massaging Neptune's invisible body. The muted light of the sea softened the dazzling green of her eyes, cooling them down to the gray-green tone of jade, the hue of the ocean itself. The skin of her shoulders and long white thighs seemed to glow with an effusive light, but I could see by the goose bumps bristling on her flesh that even the goddess was not immune to the cold. Her eyes made contact with mine, and I echoed the silent "OK" of her fingers with a silent "OK" of my own.

It's a good idea to dive with a partner; something can always go wrong. As we descended into the dusky depths, I thought of my hapless brother, snorkeling and diving for weeks on his own. He had swum in these very waters, a fact I found strangely comforting and at the same time vaguely disturbing.

Deflating my BC vest, I followed Eva's steady descent down the length of the anchor line. I was close enough behind to feel the water rolling off her and soon was entranced by the scissoring motion of her gently flexing limbs, the bare, caressing flesh of her silky inner thighs. A little bit of heaven goes a long, long way. The sight so captured my benumbed attention that I lost all thought of the coldness of the water, of the abrasive scuba tank chafing my back, of the grief I felt for the loss of my brother, even of our purpose, the reason we were here. It felt like I was following a woman in a dream, like Orpheus into the underworld, or Dante into the depths of hell.

I had no desire to awaken from the dream, but before I was even aware of it the bottom had appeared. Mossy green

jumbles of ragged boulders lay spilled across soft stretches
of gray silt and sand, gradually sloping off into darker
depths. We were exactly where Bellocheque had said we
were, on the edge of the lost point, the stony finger of land
that reached out to snag unwitting sailors and pull them into
the sea. If Dan's scribbles were to be believed—and I saw no
reason to doubt them—somewhere down here lay a cast-iron
anchor, and farther down the wreck of the boat it belonged
to, a sailing ship known as the *Argonaut*. It was still unclear
what had led my brother to this particular place; was it nothing more than the stoned ramblings of his peyote-popping
Indian friend, Sebastián? And what exactly was it Dan was
looking for on this ship? Captain Salty's mother lode? I had
my doubts. But his unrelenting pursuit of the wreck gave
credence to the notion that something of value lay buried
down here, something he wanted so badly that he had given
his life to find it.

Our own steely anchor had snagged itself in a pile of
mud-colored rocks, its sharp lines an alien contrast to the
surrounding moonscape. The occasional workaday fish
swam by, but nothing too bright or beguiling. This was a
long way from a coral reef's cornucopia; there was little of
interest in the gray and gloomy water around us. Eva
touched my arm and looked into my eyes, then made a circular motion with her hand, indicating the counterclockwise
direction she intended for us to swim. We had agreed on the
boat to search together in a gradually widening spiral, starting with our anchor as the center point. I gave her an "OK"
in confirmation, then followed alongside her as she lightly
fluttered away.

Swimming a few feet over the bottom, we scanned for an
anchor I imagined looked somewhat similar to our own,
only covered with a camouflaging crust of decay or a razor-
happy bristle of barnacles. What we saw as we swam in our
widening circles was a barren landscape of sand and rocks:
sand with an occasional patch of weedy flora, and rocks
upon which spiny black pincushions and stonelike starfish
clung. I kept hauling before my mind's eye the imagined an-

chor, placing its pattern into the passing landscape like a piece in a jigsaw puzzle.

We floated up over a mound of massive boulders, into a gully filled with gaping cracks and crevices too numerous to count. We split off and searched each side wall on our own, peering into the dark places, the hidden nooks and crannies. Fish were in abundance here, and the play of light and shadow seemed to bring the rocks alive. In one place, I saw a stone-colored lobster scuttle noiselessly back into its lair. Excited, I swam across and grabbed hold of Eva's arm, gesturing for her to follow me back. I pointed into the cavelike crevice, where the tips of the lobster's claws remained visible and a pair of antennae probed out from the shadows. When Eva caught sight of it, she looked disappointed: Apparently she thought I had found the anchor. She held out the palms of her hands and shrugged. We had no gloves with which to grab the sharp-clawed creature, and no sack or cage to put it in, so the notion that this might provide our lunch had been misguided at best. Besides, it wasn't what we had come here for. I felt childish and stupid, though she hadn't said a word. She simply moved on, swimming off into the gully.

We continued searching for over half an hour. The lack of any success fed a growing discontent that lured us into relaxing the constraints that we had set. We began to wander farther apart, expanding the search through a broader area and giving more leeway to our spiral path. Eva had remained in my peripheral vision, but after dipping into a long, narrow gulch and searching in vain along its boulder-strewn bottom, I emerged to find that she had disappeared from view. Spinning in a slow 360, I realized I had lost all track of where we were or what part of the spiral we were supposed to be on. I swam back over the gully to the place where I had entered it and searched again in the direction I thought I had last seen her. She wasn't there. I whirled in a circle again and recognized nothing around me; everything had started to look the same. I swam to the left of my original direction. Theoretically—given our counterclockwise spiral—it should have led me back toward the central anchor line, but as I swam along, farther and farther, nothing looked familiar. Nothing, and everything.

I couldn't have been so far from the anchor line, I thought. I stopped, spun around in a circle again, then went back the way I had come. If I could find the gully again, at least I'd know I was in range of Eva. I swam back, only now I had trouble finding the gully. I rose up over a high pile of boulders I had never seen before, and suddenly I had no idea at all where I was.

I hung there in the water a moment, unsure what to do. I realized I could just swim to the surface and look for the boat, but that would only waste my remaining air; there would hardly be enough left to come down again. I felt like a fool for having lost sight of my partner. Then again, she had lost sight of me as well. Perhaps she had become distracted. It was possible, after all, that she had finally found the anchor.

As I hovered above the heap of rocks and considered my next move, something strange came into view that gathered my entire attention. On the far, faint edge of visibility, a large, dark shape had appeared, welling whalelike into the light. Before I even realized it, I was swimming toward the thing, drawn by an instinctual and thoughtless curiosity. As I came closer to the dark form it seemed to lose its shape, and I realized that it wasn't a thing at all but a black cloud of silt, a billowing thunderhead expanding out in all directions. The realization frightened me at first, but I paused only a moment before a simple explanation came to me.

It was Eva. It had to be. There was no one else down here, and surely nothing else could cause such a stir. I moved closer toward the cloud. She must have found the anchor, I assumed, still half buried in the silt, and like Dan, she was fanning it free of sediment, muddying the water around her. I reached the outer boundary of the cloud and drifted along its rolling edge, peering into the murk. Soon I found myself moving into it, or it moving over me, and was surprised that I could actually still see a couple of feet ahead of me. The cloud was composed of fine particulate, a swirling storm of dark matter that seemed to swallow the ocean's light, and as I groped my way along, floating from one dim boulder to another, I felt anxious but not lost, like a blind man navigating an unfamiliar room. Eva was in the room somewhere, digging out the cast-iron anchor, and though I couldn't know exactly where she was, certainly I was getting closer to her with every kick of my fins.

The cloud grew darker and murkier the farther I ventured in. Soon my hands were touching rocks before I could even see them, and I began to wonder how Eva could possibly see what she was doing. And why in all this mess would she continue digging so relentlessly? I mean, what purpose would it serve to unearth the anchor anyway? If that was even possible. Eva did have a knife—a big knife—but it was hardly enough to pry loose the massive buried weight. The thing would in all probability be lodged firmly in rocks and sediment, unable to be moved without a team of diggers and the aid of a mechanical winch. How could she possibly do it by herself? She probably wouldn't even try.

So if it wasn't her stirring up this maelstrom, who was it? Or *what* was it?

An icy chill came over my body. My vision seemed to blur. It felt as if I had suddenly entered colder, darker water, and I flashed on the memory of the thermocline I had swum into years before—but this was no thermocline, not in the ocean, not at sixty feet. I stopped moving forward and hung still in the claustrophobic murk. I was breathing faster, using up my diminishing air. My body was shaking. Consciously, I slowed my breath. Then I stopped breathing altogether.

A sound had made its way to my ears, a sound I had not heard, or had not noticed, until now. It was a brushing or lashing sound, sporadic and violent. It seemed to come from everywhere and nowhere all at once, as if it were the sound of the swirling storm itself. The dirty water whirled only inches from my eyes. My mask was nothing more than a pocket of air trapped behind a thin pane of glass, a thousand pounds of pressure forcing it into my face, the dark water like a gloved, smothering hand bearing down on me. I felt the sudden whoosh of something above me, a turbulent swell of water. All at once a frigid panic took hold. I froze in place, unable to move. My mind stopped working.

The swell of water passed like a wave, but silt continued whirling around me. I could not see more than a few inches in front of my face. Without thinking, I turned around and started back, crawling along the sandy bottom, bumping into boulders like a blind dog, weaving this way and that, until I could no longer be sure whether I was really heading back or only moving deeper into the vortex.

That's when I saw Eva's scuba tank. It was not moving; it was not on her back. It lay instead abandoned on the seabed, covered with a powdery layer of sediment. I reached for it impulsively, lifting it and stirring an explosive cloud of silt. Pulling close, I examined the length of it as best I could in the swirling murk. The black paint was scarred with deep scratches, and the harness had been cracked and the straps torn loose. I realized with a heart-pounding shock that the buckle had been ripped clean off, leaving only the frayed end of the strap.

Blood rushed into my head. My breathing went out of control. I knew I was in a panic, but somehow I had to move, to try to find my way out of the darkness. Holding the tank in one arm, I groped my way slowly forward. Although the ocean had turned eerily silent, visibility had only grown worse; somehow the water continued to churn. Blinded, frightened, I felt my way along the bottom, afraid to detach from the tangible certainty of the ocean floor. Held down by the added weight of the tank, I pulled myself along. Sand, rock, sand, seaweed. Then my hand touched down in the soft goo of open flesh. I withdrew it instantly. Holding my breath, I lowered my face for a closer look.

The thing was a rotten, severed head! Milky-eyed, white-haired, vaguely human, and utterly grotesque—and out of its scalp poked the horns of a devil!

A chill ran up my spine that seemed to split my skull in two. In rushed the turbulent water, stirring a thousand thoughts. White devil. Obuela. Obi-man. Dan. Where was Eva? Where was I? Why couldn't I breathe?

My vision faded. My limbs went numb. My gut rose up inside my chest.

A blast of water knocked me back. The ground opened beneath me, and I tumbled into the void.

LIFE AFTER DEATH

I've heard the talk of white light, of angels singing, of departed friends and relatives waiting, of the soaring sense of relief and redemption. I can attest that all of these things happened to me. White light glistened above me, voices of angels thrummed in my ears, familiar silhouettes hovered in waiting, and a godly embrace lifted me up like a weary soul into heaven. It was Candy of the flaming hair who guided me aloft, Duff and Rock who hovered like cherubs at the surface, and Bellocheque whose vast embrace retrieved me from the sea. And the angels singing? Probably the hum of the outboard on the tender, waiting to take us all back to the boat.

Bellocheque sat me down gently on the seat and began to remove my gear. Rock and Duff dropped their fins into the boat and, with some considerable difficulty, clambered up over the gunwale. I tried to rouse myself to speak but couldn't mouth any words. I still felt the icy grip of the water, and a lingering dizziness seemed to be tugging me back down into the dark.

"He okay?" Duff asked.

Bellocheque examined my eyes, lifting each eyelid with the pad of his thumb. Then he looked at me squarely and patted me on the cheek. "He's going to be all right," he said.

Rock sat down dripping on the prow bench behind me. He put his hand on my shoulder. "Lucky we found you," he said. He pressed the release on my regulator, expelling a faint wheeze of barely compressed air. "You were down to nothing."

"Eva," I spluttered. I tried to sit up and slipped on the seat. "I never—"

"It's all right," Bellocheque said, steadying me. "Take a deep breath. Calm yourself." He was sitting across from me, watching me carefully.

Candy's red-nailed fingertips pushed Eva's tank up over the gunwale into Duff's arms. "Oh my God," he muttered, setting it down carefully on the floor of the boat.

I stared at it with dread. The tank was indeed battered and the buckle torn off—I hadn't merely imagined it. Candy handed her own tank and her fins up to Duff, then easily climbed up over the side.

"Found him on the slope at seventy-five feet," she said. "Must have passed out and rolled off the edge. He was hugging the tank in his arms."

"Anything else down there?" Rock asked.

"Nothing," she said, pulling off the rest of her equipment. "Just a lot of murky water." She took a seat at the stern and gunned the throttle. Then she shifted into gear and aimed the boat back toward the *Obi-man*. In seconds we were skimming over the water.

Bellocheque saw me staring at the tank. "We thought we might have lost you," he said. "Candy finally spotted your bubbles through the binoculars."

Duff moved onto the seat beside him. "You okay, Jack?"

I turned my woozy gaze to him. "She's gone," I muttered, my voice still weak.

"Who? Eva?" He thrust his chin toward the distance behind me. "Take a gander, bimbo."

I turned, peered over Rock's shoulder at the swiftly approaching *Obi-man*. There was no mistaking the hourglass figure silhouetted against the sun. She was perched at the rail with an open silk blouse fluttering over the curves of her suit, wet black curls clinging to her face. She smiled at the sight of me. The dog barked.

I stared at her in bewilderment. Apparently I indeed had

died for real and found my way into heaven. Eva was alive and well and looking like a million dollars. I waved at her vaguely and smiled with half my mouth. Then I turned and stared in confusion at the tank.

Bellocheque lifted it off the floor and took a careful look. "Our presumed anchor," he said. "Neither of you found the real one. It must have been this tank that triggered the magnetometer."

"But if it's not Eva's, then . . . ?"

"Your brother Dan," Bellocheque said consolingly. "It may have been this very tank that carried him into the deep." He gently laid it across my lap. The pressing metal still held the coldness of the sea. I shuddered.

There's a proper medical term my doctor uses to describe my condition. I hauled it out now to explain what had happened in that scary little episode down below, after first giving a brief history of how—just like my mother and my grandfather—I've always had exceptionally low blood pressure, a factor that apparently exacerbates the problem. I told them all about how an overload of stress, pain, fear, or fatigue can overstimulate my vagus nerve, slow my heart rate to a crawl, drop my BP into the basement, lock up my throat, drain the blood from my head, and knock me to the ground like a sucker punch. Just as Duff and Rock had years before, though, Bellocheque and the ladies all too quickly recognized that "vasovagal syncope" was nothing more than a fancy term for fainting. Given the smirking look that passed between Candy and Eva, rather than try to explain the damn thing, I might as well have waved my hand fan, picked up my doily, and retired to the parlor for tea.

At any rate, now that my shameful secret was out, nobody wanted to believe my story about the white devil's severed head. Truth is, I wasn't even sure about it myself anymore. Had it been human or . . . something else? Had it happened before I fainted or after? The more I thought about it, the more I thought it was perfectly possible I had imagined the whole thing. I'd had some hairy nightmares when I had fainted in the past; this might have been just one more vaso-vagal dream. If I hadn't brought the tank back with me, I might even have begun to wonder about that.

But something had happened that made me think twice about what I had encountered down there, something even more tangible than the broken tank or the sickening feel of the head's squishy flesh. It had occurred on the surface a short while after Eva and I made our descent. To pass the time, Bellocheque had engaged the boys in a peso poker game, while Candy read a trashy paperback about a demented serial killer up in Alaska chasing a blind girl on skis. According to Rock, Bellocheque was quite the card player; he quickly cleaned them out in a dozen hands of twenty-one. Then he gave them their pesos back and started all over again with five-card stud.

Rock was cutting the deck when they suddenly heard a splash on the water. They assumed it was a fish jumping at first, but then Candy spotted a little fishing boat with two Mexicans rowing vigorously back to shore. They called to the men in English and Spanish but got no response. Rock checked them out with his binoculars: He said one of them looked like a black man with straight hair, cut in a bowl like an Indian's; the other man he couldn't see, his face hidden beneath a sombrero. Rock said he couldn't see any fishing nets or poles, either, though they may have been lying in the bottom of the boat. They watched the two row back toward town until they grew tired of watching. Then Candy reopened her paperback and the guys went back to their game.

The story had got me thinking. Maybe the boatmen had dropped something into the water. Maybe they had dropped the head.

Later on, down in the galley, the girls were preparing lunch, Eva mashing avocados and Candy peeling shrimp. While Duff poked around them, giving bad cooking advice and snatching bites of food, I fell into a speculative argument with Rock.

"It's possible that head was Dan's," I told him.

"You said it had horns. You said the hair was white."

"The thing was all corrupted. Probably been dead for months."

"But *horns?*"

"Yeah, well . . ." I was sounding as loony as my mother. "Maybe I just . . . imagined the horns."

Rock snickered.

Duff laughed. "Maybe you're just getting horny."

This brought a giggle from Eva. Candy whispered something in her ear. Eva cracked up.

"*What* did you say?" Duff asked, feigning shock. "I can't believe you said that, Candy! I didn't think you were that kind of girl." He threw me a Groucho glance.

Candy and Eva were laughing helplessly. Candy shrieked like a banshee.

"What did she say?" I asked.

Candy threatened Duff with her fork. "It wasn't meant for your ears!"

Rock was stuffing his face with chips. "I heard what she said," he mumbled. "Shocking."

"Tell me what you said, Candy."

"Don't tell him," Eva said, clamping her wet hands over my ears. "He's got vasovagal fainting disease—"

"He faints when he gets horny!" Duff laughed.

"What did she say, Duff?"

"Can't tell you, Jackie boy!"

Candy herded us out of the galley. "All of you out— now!" she demanded. "Too many cooks!"

"C'mon, Candy."

"Out! Out!"

H aving just returned from a swim with his dog, Bellocheque was sitting on the edge of the deck with the black Lab lying beside him. The salty air, still and humid, was rife with the odor of the dog's damp fur, an earthy scent that seemed out of place so far away from the shore. Bellocheque inhabited a gauze caftan with a monk-like hood over his head. Hunched over the lower rail, with his wet paunch bulging and his dripping feet dangling beneath him, he cradled an amber-filled tumbler in his hands and absently stared at the waves.

He had promised to make another pass over the area to look for the wreck after lunch.

For now it appeared that he wanted to be alone, and I feared we were intruding on his solitude. None of us spoke, but gradually our presence roused him from his reverie. "So," he said with barely a glance. "What was all the laughing about?"

"They wouldn't tell me," I said.

"Dirty joke," Duff said.

Bellocheque sipped his drink. "Beware the demon female," he said darkly. "Boys are bred to be devoured."

I exchanged a glance with Rock and Duff.

"Enter like a lion, exit like a lamb." Bellocheque peered up from the shadow of his hood. "*Vagina dentata.* Their cunts have hidden teeth, you know."

I wondered what he was drinking. From the looks they gave me, Rock and Duff were wondering the same thing. None of us could think of anything to say after that enigmatic little tidbit, so I decided to change the general direction of the conversation toward another worrisome speculation of mine.

"Mr. Bellocheque? Do you know if there are any sharks out here?"

"Of course there are," he said, "but no more here than anywhere else."

"You're sure?"

"Sure I'm sure."

"Well, something was making a commotion down there. I don't know what it was, but it stirred up a real mess. Couldn't see a foot in front of my face."

"Don't tell me," Rock said. "An underwater dust devil."

"I'm telling you what I saw, Rock."

"Could have been the current," Bellocheque said. "You get a lot of odd currents on a submerged point like this. Water coming in has to find a way out. Did you notice a temperature change?"

"Well . . . yeah, but I thought it was just me. My blood pressure dropping."

"Might have been just you. Or it might have been a current."

I had definitely felt some turbulent water. The last thing I remembered was the blast that knocked me back. "What about the scuba tank?" I asked. "That wasn't torn off by a current."

"No idea," he said. "He might have cut it off, but . . . I couldn't say why."

Duff had an idea. "Maybe the tank was no good, Jack. An old, beat-up Mexican rental with a broken harness. Could be Dan just got pissed off and chucked the damn thing overboard."

"I doubt it," I said soberly, then added, like an afterthought, "I think there's something down there."

The four of us stared in silence at the sea. The water looked somehow different, more ominous and opaque. Bellocheque uttered something to himself. The word I caught was "dragons."

"What did you say?" I asked.

His eyes drifted skyward, as if he were following some airy train of thought. "I find it rather intriguing," he said, "your 'vasovagal syncope.'"

I replied that I found it a nuisance.

He offered a different spin. "One wonders if there isn't a purpose to fainting. It seems to be a sort of self-induced sleep."

"It's hardly under my control," I said.

"Neither is sleep entirely under our control. It's a grudging surrender of consciousness, a sort of temporal death. No one really knows its purpose. Cellular recuperation? Downtime data processing? It may in fact have an evolutionary function: enforced immobilization. Sleep as a means of survival. From the late Mesozoic, cold-blooded reptiles ruled the day, while our mammal ancestors hid in trees, paralyzed by unconsciousness. They awoke at night, under cover of darkness, to descend and steal their predators' eggs."

Bellocheque stared into his amber drink. "Perhaps dreams intermittently wake us to keep us from being eaten. Hence their content. From the time they're able to talk, children tell us they dream of monsters."

Monsters. The word lingered in the humid air like the scent of the dog's damp fur. Bellocheque appeared to be talking to himself; it didn't seem to matter who was listening. He may have been implying that I had only been dreaming, that my "devil" was the nightmare of a child. Or he may have been suggesting that some nightmares are real. I had no idea what it was he really meant. With his head hidden in the hood of his robe, I couldn't even see the man's face, but the sound of his voice was entrancing; he held our attention like the tumbler in his hands.

"Sleep," he continued, "is a vestige of history, dreams the dregs of fear. This after six million years on the ground. The memory of prey is long." He took another leisurely sip of his drink and peered at his reflection in the water.

"So what does that have to do with my fainting?" I asked.

"Everything, I imagine. Or nothing." He glanced over at me from the shadow of his cowl. "Your problem harkens back to the legends of the Greeks." Again he looked down at his wriggling reflection. "To peek at the petrifying head of the Gorgon, Perseus turned to the mirror of his shield. Passing the bone-strewn shore of the Sirens, Odysseus stuffed the ears of his men and lashed himself to the mast. How else to hear their song and survive? Blinded, deafened, bound, these ancient heroes shielded themselves with self-imposed surrogates of sleep."

"Beware the demon female?" Apparently even Duff had been paying attention.

"Beware the beauty and the horror of nature. The rose draws our eye, the thorn our blood. Lured from the trees by the promise of pleasure, we enter the unknown, the *terra incognita.* What will be encountered there can only be imagined. And so, on the empty edge of the seafarer's chart, they inscribe a baleful warning: *Here be dragons.*"

His words again were left to linger. The four of us sat staring at the water and the waves.

Then, at the sudden shriek of Candy's piercing laugh, Bellocheque fumbled his tumbler. It vanished with a plunking splash.

"Buggers!"

Candy had emerged from the kitchen below with her head thrown back in a vigorous laugh, her sunny bosom bobbing. She held a tray of sautéed shrimp and oven-warmed tortillas, with little painted bowls of green guacamole and red salsa and piles of peppers and chips. Giggling, Eva followed behind her with a full pitcher of margaritas and half a dozen plastic glasses. Demon females? I don't think so. Even Captain Bellocheque, our enigmatic monk, came alive at the titillating sight of them, though it may have been the scampi that brought him to his feet. He threw off his hood and moved on Candy's tray. "Dragons be damned," he declared. He plucked up a dripping, helpless prawn and tore off a bite with his teeth.

LIKE A VIRGIN

W ake up, everybody!"
The spike on the magnetometer looked like a full-blown heart attack. I'd been watching the marker trace an ailing zigzag for probably forty minutes when suddenly it had erupted with convulsing jitters that broke into the margins of the rolling grid. Candy closed her paperback, propped her sunglasses in her hair, and checked the trace for herself.

"Bingo," she said. "Cut it, Leo!"

Bellocheque whirled the steering wheel, his gold-banded Rolex arcing brightly in the sun. The Labrador barked, Duff stirred from his slumber in the cockpit, and Rock and Eva worked their way back from the prow.

"Who's going down with me?" Candy asked as she fastened her regulator to a tank.

"I'll go," Duff said, mustering himself.

Candy eyed him skeptically. "You drank half a pitcher of margaritas at lunch."

He rubbed his eyes and stretched. "That was an hour ago," he said.

"Alcohol dehydrates. It can lead to decompression illness."

"So I'll drink some water."

"I can go," Rock said, sliding into the cockpit. "I hardly drank at all."

"Forget it, Rock," Duff said. "I already called it."

"Go back to sleep," Rock said. "We don't need another turkey passing out at sixty feet."

"I'm going, Rock."

"I don't think so."

"You don't think so? Who the hell are you—Captain Nemo?"

"Fuck you."

"Fuck you!"

"Gentlemen, gentlemen. Please." It was Bellocheque. That voice of his. "If you wouldn't mind, I'd like to accompany Eleanor myself."

Oh. For some reason it hadn't occurred to us that the owner of this enterprise might like to make the descent himself.

"We have six scuba tanks on this boat," he explained. "We've used two. To maximize efficiency, we should stick to two divers down at a time. Four just becomes too hard to control. That means two more dives. If you'll indulge me on this one, I promise the two of you will be more than welcome to partake in the next. Agreed?"

Duff shrugged.

"Fine," Rock said. "Whatever you say."

"Splendid." He shifted the throttle into reverse and slowed the boat to a stop. "Eva, darling? Would you be so kind as to gather my gear?"

Eva dropped down below without a word. Bellocheque pressed a button; the anchor splashed.

Ten minutes later, all I could see of Leo and Candy was a soft burst of bubbles at the surface. They had traveled down the anchor line and by now had reached the bottom, which lay at roughly the same depth Eva and I had explored. In fact, we were quite close to where the two of us had made our descent, perhaps just a couple of hundred yards farther out over the point. As I watched their mingling exhalations well up in fitful bursts, I wondered again about the currents down there and hoped that Bel-

locheque was right about the sharks. Right or not, I had noticed he strapped the knife to his leg.

The ocean surface looked peaceful enough. Low, rolling
waves curled the satin glare of the sun and lulled the boat
with a gentle rock, while above us bright clouds migrated
across the blue sky like giant paper whales. I lifted the
binoculars hanging from my neck and aimed them toward
the town. The hodgepodge of stucco houses, wan and lifeless in the sun-filled haze, clung like a mirage to the hills
above the beach. There was no sign of activity on the dock,
and no suspicious fishing boats rowing out our way.

Sitting on the edge of the deck with my feet dangling
over the water, I stared down into the inscrutable depths and
found myself wondering how the devil had lost his head.
Maybe it was the same way the padre had lost his tongue.
Again I lifted my gaze and squinted toward the village. It lay
there in its languid haze, as indecipherable as the sea, its rotten secrets wrapped up like a fish in wax paper. A fish, or an
eel, or an octopus—I knew I'd have to go back there just to
check out the cuisine. Who the hell was Obuela? Why was
everyone hiding? What had happened to Dan? Every question I asked myself gave rise to a dozen more. I decided that
I needed to dig deeper into the notebook. Another sniff of
those tainted sausages might reveal the malady that ailed the
pallid town.

I rose from my perch on the edge of the bow and stepped
over to Eva sunning on the deck. She had been there for a
while; in fact, her presence had been the main reason I had
remained there for so long. Earlier she had changed into a
bikini, and for the past twenty-five minutes she had been lying on her tummy with her straps untied, entrancing me with
a view of her breathtaking back.

I picked up the Neutrogena lying beside her. "Would you
like some more lotion?"

"I'm fine," she said. She didn't even open her eyes.

As I set the bottle down, my wrist lightly grazed the side
of her thigh. It was nothing, of course, but the sensation trig-

gered a rush of feeling, and I paused there, standing over her, seemingly unable to move. It felt as if my body had been ensnared by an invisible field, a force of gravity, the same force that held my feet to the boat, and the boat to the water, and the water to the earth, the power that pulled everything together and held it where it ought to be: touching. The smart smack of a nun's ruler, my father's iron discipline, fear of embarrassment, years of schooling, books, culture, manners—this was the opposing force, the voice of inhibition and self-control, and it called on me now to hold back, to stop reaching out to touch her again. *Not now,* it insisted. *Not yet.* It was a voice I seemed unable to ignore.

"Let me know if you change your mind," I said at last. Somehow these pathetic words seemed to break the spell. Another dismal triumph of man over nature. It felt like a defeat. I stepped over her ankles and headed to the cockpit.

Duff was lying there. He had fallen back asleep on the long seat across from the wheel, while Rock, who had complained of constipation since the day we left PV, had gone down below to try his luck in Candy's bathroom. That was half an hour ago. I had to wonder if that was all he was doing down there. The Rock had long possessed a notoriously ravenous and insatiable sexual appetite; I could swear he'd been renting pornos as far back as the third grade. Duff was only half joking when he said Rock's need to screw three times a day was what had finally driven his catatonic girlfriend into the arms of another woman. Since then, the situation had not much improved. Summer in the suburbs had brought with it a long dry spell, and so far our trip into the fertile tropics had yielded little fruit. In an obvious case of beginner's luck, Rock had hooked up with a horsey Texas A&M coed the night we arrived in town, but she had left on a 7:00 A.M. flight the next day, and in the two weeks that followed, he'd never gotten lucky again. For Rock, two weeks was an eternity. I could tell from his furtive, fidgety glances, the sperm count was rising to dangerous levels. Add to that the constipation and we were talking serious trouble. Soon he'd be likely to burst into flames or embark on a killing spree—

unless, of course, as I now suspected, he had simply locked himself in an empty bathroom and placed the matter into sensible hands.

I stepped down the stairwell into the cool shade of the empty saloon. Down the hall, I noticed, the door to Candy's room was closed. I went to our room at the prow to grab Dan's notebook, but it no longer lay on the bed where I had left it. I looked around to no avail, then headed back up the hall, knocked lightly on Candy's door, and stuck my head into the room.

"Have you seen Dan's notebook, Rocko?"

"Yeah," came his voice behind the bathroom door. The door swung open.

Rock was sitting on the toilet reading the notebook, swimsuit down around his ankles, a pile of magazines at his feet. He peered up at me pathetically.

"Any luck?" I asked.

"Hopeless," he answered.

I nodded toward the notebook. "Find anything interesting?"

"Maybe," he said. He handed the open notebook to me, then flushed the toilet and pulled up his suit.

I looked at the page he'd been reading: the entry for February 20, with the reference to the old black woman, Obuela, and to *el Diablo Blanco*.

"I noticed that, too," I said. "Dan seemed to think it was some kind of cult."

Rock tied the waist of his suit while inspecting his burly physique in the mirror. "That head you say you saw at the bottom—you really think it was Dan's?" His eyes caught mine in the mirror.

"I'm not sure," I had to admit. "If it was, it no longer looked human." I watched Rock wash his hands in the sink. "If Dan is dead like the padre claims, where do you think he was buried?"

"What makes you so sure he was buried?" Rock asked.

I thought of the graveyard I crossed at the church. Could Dan have been lying beneath my feet? Somehow it didn't seem likely. "I'd like to go back to that town again. Force them to show me his corpse."

"That might not be too smart," Rock warned.

"I'm not afraid of them," I told him. "It's them who are afraid of us."

"The question is, who is the padre afraid of?"

"I think I ought to find out."

"I think you ought to give it a rest." He dried his hands on a tiny towel and tried to change the subject. "Has Eva flipped yet?"

"Eva? What—is she a porpoise?"

"She's a mermaid." He nodded toward the magazines on the floor. "Check out Charlize in the *Cosmo*," he said. "I'll keep an eye on Eva." He headed out of the bedroom.

I called after him, "Don't do me any favors!"

I kicked shut the door to the bathroom and peed in the waterless toilet. The *Cosmo* Rock referred to lay atop Candy's seaport collection of *Vogue*s and *Redbook*s and *Mademoiselle*s. The cover featured Charlize looking windswept with a dozen headlines swirling around her. All were variations on the standard theme of How to Exploit Your Power Over Men, as if it were the principal source of amusement occupying an entire gender. My eyes drifted from the magazine to the crowd of toiletries assembled on the sink. I couldn't help noticing a small golden bottle of perfume, audaciously shaped like an abstract vagina. Twisting off its clitoral cap, I lifted it to my nose and took a tantalizing sniff. The perfume smelled like roses, a scent that brought immediately to mind the blazing color of Candy's hair. It was a kind of relief to dwell on it a moment, so obsessed had I been with all things Eva. What a delicious creature, Candy! For a few dangerous seconds I considered opening the *Cosmo* and stepping up to bat.

I stopped myself. Quickly, deliberately, I turned my attention to the grungy razor on the ledge of the shower, the toothpaste smeared in the bowl of the sink, the open box of Kotex bulging from a drawer. There are two sides to everything, and women are no different. Coarse hair sprouts from their silken legs, clogged sleep turns their sweet breath foul, and once a month their golden chalice brims with crimson blood.

My brother, a well-read student of sybaritic lore and a collector of aphrodisiacs, subscribed to the theory that sexual power increases in proportion to the length of abstinence. "Use it and lose it," he liked to say. He believed the principle applied equally to both men and women. Abstinence exercised the muscle of attraction, toning the sexual persona until it exuded an irresistible aura of erotic charisma. This was the secret genius of the virgin. He talked about the vestals of ancient Rome, young girls chosen from prominent families to tend the sacred fire in the temple of Vesta, never allowing it to expire. They were sworn to celibacy for thirty long years; if one of them dared to break her sacred vow, she was taken from the temple and entombed alive.

I hoped that pondering that unpleasant prospect might dispel my beastly urge. Eva, after all, was the one I wanted, and to win her would require all the sexual charisma I could muster. *Keep the flame alive,* I thought. *Take the vestal's vow.* How else to conquer an unconquerable goddess? I would turn my passion inward, fan the flame of my burning heart. Bring on the blazing scent of roses! Stoke my loins with *Cosmo* girls! Nothing short of eternal entombment would crack my virgin vow!

After cranking one off in Candy's bathroom, I sulked through the hall to the room at the bow to brood once again over Dan's unearthed notebook. There was much that had puzzled me, and much yet unexplored. The journal entries stretched as far back as the summer he had spent in the Yucatán in the steamy drudgery of the archaeological dig. There were notes and figures relating to his pottery scams in Mexico City, references to a major cannabis purchase in Guadalajara (apparently to be unloaded in Acapulco), and plans for smuggling something called "bambalacha" (mescaline?), a scheme that appeared to have gone rather badly. He fled into the mountains. There were numerous hand-drawn maps of his trek through the Sierras, with anthropological observations of encounters with the Huichols.

The Huichols were thought to be descendants of the Aztecs; they spoke a language called Uto-Aztecan. One of the last of the world's indigenous populations, they lived in near isolation in the mountains along the coast. At one point Dan had joined a group of Huichol *peyoteros* who had embarked on a "peyote hunt" to Wirikuta, "the place of the Ancient Ones." Judging from his voluminous notes, the experience had made a considerable impression. He described in some detail their rituals and practices, how they gave each pilgrim a new name and "reversed" the names of things and places. Tangerines became lemons; gray old men became nubile young women; the dry desert became the roaring sea; the night became the day and the day the night. He described how they actually did "hunt" the peyote, shooting arrows through the plants as if they were little green rabbits that might run away. The Indians treated the precious buttons like sentient beings, touching each one to their foreheads, cheeks, and eyes before dipping their arrows in "peyote blood." He described in enthusiastic detail the peyote-induced euphoria with its concomitant distortions of time and space, its psychedelic imagery and vivid hallucinations.

I read this stuff until my eyes glazed over. Dan was one of those science-minded potheads who think of themselves as pioneering "psychonauts," exploring vast, unknown regions of the inner world—Captain Kirk on acid. Like many of those who had gone before him, he felt the need to chronicle his inner adventures, describing in minute detail everything from "glowing lava flows of brilliant, sparkling jewels" to "endless folds of glistening, iridescent fibrous wings of wonderful insects" to the alien land of the little tykes, the fairylike *cabiri,* creatures that apparently lived inside his skull. Dan used to devour whole libraries of this so-called psychedelic literature: Bayard Taylor, Fitz Hugh Ludlow, Wasson, Schultes, Huxley, Burroughs, Leary, McKenna— the names go on and on, just like their writings. Dan had

read them all, most of them more than once. He had even
lugged a 1927 edition of *Der Meskalinrausch* around Mexico with him—it was one of the books I had found in his
bag—and as far as I knew the guy couldn't read German!

None of this blather did anything for me. Narratives of
drug-induced reveries always reminded me of my flaky
psych-major girlfriend Alice and her supposedly amazing
Jungian dreams. Every morning she'd wake me up and rattle
on about them. "Archetypes" and "animas"—it all bored me
to death.

It was hot and stuffy in the airless little room. I peeled off
my T-shirt, kicked off my sandals, stretched out on the bunk,
and continued to read.

Fortunately, the notebook included plenty of more sober-
minded and potentially relevant material interspersed
among the journal entries, maps, notes, and drug-money accounting calculations: a variety of botanical drawings and
roughly sketched pencil portraits; childlike symbols and
strange, untranslated words and phrases; psalms from the
Bible and quotes from Revelations; bizarre chanting songs
and cryptic, hallucinatory poetry. Some of the symbols were
labeled "spirit writing" and looked like an imbecile's version of shorthand. Beneath one that resembled a kite with a
tail was the following little ditty:

Ay ree ah jaja	*We are searching for you*
Ay ree leh	*Wherever you are.*
Ah jaja wo goon	*Show yourself,*
Ajaja way geh	*We want to see you.*
Ay ree ah jaja	*Come, let us speak to you.*
Leh beh weh ja go	*We call you, we speak to you*
Ay ree leh eh beh weh ja go	*Wherever you are.*
Ay ree leh	

It didn't look anything like Spanish to me. I checked the
words against Dan's tattered Uto-Aztecan dictionary, and
they weren't in there, either. I wondered if it might be related
to what Dan had called the "Shango cult," which he said

came from the island of Trinidad in the West Indies. There was something African in the sound of the words. I reread a passage where he had observed similarities to Shango practices in the rituals performed by Sebastián during the peyote hunt to Wirikuta. Apparently Sebastián was a Huichol *mara'akame,* a priest or shaman; it was his description of the figurehead in the church that had brought Dan to Punta Perdida in search of the *Argonaut.*

Had that been how Dan first learned of the ship? Why would native Mexican Indians sing little ditties sprung from Africa? What had finally happened to Dan? How had he been killed? Had it been murder? I kept picking through the notebook, chasing down cross-references, following one thread of inquiry after another, trying desperately to tie it all together, until I found myself wrapped up and dangling like Kafka's beetle in a spider's web. This notebook was worse than Alice's dreams, and the whole crazy business was giving me a headache.

As I tossed the book aside, a flutter of paper fell to the floor. Some of Dan's pages had been torn loose and stuffed back in under the leather cover. I had noticed them my first time through, but nothing in these ragged pages had seemed particularly pertinent. They were drawings mostly, of plants and birds and fish, so I had simply stuck them back inside. This time, however, as I looked down at the sheets on the floor, one of them caught my eye. It contained a number of small pencil drawings, including two views of a dead fish, a close-up of a dog's diseased eye, and a delicate rendering of what I presumed to be a peyote button. The fourth drawing on the sheet was different from the others—different, in fact, from any of the drawings contained in the notebook. It was smudged and indistinct, fully shaded from the broad side of the lead, and set altogether within a small, perfect circle. The subject was indiscernible, which was why I had passed it over the first time through. This time, with the page turned upside down on the floor, a faint form emerged from the shadowy fog of lead. As I lifted the sheet closer to my eyes, the image suddenly leapt out in a flash of recognition.

Lady Liberty.

Bellocheque's quarters were luxurious. A large, frosted skylight and high, wide windows with lacy curtains admitted a generous light, imparting to the limited confines of the space an astonishing palatial air. An opulent, round-cornered, king-sized bed dominated the mahogany room, its ivory-colored satin sheets topped with sage-colored silk jacquard, pillows embroidered with tassels and trimmings, and at the foot of the bed a dark, plush fur throw, curled like a sleeping mink. Large drawers inhabited the enclosed space beneath the bed, and the walls were lined with multiple closet doors and brass-handled cabinets. Along the far wall was a foldout desk and a long bookshelf filled with an eclectic array of texts, everything from T. E. Lawrence's translation of Homer's *Odyssey* to Candy's battered paperback *Snowblind*. Beside the desk was a long, curving, upholstered couch built against the mahogany wall, and on the couch lay Bellocheque's carelessly tossed Mexican shirt, his baggy drawstring pants, and his massive silk boxer shorts, discarded during his quick change for the dive he was now on.

There were plenty of places in the room to hide the thing, if hiding it was something he felt necessary to do. I didn't think he'd find it necessary, so I went directly to the pockets of his pants and searched them like a thief. My fingers hunted blindly: thumb-levered lighter, crumpled poker pesos, Rolex wristwatch—and the unmistakable feel of an object older, heavier, and far more valuable than any of these.

I lifted out the coin and held it under the skylight. It gleamed before my eyes the way it had on Boca's beach, with a deep, luscious golden glow that seemed to give off more light than it took. On one side was the worn, nebulous specter of a proud, bald-headed American eagle; on the other, the faded profile of a woman adorned with a starry tiara. I set the coin down on the desk and laid the drawing from the notebook beside it. There was no question that the one had begotten the other—even the incidental scars on the coin were perfectly reflected in the penciled image. The drawing was not a drawing at all but a rubbing of the coin, a direct copy made from its impression on the paper.

My brother Dan had held this very coin in his hands. He had gazed on it, marveled at it, cherished it, made a visual record of it; in all likelihood, he himself had been the one who single-handedly discovered it. Yet somehow this little piece of a potentially larger treasure had fallen into Bellocheque's hands. Bellocheque the conjurer, who had tossed it with a spheric spin and offered it our fate.

I pressed the coin between my thumb and second finger and spun it on the desk. It twirled like a drunk and fell flat with a plop. I picked it up and spun it again. This time it whirled like Bellocheque's planet, finally collapsing with a reverberating din. Again I spun the coin. I spun the thing some twenty times. To my growing astonishment, it settled every time with the same side up.

Heads.

The coin had been rigged.

LIKE A RABBIT

I heard Rock shout out something on the deck. Were the divers back? Bare feet padded down the stairs to the saloon.

"Jack?"

Eva's voice startled me. I rose quickly, my thigh bumping the hinged desktop, knocking the coin off onto the floor, where it rolled neatly across the room and vanished under the wine-cooler cabinet. Scurrying after it, I dropped to my knees and lowered my head, peering into the dark slot at the base of the refrigerated cooler. I couldn't see a thing. I reached under and felt for the coin, but I could only reach so far before my forearm got stuck in the gap.

Eva called my name again from somewhere in the bow.

I got off my knees and looked across the room. The page with the rubbing still lay on the desk. I hurried over and grabbed it and looked for a pocket in which to hide it, but I was wearing only a Speedo, and a Speedo has no pockets, so I quickly rolled up the drawing and was stuffing it into my crotch when Eva appeared at the door.

"What are you doing in here, Jack?"

She asked the question with an elaborately melodic intonation in her voice, a certain deprecating righteousness mixed with a moderating tinge of genuine curiosity and a not too subtle note of amusement.

I slipped my hand out of my suit. "I, uh, I was just . . ."

She was still wearing the string bikini, which only added

to my embarrassment. She cocked her head to the side and, even more melodically, spoke my name.

"Jack . . . ?"

She stepped through the doorway into the room, and the soft light falling from the skylight lent her sculpted form a stunning chiaroscuro. It seemed as if the Platonic ideal of female beauty had stepped from the pale realm of imagination out into full-bodied life on the earth. Her presence was so real I actually found it scary. We were standing alone in the pasha's plushy bedroom with nothing more on our bodies than our scanty swimsuits and nothing more between us than a few small breaths of insubstantial air. Words bottled up in my mouth. The limp fingers of Eva's hand drifted absently up her chest to touch the delicate hollow at the base of her throat. It appeared as though a number of thoughts were passing through her mind, with each of them leading inextricably to me. Her eyes wandered down my body and lingered bemusedly at my crotch.

"Oh, dear, Jack . . ."

I was quickly growing hard—I could hear the paper crunching.

Eva looked into my eyes. "You . . . hiding something in there?"

I gulped so loudly it must have echoed through the room. Somehow words came out of my mouth. "You really want to know?"

Eva sauntered closer, her eyes clinging to mine. Her mouth opened slightly, then slowly closed again. Her flawless face, her luscious lips, her dazzling emerald eyes—all of her came closer than she had ever come before.

"What if I do?" she asked.

Again her gaze moved down my chest. Again her mouth came open.

She was so close I could smell the musky aloe on her skin and the humid sea scent in the ringlets of her hair. I could hear the sound of her breathing and see the billowing of her breasts and the catching of her nipples in the restraining stretch of fabric. She was so close I could reach out and touch her without even thinking about it—and that's exactly what I did. My hands passed slowly through the space between us, moving on an instinct all their own. The tips of my fingers landed lightly on her waist and trailed down the outline of her hips. Her skin felt smooth and slightly damp; it still held the heat of the sun, and it seemed to exude a kind of supple, vibrant awareness all its own. My fingers slipped easily under the knots of her bikini. They searched for the ends and pulled the little strings. The thong fell off like a leaf.

Eva took in a tiny breath. Then she pressed in close to me and I heard her sigh like a baby. Her top felt damp against my skin. I pulled its string behind her back and slid it off between us. Her cold breasts bobbed against my chest, while below my navel, a bristle of hair tickled my skin, triggering a quivering ache of delight. My hands drifted down her back. She brought her mouth toward mine. Her lips parted, exposing the threat of her teeth and the glistening pink flesh of her tongue. I moved to kiss her, but she drew her lips away. Her green eyes cast downward, vanishing like precious jewels beneath her feather lashes. The eyes followed her hands as they floated down my chest, caressing my nipples with the prick of her nails. Her cool palms turned toward the warm wall of flesh and felt their way down the muscles of my abdomen. Her fingers fanned out over my belly. Slowly, drawn down into the heat, they slipped in under my nylon suit to warm themselves in the fire.

Finally she untied the Speedo's knot and set my woody loose. It sprang out like a diving board, flinging out the rolled page, which soared, spread its wings, and fluttered to the floor.

I took no notice. Not with her hands gently stoking the fire. Not with her mouth wetly snailing down my chest, following the trail her fingers had traced. Not with her teeth nibbling my nipples. Not with her long locks, stiff with the sea, tormenting my flesh like a thousand fingers. Not with her buttocks splaying out as she bent to mouth that ticklish skin that lay below my navel. Not with her tongue stepping lightly onto the springboard of—

"Jack!"

"Shit!"

Bellocheque was on the deck. He called again, "Eva, darling!"

She rose up panting, looked into my eyes. "Hurry," she said. In an instant she was lacing up her bikini.

I reached for my suit, down around my ankles, lost my balance, and started to fall. Hopping across the carpet, a bunny rabbit with a boner, I noisily crashed into the foldout desk, then tumbled in pain to the floor. I landed on my sword, as they say. Excruciating, but in this case not fatal. Groaning, I rolled onto my back, sat upright, and once again reached for the suit around my ankles.

Eva had her hand clapped over her mouth, holding back a fit of the giggles.

"Very funny," I muttered.

I lay back, arched onto my shoulders, and shimmied up my Speedo, sheathing my dwindling dagger. When I sat back up, Eva was gone.

I heard heavy footfalls splashing down the steps. "Eva, dear, wonderful news. Where's Jack? Jack!"

Jack was in the master's bedroom on his hands and knees, searching for the incriminating notebook page, which, like the coin that fled before it, had disappeared. He heard Eva whisper and giggle, and Bellocheque explode with laughter. The volcano laugh, the genuine eruption.

"Jack, my friend," he called from the galley, struggling to control his torrent of mirth. "If you haven't yet done the dirty deed in there, come out and I'll tell you something that'll really get your jollies off!"

There are in such compromising situations various degrees of embarrassment. One can be abashed, shamed, humiliated, or utterly and completely mortified. Being accused—and worse, falsely accused—of masturbating in the bedroom of the captain of your ship clearly fell somewhere toward the lethal end of the spectrum. As I emerged flush-faced from the room, I tried to tell myself that it didn't really matter. I was a young, red-blooded American male, rabid with raging hormones; such behavior was not to be unexpected. If I were to be perfectly honest about it, the allegation wasn't all that far from the truth—only a few paces and a matter of minutes, really. Denying it, I was sure, would only bring on more laughter. And after all, given the diverting joy it imparted to my possibly murderous host, Eva's act of libel might have actually saved my life.

Her glance seemed to confirm it. She was setting champagne glasses on the counter when I plodded into the room, and she gave me a steady look of warning before Bellocheque appeared, dripping in his swim trunks, lumbering out of the galley with a bottle in his hand. "There he is!" he bellowed as he popped the cork and spilled the spuming contents over the glasses. "Jack, dear boy, we've got something to celebrate!"

He reached to shake my hand. Then, on second thought, he handed me a flute of the bubbly instead.

"To the *Argonaut*!" he declared, raising his glass.

We clinked and sipped. "You found the anchor?"

"Anchor?" he cried. "We found the bloody ship!"

ARGONAUTS

Bellocheque and Candy had discovered the wreck in sixty feet of water less than fifteen minutes after reaching the bottom. Bellocheque explained that directly below us the submerged point fell off sharply into the depths, and the *Argonaut* lay lodged on a broad ledge a short way down the slope. To their surprise, they had found it lying completely upside down. The hull, they said, looked like a long, peaked roof covered with a blanket of snowy sand. Apparently, when the ship sank, it landed on the edge of the point and tumbled over the slope, finally settling with its broken masts embedded in the rocky ledge. The constant wash of a slow current kept the wooden hull under a thick layer of sand and soot, slowing considerably the pace of decay. Except for the prow, which had broken off entirely when it rammed into the rocks, the ship was remarkably intact.

I wondered how they had found it so fast. "How far was it from the anchor?" I asked.

We had gathered in the cockpit to sip our champagne while Duff and Rock donned their diving gear.

"No idea," Bellocheque said, settling into the pilot's seat. "Never found the anchor."

"Really?" Rock said. He was struggling to loosen the strap of his fin.

Candy took the fin from him. "Apparently the anomaly we picked up wasn't the anchor," she said. With a simple snap, she adjusted the strap and handed the fin back to Rock.

Then she reached for the long sheet of aluminized paper from the magnetometer and spread it out on the table until she found the spike on the graph. "We think it might have been caused by something in the wreck itself."

My heart jumped. I peered again at the giant spike. Compared to the minor molehill set off by Dan's abandoned scuba tank, this one looked like Mount Everest. Rock and Duff both gave me a glance. We were all thinking the same thing, and Duff finally ventured to speak it out loud. "You think it was set off by a treasure on board?"

Eva rose to refill our glasses. "I wouldn't jump to conclusions," she said. "Gold and silver aren't magnetic. It was probably triggered by iron ballast or some part of the ship's fittings."

Candy agreed. "We just don't know," she said. Without flashlights, they had been unable to venture more than a few feet into the wreck. Its cargo remained a mystery.

I turned my gaze to the commander in chief. Bellocheque was quietly sipping his champagne, shrewdly eyeing the group of us. He seemed to be enjoying our suddenly piqued interest.

"What do *you* think, Mr. Bellocheque?"

His eyes fastened on me, and I thought I glimpsed a sly and subtle twinkle of suspicion. It may have been in reaction to the tone of my voice, which had been more accusatory than curious. That, and the naked fact that while he'd been underwater I'd been helping myself to his room. I now suspected it was not my question he was turning over in his mind but the motive for my asking it. In any case, following a thoughtful interlude, he appeared to arrive at some acceptable conclusion. With a slow swing of his arm, he carefully set down his fizzing glass, leaned back into his cockpit throne, and, in his sonorous and lordly baritone, offered his opinion.

"What I think, my friend, is based on what I've seen. And what I've seen is a nineteenth-century double-masted schooner, built roughly in the style of the Baltimore clippers, and easily over a hundred and fifty years old. The wreck is in excellent condition; for all the world it looks untouched. If this ship was indeed called the *Argonaut,* as your brother claims it was, then almost certainly it carried upon its decks those brave men once called 'argonauts,' intrepid souls who ventured west in search of their fortunes in the California gold rush. As I have told you, my great-great-grandfather was one such man, so I know of what I speak. If this ship was used in transport to and from the gold fields, then perhaps—just maybe—it was heading back home to the East Coast, loaded down with bullion, when it met its fatal end. If that is so, as we have much reason to believe, we are all of us poised on the brink of Elysium."

An enchanted hush came over us, the sort of silence one might expect if poised at the pearly gates. I had held no long-burning desire for hidden treasure; my motive had been only to find out what had happened to my brother. Several indications had suggested a murder had been committed—and that this man who had just spoken so eloquently of heaven may well have been the one who had committed that murder. Still my heart beat wildly. Bellocheque was an artic-ulate and captivating speaker. Given the authority of his voice and the power of his presence, no one among us could challenge the astounding truth of what he said. Yet some-where in that exultant beat of my heart, I felt a disconcerting thump of doom, as if he had voiced not a promise of riches but a sentence of death or a declaration of war. A final war heralding a final Day of Judgment. I suddenly wondered, in a Möbius twist of awe, if what we faced was not the entrance to heaven but in fact the doorway to hell.

We all remained silent in this meditative moment, until Bellocheque offered the divers a final bit of advice. "Be careful down there, boys. The timbers are rotted, and the bottom is soft. Keep your wits about you, and your eyes peeled for the telltale glint."

With that, Rock and Duff took up their pistol flashlights, crabbed their way across the deck, clamped their regulators in their teeth, and with a soldierly wave tumbled over the side.

• • •

I had never had a chance to tell them what I had found in Dan's notebook, and now I wondered if I had made a mistake in letting them go in the dark. Bellocheque could be dangerous, I thought, far more dangerous than rotten timbers and a soft sea bottom. A single look from Eva had said as much. The two of us hadn't spoken since our tantalizing encounter in the old man's quarters, and I yearned to know what secret those green eyes held. What had she seen? What did she know? And what did the conjurer have up his sleeve? I couldn't stop fretting about the lost gold piece and the missing page. He was bound to notice the coin was gone, and if he stumbled on the drawing he'd know at once what I'd been up to. Since he had chosen to withhold the truth, there had to be a reason. My fear was that his secret might be worth the price of murder.

I watched him now, standing with his back to us, contemplating the divers' bubbles as they slowly migrated away from the boat. As he tucked his head to light a cigar, Candy stretched out languorously on the deck beside him, absorbing the heat of the sun like a cat.

Eva glanced at me, caught my eye. She rose from her seat and headed toward the galley. "Anyone hungry for chips?"

"Please," said Bellocheque. "I'm famished. Is there any guacamole left?"

"I'll make you some," she said, stepping down the stairs.

"Let me give you a hand," I said. Bellocheque turned as I followed after her. I could feel his eyes on my back.

E va was waiting for me.

"What—"

Before I could say any more, she pulled me to her body and pressed her mouth to mine. Her wet lips opened and she gave me her tongue, a warm, live, grasping thing that entered into me hungrily. My hands roamed over her near-naked back until I could no longer tolerate the slightest space between us. I pressed her to the cupboard wall, trapping her there with the force of my body, her breasts pillowed against me. She lifted her face and looked into my eyes, then brought her lips to my ear.

"Jack," she whispered. "Forgive me. It was all I could think of to tell him—"

"It's all right," I said. I lifted the locks from her shoulder and suckled my mouth up the arc of her neck.

Her soft breath caressed my ear, and her voice came hushed and delicate, like the sound of a flower opening, exposing erogenous pistils. "I want you," she whispered.

I bit her ear and whispered back, "I want you."

"We have to be careful."

I pulled back to look into her eyes. "The coin," I said. "I took it from his pocket. It rolled under the wine cooler. I couldn't reach it."

"I'll take care of it," she said. She opened a cabinet door and emptied a noisy cellophane bag into a plastic bowl. "Take these out there," she said. "Keep him occupied." She started toward Bellocheque's room.

I stopped her. "And the page from the notebook—"

"I have it," she said. "I took it."

"You?"

"I'm afraid for you, Jack. You've got to be careful."

"Eva—"

"Go, quickly."

I backed toward the steps. "What about Candy?"

Eva shook her head. "Say nothing."

"But—"

"Trust me."

I looked at her and nodded. "Okay," I said.

A fleeting smile lit her eyes. She turned the corner toward Bellocheque's room.

I stepped up into the cockpit to find Bellocheque slumped in the pilot's seat with Candy standing behind him, massaging the rounded mass of his shoulders. They were both looking at me, Candy through the red mop of damp hair swaying in her face, and Bellocheque with his head hanging down, staring out from under his brow. Except for the cigar in his hand, he looked like a boxer in the corner of a ring.

"You look a little flushed, Jack. Feeling a bit weak in the knees again, are we?"

"Not at all," I said. "I'm feeling great." I set the bowl of chips down in front of him. "Eva's making the guac."

"Let me get us something to drink," said Candy. She started toward the stairs.

"Oh, no, let me get it," I said, moving to cut her off. "What would you like?"

"Thank you, Jack, but I'll—"

"No, I insist. Please."

Without makeup, Candy's face looked pale and gaunt, and her wet hair hung in clumps like blood-colored dreadlocks. She paused, eyeing me curiously. I was blocking the stairwell with my arms out firmly on either side. I casually lowered them and tried to look relaxed.

She glanced behind me toward the galley, where Eva presumably was. Then she looked back at me and grinned with wry impatience. "Okay, lover boy. There's an open liter bottle of Diet Coke on the bottom shelf of the fridge, toward the back. In the liquor cabinet, opposite the fridge, you'll find a bottle of Barbados rum—don't use the Bacardi. I'll have a glass of the Coke with half a shot of the rum. No ice."

"One rum Coke, no ice. Mr. Bellocheque?"

He shook his head, looking, as usual, amused. "Nothing for me," he said.

As I turned and started down the stairs, a voice suddenly called from out on the water. Bellocheque rose from his seat, and we all moved to the side of the boat, scanning the surface to see who it was.

Twenty yards off, Rock was kicking toward us, breathing through his snorkel.

"Something's wrong," Candy said. "He's alone."

I glanced behind me. Eva was still down below. A sudden wave of anxiety came over me, a feeling that something horrible had happened. Without even knowing what it was, I felt immediately responsible. I had brought us here, I was to be blamed, I was the one who had gotten us into this.

"Rock," I shouted. "What's wrong?"

He didn't answer me right away. He swam around to the back of the boat, ripped off his mask and threw it on board, and rested for a moment on the step at the stern.

"Sister Claire Blowhard," he said, wincing. "My fucking ear."

I sighed with relief. Rock had encountered this problem before. We thought he had overcome it. In grade school, an untreated ear infection had festered into a full-blown sinus inflammation that ravaged the delicate apparatus of his inner ear. When his teacher, an ancient relic of the Inquisition, Sister Claire, insisted he blow his nose as hard as he could, he obliged, blowing out his right eardrum and damaging his eustachian tube, which never properly healed. Rock had been the one to blow it, but he always blamed the nun.

"How far did you get?" I asked.

"Thirty-five, forty feet."

Not a problem in the shallow quarries we were used to diving in, but out here, if you couldn't clear your ears, you couldn't dive.

"Where's Duff?" I asked.

Rock shook his head. "I tried to get him to come back with me, but you know Bobby."

"He shouldn't be diving alone," Candy said. "And definitely not on a wreck."

I told Rock to give me his gear. "I'm going down," I said as he climbed into the boat.

"You had better not, Jack." It was Eva, standing behind us with a small glass bowl of guacamole in her hands. "I'll go." She set down the bowl and started back toward the stairs.

"No, Eva." She stopped and turned to me. "Please. Leave it to me."

She looked doubtful. "Are you sure?"

"I've had my swoon for the day," I said. "I'll be fine."

"You're certain you'll be all right?" There was a tone of genuine concern in her voice. I took it as a personal triumph.

"Positive," I said. With a wink, I added, "Trust me."

She smiled, just barely. Then, to my delight, she gave in to a sudden impulse and lightly kissed my lips. No succulent oyster, no fondling the fire, just a girl kissing a boy on a sailboat in the sun.

It was not, I'm sorry to say, offered entirely out of affection.

"I found it," she whispered in my ear. Her eyes lowered, and I followed her gaze down to her waist. She tugged open her suit a crack, and I could see, buried in the soft nest of her pussy, the gleaming gold coin.

I started to tell her to hurry back down and return it to Bellocheque's pocket—something I thought she had understood—but Bellocheque had suddenly appeared behind her. As she turned discreetly away, he stepped up close and grabbed my wrist. He looked me directly in the eye, and I half expected a reprimand for stealing the heart of the captain's maid, or some such bold transgression. What he actually said came as a surprise.

"Be careful down there, Jack. Promise me you'll be careful."

It was hard to tell with Bellocheque what was genuine and what was not, but he was right: There was certainly plenty to be careful about.

"I will," I said.

"Good!" he said with a slap on my back. "Now bring us up some of that glittering gold!"

RORSCHACH

I finned effortlessly into the depths, following the infinite line of the anchor. In the slanted light of late afternoon, the water glimmered with rippling rays, exuding a pearly luster that reminded me of moonlight. The surface above soon faded away, leaving me adrift in boundless space. It felt as if I had entered a crystal ball, that somewhere beyond the glassy edge of my vision Bellocheque was watching, able to see into my past and future in a way only God and the dead can see. I was mulling over this unsettling notion, imagining him holding my fate in his hands like a hoop-eared gypsy with her bowling ball, when all at once the bottom appeared, looking like the crinkly palm of his hand.

They had told me that when I reached the bottom I should continue in the direction of the anchor line, straight out across the plateau of the point, and right down over its bouldery edge. I headed that way now, scanning the gloomy landscape for a glimpse of bubbles or the flash of a tank. As I had expected, Duff was not to be seen. He would be at the wreck by now, searching intently for any trace of gold. He'd want to be the first to find it, a boast more precious than the gold itself, an honor he could offer to the apple of his eye. No doubt this is what had driven him ahead so impetuously—not desire for the treasure but the treasure of his desire.

The bottom sloped off precipitously; I had reached the far edge of the point. Soon I was descending down a wall of rock and sand, floating on a cascade of current. The slow drift carried me like a pale, falling feather into the darkness of a well. The schooling fish I had seen on the plateau quickly thinned to a scattered few. The water grew colder, and the light grew dim. I kept peering expectantly into the bottomless gloom, but nothing came into view. Maybe the wreck wasn't there to see, or maybe it was just too hard to see—visibility had fallen off to no more than a dozen feet.

I paused to blow some water from my ill-fitting mask, leakage from the slow-building pressure. Then I hung there for a moment to take my bearings. Around me it was murky and lifeless and bleak; below me was a void. I took a deep breath of metallic-tasting air and focused on relaxing, on keeping my cool. Everything, I told myself, was well under control. My heartbeat was regular, my mind was clear, my breathing normal—but the needle on my depth gauge read seventy feet. They had said the wreck lay at no more than sixty. I realized that somehow I had gone the wrong way, and wondered if I had misread the angle of the anchor line. Or perhaps, I thought, with some alarm, the *Obi-man* had drifted and the angle had changed. I hoped I wasn't too far off. Peering left and right, I decided the most promising terrain lay to my left—there seemed to be a gradual leveling of the slope. I hoped it might be the ledge where the wreck had lodged itself, and I started off, cruising slowly along the rocky wall.

A sudden shimmer of movement caught my eye, a flash of something light in the gloom ahead of me. It seemed too large to have been a fish; I thought it must have been Duff. I kicked the water hard and picked up my pace. I'd have to catch him if I didn't want to lose him, so I zoomed ahead, but the farther I went, the harder it became to see. Water swirled off the rocks, lifting sand like a storm in the desert. I had run into another turbulent current, a stirring brew of sediment that clouded my view.

Below me, the ledge appeared to be flattening out. I continued moving swiftly along, peering through the mist of silt, hoping for another glimpse of Duff. The ledge seemed

to be rising, while the slope beside me was leveling off.
Kicking headlong through the murk, I glanced at the depth
gauge on my wrist: sixty-four feet. As I looked back up, I ran
smack into a wall.

The impact jarred my mask loose and knocked the regulator out of my mouth. Freezing water stung my eyes and
started up my nose. I choked and coughed the air out of my
lungs. Now my lungs were empty and my mask was full of
water. Pawing blindly, I groped for the mouthpiece, but the
regulator had vanished, and I couldn't see a thing. Sixty-four
feet—too deep to surface. I didn't have time to calm myself.
Didn't have time to think. Fear triggered a buried memory:
The regulator comes off the right of your tank. When you
lose it, it should fall to the right side of your waist. I reached
down there now, frantically searching with both my hands.

Lead weights. The tank strap. And . . .

Nothing. No regulator. No trace of it at all.

My clenching throat seemed to suck at my gut. I simply
could not breathe. My vision went all sparkly, then started
turning black. For the second time in a single day, I was
fainting at the bottom of the ocean.

Then a miracle happened.

A blowing mouthpiece was plugged through my teeth. I
bit down and sucked in a watery gasp of air. Grabbing hold
of the regulator, I held my tongue against the intake port and
pressed the purge button, clearing the remaining water. Then
I took a huge breath, filling my lungs with life-giving air. I
exhaled deeply and sucked in another breath. Then another.
And another. In seconds I was breathing normally again. I
straightened my mask and held it to my face as I exhaled
stoutly through my nose. Water bubbled out through the
purge valve, lowering the level in my mask. Two more blows
and I could see again, though I wanted desperately to wipe
my eyes: The moist sting of salt blurred my vision—but not
enough to obscure the face floating wide-eyed in front of me.

Duff had just saved my life. I wanted to give him a big fat
kiss but couldn't bear the thought of taking the regulator out
of my mouth. I settled on the "OK" sign.

He waited a while, as if to be sure. I did have a reputation, after all, and seemed to be doing all I could to maintain it. I pointed to my regulator and made a palms-up, shrugging, "What the hell happened?" gesture. Through an elaborate pantomime, Duff conveyed the idea that the regulator had been knocked up over my shoulder and somehow gotten caught between my backpack and my tank. If Duff hadn't shown up, I probably wouldn't have found it. Not without a breath of air in my lungs. I could have triggered the inflator on my BC vest and sucked on the backup mouthpiece, but I hadn't the presence of mind. This was the second time I had panicked. Fear was becoming a habit.

The crash might have nearly killed me, but it also might have saved my life: The sound of the impact must have brought Duff back to find me. I'd have to verify this theory with him later, preferably over a beer on the sunny deck of the *Obi-man*. This would be a story we would one day tell our grandchildren—Duff saving my life on the day we found our fortune. For now it would have to wait; we had better things to do. Because what I had run into was, of course, the wooden hull of the wreck.

We swam up alongside it, with Duff taking the lead. I found it a stunning thing to behold. The foreignness of it, the eerie strangeness of a ship underwater. I had never dived on a shipwreck before. The closest I had ever come was a sunken school bus we stumbled on during one of our quarry dives. The bus had been dropped there like some kind of joke, a bright diversion for bored, landlocked midwestern divers. The experience here was altogether different. The size of the wreck, for one. The ghostly creepiness of it, for another. This vessel had been down here for a century and a half. Seamen had probably drowned with it. Adventurers. Fortune seekers. People not all that different from us. I felt their presence in the water around us and in the murky shadows of the wreck itself. It was a big sailing ship—Dan's notebook had described it as over a hundred feet long—but with the water stirred up the way it was, Duff and I were limited to a partial, shifting view. We were like the blind men checking out the elephant, a motley mammoth to be assembled in the mind. It gave the wreck the quality of a chimera—more the product of imagination than a hammered thing of wood and iron.

The upturned hull itself was indeed like a wall, a towering mountain of sand and silt. It rose to a long peak like the horizontal spine of a roof, slanted end to end at an unsettling angle. Waving off the sediment stirred up a cloud, revealing underneath a gray-green patchwork of corroded metal—crinkled ribbons of copper sheathing peeling off the wooden hull. We kicked up away from the cloud and floated down the other side of the vessel, swimming slowly around to the flat-backed stern. The huge, rotten rudder still hung limply from corroded iron hinges. Along the ship's side, under the gunwale, where the deck rested on the boulder-strewn ledge, black, frowning gaps appeared, none of them large enough to squeeze through. Farther up the length of the ship we came across a bigger opening, and the two of us poked our flashlights under the hull. Nervous fish quickly flickered from the light, their eyes like scattering marbles. The deck appeared rotten but remarkably intact. Below it, a jumble of decaying timbers and the massive bulk of a broken mast filled the cramped and eerie space. In the midst of them I spotted a portal in the deck, a dark entryway into the interior of the ship.

I started to venture inside, but Duff nudged my arm and led me away. He had another plan in mind, so I followed him along the hull toward the bow. Murky water draped the ship in gray veils of fog, and in the surrounding emptiness I sensed again a presence. Peering out at the empty gloom seemed to draw the presence closer; it felt as though we were being watched. Soon I was conjuring nightmares out of nothingness: spectral sailors, animated skeletons, horn-headed devils half hidden in the haze. It was as if the void itself awakened childhood terrors, wrapping hackneyed apparitions in the gauzy garments of oblivion. I could almost make out the phantom of my bearded brother Dan.

This brought the words of a psalm to my mind, words I had found scrawled in his notebook:

I am forgotten, like a dead man out of mind;
I have come to be like something lost.

I've never really believed in a supernatural world; for me it is all a mind-matter of disjointed time, past images and memories impinging into the present. Ghosts are cloud-built tricksters, as crafty and intangible as the thoughts in your head. There is no way to banish them; you can only look away. Refuse to give them the attention your fear seems to demand.

I turned ahead and followed after Duff.

The bow of the ship was exactly as Bellocheque had described it. The prow had shattered and broken off, leaving a large, open hole where once the figurehead had stood. Baring broken plank ends like a set of jagged teeth, this gaping mouth projected far out over the rocky ledge and made it appear as if the grieving wreck were wailing into the abyss. Duff swam undaunted through the teeth and was quickly swallowed by the blackness within. I watched from outside, hesitant to follow, until I saw his light flick on. Floating weightless in the inky chamber, wearing his tank and mask, he looked like a space-age Jonah passing through the open gullet of a whale.

What could I do but follow him in?

I swam through the gap and pressed the rubber button of my handgun flashlight. Marble-eyed fish scattered in terror. The conelike beam shone on a sand-coated spread of craggy debris: bottles, jars, shards of glass, splinters of rotten crates, and smashed, corroded crockery. I picked up a teapot fragment with a broken nose of a spout; it left a trail of obscuring sediment like an octopus's cloud of ink. The fragment looked to be Chinese porcelain with a blue and white floral design in the glaze. I dropped it back into the dissipating cloud and drifted over to Duff, who had found an unbroken crate of champagne. Pulling out a bottle, he saw that the cork had disintegrated and the contents had mixed with the sea. He turned to me and shook it aloft like a trophy, then tossed it away. When it landed in the powdery silt, it gave rise to a minor explosion. Odd little curlicues of yellow-orange shavings floated up in the mushroom cloud. I pointed my beam to the ceiling above (which, of course, was actually the floor) and saw that it was riddled with holes. Tiny tubeworms were eating the wood, dropping their curly debris. I realized that whatever lay in the compartment above might easily collapse down on us.

Duff had found a door in the interior wall and was struggling to pull it open. Worried that he might bring the ceiling down with it, I grabbed his arm and forced him to stop. He followed me back toward the bow's open mouth, where a section of the ceiling had badly decayed. I pushed my hands through the wafer-thin wood; it easily crumpled away. Within a few seconds, the two of us had cleared a hole large enough to swim through.

We found ourselves in a small, cramped compartment with a sharply curved ceiling, the forward arc of the hull itself. Whatever had been stored in the room had long ago disintegrated into powder, so that every move we made brought up billowing clouds of dust. Within seconds, we were unable to see more than a few inches in front of our faces. We slowly groped our way through the murk until we came to the interior wall, which had mostly decayed and fallen away. We passed easily through it. Our lights shone into a larger space, clear and undisturbed. A badly rotted column, securely mounted into the underside of the hull above, ran down at a slant through the floor below. This, I suddenly realized, was the lower portion of one of the ship's masts, anchored into the center beam of the hull and running all the way up through the deck.

Beneath us, a thick layer of heavy rocks and gravel covered the overturned ceiling. Given that the exterior of the hull above our heads was fully intact and, as we had seen, covered with a blanket of fine sand, I wondered how the rocks and gravel could have found their way into the boat. The size of the rocks and the weight of the gravel made it unlikely they'd have washed in through the bow. Perhaps Bellocheque or the women might have an answer; I made a mental note to ask them later.

Long, curved splinters of wood and corroded metal bands lay half buried in the bed of gravel. *Might have been barrels*, I thought, recalling Dan's note about smuggled tobacco. Whatever it was they held had long ago dissolved into dust. A flaming red-orange anemone suddenly caught my light, a bright island of fire in the gray sea of debris. It was the first spot of color I had seen in the wreck. Even the few darting fish had seemed ghostly and gray, their startled eyes like empty mirrors. Those flitting, soulless automatons and this little spit of fire were the only living inhabitants we had encountered in the boat. What was it, I wondered, that made the ship so repellent to life? Even I, greedy for gold, felt a recurring impulse to flee.

In the inky blackness ahead, a disembodied beam of light danced with a life of its own. Duff had joined the spirit world. I gently kicked my fins and cruised closer until his fleshy form was revealed in my light. He turned and looked at me. He seemed to be searching my eyes to reassure himself that I was all right. I gave him a thumbs-up. He nodded affirmatively, but I surmised that he shared my growing sense of apprehension. We were sixty feet down, buried in the bowels of a badly rotted ship—plenty of reason to be scared, I thought, but the fact that we had each other somehow eased the grip of fear.

The floor below soon gave way to an expanse of open space. We had entered the central hold of the ship, a long and deep compartment that ended beyond the range of our lights. Isolated from temperate currents and the warming rays of the sun, the water here was frigid. Here and there above our heads, bolted chains dangled from the floor. Presumably used to secure the cargo, they had corroded into thin skeletons of their former selves and hung at various lengths like tinsel from a tree. Our exhaled bubbles rolled past them on the ceiling, merging into mercurial ponds of silver. A second mast sprouted from the center of the hull and slanted down into the void below us. We followed it with our lights, and a school of darting minnows flashed like a sudden shimmer of foil. The water around us was still and clear, steeped in a silence that had long been undisturbed. I felt we were intruders into ancient, sacred waters, grave robbers entering the hush of a tomb.

The frigid water quickened my breath and gave me a case of the shivers. I thought ahead to the safety of the boat and the welcome warmth of the sun—and to Eva, up there waiting. It helped to think of Eva.

Duff descended. I followed after him, my light shining through the silver trail of his bubbles. The bottom was covered with the gravel and rocks, littered with rotting timbers and corroded debris, and punctured with a portal that led down under the wreck. There was no obvious glint of gold, just more of the muck we had seen elsewhere in the ship. Duff began slowly picking his way through the rubble. I drifted over to the square black portal and directed my lamp into the darkness below. It illuminated a narrow gap between the sea bottom and the overturned deck, a crawl space just deep enough for someone like me to swim through.

I dove into the hole.

Now I was under the full weight of the wreck. Above my head was the top deck, upon which sailors had trodden and mopped and danced and peered through spyglasses at passing ships. The tall masts and stout spars, the intricate rigging, and the vast expanse of canvas that had once towered magnificently above them now shone in my light as a mangled forest of crushed and rotting wreckage, a graveyard of grandeur. In a few places under the gunwale, dim rays of daylight shone through gaps between the bottom and the tangle of timbers, but none of these openings looked large enough to pass through. I remembered the gap I had seen earlier, when Duff and I had circled the wreck, a passage through which I might easily have entered. If I could find that now, we'd have a quick exit if we needed it.

I turned off my flashlight. Without that bright beam, the gaps of daylight shone clearer. I moved carefully through the claustrophobic space, looking for the opening I knew had to be there. Squeezing under the massive mast to the other side of the deck, I immediately spotted a large gap of light and started swimming toward it. I had nearly reached it when the gap of light vanished.

A shadow had fallen over the ship. It stopped me dead in the water.

For what seemed an endless moment I hung frozen in the dark. Then, as suddenly as it had fallen, the passing shadow departed. Daylight returned.

I let out my breath.

It couldn't be Duff, I told myself; he was still in the cargo hold. Whatever had passed had been larger than a diver, anyway. A whale, perhaps? A cruising shark? An opaque school of fish?

Maybe it was nothing more than a cloud passing the sun.

I moved closer to the gap of light. It lay between two boulders under the rotten rim of the ship. It was too small to pass through, but I pushed my face as close as I could and peered out into the water.

There was nothing there to see. Just the same empty limbo I had stared at before. The blank screen, home to my demons. Had my fears fabricated this shadow creature, too? I had heard of brief blackouts from nitrogen narcosis, but surely I wasn't deep enough for that. Was I?

No. I had seen something. I had definitely seen something.

My hands were shaking. Enough of this searching for holes in the dark. I turned back toward the deck portal and flipped on my light. As I slipped through the forest of fallen timbers, my lamp shone suddenly on something recognizable: a round metal rim half buried in the sand.

I was staring into the mouth of a cannon.

The heavy, open-ended barrel was unmistakable. It lay upside down and appeared to have been mounted on a circular wooden platform, now severely decayed, that had been fitted into a slot on the wooden deck above. A turnstile of some kind, not unlike a turret gun's. I moved in for a closer look. The bronze had turned to dark gray-green with mottled patches of rusty orange and verdigris. The corruption was extensive, but beautiful in its way. This would make quite a souvenir for the deck of the *Obi-man,* I thought. The barrel was massive and deeply buried, so moving it was out of the question, but all the same, I wanted to take it with me. Or take a picture of it, at least. A little something to show the folks upstairs.

Why would a nonmilitary ship carry a lethal cannon on deck? Protection? Piracy? Maybe this wreck wasn't the *Argonaut.* Either that or the *Argonaut* was a whole lot more adventurous than any of us had thought.

Back up in the cargo hold, I found Duff prowling in the gravel for a glimpse of Bellocheque's "glittering gold." He was using a stick of wood to poke into the sediment and had stirred up quite a mess. A layer of murky silt floated knee-deep off the floor, blanketing the hold like a low-lying fog. Using his stick, Duff lifted out a yard-long length of corroded chain and held it up for me to see. He jerked his thumb up toward the ceiling: It had hung with the other dangling chains on the deck high above us. He dropped the chain, then picked up something else from the gravel. A corroded iron bracket. A double bracket, two circular pieces that locked onto a bar.

Duff slipped his hands through the bracket loops and shook his fists like a man defiant. He spat out his mouthpiece and shouted something into the water. I couldn't understand, so he shouted it again.

"Slaves!"

I shuddered and nodded, feeling a little stupid for not having realized what it was—but who would have expected to find a shackle on a gold ship? Duff replaced his mouthpiece and gestured for me to follow him. A few yards away, at the base of the mast, he tossed the shackle to the floor. It landed on a pile of other iron shackles—at least half a dozen he had gathered from his hunt. When he looked at me, I shook my head in disbelief. What was a slave ship doing off the Pacific coast?

Duff reached down into his murky pile, pulled out a large round rock, and shoved it into my hands. Amazingly light-weight, given its size. I turned it over.

It wasn't a rock at all. It was a human skull.

It frightened me, and I fumbled it. Duff caught it before it landed. He held it out for me again, clearly enjoying his lit-tle scare. I took the skull gingerly in my hands. I had never held one before. I thought of Hamlet and, for some reason, the Three Stooges. It felt like a joke and it felt kind of scary, both at the same time. I pressed my thumbs into the creepy eye holes. The bone had badly deteriorated and turned a sickly olive yellow. The entire lower jaw was missing. The dome of bone at the back of the skull was dark gray-green and riddled with pockmarks; it looked like a half-dipped Easter egg. This part, I assumed, had been exposed to the sea, the rest being buried in gravel.

I handed Duff his grisly trophy, and he returned it to his collection of shackles. For a moment we just floated there, looking at one another, trying to decide what the hell to do next. We had wound our way through half the ship. I had seen a cannon and a shadow monster. Duff had found shack-les and a human skull.

Only one thing could top all that—and we were running out of time to find it.

THE WORST THAT COULD
POSSIBLY HAPPEN

The way I figured it, the worst would be getting stuck in the wreck without any air. "Be careful down there," Bellocheque had warned, and air was the first thing that came to my mind. I checked my pressure gauge now and found I had roughly fifteen minutes of air left.

If I had only fifteen minutes, Duff, who had been down far longer than I, had to be nearly out completely. I pointed to his pressure gauge. He glanced at it and gave me an "OK."

I didn't believe him. He couldn't have more than five minutes left, just enough to make it to the surface. I reached for his gauge, but he waved me away. I pointed to my watch, pointed to his tank, and drew my finger across my throat.

Duff shook his head no.

I pointed more insistently to my watch, jabbed my finger angrily at his tank, and damn near drew blood "cutting" my throat.

Duff stubbornly shook his head again and turned to swim away. I grabbed his ankle. He kicked himself free. I watched him swim off into the dark with his light beam blazing, oblivious to the fact he was about to kill himself.

I turned away in disgust, as if I were leaving without him. He wouldn't stay down here by himself, I thought. I headed back toward the place where we had found our way into the hold. When I got up there, I turned around to see if he was following me.

He wasn't. The son of a bitch had disappeared.

Duff wanted to find the gold, and he knew this was his chance. He had a woman to impress. Apparently he didn't think that gruesome little skull would do the trick. Well, who was I to stop him? Maybe there was another way out of this wreck. We had seen at least one passable gap under the hull. Besides, I knew Duff had a way of stretching his air. He was always the last one out of the water whenever we dived in the quarry. He had bigger lungs, or smaller lungs, or maybe his imbecilic brain required less oxygen than ours.

We all make choices. *Let him go,* I thought.

I couldn't let him go. The guy, after all, had just saved my life. The least I could do was make sure he didn't lose his own.

I started for the place at the far end of the hold that I had seen him heading toward with his light. Every breath was precious, and I grew increasingly aware of exhaled bubbles babbling away in my ears. The cold was starting to get to me; my skin had turned rough with goose bumps. I swam ahead vigorously, looking for the place where Duff had disappeared. I flipped off my light and stared into the dark. No sign of his light. I turned my light back on, swam to the wall, and began to search it for a doorway or a portal. The wood was remarkably intact, and wholly devoid of passage. Where the hell had he gone? I worked my way up the wall carefully, passing my light over its surface. At the top I still found nothing, no entry to the back of the ship.

It suddenly occurred to me there wouldn't be an entry. This wall separated the cargo hold from the rooms at the stern. The *Argonaut,* probably like most sailing vessels, was built with the same basic layout as the *Obi-man*: master quarters in the roomy stern, crew crammed into the narrow bow, cargo loaded in the central hold. Cargo in this case included shackled slaves. Certainly the captain wouldn't want a doorway into his crib from this angry hellhole. The entrance to his quarters—the only entrance—would be from above, off the deck.

I swam back across the floor, which was the underside of the deck, looking for another portal. Within a matter of seconds I found it. A square hole, exactly like the one I had passed through on the other side of the hold. This had to be where Duff had gone.

I swam through the hole and once again found myself in the bewildering jungle of broken booms and masts. The space here seemed even more cramped than it had been at the other portal, but I saw at once the open passage I had noticed from the exterior, a gap under the gunwale that would be easy for us to pass through. *Our emergency exit,* I thought, and made a mental note of its location. Then I turned my sights toward the stern. The reason the space was so cramped was that the roof of the rear cabins protruded above the level of the deck, similar to the raised roof of the saloon in the *Obi-man.* This left less room to maneuver as I worked my way beneath the roof looking for an entrance. I saw there were two portals. The rear one, into the larger cabin—the one I assumed was the captain's quarters—was impossible to enter; it was too tight to the ground. I moved to the other one, turned over on my back, and just barely squeezed in, my tank scraping the sea bottom.

It was a small but comfortable-sized chamber, probably a bunker for privileged crewmen—captain's mate, maybe, and the chief petty officer, and the designated whipper of slaves. The ladder and the bunks had collapsed, and the ceiling beneath me was cluttered with shattered glass and the powdery disintegration of cloth and bedding, a mix that formed a muddy gray sediment. Corroded brass buttons lay embedded in the muck, and an ivory-colored shaving mug looked like it had just been dropped there yesterday. There was no sign of Duff, and I didn't have time to poke around, so I moved on through a hatch in the floor above me that led into another compartment at the bottom of the ship.

Similar in size to the one I had just left, this room was filled with disintegrating crates and boxes, which—like all the debris on the boat—had settled on the ceiling when the ship turned upside down. From the abundance of glass jars, I guessed that the room had been the larder. There was nothing identifiable in the mash of decayed and splintered wood, and Duff was not to be seen here, either. A closed hatch to the room next door wouldn't open; apparently it was blocked or bolted shut from the other side. A few feet away, however, was another opening in the wall, a passageway that led up a remarkably sound stairwell. I could see Duff's light in the room at the end of it.

I swam up the stairwell and entered what I was sure must have been the captain's quarters. It was a large room with a single bunk, and the clutter of remains that had fallen to the ceiling gave an impression of relative luxury: ornate, badly decayed oak chairs; a massive, upturned table like a four-legged corpse; a fluted shell washbasin cracked in two; corroded wrought-iron gratings; a tall, gilt-framed mirror, amazingly intact, that blindingly bounced back the beam of my light; and various bits and pieces of china and silver, delicate wineglasses, hand-painted porcelain dinnerware—accoutrements of a prosperous life at sea. Whether through trade of slaves or gold, the fellow who had run this ship had apparently done so profitably.

Duff was busy poking into the thick layer of sediment near the slanted wall of the stern. When he saw me approaching, he flashed his light up in my face, then turned it back to the debris and resumed his rummaging, as if I were nothing more than another floating chunk of garbage, a minor distraction from his heroic quest.

Why was I chasing this imbecile? Why did I bother? If he was intent on killing himself, let him do it. Any second now he'd be out of air. Then we'd see who was garbage.

Duff suddenly swam up to me, extending his hand—not to grab my mouthpiece and gobble a desperate breath of air but to show me what it was he had found buried in the clutter.

A coin. A gold coin.

Just like the one Dan had traced in his notebook, the one Bellocheque had trained to land heads up, the one now nestled in the lap of paradise. I took it out of his hand and shone my light on its brilliant surface. Unlike the one that Dan had found, this was in nearly perfect condition. Free of wear and corrosion, its bald eagle and Lady Liberty gleamed in crisply chiseled relief, and the year, "1850," and the amount, "TEN D.," were as clearly legible as the day it was minted. Why Dan's coin had eroded and this one had not, I couldn't be sure, but I guessed that Dan's had been found outside the wreck, exposed to the wear of abrasive currents, while this one had remained in the preserving refuge of this still and secluded chamber.

Duff took the coin back from me and stuffed it into the bulging pocket of his swimsuit. It was chock full of coins. He drew his finger across his throat and jerked his thumb back the way we had come. His tank, as I had expected, was quickly running out. I started to follow him back through the passage, ready to share my air if he needed it, but he turned and stopped me, grabbed my wrist and hauled me back to where he had found the coins, and jabbed his finger toward the floor. I could see sparkling glimpses of other coins there, scattered and buried in the muddy sediment. He didn't have time to collect them all; I did. He wanted me to stay behind, to bring up all I could. How much air did he have left? Enough, apparently, to believe he could make it back on his own. Before I could argue with him—not an easy thing to do under any circumstances, all but impossible underwater—he turned and briskly swam away, vanishing through the passage.

Reluctantly, I let him go. It wasn't that far to the exit I had seen at the deck. Duff the Lung could make it on a single breath. In the meantime, I had maybe five minutes left before I'd have to leave. Then I'd have the final five to make it to the surface.

I turned and aimed my light over the field of debris. Amid the decaying rot, bright hints of gold twinkled like brilliant yellow stars. That's when it happened to me—when I was alone in that field of stars. With the same synaptic suddenness with which I had first taken the coin from Bellocheque's palm, I reached out now to grab these up, to liberate the buried treasure from the muck. First one coin, then another, then another. I snapped them up in a growing frenzy, feeling exuberant, invulnerable, a god plucking stars

from the sky. It was, I realize now, the first time I had ever
been overcome by a genuine rush of unadulterated greed.
When the world offers itself to you, when it opens like a
woman's legs and begs for you to enter, there's no holding
back, no stopping, no chain on the madman living inside
you. It's meant to happen, it's why you're here, it's yours for
the taking.

My destiny. Everything that had happened to me since the
day my father died—everything had brought me to this single point in time. This moment. My moment. A moment like
Hector Bellocheque's, a moment that would change my life
forever. There was no hesitation now. No doubts. No second
thoughts. No should or would or could or why. There was
just the thing in front of me, the golden gleaming thing that
shed its comet trail of filth and glared like a disk of sunlight.

Coins, coins, and more coins. The goddamn things were
everywhere. I poured them into the crotch of my suit and
they mingled with my balls until my cock grew stiff. I had a
golden hard-on. Tears came to my eyes.

My flashlight fell. The room went dim. The beam lay
buried in a bed of slush, and as I reached to pick it up, I saw
that the silty mud itself glistened like snow in moonlight,
with a zillion speckles of sparkly glitter.

Golden glitter.

The sediment itself was filled with gold, with tiny flecks
of gold dust. This was the stuff they panned in the rivers, the
so-called shining soil. It had spilled out from someplace and
washed through the room and settled on the sediment like a
sprinkle of golden fairy dust.

Where had it come from?

For that matter, where had the coins come from?

I wiped off the lens of the flashlight and aimed it overhead. A square black hole showed in the deck above me.
This was an open hatch into the bottom stern chamber of the
vessel, the place with the bolted side door I had been unable
to pass through. The last unseen room in the wreck. I
checked my pressure gauge: My air was very low. Just a
couple of minutes left before I'd have to leave. Slowed by

the added weight of the coins, I kicked my way up through the hatch.

The walls suddenly shook with a violent jolt. I braced myself in the hatchway. The wreck groaned, its timbers trembling. Sediment spilled from the boards overhead.

My heart banged wildly. I feared the walls would collapse around me. The flashlight had slipped from my grip and fallen into the muck. I clung in the dark to the rim of the hatch.

Several seconds after the reverberating jolt, the creaking came to a stop. The wreck settled back into silence.

I had never been in an earthquake before. Had that been what it was? I wondered if the wreck had somehow been disturbed by our presence, if our movement had tipped its delicate balance, but the jolt had been too strong. It felt as if the hull itself had been slammed. I assumed that Duff had reached the surface by now; he couldn't have had anything to do with it.

That's when I thought of the shadow I had seen. In my mind, it had evoked something menacing and massive. Could some creature have rammed the fragile hull?

There was no time to consider it now. The ship seemed more precarious than ever, and in a matter of minutes I'd be sucking for air. I wanted out.

I picked up the flashlight and brushed off the lens. Quickly scanning it over the chamber, I saw that it was another storage room, only larger, with a ceiling even higher than the captain's quarters. A ladder was built into the slanted wall of the stern, leading from the hatch to the cathedral-like peak of the hull above. Across the room, I saw the closed doorway to the larder, its iron bolt fused with corrosion. As with the rest of the ship, everything had fallen to the ceiling below. Scanning it quickly with my light, I brought the beam to a sudden stop.

Amid the muddy sediment and broken crates lay five heavy iron chests.

My heart soared. One of the iron coffers, smaller than the others, had broken open and spilled its contents. Gold coins, gold bars, gold dust—all of it spread out over the ceiling. Much of it had fallen through the open hatch, settling into the room below, where Duff had stumbled upon it.

Lifting a heavy gold brick from the sediment, I marveled at its concentrated weight and color and realized it probably held far more value than all the many coins jostling in my suit. I brushed off the brick's smooth, flat front and saw it was stamped with several numbers and a tiny lettered imprint. The back of the brick had a gently sloping indentation and what appeared to be a serial number stamped at the top. The surface was pockmarked from tiny smelting bubbles, and a small corner of the brick had been neatly chipped away.

I set the weighty brick back down in the sediment. Nearly a dozen more bars lay scattered around me, all of the same general size and description. I felt certain there must be many more locked away in the larger chests.

It suddenly seemed as if I had entered a dream. I quickly lost all desire to leave the amazing room. In this deep, hidden place at the stern of the ship, a chamber locked off from the rest, open only through the captain's quarters, I had discovered nothing less than the mother lode of the *Argonaut*.

I quickly examined the four larger chests, lying tumbled across the floor. They all had padlocks, and the lids seemed welded shut with corrosion. With a rush of excitement, I tried to wrestle one of the fallen boxes upright, but its weight was well beyond my strength, and I quickly gave it up. I found another that had landed solidly on its base, with a rotted, threadbare padlock securing its lid. I banged on it with the gold bar, which only managed to mar the gold; the lock refused to open. Grabbing hold of the smaller, open chest, I emptied the remaining contents and carried it to the larger chest. With all my might, I slammed it against the lock.

I couldn't tell whether it opened or not. I couldn't tell because I couldn't see—I had suddenly been pitched into darkness.

The bulb in my flashlight. The impact had killed it.

I flicked the switch on and off and on and off. I shook the

thing and banged it against the palm of my hand. It didn't even flicker.

My flashlight was dead. Duff was long gone. Some kind of monster was waiting outside. And I was alone, deep in the bowels of the wreck, with not a hint of light and less than five minutes to make it to the surface.

That's if the gauge had been right. For all I knew, I might only have one breath left.

Thinking about air didn't help the matter; it made me suck for more. I was hyperventilating—and heading for a faint. The pounding heart, the rush of blood, the lightness in my head. How do you know if you're blacking out when it's too damn dark to see? I groped along the bottom of the chamber, feeling for the hatchway. The sharp corner of an iron chest slammed into my ribs. I winced but kept on moving. I didn't think about the pain, or about the blood flowing into the water, or about the fact that a rib might have broken. I could only think of one thing: getting the hell out of there.

The air became harder to breathe. Or was that only my imagination? Fear was getting the better of me, like the coldness of the water. My hands shook, my shoulders trembled. The coins were like a bucket of ice in my crotch. My head suddenly banged into an iron chest, sparking a flare behind my eyes. I pushed on. A part of me had taken over that seemed devoid of mind. Call it instinct. The body's will to survive. It pumped adrenaline energy through me and forced me forward into the dark.

Suddenly I felt the hatchway. In a second I slipped through it. I came out upside down inside, like Alice through the looking glass. What room was I in? The captain's quarters? Where was the door? I couldn't remember. Somewhere across the room, I thought. I twisted around and swam ahead—and suddenly had no bearings. What was up? What was down? I couldn't see my bubbles, so I couldn't really tell. Not even when I hit the wall. Which wasn't the wall but the floor. Which wasn't really the floor but the ceiling. Covered in sediment and jagged debris.

An upturned table leg smashed my mask.

Frigid water bubbled up my nose and stung my eyes. Had the glass cracked? I grabbed the mask, held it tight to my face, and blew out air through my nose. The water receded. One more strong puff cleared it out. The glass was unbroken. But my tank was swiftly running out. This was not imagination. The air was thinner, harder to draw. I finally knew what I had left—maybe a minute of air.

I couldn't remember the way out of the room. Or even where it led to. Groping forward, I reached out for the wall, my hands falling on mangled chairs, the soft mush of sediment, an unremembered scrap of crusted iron, a splinter of wood, another goddamn coin. I gripped on something sharp that cut me like a razor. The porcelain washbasin, cracked in two. Now my hand was bleeding. I could feel the sting of saltwater entering the wound. I kept moving, feeling about, reaching for the passage.

Until something slithered over the back of my thigh.

Seaweed? No. This was not seaweed. This was something fleshy, muscular, alive. Something like an eel, perhaps. A giant moray eel. Living in the captain's quarters. I felt it brush against my ankle and slide across my foot. It sent a shudder through me and stopped up my breath. I braced myself for its touch again. Another inquiring caress.

It didn't come. Was it circling me?

I kicked with a sudden flurry and soared ahead, plunging blindly into the darkness.

I don't know how it happened, but suddenly I was pulling my way up a set of stairs. The passageway. The cook's corridor down to the larder. Upside down. It opened out into empty space, another black hole in Wonderland—but this one had a difference: a patch of light. Slight as it was, it shone like a beacon. I swam eagerly toward it, but as I drew close, I saw with disappointment it was only a tiny opening, a thin fissure in the wall of the ship. Nevertheless, I clung to it like a lifeline. The fact of daylight gave me hope, like a crack in a nightmare, a reassuring glimpse of the waking day. I dragged a long, tugging breath and peered out into the hazy light.

The moment my eyes adjusted, the light appeared to change. I realized with a sudden jolt that I was no longer looking at water—I was looking at moving flesh!

I recoiled.

The shadow monster. The white devil.

Inches from my face, it slowly glided by the crack, a moving wall of skin. The skin was milky white and scarred, and it glowed like the ancient crust of the moon. It seemed to move with grim intention, ghostly and inexorable, like the passing of Death itself. I saw no eyes or mouth, no fins or gills or teeth. Only the vast wall of flesh, gliding past in silence.

I watched, awed and trembling, until—with a sudden, whooshing whisper—the wall of flesh was gone. My view once again was a crack of light, a view of murky nothing.

The first thought that came to my paralyzed brain was a belated concern for Duff. He had had a flashlight, so he must have made it out, but now I had to wonder if he had made it back to the boat.

A second thought stumbled on the heels of the first: Could I myself make it to the boat?

I sucked on the growing vacuum of air, feeling my way down the side of the hull until I came to the flipped-over ceiling. There were four rooms in the stern of the wreck, and I had been through three. One more and I knew I'd be out. I pawed over the layer of sediment, the jumble of jars and rotten crates, until my hands finally reached into the watery void of the hatchway. It opened into the crewmen's bunk room, and from there I could see the faint light of the portal to the top deck below, and through it the rocky bottom of the ledge. I slipped through the portal and squeezed my way out from under the roof. In a moment I was heading through the dim forest of broken masts to the gap that led out from under the wreck.

I tried to forget what I had seen but could not get it out of my mind. I thought of the turbulent swirl of water and the severed head I had found. Something was stalking these waters, something monstrous and predatory. I had sensed it from the moment I had entered the depths, as if it were wait-ing for me. Now I could feel its presence again.

I peered out through the gap. After all the darkness, the dim gray water seemed flooded with light. It left me nowhere to hide, no way to reach the surface without being seen, but I had no choice. I was out of air. If I hid any longer in the shell of the wreck, I'd be dead in a matter of seconds.

I had to take the chance.

Slipping quickly through the gap, I glanced around and began to ascend, sucking an empty breath of air. There was nothing to be seen out in the water, just the great covered hulk of the wreck, slowly receding beneath me. Where had the white shadow gone? Was it circling just beyond my vi-sion, out at the edge of light? I strained my eyes, twisting steadily to check my back. Fearing the risk of an air em-bolism, I finned up slowly, exhaling air, letting my bubbles rise ahead of me. The air in the tank was expanding. The fist that had held my lungs so tight seemed to gradually loosen its grip, and I sucked in another quavering breath, more eas-ily flowing than the last.

Once the *Argonaut* faded from view, there was nothing at all to be seen in the water, no sign to tell how far I had gone or how far I had yet to go. Just the paralyzing crystal ball, the eerie netherworld. Spiraling upward, I felt a sense of stasis, of motion without movement, like the stillness in the eye of a circling cyclone. Then I came to a sudden stop. Was that a giant fin I glimpsed? That fleshy flash of white? When I had seen it before, I had thought it was Duff. Now I wasn't so sure. I whirled, peering into the misty distance.

Whatever it was, it had vanished.

I exhaled my breath of air and followed the trail of bub-bles. Far above, the soft glow of light was gradually growing brighter. My pulse quickened. In less than half a minute I could make it to the surface.

But something suddenly came into view that sent a shud-der through me. A shadow in the glimmering light. Hovering above me.

I came to a stop and hung in the water, watching my bubbles rise toward it. A pressure tightened around my throat, expelling the last of my air.

The creature didn't move. It was *waiting* for me.

My lungs burned. My vision blurred. Face the devil or die from drowning. I kicked my fins and soared up higher. The air expanded, and I sucked in a breath. That's when the sound began to emerge. The ominous roar from above.

Not the bellow of a beast, it turned out, but the moan of an outboard motor—the shadow above me was the *Obiman*'s dinghy! They must have come looking to rescue me, I realized; they had figured I had fainted again. I flew up like a soul to heaven.

Bursting through the surface, I filled my lungs with the wide-open sky. Panting, exhausted, I pulled off my mask and turned to the tender.

The boat was crowded with stricken faces. All of them goggling in panic.

One of the faces belonged to Rock. Words came pouring out of his mouth. Words that would ring in my ears forever.

I had ventured into the belly of the beast and stolen a great lost treasure. I had fallen through the looking glass, gone blind, and seen a monster. I had plucked out stars, escaped a serpent, buried my balls in glittering gold. I—only I—knew what secrets the *Argonaut* held.

All of this paled at the sound of Rock's voice, a voice on the verge of terror.

"Where's Duff?" he shouted, again and again. *"Oh my God, where's Duff?"*

LOST TO THE SEA

The puddled mound of coins on the deck steamed in the sun like a pile from the dog. They lay mere inches from my face, yet somehow they seemed far away. I felt no desire to reach and touch them. Felt repelled to even look. Instead I turned my eyes away and focused on my hand. *Pain is good,* I thought. *The sting of severed skin, the throb of ruptured vessels, the burning ache of open flesh. It lets you know that you're alive when everything else inside is dead.* I pressed my palm below the thumb and watched the blood flow out of the cut. It leaked out into the basin and turned the soapy water pink. Like dripping sweat or streaming tears, there seemed to be no end to it. *Let it flow,* I thought, *this red river of pain. Let it bleed forever.*

The long-tongued Lab licked my face, briefly sniffed the pile of coins, and ambled down the deck.

"Jack. Come on. Stand up. That's it."

Eva helped me from my knees. She stood me by the rail. She dried my hands with a paper towel and painted my palm with iodine. She pressed a bandage over the wound, wrapped it tight with medical tape, and cut the tape with her teeth. Then she started on my chest. The abrasion was high on the side of my rib cage, just below my arm. She lifted the arm, applied a bandage, and unwound a roll of gauze around my chest. She worked quickly and efficiently, like an army nurse at a battlefront. She didn't say a word.

I gazed out at the dinghy, still trolling the empty water. In minutes it would be dark, and their fruitless search would end. The air was already beginning to cool. The low sky was gray and somber. A squinting slit of turquoise still clung to the horizon, and I watched the weary eye of the sun fall sleepily into the sea.

Eva turned me around to finish wrapping the gauze. Her hair was tied up in the baby blue bandanna, and her face glowed warmly in the faltering light. As she finished taping up the gauze, she stole a look into my eyes. "There is nothing you could have done," she said.

I looked away, down at the pink bowl of blood and the grinning mound of coins. I fought back an urge to kick them into the sea.

"I could've come back with him," I said. "I could've made sure he got back safe."

"He wanted you to stay."

I reached down and picked up a coin from the pile. "He wanted more," I said. The outboard sputtered noisily, and I turned to watch the boat head toward us. "He always wanted more. More laughs. More girls. More money. More tequila."

"We all want more," Eva said, joining me at the rail. She nodded toward the dinghy. "Even a man who has everything."

Hunched at the bow, Bellocheque looked like Captain Bligh, utterly disgruntled.

"The coin from his room—do you still have it?"

Eva reached into the pocket of her shorts and pulled out Dan's beat-up gold piece. It gleamed in her elegant fingers. "I held on to it for luck," she said. She turned it slowly from virgin to vulture. "It seems to have brought us more bad than good." With a tug of reluctance, she offered it to me.

I took it from her hand and compared it to the shining coin in mine. "There's no holding back now," I said. "I'm going to ask him everything."

"That would not be prudent, Jack."

"Prudent? How can I be 'prudent' after what happened here today?"

"You need to be very careful."

"Careful of what, Eva? What is it I should be so afraid of?"

She turned and looked out at the approaching boat.

"Tell me, Eva."

"You don't know him. You don't know what he's capable of."

"What is he capable of?"

She turned to look at me but offered no answer.

"Murder?" I asked.

Slowly, she shook her head. Out of sympathy, it seemed. "You have no idea," she said.

"Did he kill my brother?"

She turned away and watched the boat. "I don't know."

"You saw the tracing from the notebook. It's the same coin—same nicks and scars, same pattern of erosion."

"Yes."

"How did he get it from Dan?"

"I don't know."

I stared at her until she turned and looked at me again. Her eyes, sharp and glistening and beautiful as ever, told me nothing. She untied the bandanna and let her hair fall to her shoulders. For a moment, she let me look at her. Then she crouched down, carefully spread out the blue square of cloth, and began to fill it with the pile of coins.

The dog barked, and I turned to watch the boat approach. Candy steered the tender over toward our stern. Rock looked up at me as they passed, but his eyes were dead. They seemed to peer right through me, as if I weren't there.

Eva finished tying off the corners of the bandanna, then picked up the bundle and offered it to me. For a moment I stood there staring at it, remembering the wonderful scent of the cloth, the aroma of her perfume I had inhaled on the beach. That had been only days ago, but it felt like years. The perfume had since faded away, and now the only scent in the air was the fishy odor of the bay.

I took the bundle in my hands and looked into her eyes. "That first morning we saw you at the beach, when you swam out to the *Obi-man* and left us your . . . souvenirs. It wasn't by accident, was it?"

She thought about it a moment before she allowed herself to admit it. "No," she said.

"Did Bellocheque put you up to it? Or was stripping in front of us your idea?"

The accusation flew like a dagger through the air, as if I had pulled it from my own heart and flung it into hers. A sad smile barely creased the corners of her mouth. There was more pity than hurt in her eyes, and when she spoke her voice was plaintive, without a hint of malice.

"He'll want to take it all, Jack. You really should leave while you still can."

She walked away to meet the boat at the stern. I started to call after her but stopped myself. Until I had found some answers, I didn't want to look into those green eyes again.

R ock had gone below deck without so much as a word to me. I found him in our room at the prow of the ship, changing out of his swimsuit. His clothes were scattered with mine and Duff's all over the V-shaped bed. He uncovered his Brown football jersey and pulled it over his head, emerging with tousled hair in his face that he shoved back with his fingers. He nodded toward the bed behind me. "You forgot to wear that," he said.

My silver cross necklace, lying among the scattered clothes.

"What are we going to do?" I asked.

He threaded a belt through the loops of his shorts. "What do you mean, 'What are we going to do?' We're going back to Puerto Vallarta. We're going to talk to the cops and call his parents. End of trip, end of story."

He sat down to pull on his sneakers.

"They're never going to find his body. You know that, don't you?"

"Yeah, they are."

I shook my head. "There's no way. I told you what I saw down there."

"Yeah, Candy saw it, too."

"A great white?"

"It wasn't a shark."

". . . What?"

"It wasn't a shark."

"What are you—"

"It was a manta ray."

"What?"

"Candy spotted it from the surface."

"Are you sure?"

"Yeah, I'm sure. She said the thing looked big as a baseball field."

"A manta ray? Here?"

"Bellocheque says there's an island to the west that's a gathering place of mantas. They call them 'devil fish.' They got those horns."

I had seen the giant creatures before, but only in pictures. Great flying saucers made of rippling flesh, their "horns" like outstretched arms gathering into their gaping mouths the tiniest life in the sea. They were black or gray on top, white underneath.

A white devil.

"So Duff . . ."

"Yeah. They eat plankton, not scuba divers."

"He's down there, then."

"Probably never made it out of the wreck."

I thought of the gap I had slipped through under the overturned deck. Could it be that Duff had missed it? That he had tried to go all the way back through the wreck? That he had gotten lost in Wonderland and finally run out of air? That would mean he was down there now, his lungs full of seawater, his pockets full of gold, entombed in one of those inky rooms.

"I didn't see his light. I never saw his light." I imagined him lying in the cargo hold, buried in bones and chains. The image was too horrible to hold in my head. "Maybe he's still alive down there—"

Rock was getting up to leave. I grabbed him by the arm. "Maybe—"

He turned and hurled me back onto the bed. Throwing his full weight over my body, he took my head between his hands and stuck his grimacing face in mine.

"Duff is fucking dead!" he cried. "The son of a bitch is fucking dead!"

My eyes locked into his, and for a moment I was terrified. Rock could kill me with a twist of his hands. His eyeballs bulged like hard-boiled eggs, and across his temples swelling vessels pulsed with purple blood. This linebacker giant had mangled quarterbacks and bulldozed linemen like cow chips into turf. Ivy League dads half in the bag would bet cash money on the injuries he'd cause. He'd pop off helmets and strip off jerseys and bury receivers up to their nostrils. He'd sent a halfback into a coma that lasted a month and a half. The Rock was a mean motherfucker when he wanted to be, and this time he didn't even want it; it just popped out raging all on its own like a grizzly out of a garbage can.

"I'm sorry," I said. It was all I could manage. A meek little murmur in the face of his fury. "I'm sorry."

He stared at me a moment, and something in his eyes made tears well up in mine, blurring his face into a watery blob. His grip on me loosened, and I watched the heat that fueled his outrage slowly leak away. He backed off and slumped on the bed, holding his face in his hands. Then I heard him weeping; not a cry but a kind of muffled whimper, a deep-down animal gut-wrenched sob. It racked his body, but he shed no tears. In all the time I had known him, he had never allowed himself to cry.

He finally fell back on the bed and stared up in a daze at the whorled-wood ceiling. "We gotta find his body," he said. "We gotta bring him back home."

"For sure," I said. I thought again of Dan's missing corpse. I wanted to find that, too.

Voices were murmuring in the galley: Candy and Bellocheque, fixing something to eat. Eva, I imagined, was still up on deck. Somehow she was separate from them, a part of them but separate. I wondered if they even knew it, knew how wary she was of them, how secretive, how hidden.

"Rock," I said, "there's something I have to show you."

At the table, Bellocheque was hunched over a bowl of milky soup. As he lifted a spoonful to his mouth, his eyes drifted up to meet our gaze. Candy had her back to us, chopping something at the counter. She paused briefly when she sensed our presence, then turned to look at us over her shoulder. "Would either of you like some chowder?" she asked.

We declined. I sat down across from Bellocheque, and set the sack of coins at my feet. Rock remained standing and raised his hands to a ceiling beam. He loomed over the table.

Bellocheque glanced between us. "I hope that you both will accept our deepest condolences," he said. "We are profoundly sorry for the loss of your friend."

"Thank you," I said. Reaching into my shirt pocket, I lifted out Dan's gold piece and placed it carefully onto the table. When Bellocheque saw it, he instinctively reached for his pants pocket—but he was still wearing his swim trunks. He turned his head slightly back toward his cabin, remembering where he left his drawstring pants. Then he looked at me, his eyes narrowing with curiosity. I asked him a simple question.

"Are you a betting man, Mr. Bellocheque?"

The hint of a smile crept into his lips, and he answered the same way I had answered him on the beach in Boca the day before. "Depends on the bet."

I lifted the bundle of coins from the floor and placed it onto the table. "How about winner take all?" I suggested. I picked up Dan's coin and admired its luster. "Heads they're mine, tails they're yours."

Bellocheque's smile turned sour.

"What's the matter, Mr. Bellocheque? Don't like the odds?"

Before he could answer, Rock stepped up and slapped Dan's notebook page down beside the coins. He took the gold piece from me and plopped it heads up next to the tracing. "You got this coin from Dan," he said. "Not your Uncle Fester."

Bellocheque eyed the drawing thoughtfully, then lifted his gaze to Rock and me. He set down his spoon, gave a little cough to clear his throat, and touched his napkin to his lips.

"Baby?" he called, and Candy turned to him. "Pour me a glass of sherry, would you? And see if the boys would like something to drink. The three of us are going to have a little talk up on deck."

THE TRAGEDY OF
THE *ARGONAUT*

I had drained my first Corona and Rock was halfway through his second by the time Bellocheque finally appeared on deck. He carried a bottle and a miniature glass of ruby-colored sherry delicately perched in his pinkie-splayed hand. He had changed out of his trunks into a pair of light linen slacks and an unusually somber, charcoal gray Hawaiian shirt—appropriate, I suppose, to the informal state of mourning we were in. Even the weather seemed suitably attired. The foggy, overcast sky soaked up every trace of light from the fallen sun and the rising moon, and the dark sea seemed to mirror and merge with it, leaving our twinkling boat adrift in an infinite, timeless twilight.

Bellocheque wordlessly offered us cigars, but both of us declined with a shake of the head. We watched him set a match to his Hugo and methodically roll the cigar through the flame, sending great clouds of scented smoke into the air. On the water the aroma seemed both odd and familiar, like incense in a church or flowers at a funeral. I wrenched open another beer, reawakening the slice of pain in the bandaged palm of my hand. Rock and I sat across from each other on either side of the cockpit; Bellocheque reclined into the broad back bench, spreading out his meaty arms, holding the smoking stogie in one hand, the teeny-weeny drink in the other.

"Forgive me for not being more forthcoming with you, gentlemen, but certain things I felt were better left unsaid until the appropriate moment. It's quite clear to me now that that moment can no longer be postponed."

Between the dressing delay and the cigar ritual and the fancy talk, Rock had grown impatient. "How did you get the fucking coin?" he asked.

Bellocheque took a tiny sip from his tiny drink. "He sent it to me."

"Dan?" I asked.

"It arrived in Nassau two months ago. Delivered by courier on an Aeroméxico flight out of Puerto Vallarta. It came with this letter." He pulled it from his shirt pocket. I reached out and took it from his hand, careful to avoid the glowing tip of his cigar.

The letter was handwritten on peach-colored hotel stationery from the Krystal Vallarta and addressed to Bellocheque care of a bank office in Nassau. It was brief and to the point. Dan had stated simply that he had found the wreck of the *Argonaut* on the Pacific coast of Mexico, that it was very well preserved and easily accessible, and that its golden treasure remained intact. He was willing to keep it secret and reveal its location only to Bellocheque. All this for a nominal "finder's fee" of three million dollars, one million payable within ten days to a bank account in Mexico City, the other two in person on delivery to the site. It was signed "D.J. Duran" and dated July the tenth.

"No doubt you recognize your brother's handwriting?"

I had to admit I did. It matched perfectly the cramped and crooked script I had been deciphering in the notebook. I handed the letter to Rock.

"Why did he go to you?" I asked.

"The simple answer is money. Your brother, as you know, had rather limited resources."

Rock looked up from the letter. "Jack didn't have much trouble picking up those coins. Why couldn't Dan do the same?"

"Retrieving the gold is only part of the problem. The harder part is getting rid of it. If word of this find leaks out, everyone will want a piece of it. The local authorities, the

Mexican marine resource commission, the American government, the archaeologists, the company that insured the vessel, the descendants of the original owners—they'll all bring in their lawyers and lay claim to the ship and the gold, and the whole thing will be tied up in the courts for years. If he didn't want that to happen, he would have to smuggle the gold secretly out of the country. Difficult under any circumstances, but particularly difficult for a young man with a criminal record. Then he would have to find a way to sell it without revealing where he had obtained it. All this would require the command of considerable resources and connections, something only a few are capable of."

Undoubtedly Bellocheque was one of those few. The Bahamas had a long history of smuggling, and it was a notorious nexus for offshore banking schemes and corporate shell games. Bellocheque was certain to be in the thick of it. He probably already had a plan in mind for the gold coins sitting in the bundle at my feet. I suddenly felt hopelessly naive and unworldly—I hadn't even given the problem any thought. Maybe Dan wasn't as reckless and brash as we had assumed. He'd been arrested for smuggling drugs in Colombia and for selling fake artifacts in Mexico; perhaps time spent in Third World jails had convinced him to never get busted again. He had been clever enough to find the gold; maybe he was smart enough to know that he could lose it.

"A lot of people have money and connections," I said. "Why you?"

"Because I'm the one who told him about the *Argonaut* in the first place."

He took a leisurely drag on his cigar and blew a cloud of smoke into the air. Rock and I just stared at him, waiting for the explanation. He didn't seem in any hurry to give it. He sipped the sherry to lubricate his tongue, stretched out his arms on either side, and extended his legs in front of him. He peered at me through the lingering smoke.

"Remember the photograph you showed me of your brother on a dive in the Florida Keys?"

"Yeah?"

"The boat he was on was mine. In fact, if I remember correctly, it was I who snapped the picture."

"Key Largo?" I asked.

"Pennekamp Reef. Your brother was the hired guide."

Dan's college roommate's father owned a dive shop in Key Largo Harbor. Dan had taken a job there one summer chaperoning day trips on the John Pennekamp Coral Reef State Park.

Bellocheque continued. "We spent three days there diving together. He seemed to have a particular enthusiasm for wreck diving. He took us out to the *Benwood* wreck, that old freighter the Germans torpedoed, and later out to Elbow Reef, to the wreck of the *City of Washington*. He told me he wanted to be a wreck hunter someday, which led me to recount for him the tragedy of the *Argonaut*."

The Tragedy of the Argonaut. It sounded like an epic poem I'd be studying in grad school.

Bellocheque gestured to me with his cigar. "You described shackles and a cannon in the wreck. This came as no surprise to me. The ship began its life as an American slaver." He paused to sip his drink. As he licked his lips, an idea came to him, and he called downstairs for Eva. "I really ought to let her tell you the story."

"Eva?" I asked.

"She's the one who's done all the research."

Now this was really getting interesting. "Was that before or after she went to work for you?"

"It's how we met, actually. Five years ago. She was looking for the wreck herself. Perhaps she hasn't told you, but she's something of a scholar of maritime history. Lost ships are her great passion. Isn't that right, Eva?"

"Finding them is." She was climbing up the stairs into the cockpit. She had tied up her white blouse again, brushed her black hair, and adorned her ears with glinting silver hoops. I fought the urge to look at her but couldn't take my eyes away. Without a glance she crossed in front of me, her bare legs as long and tanned and shapely as ever. The panting Lab followed her up and trotted over to Bellocheque. Eva pulled out a slim cigar, and Bellocheque put a match to it.

"I was just telling our friends about the *Argonaut*'s days as a slaver, but I realized you could give a far more complete and detailed accounting."

"Yes, we'd love to hear it," I said. "While you're at it, maybe you could tell us why you lied to us for so long."

She turned and spewed a puff of smoke. "I never lied to you, Jack."

"You didn't exactly tell me the truth."

"It's my fault, I'm afraid," said Bellocheque. "She was only doing what I asked her to." Eva turned away to glare at the sea while Bellocheque continued. "It's the inescapable problem of trust, you see. Much as it was with your brother Dan." He sipped his drink and licked his lips. "As you might imagine, I was rather reluctant to take him up on his offer without further proof of his claim. My interest in the wreck goes far beyond its monetary value, but sending a million dollars to a bank account in Mexico City guaranteed me nothing. As you can see from the letter, he left no other way to contact him. So I invited Eva to join us to try to find him in Puerto Vallarta. We had been there for nearly a month when we discovered someone else was looking for him, too. That someone else turned out to be you."

I thought of the words written on my back and glanced across the cockpit at Rock. Things were going down pretty much the way he had said they would. We had gone blabbing about Dan all over Puerto Vallarta; if Bellocheque had heard of it, every drug-dealing weasel with a score to settle with Dan must have found out we were looking for him. I suppose I should have considered us lucky: Bellocheque might have been sly and deceptive, but at least he wasn't a deranged cokehead with a penchant for knives and baseball bats.

"At first," he continued, "I wasn't sure how much you knew or what your intentions were. Certainly you can understand my concern for discretion. We needed to meet you properly and get to know one another. So I asked Eva to help

draw your attention. I hope you don't mind. You didn't seem
to at the time."

Rock and I exchanged a glance. Did we mind? He must
be kidding. We had loved it—but we didn't like to be had.
Especially the Rock. For him it signaled a major failure of
his analytic powers.

"After we had met and talked," continued Bellocheque, "I
was still uncertain you could be trusted with the secret. If I
had told you what we knew from the start, you might have
left us and set out on your own. It's important, I believe—
extremely important—that all of us stay together on this.
Wouldn't you agree?"

Again I glanced at Rock. The look he gave me told me
everything. We'd been had once; it wasn't going to happen
again.

"Absolutely," Rock said. "We all stay together. Right,
Jack?"

"Yeah. I agree. Definitely."

Bellocheque smiled. "Splendid." He reached for the bottle to refill his glass. "Now. The tragedy of the *Argonaut*.
Eva? I want you to tell them the whole story."

Eva was leaning back against the rim of the cockpit with
her elbow propped in her hand, the cigarillo poised in her
upheld fingers. She drew in a breath of smoke and held it for
a moment in her open mouth; it hovered there over the bed
of her tongue until she began to speak, then flowed out
through the gate of her teeth, trailing her words like the
cloak of a ghost.

It seems that *Argonaut* was not the ship's original name. It
was called the *North Wind*, designated so by the man
who built it, the Boston shipping magnate R. W. Freirich.
He sold it to a Southern cotton trader, James Pierson
Cliburn, who in turn sold it to a rogue American trader based
in Cuba, a man named Cesar Luiz Braga. Braga had been
born in New York in 1810, the son of a Portuguese immi-
grant, a wealthy trader who had fled from Lisbon when

Napoleon invaded in 1807. The father had lost his ships and his fortune, and the son had taken over a dwindling and increasingly perilous business in the African slave trade, an enterprise outlawed in the United States, Europe, and much of South America. Because markets were limited to Cuba and Brazil, where the importation of slaves was still tolerated, Braga often brought them into Cuba and then smuggled small groups into the States by landing them on the coasts of Florida and Georgia.

It was dangerous work. The coasts were monitored by schooners from the U.S. Revenue Marine, and slave routes out of Africa were vigorously patrolled by squadrons of the British Royal Navy. This situation made the *North Wind* a particularly valuable player in the trade. She had been designed for speed and was limited in size, making it easier for her to outrun cruisers and to slip unnoticed into African ports. It also meant a shorter voyage, and given the high mortality rate among its overcrowded cargo, shorter trips meant higher profits. Braga sought those higher profits through the late 1830s and into the '40s, but he knew the days of the trade were numbered. While American efforts to stop the traffic had never been more than halfhearted, the British pursued slavers with an ever-increasing vigor, employing faster brigs armed with devastating batteries of long guns and carronades.

"I guess that would explain the *Argonaut*'s cannon," I said. "There are probably even more of them I didn't see."

"I don't think so," Eva said. "Slavers trusted their heels more than their guns. Crews were too small to man a battery. Most carried only a single carronade on a pivot—enough to fight off hijackers at sea, or to repel attacks by Negroes when buying slaves in port."

Negroes. Hadn't that been consigned to PC oblivion? Apparently it still held a place in Eva's lexicon of maritime history, right there alongside "carronades" and "brigs." I glanced at Bellocheque, wondering what he thought of her using the term. He seemed oblivious, lost in thought, his mind somewhere out there off the Ivory Coast.

By the late 1840s, the slave trade had grown too dangerous and difficult; Braga knew he'd have to change his ways
or he'd end up stretching hemp. He began looking for a more
legitimate avenue to regain his family's lost wealth and
glory. Following a fruitless foray into the opium and tobacco
trade, Braga heard of the discovery of gold in California and
leapt at the chance to make his fortune. Investing all the
money he had, he hired a crew out of Havana and purchased
a black Jamaican slave to do the cooking and seven fresh im-
ports from West Africa to do the digging. Then he set out on
the newly christened *Argonaut* for the long voyage south
around Cape Horn and up the Pacific coast to San Francisco.

Shortly after shipping out, the cook was killed in a galley
brawl. Braga stopped at the island of Tobago, off the coast
of Venezuela, to pick up a replacement. Tobago was a
British colony, and slavery had been abolished there since
1834, but many former slaves still labored on the same sugar
plantations as they had for generations. It was from one of
these plantations that a new ship's cook was recruited, an
ambitious young black man with a wife and child. So enthralled was he with the prospect of finding gold in California, he left his beloved family behind to join the expedition.

The man's name was Hector Bellocheque.

"Your great-grandfather?" I asked.

"Great-great-grandfather," Bellocheque replied. "The son
he left behind was my great-grandfather, Gabriel. But we
don't want to get ahead of our story. Please, Eva, continue."

The *North Wind* had been designed for speed and the
steady, moderate trade winds of the slave routes. Now the
Argonaut faced more challenging seas, but with luck—and
his considerable sailing skills—Braga expected to make it to
San Francisco in record time. Early into the voyage, however, his hopes for a swift trip were dashed. A heavy squall
off the coast of Brazil damaged the ship's sails and forced
him into a lengthy stopover in Rio de Janeiro, where he re-
paired the ship's canvas and reconfigured its rigging. For
ships making the trip around the Horn, a stopover in Rio was

not all that unusual, nor—according to Eva—all that unpleasant. It was typically the first landfall made by gold
seekers who had departed from Boston or New York, and the
city was quite cosmopolitan, with a reputation not unlike the
one it has today. Eva cited records she had found at the naval
academy, noting the *Argonaut*'s stay at the port's dockyard;
but she had also found Cesar Braga's name on the guest lists
of Portuguese gentry, friends of his father's who had fled to
Brazil when the royal court was exiled from Lisbon.

"Captain Braga, party animal?" Rock suggested.

"According to descriptions," Eva said, "he was a dark and
handsome man with courtly manners and considerable
charm. But above all he was a man with connections. The
foundations of his trade."

I thought she might as well have been talking about Bellocheque. "I guess it was a small world even back then," I said.

"In some ways," Eva said. "Not in others. The voyage
around the Horn from Boston to San Francisco could take
easily six, seven, even eight months. Leaving from Havana,
with a monthlong stop in Rio, the *Argonaut* made it in a
mere 172 days."

Even with the delay, Braga's early start had put him
among the first major wave of "forty-niners" arriving in San
Francisco. In the spring of 1849, the city was already a ram-
shackle boom town bustling with adventurers hungry for
gold. The harbor bristled with sailing ships from around the
world, and the first of the Pacific steamers had arrived,
carrying overland passengers up from the isthmus of
Panama. The gold country was largely lawless, with little
government and no bureaucracy; hence, few records from
which to trace what happened next.

"You don't know what happened?" I asked.

"If Braga kept a journal, it's never been found," Eva said.
"The arrival of his ship was recorded by the harbormaster,
but nothing else was left behind."

Rock turned to Bellocheque. "No letters home from Papa
Hector?" he asked.

"Postal services in the mining country were practically nonexistent. Besides, it's unlikely my ancestor could either read or write. No correspondence has ever been found."

"So how do you know what happened?" I asked.

Eva answered. "Their names come up in records from an El Dorado County court case in 1851."

"A lawsuit?" I asked.

"It seems that fortune did not smile on our dear Captain Braga," Bellocheque said. "If he ever did find any gold, it couldn't have amounted to much. He had to sell off two of his African slaves in order to pay his legal expenses."

"But the coin—you said Hector found gold—"

"He did," said Eva. "Apparently they'd had a falling-out, and Hector had ventured off on his own. Soon afterward he discovered one of the richest veins in El Dorado County. When Braga got word of it, he came back to claim Hector as his slave and the gold as his own."

"But wasn't Hector a free man?" I asked.

"He was a free man," said Bellocheque, "but no one in California knew it. Braga used the papers from his dead cook, claiming Hector was the Jamaican slave he had purchased in Cuba. He demanded all the gold that my great-great-grandfather had found on his own."

He got it, too. California, admitted as a state into the Union in 1850, had failed to emancipate the slaves brought into its borders; masters retained rights to their services, and in contested cases of captured runaways, judges often ruled in the owners' favor. Such was the case of Hector Bellocheque. Pleading before a judge in a Sacramento courthouse, his testimony could not stand up to the certificate of ownership in Captain Braga's hand. The "slave" was remanded to his counterfeiting master, who gladly took ownership of Bellocheque's fortune.

Braga packed the gold aboard the *Argonaut* and set off at once on his return trip, carrying with him his five remaining African slaves, a crew of four seamen, and a shackled Hector Bellocheque. Like Dan, whose research had been recounted in his notebook, Eva had scoured logbooks of passing ships and records of harbor activity along the coast, looking for traces of the *Argonaut* following its departure from San Francisco. There was an exchange of signals with the northbound steamer *Sonora*, and a stop to resupply at the dock in San Lucas, but beyond that, nothing more was ever heard from Captain Braga or the men aboard his sailing ship. Shortly after the *Argonaut*'s departure from Baja, the steamer *Diamant* reported an approaching gale off the coast of Puerto Vallarta, hinting at a possible end to Braga's story, one that only now could be confirmed. The ship, floundering in heavy seas, had crashed headlong into the rocks off Punta Perdida and sunk with its crew, its slaves, and its purloined cargo of gold.

I thought of Hector Bellocheque, who must have been chained in the cargo hold I had floated through only hours before. I had felt a presence in the shadows of the wreck, and wondered now if what I had sensed had been his lingering soul, the intangible echo of his outrage and anger, haunting the depths for a century and a half. Perhaps it was he, unwilling to relinquish his golden treasure, who had captured Duff and held him with the cold grip of the sea.

"Maybe they didn't all die," Rock said.

I asked him what he meant.

"The men we spotted in the fishing boat this morning—one of them looked like a black man, a black Mexican Indian."

"Just like Dan wrote about in his notebook," I said. "The villagers—they're descendants of the slaves!"

We both turned with excitement to Eva and Bellocheque, but the two of them continued smoking in silence. It was obvious they had long before arrived at the same conclusion.

"What about your great-great-grandfather?" I asked. "Do you think he might have survived as well?"

"I sincerely doubt it," Bellocheque said. "Hector had a wife and a child in Tobago; he would have done all that he could to return. The Africans, on the other hand, had no one to return to and nowhere else to go."

"What about Braga and the crew?" Rock asked. "They might have made it to shore."

"It's unlikely," Eva said. "Nothing was ever heard from them again. They either drowned when the ship went down, or . . ."

"They were killed by the slaves," I said.

It didn't seem all that far-fetched a notion. Given the cruel shackles we had found in the hold and the ruthless way he had dealt with Hector, I was certain that Captain Braga had gotten the fate that he deserved. The true tragedy of the *Argonaut* was the tragedy of Hector B. From plantation laborer to galley cook to millionaire—only to die in chains at the bottom of the sea. I glanced across the cockpit at his great-great-grandson. He sipped his sherry silently and puffed on his cigar, contemplating this story as he must have done a thousand times. *Eva was right,* I thought: *He'll want to take it all.* Who could blame him? His family had been denied its rightful fortune. A wife had lost her husband and a son his father. A flagrant miscarriage of justice had been perpetrated, an outrageous theft, a humiliating dishonor—all due to the overweening greed of a slaver.

He'll want to take it all.

"There are five chests in a room down there," I said. "Iron chests."

Bellocheque and Eva stared at me.

"The coins came from one that had broken open. The others are sealed with corrosion."

They continued to stare at me, both of them speechless.

"They're probably what spiked the magnetometer," I said.

Bellocheque's voice came in a whisper. *"Very likely, yes . . ."* He seemed to be visualizing the chests in his mind, peering inside them with X-ray eyes. Finally, he aimed the eyes at me. "Along with the coins, did you happen to notice—"

"—gold bars?" I said. "As a matter of fact, I did. About a dozen had spilled out of the open chest."

Bellocheque's eyebrows lifted appreciatively.

"How much gold is down there?" I asked. "What's your granddad's fortune worth?"

He threw a glance at Eva, then looked back at me. "Difficult to say."

"Try," Rock said.

Bellocheque puffed his Hugo. He looked to Eva.

Eva smashed out her cigarillo. "According to court records," she explained, "most of the gold was in the form of bullion—a hundred and ten gold bars, roughly four hundred ounces each. At the time, gold was worth about sixteen dollars an ounce. Today, an ounce is worth about three hundred and fifty dollars. But you have to add to that their historical value. Gold rush ingots in their original form are extremely rare. As Leo said, their value is nearly impossible to estimate. It's usually determined at auction."

"How much?" Rock said.

Eva glanced at Bellocheque. "If I had to guess," she said, "I'd say each bar is worth at least a quarter of a million dollars."

Rock and I, awestruck, quickly started calculating numbers in our heads.

"You're talking . . . over twenty-seven million dollars' worth of gold," Rock said.

"Easily," Eva said.

My pulse was racing. "So what do we do now?" I asked Bellocheque. No reason not to play along. Better to work with him than against him, for sure.

Bellocheque glanced between Rock and me. "Your friend is gone," he said. "You have both suffered a heartbreaking loss."

"Yes," I said.

"But you realize that nothing you can do now can bring him back to us."

"We can recover his body," Rock said. "Bring him home so his parents can bury him."

"Yes, most definitely," Bellocheque said. "I couldn't agree more. It's the least that we can do . . . and the most, I'm afraid."

"Assuming we can find the body," Eva added.

"We'll find it," Rock said.

"Whether we find it or not," Bellocheque said, "you'll both have a choice to make. Return to Puerto Vallarta, call his parents, and tell the police. Or wait. Wait until we've recovered the gold and smuggled it out of the country."

Rock and I stared at him a moment, then glanced at one another. It was the same look we had shared before, the one that said we wouldn't be had, we'd keep our eyes open, make ourselves rich, come out alive in the end.

Rock looked to Bellocheque. "What's in it for us?" he asked.

Bellocheque studied him for a moment.

"My brother gave his life for that gold," I said. "So did Duff."

Bellocheque dragged on his cigar, blew out a long exhalation of smoke, and peered at me through the haze. "Why don't we take up your brother's offer?" he suggested. "Now that I know it's for real." He glanced between the two of us. "All of the gold goes to me," he said, "and three million dollars goes to you."

"Three million dollars . . . *each*," Rock said.

My mouth fell open. Bellocheque glanced at Eva. Then he gazed into his glass of sherry, brooding over its bloody hue. "Very well," he said after a long silence. "Three million dollars—each. But I will require your continued assistance in recovering the gold."

Life is lived in the moment, he had said. I looked to Rock and felt the moment closing around us, sealing us in our fate like insects in amber. I was aware of it happening but seemed unwilling or unable to stop it. I watched my hand reach out to Bellocheque and heard a promise come out of my mouth. "You'll have it," I said. "All the help we can give you."

He stuck the cigar in his teeth and shook my hand. "Splendid," he said. "Splendid."

I glanced at Eva. Her green eyes told a different story.
Things, dear Jack, will be anything but splendid.

Part Three

UNDERWORLD

GRACCHUS

What's that barking? Where the hell am I?

Oh, yeah. The beach.

I'd been hearing that dog for hours in my dreams. I propped up on my elbows and looked out toward the sound. It seemed to be coming from somewhere down the shore. The narrow strip of beach looked like an empty stretch of road. With the moon still hidden in the overcast sky, the jungle behind me was utterly opaque and the shoreline vanished into darkness. Black waves swept the sand with a steady, plaintive rhythm, a softly pleading background to the yammer of the dog.

I climbed out of my sleeping bag, pulled on my jeans, and followed the sound along the water in the dark. A slight sea breeze chilled my back, and beneath my bare feet the sand felt icy, as if it had never been warmed by the sun. The dinghy lay where I had left it, pulled up to the edge of the trees; I probably would have missed it if I didn't know it was there. I had come ashore up the coast from Punta Perdida, straight in from the rocky point where the *Obi-man* had anchored. The boat had departed at sunset to refill the tanks and replenish our supplies; it had to be halfway to PV by now. Without its reassuring presence on the water, the ocean looked cold and forbidding.

"Gracchus!" I shouted. Weird name for a dog, but these yachties weren't exactly the folks next door. Bellocheque said Gracchus was a hunting hound, far more at home in the

woods than the water, but I had seen the dog swim; he
seemed to like it all right. Maybe it was the incessant sawing
of the surf that had sent him running for the hills.

"Gracchus!"

Taking the dog ashore had been Bellocheque's idea. He
had tried to dissuade me from staying, but when I insisted,
he told me that I should take Gracchus along. I had agreed,
thinking the Lab would keep me company, but now all the
barking just made me feel more alone. I suddenly regretted
staying behind. Whether they needed me or not on the boat,
it would have been refreshing to be back in the city, to shake
off all the weirdness that had happened since we left. It
clung to me now like the saltwater grime. I could have used
a shower, a hotel room, a meal in a crowded restaurant, pretending for a while I was just another tourist, that nothing
horrible had actually happened.

Staying was a choice I had made on my own, though; no
one had talked me into it. It was something I felt I needed to
do. In the morning I would hike into Punta Perdida. Dan had
spent his last days in that town; I still hadn't found out what
happened. The least I could do was to locate his body and
transport it back to my mother. She'd want a proper burial. A
coffin, a priest, a prayer. Without it she'd never believe he
was dead. I couldn't believe it myself. The only way I could
know it for sure was to look it square in the eye.

Eva had voiced reservations, but Rock had not tried to
stop me. Apparently any fraternal concern had been trumped
by his paranoia, what Bellocheque had called "the inescapable problem of trust." Rock had no more trust in Captain Bellocheque than he would have had in Captain Braga.
He didn't want the two of us sleeping on the old man's boat.
Not tonight, anyway. Not after demanding six million dollars to keep our mouths shut. There was another way to in-
sure our silence, and Eva had implied our captain might use
it. Rock said he'd sleep with one eye open but thought it was
unlikely anything would happen unless it could happen to
both of us at once.

I finally spotted the dog. He was barking at a throng of

men gathered along the shoreline. I assumed they must have walked all the way from the village. What could they be doing out here so late? I couldn't read my watch in the dark, but it had to be three in the morning. Did the clammed-up people of Punta Perdida only come out at night? I moved closer, stepping carefully through the rocks. Why didn't somebody shut up the dog?

"Gracchus!"

He kept on yapping at the cluster of men. They were all dark-faced Mexican Indians, dressed in loose white clothes, staring down grimly at something in the water. Gracchus continued barking even as I approached. I went past him to the edge of the crowd, peering over their hunched shoulders to see what lay at their feet. The men took no notice of me, their mute faces blank, their downcast eyes dark as the sea. I squeezed my way through the crowd, brushing past them to the edge of the water. What I saw there made me gasp.

A mangled corpse rocked in the surf. Its head had been hacked off and so had its limbs, leaving only a bruised and bloated torso. A wave rolled in and tumbled it over. The belly had an appendectomy scar.

I vomited onto the sand. It washed away in the foam of a wave. The cluster of men closed around me. I dropped to my knees in the surf and saw there was blood in the water. Bile again rose up in my throat; I dared not look at the corpse. When at last I lifted my face, a figure was standing before me. A bent old woman in a black cloak. One hand held a bloody machete; the other clutched the hair of Duff's dangling head. She looked at me and grinned. She had no teeth.

The sun blazed high in the sky, and a thunderous wave crashed behind me. My head seemed filled to the brim with pain. A thick sweat covered my skin, and the sleeping bag beneath my feet was wet with perspiration. I could not remember climbing out of it, but there I was, completely naked, standing in the sweltering heat. The jungle stared back silently, and the beach lay empty on either side.

The dog was gone.

I looked down and noticed something stuck into the sand. Bottles. Old bottles. Someone had buried them in a circle around me, leaving only their necks protruding. I pulled one out and brushed it off. It was partly filled with liquid but had no label or cork, and I couldn't see through the bronze-colored glass. I brought it to my nose, then abruptly threw it at the ground. Never in my life had I smelled anything so foul.

I fell to all fours and heaved again. Nothing came out— my stomach was empty—but blood surged noisily into my head. Behind me, the crashing sea went silent. A drop of sweat dripped off my nose, exploding in the sand, leaving a tiny crater on the shadow of my face.

Then my head dropped like a bomb, bursting back to blackness.

CORPUS DELICTI

It was dark by the time I opened my eyes. I rolled over onto my back in the sand and watched the moon emerge from a cloud. Half a moon, anyway—enough to reveal that the ocean was empty and the long stretch of beach completely deserted. My clothes and backpack lay where I had left them, as though I had never climbed into my jeans and wandered down the shore. The humid air was still and pungent, filled with the disgusting odor of the bottles. Seized with revulsion, I yanked them up one by one and chucked them into the sea. Twelve crusty bottles in all, each one sailing off into the dark, pissing a trail of poison until it plummeted into the water with a gratifying splash.

When I could find no more to throw, I stood there with my headache throbbing and gazed down at my naked body. My front half was caked with sand, and my backside had been burned in the grueling sun. Brushing off the sand, I found my chest and abdomen marked with swollen spots of pain. They were tiny, slitlike punctures in the skin. What they were, or how they had gotten there, I had no idea. Perhaps it was something in the sand, I thought—ticks, mites, chiggers, scorpions. Whatever it was, it was worse than anything I had encountered on Sand Fly Beach. Maybe it was what had gotten to the dog.

"Gracchus!"

I found a water bottle in my pack and gulped down nearly all of it. Then I walked down the sandy slope, stepped carefully through the shoreline rocks, and plunged into the surf. The water felt bracingly cold and cleansing and seemed to relieve the pressure in my head. Farther out, I rose up with a surging wave and searched out the horizon.

The *Obi-man* had not returned.

According to my watch it was nearly midnight, more than twenty-four hours since the boat had sailed away. They had hoped to be back by nightfall but had left enough food and water to last me another day. I felt like a castaway, long forgotten. Rock, Bellocheque, Candy, Eva—they seemed like fragments of a disintegrating memory that had broken off and floated into the irretrievable past. Wherever they were was a lifetime away from the place where I'd just been.

What in the hell had happened here? I turned around and scanned the shore, filled with doubts about what I had seen. The men on the beach, the dog's mad bark, the bloated torso, the crone with the knife—all of it so tangible and real, yet all of it as strange and elusive as a dream. It had to have been a nightmare. A journey on the highway of those airborne fumes.

How could it be otherwise?

"Gracchus!"

My call brought no reply beyond the breaking of the waves. Had the dog simply wandered off, or had it been lured or taken? Somebody had come and planted the bottles; maybe Gracchus had followed that somebody back into town. I remembered the barking I had heard in my sleep but couldn't remember it stopping. *He can't have gone too far,* I thought; *I'm going to have to find him.*

Back on shore, I ate a PowerBar that Eva had put in my pack. I was weak from hunger, but my stomach was queasy and I had to force it down. I finished off the bottle of water and opened up another. If the toxins were still in my system, I'd have to flush them out. Other than drinking water and downing aspirin, there wasn't much I could do. I dressed, pulled on my sandals, dropped my pack and bag in the boat, and headed up the shore toward the town—the same direction I had ventured in my dream.

Unless it had not been a dream. I decided to look for clues. If I had indeed been this way before, I would have left footprints in the sand, but as I walked along now I could not find a single print—at least none I could discern in the dim light of the moon. Finding nothing, not even the tracks of a seabird or crab, I realized the tide had come in and gone out during the time I had spent passed out on the beach. If this had been where I had walked before, I was unlikely to find any trace of it now.

I peered ahead into the darkness as I continued down the shore, but the town was still too far away to see. This came as no surprise, given its lack of electric lights, but eventually a soft glow emerged out of the darkness, and I realized a bonfire must be burning on the shore. It was far ahead, probably at the edge of the village, on the beach that Dan had called the Playa de los Muertos. I aimed for it now, walking swiftly. That's when I stumbled into the mound.

It was a pile of dry sand, maybe two feet high and three feet wide, surrounded by a dozen half-melted black candles. The mound itself was ornamented with an odd assortment of collected objects: a turtle shell, black seeds, several corked bottles, a clay pot of water, a crow's black feather, a jar full of dried leaves, two tiny crucifixes, a brass hand bell, various roots and bundles of grasses, Mexican coins, scattered flowers, a strip of yellow cloth, and the small, painted plaster figure of an unidentified Christian saint. The sudden sight of all this was shocking, an impression only intensified by the destruction I had caused: My sandaled foot had plunged into the mound, far enough to collapse a portion of it, toppling the haloed saint and spilling the pot of holy water. I froze on the spot, then slowly withdrew my foot.

No doubt a sin had been committed. A curse would hound me to my grave. I quickly pushed back the sand, leveled the bowl, and returned the saint to its prayerful position. Then I stood back and looked at the pile. Obviously someone had deemed this nameless site worthy of sacred honors. It reminded me of the crosses and flowers I had seen on Mexican roadsides where fatal accidents had occurred. I glanced around and saw that the beach was covered with shoe prints and bare footprints, all the way to where the tide had washed them away. Searching for my own footprints among them, I found nothing obvious in the jumbled chaos of marks. One thing was clear enough though: A large group had assembled at the edge of the water here, and within the last day or two. Suddenly I could not help but believe that what had happened in my dream had happened for real. Duff's body had been found washed up at this very spot. The men had come to look at him. The old witch had cut him up and . . .

I hurried back to the mound and tore into it, my hands digging deep, knocking away the bowl and the statue, the feathers, candles, seeds, coins, crucifixes—all the way down through the core of the mound, then deeper into the ground. I clawed an open hole, pulling out the sand and spreading it around me, combing through it with my fingers, searching for what I was certain must lie hidden within it.

I dug a pit two feet deep before I finally reached it. The feel of the flesh felt sickly familiar. I dug out the hard-packed sand around it, freed the head, and held it up before me. The moon came clear of a cloud and shone its morbid light on the face. I drew a breath in horror.

The devil's head. Exactly like the severed head I had found in the ocean. White hair, stubby horns, long, tufted ears, its milky eyes filled with sand—and something moving in its mouth.

Maggots!

I flung the head away and retched.

After a long, nauseous moment, I rose to my feet and shuffled across the sand to look at the thing again. It had rolled down to the edge of the water, where the surf gently nudged it, lending to the lifeless form a mechanical parody of liveliness, a movement mimicking a shaking head. "No," it seemed to be warning me. "Go back to where you came from. You do not want to know."

But I did want to know. Despite the message carved on my back, despite the horrors I had seen—because of them, in fact—I wanted more than ever to know. I had to know. It was why I had brought myself to shore and spent a harrowing night. It was why I had come to Mexico. My brother had disappeared, and I was bound to find out what had happened to him. I wanted the truth. It went beyond the promise I had made. It went to the heart of who I was, that question flung out into space that called itself my fate.

I crouched down to look at the head. This was no devil's noggin. It was, in fact, the head of an animal. A sacrificial sheep, most likely—but sheep had no horns. No, this head belonged to a lower, meaner creature. A ghostlike imposter, a counterfeit, a proxy, a stand-in for the devil. Those long, tapered ears with their furry, fiendish tufts. A mouth with the snout of a hound and the grimace of a cat. Those cadaverous eyes with their unnerving stare, fixed on some final and immeasurable terror—a tin can, perhaps, lodged in the throat?

The head belonged to a miserable goat.

How could I have let the damn thing scare me half to death?

I left it lying on the shore and walked away in disgust. By morning the tide would roll in and carry it out to join its evil twin at the bottom of the sea. With any luck, the mound and all its superstitious bric-a-brac would wash away with it. Let it all go to hell, what did I care? I had had enough of my pious trepidation and fear of fatal curses. If uncovering buried goat heads was a damnable sacrilege, so be it. I wouldn't confess my sin to a deaf-mute priest or light a black candle on a holy hump of sand. I'd leave that for the upstanding citizens of Punta Perdida. In the meantime, I'd try to steer clear of their poisonous bottles and machete-wielding witches. I wasn't looking for trouble.

In the ghost town of Punta Perdida, the ghosts had come to life. I had been hearing the noise they made from a long way up the shore. A clamor of flutes, rattles, and drums accompanied a high-pitched, whining chant. It sounded Spanish and undoubtedly was Christian, but it had the percussive rhythm of an African tribal hymn. The weird ruckus permeated the stillness of the night. As I walked the darkened shore it seemed always near at hand, yet the ghosts themselves remained elusive. By the time I reached the enormous bonfire, blazing at the water's edge, most of the revelers had abandoned the beach and were heading up into the town. The slow-moving mass of their ragtag procession, snaking up the daunting hills of the village, was hidden by the dark stone walls of the road. All that could be seen from my lowly vantage was their high-held crosses and smoke-trailing torches, a bodiless caravan of bright brass and fire.

I stayed back, crouched in the shadows behind the low wall of a boatyard strewn with fishing nets and upturned hulls, and watched a group of old women who had remained behind to tend the blaze. They circled it slowly, wearing dark shawls over their heads and leaning on crooked sticks of driftwood, which they lifted impulsively to poke at the fire, sending up great swells of sparks and cinders. As if to help in stoking the blaze, they spat into the flames and shouted curses into the air.

What it was they were burning was difficult to tell. Plenty of wood from the forest, no doubt, but something lay at the center of the blaze that looked suspiciously like a coffin. A small coffin, like that of a child. The sides had burned away, but the broken outlines of a glowing frame remained, and within the frame lay a dark, crumpled form wrapped in orange and yellow flames. It sent forth whirls of black smoke that rose up with the floating cinders and blended into the dome of darkness hovering over the beach.

Was it Gracchus they were burning? I couldn't quite see. The form was larger than a child but smaller than a man. I was still crouching uncomfortably behind the wall; my legs began to tremble. I felt that I was witnessing some secret, twisted rite. This was not a bonfire of joy and celebration. Nor was it a funeral pyre—there were no mourners here, no sense of bereavement, no anguished display of grief and loss. There was spitting and cursing and the stoking of flames. Flesh was being burned, being turned into ashes and delivered to the sky. Like the head of the goat, the body of the dog could be an offering of sorts, an act of appeasement or of supplication, a sacrificial tribute to their darkly brooding god.

I slipped over the low wall into the boatyard. Hunching down, I snuck from hull to hull, keeping to the shadows as I crossed to take a closer look. The opposite wall was draped with a ragged fishing net that stank of the sea. I peeked over it cautiously, and the brightly blazing heat of the fire warmed the skin of my face. As they shuffled their way around the blaze, jabbing their sticks and barking their curses, the bent little women cast mighty shadows that moved across the ground around them, plunging me in and out of darkness. One squat little crone, tightening her shawl around her head as she ambled along, suddenly turned her crinkled face and stared in my direction.

Her shadow leapt into my face.

The dog! Not Gracchus but Pancho, the mangy mutt who had followed me on my visit to the priest. Resting his paws atop the low wall, he licked my face until I pulled away, then let out a raspy bark. I ducked to the ground and quickly crawled away. Pancho jumped over the wall and followed me. Hiding behind the upturned hull of a freshly whitewashed rowboat, I pulled the dog close and held him still, then peered back cautiously at the fire.

"Easy, boy," I whispered to the mutt.

The crone who had spotted me had vanished, an anonymous spoke in the shadow wheel of circumambulation.

Pancho licked my chin. "Glad to see you, too," I told him, "but you better keep your mouth shut." I released him gently and snuck back across the yard and over the first wall. Without looking back, I raced across the beach and down a narrow alley, turned a corner, and came to a stop beneath the shadow of a high stone wall.

The dog loped up behind me.

"Okay, Pancho. Which way to the parade?"

The houses and streets near the beach appeared deserted, as though everyone in the town had been drawn into the procession. I could hear, floating down from the streets above, the jangled noise of their eclectic instruments and the high cry of their song. Moving furtively through the shadows, I scurried up another alley, crossed an empty street, and found a stone stairway that had been carved into the hillside.

I began the ascent at once. The climb was steep, and I took it carefully; many of the steps were broken, and the way was twisty and dark. It brought me alongside numerous houses with crumbling stucco walls, past windows offering glimpses of dark and vacant rooms, over yards with nervous chickens, cats prowling high and low, and sullen dogs that— strangely enough—didn't bother to bark. One pen I passed housed a massive hog, sleeping like a giant baby, and on the steep incline beside it a single munching goat, who observed my passing with complete disinterest. No horns, I noted— unlikely this one would donate its head! I continued on strenuously, and each time I looked back I found Pancho staring sadly up at me, exactly as he had done before.

Tiring from the climb, I paused to catch my breath. Though I could not see the procession itself, I could hear it making its way up the street, and for a long moment I listened to the sounds of the marchers floating through the air. The chant had changed to a kind of lament: The whining had turned to wailing, and the drums and rattles had softened their beat. Then, suddenly, a man's deep voice cried out, and the lamentation transformed at once to a joyful exaltation. The man called out and the marchers answered, happily echoing back and forth, until the spirited exchange exploded in a rising tumult of song.

The sound was electrifying. I scurried up the remaining steps to spy on them before they passed. Finally reaching the top, I was relieved to find that I was well ahead of the on-coming procession. Their torches could be seen approaching in the darkness down the street. Quickly, I slipped through an unlocked gate, entering into the courtyard of a dark and seemingly deserted house. A leafless, black-limbed tree jut-ted out from the stone floor and reached up over the crum-bling roof, while below, rimmed with ancient flagstones, a small, round, algal pond reflected the stark branches of the tree and the half-lit face of the moon. The dog followed me in and went immediately to lap at the water, turning the placid pond tableau into an abstract riddle of ripples. I gazed up at the pale facade of the forlorn little house, its stucco pockmarked with rotten brick, and thought it resembled the face of a spook: its high, empty windows a pair of eyes, its arched doorway a gaping mouth. Despite the sense of disquiet it provoked, it was clear to me that the house was vacant, perhaps even abandoned; I turned my back on it without another thought. Closing the wooden gate to the street, I peered out through a crack in its slats and awaited the approaching parade.

In less than a minute it was close enough for me to see the revelers' faces. They were like those of the fisherman Rock had described seeing from the boat, and of the crowd I had passed through in my nightmare on the beach: black-skinned Indians, a blend of two races—men, women, and children alike. Only here they had shed their meek white cottons, exposing flesh in flagrant display. Men wore loincloths and turbanlike headbands, their faces and bodies adorned with paint. Some of the men and the children wore masks: wooden masks with carved-out eyes, painted white like skulls, and masks with gourd-stem horns and noses, ablaze with the colors of fire. Women wore swirling skirts of brilliant colors, with dazzling sashes, headwraps, and scarves. Many went bare-breasted, bouncing beneath a bib of beads, their peeping nipples painted gold. The women's faces, without exception, were painted a ghastly white. It gave the otherwise colorful crowd the look of the skeletal dead.

Leading the congregation, with an ornate cross turned upside down atop a golden staff, was an aged black priest in a flowing black robe. His white-bearded, white-haired head was crowned with a wine-red turban, and he wore a pair of round, thick glass spectacles that seemed—amid the exuberant wantonness—soberly out of place. It was his voice that I had heard before, crying out in counterpoint to the chanting crowd, and now, holding high above his head a painted rattle, he sang out in his sonorous wail, leading his parishioners in the exhilarating hymn. Distributed around him, several young altar boys in fluttering white smocks and skull-head masks held framed lithographs of the Virgin and the saints, carrying them deliberately upside down. One of the boys held aloft a sloshing bowl of blood. The priest dipped his gold-ringed fingers in the bowl and flicked a wet blessing out over the crowd. As he crossed before the gate from which I was peering, I tried to get a closer look at his face, but yellow torch fire danced on his glasses, hiding his eyes like a pair of gold coins.

When the priest had passed ahead so I could no longer see him, my view through the crack became a kaleidoscopic blur, a whirl of dancing worshippers. They joyfully cavorted in their bare feet and sandals, blowing on whistles and pipes, shaking rattles, banging drums, shouting their jubilant song to the priest. Most of the men carried tar-tipped torches that gave off an oily smoke, while a number of women held wax-dripping candles and blazing, multiflamed candelabra. While some wagged Bibles in their hands, others clutched plumed arrows, shaking them vigorously over their heads. Several men brandished machetes and clubs, playfully waving them about like toys. The clamor they all made was a joyous cacophony, contagious and ecstatic, yet savage and frightening. They rolled and shook and bobbed their heads, and I thought for sure they were all intoxicated, though on what I couldn't say. I smelled no telltale weed and saw no one imbibing as they danced along the street. Whatever they were on had been taken on the beach. Their eyes were clear and moist and bright, their bodies full of vigor and their minds delightfully free of thought.

It took several minutes for the procession to pass. When it finally dwindled down to the last, I saw a figure trailing in the dark, and the sight of him brought my heart to a stop.

He was being led up the street on a tether, tied to a barefoot, shambling boy who clearly suffered from a severe and untreated form of mental and physical retardation. His curved spine forced him forward, and his head was bent grotesquely to the side, revealing a wildly wandering eye. All the while he shuffled along he mumbled incoherently, and a white froth of saliva had caked around his lips. Following so suddenly on the happy heels of the bacchanalia, the sight of him appalled me; yet far, far more horrible to see was the man he towed behind.

The padre had been stripped naked, flogged, and fitted with a Christlike crown of thorns. With the tether roped around his neck, he stumbled clumsily up the street, his bare feet soiled and bloody, his hands groping the empty air. The man had been blinded, his sight gouged from his face, leaving black, bloody sockets where his eyeballs once had been.

The gruesome shock of it revolted me. I felt a sickness welling up, a bile in my throat that turned into anger. I reached for the latch to open the gate. My impulse was to rescue him, to take him far away, or at least to offer some gesture of comfort—but I could not do so without revealing myself. The noisy crowd was only just ahead, and a move to the street would immediately be noticed. The parade of pickled revelers could easily turn into a mob. I myself might end up like the priest. And what, I thought, as the padre staggered past my gate, could I possibly do or say to assuage his awful state? The evil that tormented him lay too far out of reach. The man could neither hear me nor speak to me nor see.

I watched him hobble away up the road.

When at last the crowd had disappeared, I eased open the creaking gate and stepped out guardedly onto the street. I could still see the glow of their torches as they rounded the bend, and hear the sound of their voices and the clamor of their instruments. They were heading, it appeared, to the top of the hill above me. I looked up there now, over the rooftops, and discerned a lone, moonlit cross standing against the sky. The church, I realized, was their final destination.

A small object was lying on the stone pavers, and I walked over to see what it was. The rattle—a painted gourd filled with seeds or gravel—had been left behind by one of the revelers. I picked it up. The black gourd was painted with swirls of green and gold and carved with a strange symbol on the rounded end: a squat white diamond shape with a long stem. It reminded me of the kitelike symbol I had seen in Dan's notebook. Taking the gourd by the handle, I shook it gently in the air. It made a hollow, scratching sound.

An echo of the rattle sounded in the courtyard behind me—strangely so, for it came too long after the sound I had made. I turned abruptly but saw nothing in the darkness through the gateway. I glanced around. It was clear there was no one left on the street, but far down the road, moving slowly up the hill, a group of shadowy figures was approaching: the band of shawled women, I thought, those mysterious tenders of the fire. They moved in a slow sinister swarm, as though they were not walking but flowing over the stones, like the shadow of a flock of flying crows.

Out of the courtyard came a menacing growl.

"Pancho?" I moved warily toward the open gate, peering into the darkness. The silver moonlit pond appeared, and the black tree loomed above it. The shadow of the tree seemed to reach out toward me, taking on the form of a dog.

"Pancho?"

A sudden thrill went through me—it wasn't Pancho, but the black Lab.

"Gracchus!"

The dog crept slowly out onto the street, his head low and wary, his eyes staring strangely, as though they belonged to a different creature, one who did not know me.

"Gracchus . . . What is it?"

I squatted down, reaching out to him with my bandaged hand. "What's the matter, boy?"

With a sudden flashing snarl, the dog sank his teeth into my wrist, biting down hard and holding firm. Blood flowed at once, and I dropped the rattle from my other hand and tried to pull him off. "Gracchus!" I could feel the edge of his teeth on my bones and dared not tear my hand away. "Gracchus!"

I looked up. A shawled figure stood in the gateway. From the shadow of her hooded head, a pair of glistening eyes glared down from a cruelly crinkled face. This was the crone who had spotted me in the boatyard. I recognized her now as the butcher from my dream, the hag with the crowd of men on the beach.

She clutched her shawl with her bony hand and grinned her toothless grin.

"Who are you?" I asked.

The woman moved slowly toward me, spitting out words in an arcane tongue, words not meant to communicate but to summon spirits, or ward them off.

Gracchus, growling, held firmly to my wrist. Blood dripped on the pavestones, flecking the fallen gourd. I looked up and saw the shawled flock of crows slowly closing around me, their eyes like pairs of black seeds, their hands like gnarled roots.

The old crone reached into her cloak, babbling her baleful chant. I glimpsed a moonlit glint of metal.

"No!"

The machete flashed above me. Thrusting it high in the air, she shrieked, *"Ayalaba!"*

I wrenched away my hand, tumbling back from the plummeting blade. Gracchus held tight, his body pitching over me, and the falling steel came down on his neck. A spray of blood splattered my face. I scrambled in horror to my feet. Blood continued spuming as the dog jerked in squirting spasms—his head had been severed from his body. Lifting my bleeding arm, I saw his teeth still locked on my wrist. I ripped open the dog's jaws and flung the bloody head at the crone. Then I burst through the circle of women and fled in terror down the street.

When I reached the beach, I kept on running. I ran along the crashing waves, away from the flickering light of the bonfire into the darkness up the shore. When the light had faded behind me, I did not pause to rest. I didn't look for the sacred mound or the severed head of the goat, for footprints or corpses, or dogs created out of night. I didn't look for evidence that dreams were not dreams, or nightmares not reality. I heard the roar of the waves, felt the grip of the sand on my feet and the throb of dripping pain in my wrist. I didn't need to wake myself. Had I entered some kind of underworld? Had it entered into me? For now I didn't want to know; it mattered not a bit.

I hauled the boat down into the surf and launched it boldly onto the sea. Plunging through the hurtling waves, I finally brought it deep enough to lower the prop and start the motor. I charged out over the black water. Blasting through the heavy rollers toward the open ocean, I headed out as far from shore as fear would dare to take me. Then I kept on going. I screwed my eyes toward the western horizon, that delicate darkness at the rim of the sky. Chasing the long-lost light of the sun, I yearned for the blinding blaze of its fire to burn my world away.

THE LUST OF THE EYE

She called to me. *"Buenos días!"*

It's one of the few phrases we all know in Spanish. That, and *hola, por favor, hasta la vista, baby,* and *gracias*—polite terms of greeting and good manners essential for any visitor to Mexico. Serious travelers, of course, will be eager to pick up a new phrase or two and with a little study and practice might even find themselves chatting with the natives. Learning new words and phrases can prove useful in avoiding embarrassment and may even keep one out of harm's way. Take, for example, the delightful term *"ayalaba."* Charming sound—trips off the tongue—but if you don't know what the hell it means you might end up with your head on a plate!

Okay, okay. Let's not get into all that now. Let's return to a more pleasant subject. Let's return to Eva.

Shall I describe the way she looked as she rose up out of the water and shouted the local greeting? Let's do. Unless you'd rather hear about the pain I'd been feeling on nearly every square inch of my tortured body. The blisters, for instance. After lying for nearly two days unprotected in the sun, I was not a pretty sight. On my back, bubbling skin pushed up the neatly lettered knife-cut scars, opening the half-healed wounds, brutally exposing them to sun and sand. I'd reach back to relieve the unbearable itch, and my fingers would return all smudged with blood. Speaking of blood, I should mention the peculiar numbness in my arm after losing a quart of the stuff into my shirt—the one I had so hastily torn from my back to wrap around my punctured, bleeding wrist. I should also mention the strange bites on my chest and abdomen. They had swollen into tender welts and were now spewing forth a mixture of yellow pus and blackish blood. Those bites, by the way, were so evenly and precisely placed—one above each nipple, one below, and two on either side of my belly—they could only have been made by a human being. A sick and twisted human being, but human nonetheless. So who exactly was it? I had a good idea. That grinning crone, after all, had damn near fucking killed—

All right, all right. I know I shouldn't dwell on it. Life is a catalog of suffering and evil. Let's look instead on the bright side of things. Let's turn our gaze upon Eva.

I must ask you, of course, to trust me on this. My claims are sure to be doubted, but what I saw from the shore that day was greater than any gold or treasure. This was not a coin from the bowels of a wreck, or a pearl from the mouth of an oyster. Its worth could not be calibrated in capital or pleasure. It was instead a revelation, a miracle of the sea, the Infinite brought into being through the bleary eyes of Man.

Granted, I was not exactly at the peak of my faculties. I had drifted back to land sometime shortly after dawn and had been lying strung-out under the receding shadow of the beached dinghy for probably six or seven hours. I had finished off the last of the water in the first hour of the sun beating down, and I had had nothing to eat since the night before when I had gagged on that measly candy bar. On top of that I hadn't slept—really slept—in nearly three days. Plenty of heated REM in that time, but not enough deep-down, delta-wave, stage-four shut-eye. That lazy vapor poison still loitered in my system, and, of course, I had lost a boatload of blood. My strength was nearly gone, my brain was more than a little fuzzy, and I suppose my eyesight was not up to par: I hadn't even noticed the boat in the bay. I was also, to put it mildly, slightly out of my mind. Somehow I had gotten the idea in my head that a witch with a machete was—

Sorry. Can't seem to help myself. Rancor grows rampant as ivy. The point is, none of this made a damn bit of difference. One little glimpse of that heavenly paragon, one little eyeful of Eva, and I knew in my heart I was saved.

There was Beauty in the world.

I confess I never actually saw her rise out of the water. She was already waist-deep when I lifted my gaze. It was as if she had been born there, fully developed, presented to the world on a cockleshell, blown in to shore by the gods of the wind. Her dark hair lay like satin on her shoulders, a veil drawn back to reveal her stunning face. Even from a distance of twenty-five yards I was struck by the long black lashes of her eyes and the strong lean angles of her cheeks. She moved through the surf with slow, forging strides, balanced by graceful, slender arms held slightly out and back, her fingers trailing lightly in the unresisting sea. With her chest thrust forward and her head held high, her wet breasts shifted gently side to side, barely yielding to the tug of her top while offering every pleasure to the sun's grinning eye. The silvery water, greedily enveloping her hourglass waist, opened with slow, astonishing splendor as her hips rose magnificently out into the light.

I swallowed. I squinted. I elevated my view.

The emerging legs went on forever, the water like a slip slowly falling to her feet. Yes, she was wearing a bikini, of course, a black one I had not seen before, but it would serve little purpose to describe it here. The impression I had was not of a swimming suit revealingly cut, of a disappearing thong or a cantilevered cup, of strings waiting to be untied or of fabric yearning to elope with the breeze, but of the woman as a whole. It was not the suit or the sunlight or the color of her hair but all of these things and more, together and at once—joined, I freely admit, by my unremitting lust and my desperate need for succor. All of this together created the vision, beheld as much in the eye of the mind as in the bloodshot eyes of the flesh, a creature of divine and immortal conception, a thing, as I've said, of Beauty.

The magic vanished in an instant, of course, the moment she saw my wretched state. The sudden shock that shadowed her face, the outright fear that stiffened her limbs, punctured the burgeoning balloon of my vision and brought the woman gasping down to earth.

"Jack—*my God!*" she cried, crouching beside me, looking me over with utter disgust.

"I missed you, too," I said. My elbow gave out and my head fell into the sand.

"Jack!"

I murmured something.

Eva lowered her face. "What *is* it, Jack? What are you saying?"

I mumbled again. "You look great," I said.

People had warned us about the rainy season. They had said it poured every afternoon all summer long and you couldn't go anywhere without getting drenched. This had not been our experience. Though it had certainly rained, and on occasion rained hard, it definitely had not been every day; we had gone three or four in a row without so much as a drop. More often than not, when it did rain, it was only a cooling shower that came and went so quickly we'd hardly even notice it.

Not so this time.

It had started imperceptibly, like cat paws on the deck, a light, lulling patter stealing sinuously through my sleep. Eventually, however, the kitty cat grew into an MGM lion, and the roar that eventually filled my chamber drove me scrambling out of bed. So quickly, in fact, that I nearly toppled back in. The boat was steady; I was not. Though my bite wounds had been neatly dressed and my back expertly attended to, the ache that had entered my head on the beach had taken a definite turn for the worse, and despite Eva's efforts to get me to eat, I had yet to develop an appetite or a stomach able to keep anything down. Sleep, it seemed, was all that I could do—but under this relentless, pounding rain, even that had proved impossible.

I staggered toward the door. "Eva!"

A pin dropping in a thunderstorm. Hearing the feeble cry of my voice made me frightfully aware of how weak I had become. I plowed through the door and lumbered down the corridor, my hands holding the wobbly walls to keep them from caving in. Eva's cabin was empty; so was Candy's. I stumbled into the saloon and found it empty, too.

"Eva!"

I heard her voice, then Rock's, up on deck, shouting over the rain. It took some effort to climb the steps, but I made it through the gangway and out into the weather. The rain was falling in a crushing downpour, as if the bowl of the ocean had been turned upon itself, yet the sea was surprisingly windless and flat. The keen slap of water on water sounded like breaking glass, and the surface churned with a scintillating spray, a frosty sheen of velvet. Above the boat, in the leaden sky, the ragged clouds hung open and raw, and I guessed from their sallow, greenish light it must be late afternoon.

Rock stood at the stern with his back to me. He was barefoot, wearing his swim trunks and a sopping Cuervo Gold T-shirt, peering out over the water. I started toward him, and Eva grabbed me from behind.

"Jack—what are you doing out here?"

I stared at her without answering, as if I didn't know myself why I had stumbled out on deck. Eva was drenched, her open white blouse the color of flesh. Her wet tresses clung to her cheeks and her neck, and the rain splashing her face made her squint her long-lashed eyes. She dropped her gaze to my chest and abdomen. I was shirtless, and the bandages over the strange bite wounds had come undone, washed off by the drowning rain. Thin trails of a black, silty blood coursed down my stomach and into my jeans.

Rock's big hands gripped my shoulders. He had to shout over the din. "What's wrong?" he asked. He came around and looked into my eyes. "You all right?" Then he looked down at my chest and his expression went from bad to worse. "Take him downstairs," he told Eva. "I'll keep watch up here."

I managed to emit some kind of a question. Without quite hearing me, Rock gave an answer. "Candy and Bellocheque went down to look for Bobby's body. We lost their bubbles when it started raining." He glanced out over the water, squinting into the spray. "They should be back any minute now."

"C'mon, Jack." Eva guided me into the gangway.

I hadn't noticed how humid it was down in the saloon, but now, as Eva pulled shut the gangway hatch, the air seemed to close in around us like a pair of latex gloves. The steady rumble of rain outside added to the tactile sense of enclosure, and I paused in the middle of the room for a moment and tried to allow myself to relax. My brain, however, seemed to be on a spiraling course all its own, and soon I was caught in the rushing narrative of a vivid childhood memory: the mindless hum of a humidifier in the misty cocoon of my lower bunk; the blur of a shaken thermometer and its clinking insertion under my tongue; my father's sanguine pronouncement of "pneumonia" with the steely grin of Mr. Clean; and finally, the terrifying midnight abduction, ending in the long-needled horrors of hospital imprisonment.

"Jack?"

Eva touched my arm, eyeing me inquisitively. "Why don't you lie down over here?" She cleared a space on the upholstered bench along the wall, then went to the sink and ran the tap. I did what she told me, stretching out carefully on my back, and, without any effort or maneuver on my part, immediately began to sink into sleep. It seemed as if, ever since I had awakened, a vast realm of blackness had been waiting just below the shimmering surface of my thought. Willingly now I plunged, letting my consciousness escape like exhaled bubbles in a watery abyss.

I might have dreamed of a dark-haired mermaid rescuing a drowning sailor from the sea, but I can't say that I did. I can say, however, that I awoke to find Eva sitting beside me, gently wiping my chest and belly with a warm, wetted cloth and offering an utterly enchanting smile.

"You were dreaming," she said. "I could see your eyes moving beneath your lids."

"I've been doing a lot of that lately," I said. "Sometimes even while I'm still awake." I lifted my head and watched her clean the pus-leaking bites on my belly. If it hadn't been so disgusting, it might have turned me on.

"It's not as bad as it looks," she said. "The black gunk is an herb paste I put on under the bandages. Leo says it will help in healing the wounds."

"Wounds? I thought they were bites. They're swollen. Each one has two punctures, like teeth."

"Leo called them *el beso del diablo*. Kiss of the devil."

"What would Leo know about it?"

"You'd be surprised," she said, with a tone more of admonition than admiration. "Leo knows all manner of things."

"Kiss of the devil?"

"He grew up in a village like Punta Perdida. On the island of Tobago."

"Believe me," I said, "there's no village like Punta Perdida anywhere this side of hell."

Eva ignored me. "He recommends a tea as well. I was to make you some the moment you awoke."

"How long have I been sleeping?" I asked.

"Only a few hours. I found you this afternoon on the beach, remember?"

Of course I remembered, but it seemed impossible. It felt like days, not hours, ago. I asked her why it had taken so long for them to return.

She hesitated before she answered. "We had some . . . difficulties. After leaving Puerto Vallarta."

"Difficulties?"

"You really ought to rest now, Jack."

She was trying to protect me, didn't want me to worry— but that was all I knew how to do. "What kind of difficulties, Eva?"

She looked at me a moment and resigned herself. "Leo thought a boat was following us. He decided we should stop in Yelapa for the night."

"A boat?"

"Thirty-foot cruiser. Named *Orchid*. Two men on board."

"Did you lose them?"

"We waited for them to go ashore. We waited a long time. Finally, in the morning, Candy and I went ashore ourselves. When they followed, we snuck back to the boat and slipped away."

"Who do you think it was?"

"We don't know, but Leo is afraid we don't have much time. It's why he insisted on going down this afternoon."

Eva folded up the gunk-soaked cloth and headed back to the sink. Apparently she hadn't liked the idea of diving with a storm coming on. I watched her rinse the rag and dry her hands and move about the galley. Her hair and skin, still damp with the rain, gave off a kind of luminous sheen that made her presence glisten. Beneath her wetly translucent blouse, she was still wearing the black bikini she had worn on her rescue swim to the beach. A filmy wrap skirt clung to her legs, and I watched for the flash of her naked thighs in the fabric's wavering rift. Opening cupboards, lifting out china, adjusting the obedient blue flame under the kettle, bending, stretching, turning, reaching, she glided through the cluttered room with the unerring grace of a Latin ballerina. Probably a full minute passed like this, with me in a silent, gawky trance, watching her move her various limbs, before I finally realized she was looking for something.

I sat up, cringing with the surge of pain in my head. "What is it, Eva?"

"I thought he said he put it out, but I can't seem to find it." She headed up the hall to Bellocheque's room.

I looked down and ran my fingertips over the swollen bites that were not bites, the *beso del diablo*. Whatever they were, they were ugly as hell. I reached for the protruding black arm of a T-shirt in the pile of discarded clothes that Eva had pushed to the foot of the bench, and as I tugged it loose, a glass jar tumbled off the edge and rolled along the floor to my feet. I picked it up and found myself suddenly transfixed. The jar was full of leaves, dry and brittle and crumbling, and exactly like the ones I had seen in the jar at the sacred mound on the beach.

The kettle began to whistle.

"Eva!" I called. "I've found the tea!"

It was still raining hard when Bellocheque and Candy surfaced from their dive and boarded the boat. I had fallen asleep again, pleasantly relaxed after two steamy cups of the mysterious brew, and didn't come awake until I heard voices murmuring around the table in the galley. Actually, it was Bellocheque's booming baritone that woke me; his voice always seemed to be louder than the rest. I sat up and shook off the remnants of sleep. Nobody noticed me. They were sipping coffee, slicing an odorous cheese, and passing loaves of the crusty Mexican bread they call *bolillo*.

I was suddenly overcome with an urgent need for the bathroom. I raced down the corridor, slammed through the door of the head, and plopped my ass on the pot. Bladder and bowels exploded at once. The prodigious quantity and duration of the release—pouring forth with a violent, unceasing intensity—stunned me. This was not simply a case of diarrhea or loose stools and a full bladder. This was an unprecedented phenomenon, utterly effortless and perfectly expressed. I sat there for what must have been a full minute of uninterrupted discharge, marveling at the vastness of the body's inner labyrinth and the miracle of Bellocheque's mysterious tea.

It came to an end in the usual way. I cleaned up and pressed the button and buckled my pants. One might expect, after such a record-breaking elimination, a satisfying sense of lightness and relief. All I felt, however, was a dispiriting sense of depletion and loss, a hollowed-out sort of emptiness, as if some vital part of my being had been flushed away in the swirl of waste. Stepping out into the corridor, walking back toward the galley, it seemed as if I had been disembodied, as if the fragile flesh that held me was only a tenuous membrane, illusory and insubstantial. I felt like a shadow of my former self.

The poison seemed to have fled, however. My headache was gone, and the queasiness in my gut had disappeared completely. It should have come as no surprise that I felt so very different. Maybe all that was missing was the darkness that had weighed so heavily upon me these last few days. Inspired by this turn of thought, I decided to take my lightness of being for a newfound state of health.

"Hello, everybody," I said as I strolled into the room.

Rock and Eva and Candy glanced up from the table. Bellocheque had his back turned and declined to make the considerable effort required to wheel himself around. "Feeling better, are we, Jack?"

There was an edge of skepticism or anger in his voice. That subtle tongue of his. Why did he always sound like Admiral Nelson? "Tobago," I said. "Was that a British colony?"

"British, yes. And before that, French. And Dutch. And Spanish. But if it's my accent you're wondering about, it came from my years at Oxford."

I remembered having recently watched his dog get killed. *Can't blame the man for being angry,* I thought. On the table at his elbow was a bottle of rum. "You didn't find Duff, did you," I said, more an assertion than a question.

Bellocheque didn't answer.

"We went through every room in the wreck," Candy said. "Not a trace of him anywhere." She looked a bit pale and drawn, and the blue of her eyes had faded to gray.

"You saw the treasure, though, right?"

Candy glanced at Bellocheque before she answered. "Yes. It's just like you said, Jack. We'll have to take some tools down to crack open the trunks."

I sat down next to Rock. He was slumped back in the seat with his head resting against the wall, palming a warm mug of coffee. His eyes were bloodshot; he looked exhausted.

The "sleeping with one eye open" policy had obviously been taken to heart. "How was Puerto Vallarta?" I asked.

He rolled his head toward me and looked me over. I was wearing a black *Newport Lobster House* T-shirt of his, at least two sizes too big. "Better than Punta Perdida, I'm sure." He gazed down at my bandaged wrist. "Why don't you tell us what happened to you?"

"Yes, Jack," Bellocheque said, tipping a trickle of rum into his tea. "Tell us about your adventures. And don't forget the part about what happened to my dog."

There it was: simmering but seemingly under control. Eva rose from the table, eyeing him with a look of mild reproach. He glanced at her begrudgingly, then took the loaf of bread in his hands and ripped off a sizable chunk.

Eva asked me if I'd like some more tea.

"Absolutely not," I said. "Just water, thanks."

She went to the cupboard. I looked for the torn loaf of bread. It lay within the bulwark of Bellocheque's elbows. "I'll have a bite of that . . . if it's all right with you."

Bellocheque raised his gaze to me. He looked fairly exhausted himself. One night spent at the wheel of the ship, the next with an eye on the mysterious *Orchid.* I had never seen rum mixed into tea before, but the two of them appeared to be having some effect. A surliness tugged down the corners of his mouth, while his eyes looked alert and discerning. He passed the mangled loaf of bread, then shoved the bottle across the table. "Have a swallow of this, Jacko. It'll whet your appetite."

"I don't think so—" I started to say.

He interrupted me, calling over his shoulder to Eva, "Bring him a glass." Turning back, he looked at me again, his eyes probing deeply into mine. *"It'll fill that empty hole inside."*

I shuddered. It felt as if he had peered through the windows to my soul—and found the soul was missing. I looked away.

"So wise so young," he said cryptically.

Eva set down a glass of water and, with a deprecating frown, placed beside it an empty tumbler. I glanced around me. They all seemed to be waiting to see what I would do. I stared at the bottle a moment, then poured a shot of rum into the glass and—much to my own surprise—knocked it back in a single gulp. Bellocheque smiled. I choked and gagged, and he began to laugh, his broad, bright teeth filling the gloomy room with light. The others joined in the laughter as a fire blazed its way through my belly, sending flames up my throat and burning the cobwebs out of my head. I chugged down some water. This transformed the heat into a soothing steam that seemed to suffuse the whole of my being.

It felt wonderful. A smile came to my face.

"Much better," I said. I tore hungrily into the bread. Bellocheque watched me eat.

"I'm sorry about Gracchus," I told him, "but that dog of yours nearly got me killed."

I told them the story. My whole bloody adventure. The crowd on the beach with Duff's corpse. The old crone with the machete. The circle of poison bottles. The sacred mound and the goat's head. The bonfire and the weird procession. The tortured priest and the beady-eyed flock of witches. And Gracchus—how his vicious effort to help kill me had somehow ended up saving my life.

My sleepy companions seemed a good deal more alert at the finish of my story than they had been at the start. Maybe it was all the coffee, but I'd like to think it had something to do with my harrowing tale of terror. For nearly an hour they peppered me with questions, most of which I couldn't answer. What was in the bottles? How could Duff's corpse have washed up so soon? Why would they chop it up? Was I absolutely positive I wasn't just dreaming? What was the meaning of the sacred mound? What was the crazy procession about? If it wasn't Gracchus they were burning in the fire, then what was it? How had the old hag gotten into the courtyard? What had she done to the dog? Why on earth would she have wanted to kill me?

Among the five of us at the table, Bellocheque was the only one who didn't seem surprised by the tale. To the world-weary chap from the island of Tobago, burnings, beheadings, bacchanalian reveries, roving bands of bloody-minded witches—none of it apparently seemed too far out of line. He did ask a few peculiar questions: How tall was the priest? Were there any severed fingers in the mound? Was there blood on the quill of the black feather? Did Gracchus's tail wag? And a few I thought were perversely voyeuristic: Were the altar boys naked? Did the women expose their pudenda? Were there acts of fornication? But mostly he just listened. Our lame speculations seemed to interest and amuse him. At times he acted impatient and annoyed; other times he laughed. Only one thing appeared to bother him much: the fact that they had gotten his dog. This made him disgruntled and upset with himself.

"I should have known better," he grumbled. "These people are barbarians."

"The parade," Rock said. "Do they have those in Tobago?"

"They have Carnival. This was different. This was *un Día de los Muertos.*" He lifted his eyes to meet our gaze. "A Day of the Dead."

Something in the way he spoke the words frightened me. The finality, the foreboding of it. It reminded me of the bellowing of the four-eyed priest and the bone-white skull masks of the altar boys around him. Why did Mexicans make a holiday out of death?

I noticed Rock's Adam's apple bob with a gulp. "Doesn't that come at Halloween?" he asked.

"The Days of the Dead go back three thousand years. Among the Indians, they were celebrated at the start of their harvest. At summer's end."

Summer's end. For a schoolboy like me, it sounded like a death sentence. "But these people aren't, like, Aztecs," I protested.

"And they're not even farmers, they're fishermen," Rock added.

Bellocheque stared vaguely at the crumbs on the table. "Perhaps this was a . . . special occasion," he said.

Rock and I stared at him in silence. Both of us knew exactly what he meant. That corpse on the pyre was no dog.

I looked up at Eva. Her eyes fell away. I turned back to Bel-locheque. "Why?" I asked. "Why would they do that to him?"

He didn't seem to be listening. He was staring into his drink. "The Spaniards thought the rituals were sacrilegious. They tried to eradicate them, but of course they failed. All they managed was to move the celebration to coincide with theirs—with All Saints' Day and All Souls' Day. 'All Hal-lowed's Eve.' But the Spaniards never really understood. Their view of death was completely different. They mourned the loss of life. To the Indians, death was deeply revered. Life they considered nothing more than a dream. Only in death did one truly awaken."

Awaken to what? I thought. The procession had looked like a nightmare to me. I asked him about the devil masks, the sprinkled blood, the upside-down crosses and pictures of the saints.

"It may have been the prelude to a Black Mass," he said. "A Feast of Fools."

"They worship the devil?" I asked.

"Not worship—respect. They give him his due. Turn the Church on its holy head."

"Why?" I asked.

"So all can see what lies in the dark. A face-to-face en-counter with the shadow of the tribe. Among the medieval Christians, these counter-religious celebrations used to be quite prevalent. They'd curse the name of Christ, kiss an an-imal on the anus in the name of the devil, use a naked woman's back as an altar, on and on, all the complete re-verse of what is normally considered right and holy."

I thought of the Huichol Indians described in Dan's note-book, those peaceable descendants of the homicidal Aztecs, how they had "reversed" the names of things while on their peyote pilgrimage. Perhaps these violent, decapitating vil-lagers had reverted to their ancient, savage ways. "What about these cuts on me?" I asked. "Is that a part of their black magic? They look like bites from a vampire."

Bellocheque chuckled dismissively. "Cut with the quill

of a crow, most likely—the feather you saw on the mound. The *bruja* used it to draw out your blood and replace it with poison."

"She could have picked an easier way to kill me," I said.

"At that point she wasn't trying to kill you. She was trying to drive out the devil."

"You think it's all just superstition, then?"

Bellocheque leveled his rummy gaze on me. "Superstition is born in fear, and fear is born of an experience of the world." He downed the remainder of his inebriating tea. "Nature creates and annihilates," he continued. "The Spirit lives both high and low; the demon shadows the divine. We fear this shadow and flee from it; we seek and are obsessed with it. But it cannot be escaped, and it cannot be possessed. All we can do is acknowledge it and attempt to discern it in ourselves."

With that, Bellocheque capped his bottle and rose unsteadily from the table. The big man apparently had had enough to drink; he seemed to be teetering, as if he might collapse. Rock and I were not about to let him go to bed, though. We followed him around the galley, demanding answers. He told us that the Shango cult of Trinidad and Tobago combined Yoruba, Catholicism, and the Baptist faith; that believers think a man blinded by desire can turn into a living devil; that the mound on the beach was an "apotropaion," built to ward off these pestering souls; that "*ayalaba*" was an incantation to cast them to the fires of hell.

Bellocheque guessed that during the six-month voyage to California aboard the *Argonaut* his great-great-grandfather had taught these arcane island secrets to the African slaves, who themselves were no doubt already imbued with the magical beliefs of their tribal homeland. Here in this isolated village on the coast of Mexico, it had all combined with Huichol peyote rites, ancient Aztec sacrifice, and Latin Catholic ritual, creating a uniquely volatile brew of savage spiritualism and eccentric ceremony.

At the door to his cabin, Bellocheque turned to us to say good night.

I stopped him before he could. Something felt amiss. "Why would they hack up Duff's corpse?" I asked. "Why would they burn it and spit in the flames? That's not religion or magic. It's *evil*."

"You fail to grasp the mind of the believer. To them it is we who are evil."

"Duff was no angel," Rock said, "but turning him into a devil is going a little too far."

"How far is too far?" Bellocheque asked. "Plato said that if one merely looks at something evil, something evil falls into one's own soul. The Bible calls it 'the lust of the eye.' For the people here, it's not merely a question of morality; it's an essential, practical problem. Evil is a force of nature, and your friend had fallen under its power. He had to be reckoned with, like a flood or a drought or a plague of disease. To them he was no longer human."

"Not *human?*" I asked.

"When a man has fallen to the devil, he loses his humanness. He acts as if divine, and so he must suffer the fate of the divine. Men burn their devils and crucify their gods."

Duff a devil? Duff a god? "You mean . . . because he was diving—breathing under the sea?"

"No, no," he said. "Because he was diving *for the gold*."

I glanced at Rock. He looked as confused as I was. "The gold?" I asked.

Bellocheque fixed me with a tolerant stare. "Don't you see? For them it's cursed. That ore was the source of all their troubles. Tribal Africans abducted from their homeland, clapped in shackles and shipped like animals halfway around the world, forced up into frigid mountains to dig for a yellow rock, 'the buried sun' they knew nothing about. All to satisfy one man's greed." He glanced between the two of us. "Is that not the epitome of evil?"

We stared at him without speaking.

He glanced up to listen to the rumble of rain still pounding hard on the deck. "You'll be wanting to get some sleep," he said. "We'll be diving in the morning if this storm ever stops." He stepped into his room and started to shut the door, then turned to us, smiling slyly. "Don't forget to say your prayers," he said.

I thought I heard him laughing behind the closed door.

THE FALLEN ANGEL

Bellocheque's laughter echoed through my sleep. Slipping into a variety of audible disguises, it strolled like the devil through a masquerade of dreams. I heard it in the song of the red-turbaned priest and in Gracchus's black, rattling yap. I heard it in the deafening crash of the waves and in the bonfire *brujas'* wrathful rant. It finally took the form of a hacking chortle spurting from the mouth of the toothless crone. Lowering a crow quill over my chest, she turned her ugly face to cackle in my ear.

I woke up and realized it was thunder I'd been hearing. Lightning flared in the skylight, and the boat vibrated from the boom of the blast. Rock was gone, and the door was flapping open. The vessel was rocking violently. I looked at my watch: a little after two in the morning. Climbing out of bed, I held on to the overhead bin to steady myself. Another flash of lightning filled the room, followed by a louder blast of thunder. Pulling on my clothes, I stumbled into the swinging door and banged the bone rim of my eye on the flying globe of the knob. I grabbed the knob, stepped into the hall, and closed the door tight behind me. Making my way down the quavering corridor, I couldn't shake off the feeling of déjà vu, as if this routine were part of a nightmare I was destined to repeat again and again. Before I even entered the hothouse saloon, I knew it would be empty.

I was wrong. Candy and Eva were sitting by the chart table. Candy was encompassed in what must have been Bellocheque's oversized terry cloth robe. She was staring into the radar screen, and her eyes looked tired and bloodshot. The radio crackled with empty static. Eva sat on the bench nearby with her knees pulled up and her arms clasped around her legs. She wore cotton pajamas and looked like a little girl.

"Can't sleep?" I asked.

They shook their heads. Eva hugged her knees. "You, too?"

"Yeah," I said. "Where's Rock?"

A flash of lightning lit the windows. "Outside," Eva said.

"In *this?*"

"We told him he was crazy," Candy said. "He said he was too sick and had to get out."

"You feel all right, Jack?" Eva asked.

"I'm okay. Where's Bellocheque?"

Eva glanced at Candy. "Sleeping like a baby," Candy said.

As I started up the gangway, Eva rose to her feet. "Not you, too!"

"I've got to bring him in," I said. "He'll drown out there, if he doesn't get fried first."

"Wait, Jack." Eva crossed the room, opened a locker, and pulled out a heavy yellow slicker. "Put this on."

She helped me into it, turned me around, and worked her fingers up the loops and buttons. Now I felt like the little kid. I let her do it and looked into her face. Her long black lashes hid her downcast eyes, and her lips, pale pink and plump, moved slightly with the effort she was making. When she finished, the hidden eyes flashed up at me and the lips began to speak.

"Be careful out there," she said. "Remember the sailor's three-point."

"Two feet on deck, one hand holding on." A practice she had taught me my first day on board.

She grinned proudly, and I started off. She held to my coat. I looked at her again. Her eyes twinkled with a childish hint of mischief. I took it as an invitation and kissed her. I was right: She generously offered her mouth to mine, and I tasted the honeyed plum of her lips and the salty stroke of her tongue. There was something utterly enticing about her; I felt I could have kissed her there all night. But Eva pulled away and looked into my eyes. Then she released her grip. I started toward the steps without looking where I was going. From the kick of the kiss or the roll of the boat, I lost my balance and stumbled, crashing into the table. I grabbed hold of it and pulled myself up.

Candy was laughing. "That's a four-point, Jack." They both continued laughing as I hobbled up the stairs.

Outside, the sky was boiling, and rain poured down in blustery sheets. Lightning veined the clouds above; toward the unseen shore, bright bolts reached out to light the peaks and shake the shimmering air. I pulled myself through the cockpit. The big wood-rimmed steering wheel was moving on its own, and though the sails were rolled up tight, flaps and rigging rattled in the wind. I peered through the rain out toward the stern. In a flare of lightning, I saw that Rock had crawled out onto the transom and was hunched at the boat's back edge, the sea crashing around him like an angry fist. The deck swayed steeply side to side. Rock had found the steady center, grabbed on tight to the taut rope rail, and hung his head over the water. I climbed up from the cockpit, crawled over the rear skylight of the raised cabin, and slipped down onto the deck beside him.

"What are you doing out here?" I shouted.

He turned his dripping, pallid face to me, wiping a trail of spittle from his chin. "Feeding the fishes," he said.

I glanced at the water, black and forbidding. "They like it?"

His eyes widened, leering into mine. *"They love it,"* he said intently. The words were spoken without irony or humor. I began to think he was suffering from something more than motion sickness.

"You about through?" I asked.

"Yeah, I'm through."

"Then why don't you get your crazy ass back inside!"

He shook his head no and continued staring at the water.

"What the hell's the matter with you?"

His white T-shirt, sopping wet, hung from his shoulders

like a flaccid sail. He looked weak and ghostly, almost as if in a state of shock. He said something, spoken out over the sea, but with all the blowing wind and rain I couldn't hear what it was. Then a flash of lightning cracked overhead. It perked him up like a shot of adrenaline, filling his feverish eyes. I wondered, for a scary second, if he hadn't lost his mind.

"Rock—"

"Wait," he said.

"*Wait?* For what?"

He looked at me again. Slightly crazed. "The Thunder Bird," he said.

I stared at him, dumbfounded. "The *what?*"

He smiled. Gap-toothed. For a moment he looked like the goddamn witch. "You'll see," he said.

I was right. He had lost it. Come unglued. Too much time on the boat, maybe. Not enough sleep in the last three days. And not enough time to grieve for his just-dead friend. I suddenly remembered something my brother Dan had talked about the day we ingested mushrooms at the Bronswood Cemetery. He was sitting under an umbrella in the pouring rain, staring at our father's freshly covered grave. He had a look on his face much like the look on Rock's face now. His eyes reflected a numinous light. The light was not of the earth and not of the sun but came from somewhere out of the night, from the cold glint of the frozen stars or the hollow skull of the moon. He said we had to be wary now, that our family was in danger. He said that people who are killed before their time leave behind a residue of unlived life, an unexhausted energy that flows back to those who were close. The grieving souls have no use for it. It turns into a ghost or a guilt or a nagging emptiness, a kind of sick yearning for the yawning grave. He called it "the death pull." If we didn't watch out, if we didn't stay alert, we might absentmindedly walk off a cliff, or drive through a red light, or step in front of a hurtling bus. The danger was real and deadly as hell. It happened all the time.

I thought of that now as I watched my friend, peering over the edge into the angry abyss with that slightly lunatic look in his eyes.

Wait, he had said. *You'll see.*

I did see. I saw astonishing, terrifying things—and nothing at all of what I had expected.

It happened all at once, literally in a flash. A gash of blinding light pulled the brooding sky apart. With a deafening crack, the cleaving bolt struck the metal mast, igniting a towering pillar of fire, spewing sparks and lighting up the air. The blaze clawed out in all directions, coursing down the metallic rigging, flaring onto stanchions, handles, and hinges, arcing spidery tendrils out into the sea. Rock was rising to his feet, pointing a finger out from the stern like Adam at Creation pointing to his God. I peered in that direction through illuminated rain. There, out on the water, caught in the bright snapshot of light, I saw a thing more astonishing even than the lightning strike itself.

A miraculous and demonic thing. Unearthly and bizarre. A prehistoric bird with fins. A diabolic fish with wings.

The creature exploded out of the sea. It flew from the water and soared through the air. I saw in the flash its great, gaping mouth and its curled pair of outstretched horns. Its belly was slit with a double grille of gills, but its wings were a solid expanse of flesh, their vastness tapering gracefully to a long, spiny tail. The massive diamond disk of muscle wheeled above the scowling waves, igniting the somber water below with skimming mirrors of light. This perhaps was strangest of all, this supernatural light of the creature. Its flesh was a luminous ivory, a ghostly whiteness squeezed like ice from the nipping black of the night. It glowed with the hue of an eyeless moon. The color of bone, the color of death. The haunted color of Rock's stricken face. The two of us stood entranced, awed by its strange and startling splendor. In that convulsive instant, captured in the lightning's aching glare, the sea had given birth to an infernal god, an angel with the horns of a demon, a manta beastly and divine.

As quickly as the lightning vanished, the creature disappeared. All that was left was a pale shadow, a fading moon or a falling angel, surrendering itself back into the sea.

Rock was still standing, holding on to the nylon rope of

the rail. I had for some reason fallen to my knees, though I had not been touched or even tingled by the bolt. The sizzle of lightning had left in the air a troubling yet tantalizing scent—an ionized freshness that smelled like heaven, and a tarlike odor that smelled like hell. A mysterious silence had descended upon us. We were both staring into the empty sea, which had merged with the inky blackness of the sky. The waves appeared to be settling down, and the lightning was tapering off in the distance. The storm had apparently reached its peak at the moment we were touched by its power.

The manta ray was gone.

I rose to my feet and rested my hand on Rock's sopping shoulder. He turned to me with a calmness in his eyes. I had seen what he had seen. His Thunder Bird was not a dream but real as the gaping grave and graceful as an angel's flight. We had witnessed a kind of miracle together.

Eva called out from the gangway. I saw her step out into the rain holding a slicker over her head. She wanted to know if we were all right. Rock climbed down into the cockpit and walked past her through the door. Eva called again to me, waiting for my answer.

I turned to gaze once more at the sea.

CONSUMMATION

The lightning strike did it to us. Turned us into animals. Nothing like a close call with eternal Death to make you want to fuck your brains out.

No one on board had been hurt, but we had all definitely been charged. The lightning had streaked down below deck as well as above, arcing off the mast and chainplates into the stove, the refrigerator, the engine room, and the breaker box, burning into the labyrinth of the ship's electronics. The radio and radar were dead. The cabin lights had all blown out like candles on a cake, plunging the boat into an eerie, smoky darkness. I found this darkness strangely stimulating. Our blind gropings heightened the shared state of arousal still lingering from the lightning blast and lent to the chaos a peculiar but not unpleasant element of intimacy. I babbled on excitedly about the manta ray, but neither Candy nor Eva seemed interested, preoccupied as they were with the catastrophe at hand. Poking like a snail from the shell of Bellocheque's robe, Candy futilely banged at buttons and flipped dead switches on the instrument panel. Eva hurriedly hunted through the galley, opening appliance doors and pressing inoperative touch-panels, looking for some vestige of utility that might have survived the blast. I removed my slicker and hung it back in the locker, while Rock pulled open the refrigerator, grabbed a bottle of beer, and chugged the whole thing down in a single pull. He let out a prolonged, satisfied "ahh" and proclaimed that he felt like a whole new man.

The same could not be said of our skipper. Emerging from his suite in a king-sized pair of boxers and carrying a flashlight in his hand, Bellocheque noisily groused about, cursing his ill luck and the failure of the boat's supposedly fail-safe grounding system. He flipped on a battery-operated emergency lamp on the wall above the electrical panel, casting long shadows out across the saloon and uplighting his face with a ghoulish glow. After scrounging around in the fuse box, tripping switches and banging with his fist, he decided there was nothing to be done until morning. He trained his beam into the liquor cabinet, pulled out the bottle of rum, and poured himself another shot. "Buggers," he growled, and downed it, then shuffled, grumbling, back to his room.

We heard his door slam shut, and for a long moment no one among the four of us spoke, not a single word. The storm had died down to a pattering rain, the boat was rolling gently, and in the silence of the saloon you could hear the simmering sound of our breathing.

Rock stood up then and crossed the room, passing in front of the emergency bulb, casting a monstrous shadow on the wall and ominously onto the ceiling. To my amazement, he stopped in front of Candy and stared down at her, looming over her in his wet T-shirt and soggy boxers, his hair pushed up and his neck and face still damp from the rain. She was sitting at the chart table with her robe partly open, and she turned her face up to his. I watched in stunned silence as Rock reached out his meaty paw, took hold of her terrycloth collar, and gently guided her up from her chair. They stood there for a moment, just looking at each other, face-to-face, without so much as a blink between them, before Candy finally turned and walked out of the room. Rock followed her down the hall, and we heard the door to her bedroom suite close.

Eva was standing across from me. She couldn't help noticing the look on my face. "It started in PV," she said.

"The *Rock*? With *Candy*?"

"They've been at it every night for the past three days."

The news was a shock, but only for a moment. As I thought about it, I realized the clues had been there all along. Their tired eyes, their exhaustion. Rock's sly silence. I had thought he'd been unable to sleep, worrying about Bellocheque. Turned out he was screwing the old man's girlfriend right under his nose.

"What about the skipper?"

Eva opined with a shrug.

"He doesn't care?" I asked.

"Leo is never lonely," she said. "Just doesn't like being alone." She came toward me.

"I'm not sure I get the difference."

"He doesn't want anyone. Doesn't need anyone. He's not like the rest of us."

She was touching me as she said this.

I gulped. And shivered. "You should have seen the manta ray," I said, inanely.

"Oh?" Her fingers—the way she was moving them—touched me in places she wasn't even touching.

"Yeah." I said. "Yeah, it was . . . It was . . ."

A tingle climbed up the back of my neck. A little leftover lightning.

"What, Jack?" Eva's alluring whisper was spoken as much with her eyes as with her mouth. "What were you going to tell me, hmm?"

"I was . . . It was . . ." I forgot what the hell I'd been talking about.

"Jack?"

"Eva . . ."

"Jack . . ."

We went into her room, not mine.

The bed was bigger, for one—twice the width of my slim V-bench—and the sheets on her bed were silk: a ripe pink, the color of her mouth, and so thin and supple their touch on the skin could barely be felt. But the real reason we went to her room was that her room was where she took me. She led me down the darkened hall, lightly holding on to my hand while searching the wall for her door. I would have followed her into the cold sea if that was where she wanted to take me. It wasn't. She wanted to make love in her private boudoir, on her luxurious sheets, in her comparatively commodious bed. I accommodated.

I don't know how her pj's came off. I had nothing to do with it. The room was pitch-dark, and I couldn't see a thing. All I know is that Eva was suddenly on the bed with me, taking off my clothes. While she was doing so, various parts of her naked body were softly brushing against me, parts that were usually concealed and that guys like me spend their lives dreaming about, conjuring up in their mind's eye while they lie alone in their tangled bed, or for that matter every thirty seconds of their waking life, and certainly every time a beautiful woman passes by and they try to imagine what lies beneath that lovely, breezy sundress or that halter top that's cut so low. Those hidden parts were touching me now, touching me incidentally, as if there were nothing so special about it, as if it were just bare flesh and not some magical, aching beauty withheld for far too long until finally generously shared with a man. A nipple grazed my belly like a tiny, pliant finger. My ankle nestled between her thighs. Reaching down to help free my pants, I felt on the back of my outstretched wrist the shocking scratch of her bush. Instinctively I turned my hand to stroke the shaved bristle and fondle the tender, pudgy flesh. My fingers sank deeply into her, and she let out a sigh that wounded me, striking me deep in a place I didn't know I had inside.

I kept my fingers in her silken flesh and felt her crawling over me, an unseen giantess mounting my bones, invisible hair trickling down, a creature made out of darkness, like a goddess who had abandoned her constellation to lie with a mortal on the satin sea. She pressed a bulging breast in my mouth. I tasted it, just barely, and she pulled it out and gave me the other. I sucked on that one, too, hungrily, until she abruptly wrenched it away. She gave me the first one again, now cool and wet, and I took her nipple between my teeth and tickled its nubby end with my tongue. She tugged it from my teeth, then plunged the other back into my mouth, pulling it out again without giving me enough before pushing the other back in. It went on like this, one breast and then the other, back and forth in the darkness until the nipples grew fat and hard and numb from all the kissing and the biting and the sucking they took.

Then her lips found my mouth in the dark. Coming as it did after the Feast of Breasts, the tender caress of her lips and the warm, inviting wetness of her mouth made me feel I was coming back home where I belonged, a newborn crawling back into the womb. But everything was vulnerable, and all would be plundered. A fierce encounter with her tongue mingled with the wetness I felt with my fingers and the groans that were coming from somewhere inside us, from the place I had not known about, where the soft collision of flesh gave way to clawing nails and hardened nipples and probing tongues, making way for the mindless monster, hard as stone, that pressed its way between us. She slowly withdrew her mouth from mine, and then the rest of her body, leaving me lying on the bed alone, damp and hard and yearning. A cool breath blew out over my skin and breezed around my navel, then swirled toward the burning tip reaching up to meet her. Her silky hair fell on my thighs, and then her hands came out, and with a sudden, shocking plunge, she had her mouth around me.

I cruised her unlit landscape of flesh, searched unseeing with nose and tongue until I sensed the trail of liquid lust in the deepening heat of her pleasure. She was creamy, wet and bristly, and redolent of perfume, a fragrance she had touched herself with hours ago, knowing I might get lost in her bedroom and have to find my way in the dark. I found her, and I liked her, and in the bedroom of her thighs I lost myself again.

We licked each other longer than any two people should. There was something compulsive and merciless about it. Eventually her moaning reached a painful peak and my cock burned like a white-hot ember, so there was nothing else to be done but the final thing, the thing we had wanted to do and dreaded to do: dreaded because it would end what neither of us wanted to end; wanted because the end was the dreaded thing we wanted most.

We pulled apart, then found each other again. She opened her legs, and her greedy fingers guided me toward the hunger of her body. It took all the will I could muster not to abandon myself in her hands. I pulled free, and slowed down, and let the monster temper into hard-hearted rock. Then, cruelly, I dawdled in the tickling brush. Hair as fine as eyelashes lashed my tender tip. Eva's breathing reddened my ears.

I went into her slowly. Millimeter by millimeter, inch by inch. Eva began to plead with me. Whispered words in Portuguese I did not understand. Words repeated, over and over. Her hands were somewhere out in the dark; she did not deign to touch me. Only her imploring voice caressed me, strange words in a foreign tongue, spoken in a desperate murmur.

I was fully inside her now, held in her heat, our two worlds locked on a single stem. I slid out slowly, all the way out, and for a moment her whimpering pleas abated. Then I plunged back in, hard and deep, and she gurgled and moaned and murmured again. Once more I pulled out and pushed back in, and then I stayed in, thrusting. Painful, blissful cries of longing fled like black birds out of the night. I rammed her hard and hard again, with the sibilant whisper of her tortured cry calling out in rhythm. *"Is this it?"* she begged as I banged her down. *"Is this it?"* she pleaded with every thrust. *"Is this it? Is this it? Is this it? Is this—"*

With a gasp her legs went straight and her thighs began to quiver and her hands came out of the dark, slapping at my flesh and grasping at my neck while a throttled shriek rent the air. She grabbed my hair and tugged me toward her, but I fought her off and held her down and pumped her without pity. She thrashed and screamed beneath me. We clawed our way to forbidden realms of pitch-black, savage fury as a mindless frenzy overcame us, a gleeful burst of cruelty. It pushed us to the painful edge, a long, suspended moment, until all at once, in reckless abandon, like a penis-tingling jump off a cliff, with a groan leaking out of my throat and a shudder rippling through my plummeting body, I came.

We made love two more times that night, if love is what you'd call it. It had an increasing violence about it, an intoxicating ferocity. Eva was unstoppable, and I had that unnamed something inside me, that vacancy that had filled up with a blood lust that would not let go. I don't know where or how I had found it, or it had found me. On the shore, perhaps. The things I had seen. My brutal brush with death. Or on the boat, the lightning strike. Whatever it was, it made me different. Something had clearly changed. My heart or my soul, I didn't know which. I had never felt anything like it before. It might have been nothing more than desire, or nothing less than love, but it seemed to me to be something frightening, it lived so deep within me.

I didn't think about it—I dreamed about it. More like a nightmare, really. Plato at play in his shadow cave.

When I awoke, I saw that a shadow had come back to life. One I had tried like hell to forget.

The shadow took a seat at the foot of our bed. He had a black eye and a black cowboy hat. The hat the bad guys wear.

Part Four

DEVILS

THE DEVIL YOU KNOW

He woke us up by slowly sliding off our satin sheet. I thought it was Eva. I thought she must have been getting cold and was tugging the cover down over her feet. Then I realized my arms were around her and the woman was sound asleep.

I bolted upright. Horizontal sunbeams glared through the oval windows, and I squinted, staring stunned at the dark figure perched at the foot of the bed. It was as if, having grown bored with being confined for so long to the back of my mind, the cowboy had stepped right out of my skull into the morning light.

"You are sleeping like branches," he said. He was peering over the clump of wadded sheet in his hands, surveying our naked bodies.

"Logs," I said. His black-and-blue shiner had started to yellow. I tried to remember how many days it had been since I poked the eye with his bat.

Eva sat up and covered her breasts with her arms. "Who are you?" she hissed.

His eyes grinned. He let them rove over her nakedness without the slightest trace of shame. "José Ludwig van Bustamante Alvarez de la Cadena," he said. "I am a friend of your *Yanqui* lover."

Eva glanced at me, terrified. "Jack, what is this?"

"I don't know," I said.

We watched him bury his hawklike beak in the crumpled

wad of sheet. "Hmm," he uttered, apparently pleased. He threw his leg up onto the bed and casually leaned on his elbow. He wore a long-sleeved black silk shirt, black Levi's, and black leather cowboy boots. With the black felt hat and the black toupee, you might begin to think it was his favorite color. I thought of Gracchus and wished he weren't dead.

"What are you doing here?" I snarled.

He wryly regarded the scratches on my chest. They were almost as bad as the cuts on my back. "The *señorita,* she try to tell you something, too, eh?" He smiled, allowing us a view of his dental work, something I'd been denied in our previous encounter. It appeared to be the result of some unfortunate accident, like wandering into the butt of a gun or the oncoming trajectory of a brass-knuckled fist. The spiky white ruins, oddly bleached and brightened, shone like a set of broken china.

I called out, "Rock!" and immediately felt absurd.

The Mexican offered his smile again. "Rock," he repeated, and laughed. "He the big one, no?"

"Go away!" Eva shouted, and whipped her satin pillow at him.

His arm shot up and the pillow impaled itself on the blade of a knife, a switchblade that had popped out from his fist like a silver finger. He slammed the stuck pillow down on the bed and held it there, motionless, as if waiting for all the life to drain out of it. Then he withdrew the bloodless blade and held it before his face, eyeing his narrow reflection and briefly admiring his graveyard of teeth.

"What do you want?" I demanded.

He turned his gaze on me, and the grin went sour. "I want the *oro,* gringo. The *gold.*"

I stared at him, probably a moment too long, before I spoke. "I don't know what you're talking about."

He leered at me, then reached back with his knife, slowly lowering it to the floor behind him. We heard a muffled jingle as he raised the bulging baby blue sack, dangling it from the blade, and set it down gently in front of us on the bed. He slashed the knife up through the knotted loops, and gold coins spilled out over the pink satin sheet.

I stared at them for a moment, frozen in thought. The sack had been locked in a safe in Bellocheque's room.

"Where's Leo?" Eva asked, with a rising note of panic. "What have you done to him?"

"Tell me where is the rest of the gold," he said.

I wondered how much Bellocheque had told him, and if he was still alive. "That's all there is," I said. "That's all the gold we've got."

He smiled. With a practiced expertise, he began to twirl the switchblade in his fingers, spinning it effortlessly in glittering circles, his eyes locked on mine all the while. "I no believe you, *gringo*. Your brother, he tell me different."

I felt a surge of anger. "What do you know about my brother?"

"I know what he tell me. He tell me he find *mucho oro*."

"My brother's dead," I said.

"So are you," he said, "if you no tell me about the gold."

Eva touched my arm. "Jack . . ."

I watched him twirl his deadly baton. "That's quite a talent. You should try out for majorette."

He instantly stopped the spin of the knife and held upright its gleaming blade. "You calling me a Nancy boy?"

I gulped. "More of a lazy Susan, I think."

He expelled a tiny laugh through his pearly piranha teeth. "I like you, *gringo*. I no want to kill you."

"You don't have to," I said. "I've told you the truth. That's all the gold we found."

He stared at me a moment, then turned his leering eyes on Eva and uttered a final threat: "I hope you are not lying, *amigo*." Using only the nimble fingers of the hand holding the knife, he deftly folded the blade back into the handle, then rose in an instant and briskly departed.

José Bustamante Alvarez Whatever-the-Hell was searching the forward cabins, rummaging through drawers and closets and storage bins, and making a heck of a racket, when Eva and I, hastily dressed, made our way warily through the saloon and climbed the stairs to the cockpit. It was bright outside and growing hotter by the second. All the clouds from the night before had been swept from the sky and piled like trash on the rim of the mountains. Candy and Rock, seated beside each other on the teak side bench, looked glumly up at us as we stepped out onto the deck. Bellocheque sat pitched forward on the pilot's seat in front of them, his hands tied behind his back and his mouth sealed shut with a strip of duct tape. Behind him, sitting casually on the edge of the deck, was a man with a revolver dangling loosely from his hand.

"*Buenos días, señor, señorita.*" He wagged the gun toward the bench across from Rock and Candy, indicating that we should take a seat. I glanced out over the water and spotted the bad guys' boat, anchored a couple of hundred yards away, a big, ugly cabin cruiser with a cursive purple ORCHID stenciled across the stern. Just behind the gunman, down in the water and tied to our boat, a yellow inflatable rubber dinghy lolled on the waves. The Zodiac sported a miniature outboard but also held a pair of short aluminum oars. They must have paddled over; none of us had heard them coming. Bellocheque, the only one of our party muzzled and bound, must have been their first captive. Once they had a gun on him, there wasn't much anyone could do to resist—even Rock, "the big one," who by now I could tell was chafing at the bit.

The man with the gun was staring at me as I took my place on the seat. His blue eyes glistened behind his squinted lids, and between his unruly beard and his untrimmed mustache I saw that a corner of his mouth was curled in a creepy sort of half-grin, as if he were musing over some private joke that had passed between the two of us. He was in his forties or early fifties, a stout man with a slouching, sedentary build, tattoos nearly hidden in the hair of his arms, a darkly tanned, weathered face, and long, floppy, hair-filled ears, a tiny diamond stud in the lobe of the left. With a sea captain's cap nestled on his reddish-brown curls, he had the crooked look of a salty dog who spent half his time running drugs in his boat and the other half hunched at the harbor bar. His billowy cheesecloth white cotton shirt was buttoned only in the middle, revealing the great bulge of his belly below, and above, an abundance of chestnut hair and a fat gold chain dangling from his neck.

The gaudy chain was what finally triggered it: the biker bar, the man with the gun. This salty bloke was my Tennessee Williams.

I turned my gaze away and saw that Rock had been watching us. Glancing at Tennessee, he looked inquisitively back at me. I nodded, subtly, in the affirmative.

Then I noticed that Bellocheque, immobilized, was eyeing the two of us like a frozen spectator at a tennis match. He was not a happy man. Forced from his bed wearing only his boxers, he'd been tied like a captive king to his throne, made to witness the humiliation of his court and the pillaging of his kingdom; and now, as he sat there, bent forward, neck straining, with his big bare feet bristling beneath him, his beefy black body bulging from the seat, and his polished ebony pate shining hotly in the sun, he gave the impression of a seething giant, a bottled-up force of nature.

José What's-His-Name climbed up through the gangway, twirling a small gold pocket watch on the end of a delicate chain. Sauntering up to Eva, he swung the fob in a final loop and jauntily caught it in the palm of his hand. He popped open the lid, wound the knob, and pressed the crystal up against his ear. His eyes lit up.

"She is old," he said, "but still ticking, no?" He noticed an inscription on the inside of the lid. "A gift from your lover?"

"From my mother," Eva sternly replied.

The watch was obviously a family heirloom. José snapped the gold case shut, dropped the watch into his shirt pocket, and smiled his ingratiating smile. *"Gracias, señora.* And please to thank your mother."

She stared back at him coldly.

He tipped back his hat and, with the emptied baby blue bandanna, wiped the sweat from his glistening brow. Then he lowered his hat and stepped in front of Bellocheque, peering down at him without the smile. "You never find the *gringo,* eh? The Dan Duran?"

I doubt that Bellocheque would have answered even if his mouth were not taped shut.

"You find the brother, instead, no?" He turned and gazed at me. "Or the brother, he find you."

"*Sí, en Boca,*" added Tennessee, grinning. Judging from his beam of self-satisfaction, I surmised that he or one of his cronies had witnessed our meeting on the beach.

"*Mi amigo* Gonzalo," the cowboy said, nodding toward Tennessee, "in Puerto Vallarta, he very . . . how you say? *Exitoso.* He very *enterprising,* no? He own, not one, but two—*two* of the shops for the scuba."

"*Cinco!*" Gonzalo corrected, the proud grin erased from his face.

"*Dos,*" the cowboy insisted. They argued back and forth in Spanish. From what I could tell, the number of dive shops the fellow owned depended on whether or not you counted hotel concessions as entirely separate, profit-generating enterprises. I heard the names Ramada and Holiday mentioned, and Mismaloya, a resort I had noted on our bus ride to Boca. Ultimately the dispute seemed to be settled in José's favor, which allowed him to continue his discourse with Bellocheque.

"Gonzalo tell me you come to his shop. In the *puerto deportivo.* He say you buying all the tanks for the scuba. They asking you where you are taking, but you no want to answer. You say for the *pleasure.* For to see the fishes." He reached out to Bellocheque's face and began to peel the duct tape, slowly, painfully, from his mouth. "I no think you want to see the fishes," he said.

It was difficult to watch. Bellocheque grimaced but did not let out a sound. His eyes were locked on the cowboy's eyes. The cowboy seemed to like it.

"*Capitán,*" he said when he had finally removed the tape. "Your friends, they all tell me there is no more gold, just like you say." The knife appeared in his hand and the blade snapped out. Slowly leaning forward, the cowboy lowered the long, tapered tip to Bellocheque's knees and peered curiously into his eyes. *"You sure you no want to change your mind?"*

Bellocheque eyed the steel blade. It was six inches long and probably sharp enough to pass through bone. The cowboy was not a big man, but he was trim and sturdily built, and you got the sense from the way his hands hung from his wrists and his sinewy arms were angled at the elbow that this man with the dead eyes and the hawk's beak and the taste for funereal attire might be capable of the most brutal violence; that out here on the lawless sea, with a gunman to back him up and no one around to hear the screams but his captive audience of *gringo* college boys and beautiful women, he might, in fact, take pleasure in the act.

Candy started up from her seat. "Leo—"

Gonzalo pointed his pistol at her. *"Señora—por favor."*

Rock stood up and so did I. Eva reached out and held my wrist.

Gonzalo waved his gun at the bunch of us and said something heatedly in Spanish.

None of us moved. Our eyes were locked on José's knife. *"Capitán?"*

Slowly, Bellocheque lifted his gaze. His eyes reached the cowboy's eyes and held them with a look of palpable loathing. Then he told the man exactly what he knew.

"There are five iron chests in the bowels of the wreck," he said. "One of them held the gold coins and a dozen gold bars. The gold bars are still down there, and the rest of the chests are sealed shut. None of us knows if there is anything inside them."

José continued staring at him and gradually released a guttural groan from deep within his throat. He stood upright. "We are going to find out what is keeping in these boxes, no?"

Bellocheque looked away without answering.

José glanced around him, scrutinizing each one of us, making some sort of psycho-social-sexual calculation. Somehow it all added up to the woman with the big tits and the flaming red hair. "You," he said, pointing his knife at Candy. "You are taking Gonzalo to these boxes."

Gonzalo immediately began to complain. He pointed to me and Rock and pleaded with José in Spanish, bemoaning, apparently, the prospect of diving for untold treasures in the company of a beautiful woman. José was insistent, however, and they argued vehemently for at least a full minute. During this distraction, I noticed Bellocheque and Candy exchanging a look; he seemed to tell her something with his eyes, like "Do whatever you have to do, but don't let these assholes steal our gold."

Gonzalo finally acquiesced. He handed his pistol to José and, mumbling curses under his breath, followed Candy below deck to collect the diving gear.

Bellocheque raised his head and glared at the cowboy. "How long do you intend to keep me bound to this chair? I've told you all I know."

Gently, with the tip of his gun barrel, José lifted up Bellocheque's chin. "Maybe you tell me a lie," he said.

He didn't withdraw the gun, and I suddenly thought he might pull the trigger. "You don't have to do that," I shouted. "He told you the truth."

José instantly swung the pistol at me. "Then why *you* no tell me, *gringo*?"

The gun was aimed directly at my face. All I could see was the black hole at the end of the barrel. I suddenly realized how easy it is to kill a person. It takes just the twitch of a finger.

"Why don't *you* tell *me* what you did to my brother?" I said.

"Your brother." He scowled. "He is also very *enterprising*. He say he has a buyer for the bambalacha. I trust him. But they take the bambalacha and he lose my money. Then he disappear, hide into the mountains. When he come back, he say he knows where there is gold. He say he take us to it. But he *lies!*" The hand holding the gun trembled, and the eye with the shiner twitched. I began to think bringing up my brother had been a bad idea.

"Did you kill him?" I asked.

"He dive for the gold—but never come back!" The cowboy glared with his twitching eye. Then he noticed his hand was trembling and slowly lowered the gun. "I no kill him. But I would. If I had the chance."

Candy and Gonzalo hauled the dive gear up through the gangway, along with a packet of tools and two large inflatable lift bags to bring the gold to the surface. José sat down with the gun at his side and watched them strap into the equipment. While below, Candy had changed into a one-piece swimsuit, but Gonzalo waited to strip down in front of us, revealing a tiny green Speedo beneath his overflowing belly. His ass appeared absurdly small, and his broadly curved back was covered with hair and prison tattoos; he looked like an overgrown satyr in a jolly-green jockstrap. Although he was obviously an experienced diver, he seemed rather huffy with the effort to prepare, grumbling frequently and scowling at Candy. Cool and efficient, she donned the gear quickly and was ready to go long before he was. She opened the packet to check the tools—hammer, saw, chisel, crowbar—then went about strapping the dive knife to her leg.

Gonzalo protested to José about it. José told her to take it off, gesturing with his gun.

"There are sharks," she said. Gonzalo scoffed, but Candy insisted. "I won't go down without it."

José considered a moment. "Give it to Gonzalo," he said. "He swim behind you."

Candy looked to Bellocheque, who nodded almost imperceptibly.

She obliged and handed the knife to Gonzalo. He strapped it to his calf. Candy rolled up the packet of tools and tucked them under her arm. Finally, Gonzalo was ready to go, and they climbed to the back of the boat.

Gonzalo stepped off into the water.

"*Señora*," Jose called. He stood behind Bellocheque and touched the gun barrel to his head. "The *capitán,* he no like to be tied to the chair." He looked to Candy. "You bring up the gold, I let you untie him. You no bring the gold," he showed her his teeth, "I kill him."

Candy looked at Bellocheque. All she could see was the back of his head. She glanced at Rock, and at Eva and me.

Rock rose to his feet. "Candy—"

She pulled the mask down over her face, stuck the regulator into her mouth, and stepped off the back of the boat.

THE DEVIL YOU DON'T

T ell me where she go!" he demanded.

Once again I was staring into the barrel of the cowboy's gun. He could do this to me every day for the rest of my life, I would never, ever get used to it. "I don't know," I said.

Nearly an hour had passed, and Candy and Gonzalo had not come back. No bubbles in the water, no hint of what had happened. We were all in a panic.

José pressed the barrel into the soft flesh at my temple. "You lie," he said. "Like your brother."

"No," I said. "Please—"

Eva cried out. Jose raised his other arm, and the knife blade popped from his hand.

Rock had come out of his seat and was charging toward us. José's knife stopped him, cutting through his shirt and pricking him in the belly. Rock backed off, looking down, touching his fingers into blood. "Son of a bitch!" He seemed to be amazed by the puncture in his flesh and looked up at José in disbelief. "He cut me! The little cocksucker cut me!" He started toward the cowboy.

"No!" Eva jumped in front of Rock and tried to hold him back. Perhaps he hadn't noticed José was still holding a gun to my head.

"Tell your friend to sit," José said calmly.

With Eva's urging, Rock relented, backed away, and plopped down into his seat.

Eva turned. "Don't you see?" she pleaded. "None of us knows what's happened!"

Pointing the gun with one hand, clutching the blood-tipped knife in the other, José took a step away and turned his sights on Bellocheque.

Bellocheque was the only one of us who hadn't said a word. He had sat there, bent forward, eyes buried beneath his brow, silently brooding while the commotion stirred around him. I couldn't tell exactly what he was feeling—anger? sadness? loss?—but there was a morbid intensity about him I had not seen until now.

José remained oblivious to it. He put the gun to Bellocheque's head and held the knife blade under his throat.

"What you like, *Capitán?* The fast . . . or the slow?"

The three of us stared at him, holding our breath.

"Where is the woman?" José demanded. "What happen to Gonzalo? You tell me. Now."

Bellocheque was not a man used to taking orders, and certainly not from a punk like José. It took a long moment for him to respond, even with the threat of the gun and the knife. Slowly, he lifted his gaze and glared at the cowboy. For a second I thought he might spit in his face. Instead, he asked him a simple question, one that nearly knocked me clear off my feet.

"Have you never heard of *el Diablo Blanco?*"

A paralyzed moment of silence followed, with a vision of the Thunder Bird sweeping through my head. Rock sat gaping. Eva looked alarmed. Even cool José betrayed a passing flash of fear. It was as if he had recognized a long-forbidden fantasy, born in his childhood, nursed in his dreams, then banished from his consciousness for fear it might be real. He lowered the knife and the gun, expelling his toothy piranha laugh. "There is no *Diablo Blanco,*" he scoffed. "Is only a story. Told to children by ignorant fishermen."

"Perhaps it is not a story," Bellocheque said, "but a thing as alive as you or I."

Jose snarled. "I no believe your lies."

"*El Diablo Blanco,* the manta," Bellocheque said. "*Manta,* as you know, means 'cloak' in Spanish. A creature of illusion, descended from the shark. It is the most evolved of all the creatures in the sea. I know this because they live around the island where I was born. The sea there is also a great gathering place of mantas, as is the western shore of Africa, the land of my ancestors. But in all the seas of all the world, there is only one *Diablo Blanco*. It lives here, beneath this boat, hunting these very waters."

The cowboy hesitated; his black eye twitched. "Is no true," he said. "Is no real." Suddenly the knife was at Bellocheque's throat. "*This* is real."

"Wait!" I said, jumping to my feet. "It *is* true. We've already lost one diver. Two days ago. He was our friend. He went down and never came up."

José stared at me, the edge of his blade nicking Bellocheque's throat. He turned as Rock rose to his feet.

"We saw it," Rock said. "Last night, during the storm. It came leaping clear out of the water. Right at the moment the lightning struck."

"That's right," I said. "Both of us saw it."

"It was huge," Rock said.

José scrutinized us. "The color. What was the color?"

"White," I said.

"All of him white?"

"White as my ass," Rock said.

José lowered the knife. A slow grin filled his face. His eyes sparkled in wonder. He glanced between us. "*El Diablo Blanco*. The White Devil, no?"

"*Sí, sí!*" I said, nodding enthusiastically. "The White Devil!"

He turned and pointed the gun at me.

"Then you must be very careful, *amigo*, when you go down for to bring up the gold."

Fish have eyes on the sides of their heads. They can see in two directions at once, nearly all the way around them, front to back. It's because they're prey, and live in constant fear, that they developed this protective omnivision. I thought about this as I floated through the water, watching them flutter through my narrow field of view. Human sight is limited to begin with, but when you add a dive mask, you're adding blinders, restricting your peripheral vision even more. You can't see anything but what's straight out in front of you, and that for only maybe fifteen feet. Above, below, behind, to the sides—you're vulnerable from every quarter, blind as an earthworm wriggling on a hook.

Eva had wanted to join me, but the cowboy refused to allow it. He said if I didn't come back, he might just have to kill her. "Then what?" I asked him. "Rock can't dive—you going to kill him, too?" The idiot would end up with a boatload of corpses and a wreck full of gold lying just out of reach. The prospect might discourage him from acting rashly, but I'm not sure he was capable of rational thought. A man who points guns and knives at people is not a man who lives by his wits. He told me to shut up and get in the water, and poked me with the gun until I did what he said. Now I was the one who'd have to live by my wits. Either that or sprout eyes from the sides of my head.

I scanned the water as best I could and continued descending into the depths. If the manta was around, it was keeping to itself. Maybe two divers was all it could devour in a day. Surely it wouldn't have room for—

What was I thinking? Weren't mantas harmless? *El Diablo Blanco* must have been a local legend, a Mexican version of the Loch Ness Monster. I recalled the midget Indian woman peddling beads in Boca. She had been the first to mention the thing, as if she were giving us some kind of warning, complete with a somber sign of the cross. This morning, when I had changed into my suit, I had impulsively put on the necklace she gave me. Now I found myself clutching its cross, praying the big silver trinket would save me.

Don't be ridiculous, I tried to tell myself. Bellocheque had only been grasping at straws. What could he know about *el Diablo Blanco*? He lived in the Caribbean, a thousand miles away. He had obviously picked up on the local myth and turned it to his advantage. A clever ploy that had saved his life, at least for a while. I wondered what other tricks he had up his sleeve.

The White Devil couldn't be entirely a myth, though. I had seen the creature passing by the peephole in the wreck, and Rock and I had watched the manta soar into the storm. But was it a manta that could actually *kill*? How else to explain the disappearance of Candy and Gonzalo—not to mention Duff? What had happened to them all?

The question made me paranoid. The water seemed alive with shadows and glimmers, with hidden creatures lurking just beyond the reach of sight. Peering warily into the gloom, searching out any suspicious semblance of form, I was startled by the flash of a pan-shaped fish a few feet away from my face. The silver swimmer darted off in a spurting, zigzag course, turning first one eye at me and then the other, as if it couldn't trust either one. In a kind of parody of this panicky prey, I twisted and turned as I continued my descent, trying to see in all directions at once, all the while yearning for the shelter of the wreck.

At forty-six feet, I reached the steeply sloping cliff that led down to the *Argonaut*. A silt-filled current flowed down its granite face, fed from the turbulence of the previous night's storm. I joined into the flow, descending into the darkness of the murky water, and found it strangely comforting: If I couldn't see the creature, perhaps the creature couldn't see me.

The wreck emerged abruptly. Hunched on the ledge under its blanket of silt, its open prow yawning out over the rocky precipice, the leviathan lay silent and still. I swam along the upturned hull, searching for a trace of Candy and Gonzalo. There was nothing. Even the marks that Duff and I had fanned into the silt had already been covered by the steadily flowing current. Not a hint of our visit remained. The hibernating ship had shuddered us off and drifted back into its slumber. I aimed my flashlight into the gaps beneath the hull. Fish fled, and particulate hung in the lighted water like floating dust in a sunbeam, but again I found no trace of anyone, as if no living human being had ever been down here before.

Days ago, with barely a breath of air in my tank, I had slipped from a gap and swum for my life. I looked for that gap now, and soon I found it, tucked between two boulders nearly halfway down the length of the wreck. I swam into it, leading with my light, which shone once again on the mangled forest of masts and booms, scaring off reclusive fish and casting deep shadows into the gloom. For the hell of it, I poked up through the square portal of the cargo hold and shone my light around. Except for the broad mast slanting through the dark, the huge space looked empty, without a light in sight. With its cold, still water and impenetrable darkness, the vast hold once again filled me with unease. Although I couldn't see it from where I stood, I remembered the two-toned skull Duff had found, and wondered if it was still lying amid his pile of collected shackles.

No time for that now; I had to find Candy.

I backed out of the hole and slithered through the forest toward the hind end of the ship. At the raised roof of the rear cabins, I turned onto my back and slipped underneath, scraping my tank on the rocky bottom. A few feet in I found the square portal to the officers' quarters and pulled myself inside. I saw at once that the room was empty and started for the next hatchway. Still filled with thoughts of the uncovered skull, I paused abruptly when my light struck something white. Not, it turned out, another bit of skeleton but the ivory-colored shaving mug I had come upon before. I swam on past it and moved up through the hatch above, entering the jar-filled food locker.

Nobody in there, either; just the memory of a crack in the wall through which I had glimpsed the manta ray. I considered turning off my light and finding that narrow hole again, but I couldn't bear the thought of flirting with the dark. Somewhere in this wreck was that slithering eel. Last I had seen it—or rather, felt it—was in the captain's quarters, just up the stairwell I was peering into now. I swam up slowly, watching every corner, and pushed out swiftly into the room.

The beam of a flashlight shone in my face. Candy? Gonzalo?

I pushed closer, peering past the blinding light. I could just make out the glint of a mask, bubbles of air and the sheen of a tank. My pulse raced. My eyes widened.

There, staring back at me, was an imbecile with a silver cross necklace and a flashlight just like mine. I was looking into a full-length mirror—the ornate, gilt-framed vanity mirror I had stumbled on before and forgotten about. Eyeing my reflection now, feeling like a fool, I thought of Captain Braga, posing in this room, admiring his visage in this very pane of glass. What kind of man carries a mirror like this halfway around the world with him? Not to mention a cargo of slaves and a stash of pilfered gold. What kind of man? A man with a limitless ego and a heart of stone. A man who, to get what he wanted, would do absolutely anything.

I kicked away from the mirror and drifted through the room, passing over the jumble of chairs, the upturned table, and the broken basin, wary all the while that the moray might be near. If it was, it didn't deign to show itself; maybe my light had scared it away. At the back wall, I floated up to the ceiling—actually, the floor—and came to the hatchway that led to the treasure room. A cloud of silt was wafting down from the opening. I swam through it and poked my head up through the hatch. The water in the room was nearly opaque; the sediment had been stirred up, and I couldn't see more than a couple of feet in front of my face. I pushed up through the hatch and moved out slowly into the room. Somewhere deep in the murk, a soft glow of light was showing. I turned off my flashlight and saw it more clearly: a light beam shining faintly through the haze, silhouetting the jumble of iron chests before me. Oddly, the light didn't move.

A shiver of fear went through me. I turned my flashlight back on. Slowly, I moved toward the mysterious glow, floating over the iron chests and the scattered bars of gold. My heart was pounding. Silt was still moving through the water, as though whatever had stirred it up had not yet left the room. Unlike the chambers I had just been through, I saw in this one not a single fish. They might be concealed in the murk, I thought, but it seemed more likely they had been frightened off and hadn't yet returned. I steeled myself and ventured forward.

Among a scattering of broken crates and rotting debris, I came upon the source of the glow: a fallen flashlight, abandoned in the muck. It shone still against the wall, lighting the bolted door to the larder, casting shadows into the silty water. I didn't know whether it belonged to Candy or Gonzalo, but it was clear now that whatever danger they had encountered, they had encountered it in this room. I peered through the murk, searching the area around the lamp for some hint of what had happened. Stirred silt filled the beam of my light, and shadows clung to the crates and chests. In one of these shadowed spaces, I found the two lift bags and the packet of tools lying open on the floor. Nearby lay a silt-dusted chisel, and beside it a hammer protruded from the muck.

As I picked up the hammer and waved off the dirt, I noticed that the chest before me was the only one sitting upright. This was the chest I had tried to smash open, an act that had plunged me into darkness and sent me scrambling blindly through the ship. I could see now the lock had been broken off, though I couldn't be sure I had been the one to do it. It was clear that Candy and Gonzalo had been at work on the chest as well. All along the joint of its lid, completely around to the hinges on the back, I could see the impression of their chisel marks. The fusing crust of corrosion had been cracked off, and gouges of metal shone brightly in my light. With a sudden flush of excitement, I dropped the hammer to the floor and began to push up hard on the lid.

For a moment, struggling with it, I thought they might not have completely severed the bond. I had to set down my flashlight and use both hands. Finally, with a scraping crack, the lid tore loose, and the chest yawned open like a toothless mouth. A gaping darkness lurked within, but the heavy lid opened only halfway, refusing to fall to the back of the trunk. I had to hold it up with one hand while I reached for my flashlight with the other. I lifted the light and aimed it like an eye into the dark.

The brilliant glare of gold beamed back at me. Not coins

or dust but gleaming gold bars, stacked solid in the trunk. I stared at them in wonder, then gasped in shock. Lying there on the golden bricks was a diver's mask.

I reached inside and pulled it out, then let go of the lid, which descended and shut with a watery thump. Examining the mask, I couldn't tell who it belonged to. All the masks were rentals and looked basically the same: an oval-shaped glass with a black rubber flange, an adjustable strap, and a purge valve underneath. Though the glass on this mask was unbroken and the strap was completely intact, I knew at once that someone was dead.

The undeniable reality of it fed a growing terror. Death had reared its head again and was lurking down here in the dark. I felt a sudden urge to flee, to race out of the murky room and head back up to the surface. Better to face the devil I knew than some unnamed devil I didn't. The cowboy might have been out of his gourd, but at least he had clear motives—greed and the collection of debts, not some ghostly, underwater curse that snatched unwary gold seekers and whisked them out of sight.

I turned and started for the hatchway. That's when I spotted the moray's tail. It sent a shiver through me.

It slithered through the beam of my light, slipping into the shadows behind an overturned chest. Judging from the tail's thickness, the eel had to be huge. My heart raced wildly. I tried to calm my breathing. Cautiously, I aimed my light around the upturned chest. The tail snaked away. I followed it with my beam of light, fighting back my fear, until I glimpsed the tail's tip vanishing down the hatchway.

I sucked in a breath and sighed in relief. Now it was back in the captain's quarters, doing who knows what. Admiring itself in the mirror, perhaps. Whatever it was up to, if I wanted to exit the ship, I'd be forced to cross its path again.

But maybe not. I remembered the other door, the bolted one that led to the larder. If I could break the bolt, I'd have another way out. I swam back to the upright chest to recover the hammer and chisel. Then I moved on toward the glow of the dropped flashlight, which shone on the bolted doorway.

The bolt was badly corroded, and the wood of the door was rotted and thin. I set down my own light and went to work.

Hammering underwater is a strange undertaking; the action is direct yet oddly ineffectual. Nevertheless, within a matter of seconds, I managed to wedge the chisel deep behind the bolt and, using it like a lever, pounded down until the latch broke loose. I pushed on the door, and it popped wide open.

A wave of silt billowed out into the darkness of the next room. I reached back to grab my flashlight. As I did so, I spotted at the edge of its beam what looked like a stretch of blackened flesh. I picked up the light and took a closer look. It was a rubber fin, lying bottom up and coated with a fine layer of silt. I panned my light up the length of the fin and saw that it was still attached to a foot, and the foot was attached to a man's hairy leg.

Gonzalo lay twisted on his belly in the muck. His tank was gone, and the hair on his back was dusted with silt. I held my breath, took hold of his arm, and flopped him over. This brought up a great burst of sediment, clouding the murky water even more. I moved in for a closer look and trained the beam of my light on his face. What I saw made me gag. I choked for breath.

His mask was gone, along with an eye and the flesh of one cheek. The moray had taken to munching his face.

I backed off and struggled to stop my choking. Finally I managed to take a full breath, and that's when I noticed the knife in his chest. It was stuck up under his rib cage, the blade buried all the way up to the handle.

I took some more breaths and stared at the corpse. Candy had done a hell of a job. She must have waited until the moment he opened the iron coffer. Gonzalo probably held the lid up himself, and when he poked his head in to look at the gold, Candy ripped his mask off and yanked the regulator from his mouth. Then she grabbed the knife from the sheath on his leg and shoved it into his gut.

Judging from the amount of sediment stirred up, Gonzalo had not gone quickly. I pictured him thrashing blindly as the water filled his lungs. Candy, I assumed, must have backed off until he was dead. Then she had taken the tank and fled the room. Later, once things had settled down, the moray must have smelled his blood and come looking for a meal.

What had happened to Candy? Why had she taken his half-empty tank? Could it be she was hiding out in another part of the wreck?

I started for the doorway, then stopped myself. Wasn't I forgetting something? I turned back to the body and, trying to act without thinking about it, took hold of the imbedded knife and attempted to pull it free. It was surprising how difficult this was; it seemed as if his body didn't want to let it go. Finally it tore loose, releasing a dark cloud of blood. I saw at once what had held the blade: The base of it was notched with a deeply hooked gap. It had been thrust in all the way, and the pierced flesh had closed around it, holding it in place. Apparently Candy's knife wasn't made for stabbing; it was designed to go in and stay there.

I wiped the blade off on Gonzalo's hairy leg. Then I unstrapped the sheath from his calf and tied it to my own. I didn't put the knife in there; though; I decided to carry it ready in my hand.

I headed through the door into the larder and shone my light around. No moray eel in sight. I swam down through the hatch to the officers' quarters, then down to the space beneath the overturned deck. It took me another five minutes to search through the remainder of the wreck. I saw Duff's pile of shackles and the half-dipped human skull; the chains dangling from the upturned floor; the layer of rocks and gravel, which Eva had explained was the ballast of the ship; and the storage and crew rooms jammed in the bow. There was no sign of Candy anywhere, and when I finally swam out through the hole in the prow, I hadn't a clue where she had gone.

For a moment I hung there alone in the water. Below me, the sheer cliff dropped off into a fathomless void. Some sixty feet above me glowed the faint light of the surface. The prow of the wreck lay gaping behind me, while out in front stretched the vast reach of the open ocean. Candy had taken Gonzalo's tank. She must have wanted to stay down for a while. Why? Where? We were easily over a mile from shore, too far to swim underwater, even with both of the half-full tanks. If she surfaced there, she might be spotted. Why would she have wanted to go to shore, anyway? Surely my gruesome adventure had dissuaded her from that.

I started to wonder about the manta ray again. Could it be that Candy had tried to swim for the surface, just like Duff, who had never made it back? The longer I thought about it, the more it seemed absurd. Candy had just whacked the cowboy's partner. Returning to the boat without him would surely bring the switchblade to her throat.

If she hadn't gone up or down or back, that left only what lay out in front of me. But there was nothing out there, just endless open water and—

And the *Orchid.*

That's where she'd gone! Of course! Hiding on the boat was her only real option, and it was sure to have a working radio, or perhaps a gun, or maybe something valuable to be used against José.

I needed to find her and help her with her plan. The boat, I knew, was anchored no more than a couple of hundred yards away, off to the west of the *Obi-man,* and farther out from the shore. Determining my position from the compass on my wrist, I began at once to swim in that direction, away from the cliff and the gaping *Argonaut,* out into the open water.

ZOMBIE

The *Argonaut* faded behind me in the silty fog of the cliff, and the sea before me grew clearer. Soon I was finning through wide open water with nothing to give me bearings but the needle on my wrist. I clung to that jittery arrow as if my life depended on it, and in a way it did. If somehow I was heading in the wrong direction, and came up too far away from the boat, I'd blow my chance of reaching Candy. Worse, if I came up near the *Obi-man,* the cowboy would be sure to spot me.

Faced with this uncertainty and the vast expanse of water, my initial rush of enthusiasm rapidly dissolved. It was replaced by a now familiar paranoia, and by tremors that seemed to take hold of my limbs. Nothing like a bottomless void to bring out thoughts of annihilation. I couldn't stop wondering about Duff's mysterious fate. Had it been his quartered corpse burning in the witches' fire? Maybe what had happened to him had happened to my brother Dan. We had never found a body, just a half-empty scuba tank. The vision of the manta ray kept swimming through my head. That huge, open mouth it had; the fins like massive wings. What did I really know about these creatures? What did anyone know? They had probably been around for millions of years. Who could say what flukes might occur, what genetic aberrations? Perhaps what turned this creature white had also made it deadly.

I began swimming closer to the surface, as if it might offer protection—but I knew, swimming through the open ocean, there was no real safety. There was nowhere to run to and nowhere to hide, and nothing to do but pray.

I did, however, have a knife in my hand. If the manta came at me, I could bloody its nose. Did manta rays have noses? I wondered if they even had eyes. All I remembered was a giant mouth—a giant mouth with wings. The wingspan had to be twenty-five feet, twice the width of my bedroom at home. And who could say how many tons it weighed? It appeared to be a solid sheet of muscle. Suddenly the knife in my hand looked pathetic. What could I do with a six-inch blade in the face of this flying giant?

I'd been swimming now for at least ten minutes. It may have been increasing panic that drove the impulse, but I suddenly decided I had gone far enough. I swam for the surface.

Just beneath the waves, I paused a moment and faced back east. I'd have to peek up quick and low to make sure no one saw me. I eased upward through a passing wave. My mask broke clear, and water coursed down the glass. I saw nothing but the deep blue sky. Another swell washed over me, and then I broke through the surface again. The masts of the *Obi-man* appeared in the distance. I wheeled around.

The *Orchid* was only twenty yards away to the north. No sign of Candy on board, but the view through the mask was blurry, and I didn't take time for a careful look, just enough to get a bead on the boat and start off in that direction. I checked the compass needle and tried to hold it steady while swimming slightly under the surface. The fear of being spotted and the sight of the *Orchid* had filled me with a rush of excitement, and for a while I completely forgot about the real or imagined dangers of the sea. Instead I focused intently on the water ahead, the unending sameness of it, and as I was beginning to think I must have wandered off course, an anchor chain came into view. Passing it, I swam down under the algae-covered bottom of the boat toward the side that was hidden from the *Obi-man*. A crusty beard of barnacles rimmed the hull at the waterline, and at the stern a scarred set of twin props hung down menacingly.

For the last half hour, exhaled bubbles had been blasting in my ears. As I rose through the surface now and pulled off my mask, the thing that struck me suddenly was how very quiet it was. The air was still and the boat was silent, the only sound the soft lap of waves against the hull. The morning sun, a quarter of the way up the sky, lay hidden behind the looming vessel, casting a deep shadow around me that blackened the water and darkened the air. Once painted white but now a moonlike gray, the boat was a reconstructed fishing trawler, turned into a pleasure yacht, with a big-windowed cabin on deck and an open-air pilot bridge up on top. The vessel was decrepit and sorely in need of paint. Brackets were loose and fittings corroded. The wood trim was warped and splintered. The caulking on the windows was dry and shriveled, and one of the panes was marred with a crack and what looked like a bullet hole at the edge of the frame.

I couldn't see anyone on board. Toward the stern, off the side, I found the rope ladder from which José and Gonzalo had boarded their Zodiac. Grabbing hold of it, I sheathed my knife, then pulled off my fins and slipped them on board. The offshore breeze had blown the boat parallel to the shore, and as long as I stayed on the shadowed side, I was hidden from the view of the *Obi-man*. Creeping up the ladder, I peered over the gunwale and checked out the deck.

From what I could see or hear, there appeared not to be a soul on board. On the back deck, beside a rusty gas grill, a man's white shirt and a frayed beach towel lay draped over a canvas hammock chair. Through the unwashed windows of the rectangular cabin, I could see a wooden steering wheel, an empty red vinyl pilot's seat, and the reflection of glassware on a dining table. An overhanging roof above the cabin blocked my view of the bridge, but I didn't hear a sound from up there, either. If Candy was on board, she was keeping awfully quiet and staying out of sight. But there was no sign of her diving gear, and the deck in front of the ladder was perfectly dry.

I climbed up over the gunwale and stripped off my weight belt and tank. The cabin safely hid me from the sailboat's view; I could just make out, in the distance through the windows, its bare silver mast and gleaming white hull. The sight of it quickened my pulse. If I wasn't back there within half an hour, José would be calling for blood.

So where the hell was Candy?

A ladder on the back wall of the cabin led to the bridge above. I climbed up a few steps, poked my head through the hatchway in the roof, and looked around. There was another empty pilot's chair in front of a steel steering wheel, side benches with badly faded cushions, a torn canvas hood shading less than half the deck, and a bright brass lantern hanging from above. A purple plastic drinking glass lay on its side on the floor, along with several smashed beer cans, an empty pack of cigarettes, an uncapped bottle of aloe vera gel, and a pile of discarded clothes. The view from this deck was far and wide and largely open to the sea; it was unlikely Candy would venture up this high for fear of being spotted. I started to climb back down the ladder.

Then, suddenly, I stopped. Something had tickled my eye in the tangled pile of clothes. I poked my head up and took another look. Along with the blue jean cutoffs and the hooded sweatshirt was a slim strip of clothing, lipstick red.

A bikini top.

I froze. Eva had said they had seen only the two men on board. From the distant vantage of the *Obi-man,* waiting for more than an hour while Candy and Gonzalo made their dive, none of us had noticed anyone else on the boat. We had thought for certain the two men were alone.

But how to explain *this?* Whatever their sexual orientation, I doubted that José or Gonzalo was into wearing bikinis. Probably left from a previous outing, but how could I know for sure?

I eased back down the ladder. On the rear deck, I peered through a cabin window and verified again that the room was empty. Then I crept along the side of the cabin to the front of the boat and saw that the deck there was empty as well. I carefully opened a side door and slid into the cabin. The refrigerator was whining loudly. A moldy odor filled the air. As I edged past the pilot's chair into the galley, my bare foot fell on the salsa-stained half moon of a torn tortilla. The kitchen was filthy. Dirty dishes littered the counter and filled the tiny sink. Crumbs were scattered over the grimy floor. In the saloon, an ashtray on the cluttered dining table bristled with butts, and an empty bottle of tequila lay on the tattered vinyl seat. When the refrigerator suddenly stopped its whine, I thought I heard a creaking noise coming from behind me. I turned and saw, descending from the galley, a stairwell that led to the bedrooms below. I started down.

At the end of the brief, bulbless corridor, a darkened door was closed tight. To the right, a half-open door revealed a toilet and sink, and to the left, another door, nearly but not completely shut, was outlined with a seam of daylight. I quietly pushed it open.

An empty double bed filled the room. A sunbeam slanted through the oval window and fell like a pee stain on the grass-green sheet. A blanket lay piled at the foot of the bed; at the head, a white pillow mottled by a coffee spill sat propped against the wall. On the floor, a canvas Nike bag, half unzipped, held a pair of men's trousers, a coiled leather belt, and an unopened bottle of crystal-clear mescal, complete with resident worm. On the built-in bedside table was an empty glass, a half-eaten strip of beef jerky, and a well-thumbed Mexican porn magazine. Poking out from under the magazine was what looked at first glance like a dead snake but turned out on closer inspection to be a two-foot length of surgical rubber tubing.

I left the room. In the hallway, my eyes took a moment to adjust to the dark, and I listened for sounds from the suite at the end. It was silent. I walked to the door and listened again. Nothing but the wooden creak of the boat, the splat of waves on the hull, and the noise of my own breathing, which had grown short and tense. My fingers found the brass knob and gently turned it clockwise. The latch clicked, and without the slightest push, the door drifted open by itself.

In front of me was a disheveled king-sized bed, empty. To the left was a built-in desk with a single chair; to the right, a closet with double louvered doors, a wall-mounted mirror beside it. The oval windows had all been curtained off, so the only light that filtered through was a dim, aquatic green. Clothes were scattered everywhere: patterned silk socks, tire-tread sandals, blue underpants, jeans, a woman's straw hat, and a black leather vest—undoubtedly the cowboy's— hanging neatly on the back of the chair. On the desk in front of the chair was a razor blade and an American twenty-dollar bill, loosely curled. I wiped my finger past it, leaving a trail in the nearly invisible trace of angel dust. Then, turning to the bed, I saw amid the tangle of sheets and clothes a blackened spoon, a Zippo lighter, and a hypodermic needle. I was reaching for the needle when I heard the rushing patter of bare feet behind me.

That was the only warning I had. There was no cry of fury, no primal scream to put her in the mood. The girl just appeared out of nowhere, lunging at me with a fillet knife in her hand. If she hadn't been half blind from the crack, she might have killed me right then and there, but I spun away instinctively, and the plunging knife merely grazed my hip, tearing a gash in my surfer suit. She dove at me with the knife again and we tumbled to the floor. I gripped her wrist and held it off with both my hands. Her lank hair hung in my face, and through it I saw the trembling blade. I turned and drove her wrist to the floor. She fell to the side and the hair came at me and suddenly her teeth were locked on my nose. I hollered as blood ran into my mouth. Releasing her wrist, I forearmed her head and knocked her back. Again the knife rose up. I spun away and the plummeting blade went into the floor. I started to my feet. She yanked the knife loose and charged me again. I dove at her feet. A rolling body block. She flipped and crashed into the louvered doors.

Then it was suddenly quiet. She didn't move at all.

My nose was dripping blood on the floor. I pinched it between my thumb and forefinger and staggered to my feet. She was lying in a twisted heap, half in the closet, half out, broken louvers dangling around her. For the first time it registered: The girl was naked. On closer inspection, not quite—she had on the red thong bottom of her suit. It looked like the suit was melting onto the floor. Blood was pooling at her hips. I reached and pulled her shoulder back.

The knife had gone into her chest, just under her left breast. The entry could not have been more lethal. Judging from the gush of blood, the blade had slipped between her ribs and pierced her pumping heart. I stared at the unrelenting flow in utter amazement and horror. Involuntarily stepping back, I caught sight of my reflection in the mirror. My body was dark, my face in shadow, but the silver cross blazed like a shield on my chest.

I had been protected. My assailant was dead.

I didn't have to feel her pulse to know it. I could tell from her stillness and the massive loss of blood. Her face was wax pale and shiny, her hair a greasy tangle of straw. Her silver-blue eyes, which may once have been pretty, were locked in a stare that was anything but.

The girl had been on a coke jag for who knows how long. There were tracks up and down the insides of her arms, and the rims of her nostrils were swollen and raw. She looked emaciated. A tattoo on the small of her back said SPENCE, and another one, on the meager mound of her breast, showed a tiny, open rose with a falling, tearlike petal.

She was probably an American. A runaway. Bumped from a boat in Puerto Vallarta, she had turned herself into a hooker crackhead and taken it over the edge. She might have been sixteen, she might have been twenty. She might have been somebody's long-lost daughter.

I didn't want to know. Whatever she was, the girl was dead. Nothing else mattered. Not even the fact that it was I who had killed her.

This terrible truth didn't bother me—not in the way I would have expected it to. I felt no sense of guilt or sin. No feeling for the loss and tragedy of her death. In fact, aside from the painful bite on my nose, I had no feeling at all.

It might have been for the simple reason that the girl was

a total stranger. That she had attacked me with a knife meant for gutting dead fish. That all I had tried to do was to defend myself. No, there was something deeper and more disturbing in my lack of a response. A bloodless chill had taken root in that empty place inside me. It seemed a strange source of strength, a kind of cold power. It went through me and beyond me, like the force of nature itself. I found it oddly invigorating and wasn't sure at all that I wanted it to end.

My only real concern was with not getting caught. The last thing I needed—that any of us needed—was to deal with the Mexican police. We'd lose any chance we had for the gold. I'd end up rotting in some godforsaken prison, charged with this young girl's knife-stabbing murder.

I sat down on the edge of the bed, clutching my bitten nose, and watched the girl's blood flow out over the floor. There seemed to be no end to it. Soon the whole room would be inundated. How could I begin to clean it all up? What could I do with her body? And what would José do when he found out she was dead?

The blood was at my feet. I lifted them up and moved back on the bed, and my hand fell on the hypodermic needle. I let out a shout. The needle had punctured the web of flesh between my thumb and forefinger. Cursing, I pulled it out and squeezed the skin to make it bleed. Now I could add AIDS to my list of worries. I wiped my bloody hand off on the bedsheet and angrily chucked the syringe across the room. Then I grabbed the Zippo and started to throw it, too.

That's when the idea came to me. Slowly at first, then all in a tumble—the girl, the boat, the cowboy, the cops—a way to take care of everything at once.

The stove in the galley was electric, but the grill on the back deck was gas. The propane tank underneath it felt light; I guessed it was only half full. I unhooked it and carried it inside. Then, after checking through the engine room and nearly every cabinet and storage bin in the boat, I finally came across a second propane tank, stored in a crawl-space equipment chamber next to the engine room and under the cabin. This tank was full.

I searched for a candle in the galley but couldn't find one. Then I remembered the brass lamp up on the bridge. Climbing up there in broad daylight would be a risk, but I was running out of time and didn't have a choice. I went up the back ladder and crawled out onto the top deck. As long as I stayed low, the wind panel up front and the benches on either side kept me out of view. The trick was in reaching for the lantern, which hung from a bar supporting the canvas roof. I'd have to stand up.

Cautiously, I peered over the dashboard to check out the *Obi-man*. It appeared that Bellocheque was still tied to the pilot's seat; Rock and Eva sat on either side of him. The dark figure of the cowboy was perched at the rear, undoubtedly with his gun trained on Bellocheque's back and his eyes on Rock and Eva. Rock was the only one facing me, but if I was standing up, all it would take is a glance in my direction and the Mexican was sure to spot me.

I tried to make it as quick as I could. Glancing briefly at the cowboy again, I rose up and took hold of the lamp. When I tried to pull it away, however, I couldn't release the hook from the bar. For a long and perilous moment, I was standing fully upright, both arms extended over my head, jerking at the lantern to try to set it free. Finally it broke loose with a loud snap. I ducked. For several seconds I crouched there, frozen behind the bench, the lantern clutched in my trembling hands. Then my heart leapt into my throat.

Somebody was shouting.

It came fitfully over the water, and I quickly recognized the Mexican's voice. He had spotted me, I was sure of it. Sneaking a peek over the bench, I saw that he and Rock were on their feet. The cowboy appeared to be threatening him. To my relief, neither of them was looking or pointing my way. Rock finally returned to his seat, and the Mexican backed away. That seemed to be the end of it. The cowboy sat back down at the rear without once looking toward the *Orchid*. The entire outburst hadn't lasted for more than half a minute.

Rock must have seen me, I thought. Calculating Rock. He had probably been keeping an eye on the *Orchid*. When he saw me go up top, he was afraid I might be spotted and had done or said something to distract José. Whatever it was, it had worked. I had gotten the lantern without being caught.

Back in the cabin, I closed all the windows and shut all the doors. Then I went down to the bedrooms and locked those windows, too. Crawling into the equipment storage room, I reached the two propane tanks I had left there and opened up their valves. Immediately I smelled the rotten onion odor. I backed out, leaving the hatch wide open. Propane is heavier than air. In a matter of minutes, the escaping gas would fill the storage room and seep down into the bilge, as well as across to the engine room, where I had already uncapped the fuel tanks. Eventually it would flow out into the hall and into the bedrooms, and begin to climb up the stairs. By the time it reached the kerosene lantern on the floor of the cabin, most of the boat would be filled with the highly flammable gas.

There was going to be a big, big boom.

When it happened, I wanted to be back on the *Obi-man*. The explosion was certain to startle José and give me a chance to disarm him. The trickiest thing was the matter of timing. I figured it would take no more than twenty minutes for the gas to reach the flame. That meant I had to hurry.

I set the brass lamp at the top of the stairs, lifted the glass, and lit the wick with the Zippo. The white flame sent up a wisp of black smoke, then burned unwaveringly. I closed the cabin door behind me. Two minutes later I was strapped in my gear, and with my mask propped on my forehead and my fins in my hands, I climbed over the side and down the ladder and slipped quietly into the water.

I had given up on finding Candy. And I had totally forgotten about *el Diablo Blanco*.

BLACK WIND

A t first I thought it was a trick of the light.

In my rush to leave the *Orchid,* I hadn't taken time to wipe spit in my mask, and now, halfway back to the *Obi-man,* twenty feet under the surface, the glass had begun to fog. Fluttering sunbeams flared on the fog and bleached my field of view. One of these blossoming cataract flares dissolved to a solid white spot, like a pale moon in the evening sky, or a nickel at the bottom of the ocean. The spot grew steadily larger, gradually taking on a sinister shape. By the time I recognized what I was seeing, it was too late to try to escape. I stopped swimming, hung in the water, and stared down gaping in mute suspense.

The manta had emerged from some imponderable depth. How else to explain its colossal change in size? Nothing had prepared me for the enormity of it—not the glimpse from the wreck, not even the sighting in the storm. The creature was the largest living thing I had ever seen. The sheer immensity and power of it filled me with awe and chilled me to the bone. It appeared to move with remarkable speed. Peering through my fogging glass as if through a ring of clouds, I watched it rise up out of the depths like a phantom out of a dream. In seconds it was before me. Ghostly and fantastic, it looked like an alien being, released from some infernal region beyond the natural world. I couldn't move and didn't try. Its presence overwhelmed me. I watched the white beast cruise on by and peer into my eyes. It had enormous eyes it-

self, on each side of its mouth. The great black orbs held no
light and gave no hint of feeling. They moved independently,
like creatures all their own, gazing out from languid lids
creased with age and worry. Below the eyes, jutting forward,
long white horns of curled flesh pointed like probing fingers,
and in the cavern of its mouth a crimson tongue was wagging, like the beckoning ribbon in a viper's fangs, or the
blooming breath of a dragon.

With a leisurely flap of its outstretched wings, the manta
turned up toward the surface and swiftly looped back over
me. The vast diamond spread of wings blocked the shimmering sunlight, turning the creature an inky black and
tenting me in shadow. Then it came down, swooping past,
its wide wings once more turning pale, and I saw in the
light its leathery hide, as old and scarred as the surface of
the moon or the time-tortured face of a fossil, and its long
white tail, the length of a whip, stiff as a spiny erection.
The creature looked as old as the ocean itself, and when
again I peered into the black orb of its eye, I felt as if I
were looking back to the origin of time, to the great black
Nothing from which everything was born. It seemed to
harbor an ancient intelligence, infinite and unknowable, a
consciousness that reached out of life and touched what lay
beyond it—the vast, heartless void of space, the depths of
the bottomless sea.

The manta slowly floated off and began again to circle,
this time in a dreamy, horizontal orbit at the outer edge of
visibility. The fluid, flowing fins seemed to merge with the
misty water, disappearing and reappearing, as if the ocean
itself were taking form, growing wings and losing them
again, an endless dance of creation, in and out of nothingness. The effect was mesmerizing. For the longest moment I
forgot where I was, what I was doing, the danger I was in.
Twirling in a whirlpool of wavering light, I became like the
thing I was looking at, half made of nothingness and half
made of skin.

It wasn't until the monster started toward me that I was

jarred back to my senses. I felt the cold and held my breath and stared through the foggy lens of my mask. I realized that this ethereal being, this creature of illusion conjured from the void, was perfectly capable of devouring me whole. Its mouth was a vast, advancing cavern. I was little more than a loitering fish. For the first time I thought of the knife on my leg and reached down to pull it out of its sheath, but something caught my eye and froze me in place—the blood-colored tongue in the manta's gaping mouth.

As I peered through the sweating glass of my mask, drops of condensation streaked through the fog, and I saw with sudden clarity the white-capped tip of the crimson tongue. I recoiled in horror. The tongue was not a tongue at all but the dark-eyed death's-head of Candy's face and the flowing flame of her hair!

She might have been screaming when the creature devoured her. Her mouth was locked in a gaping shriek. Her body had been crushed and her mask knocked off, and her eyes were frozen in terror. Her arms hung twisted and broken at her sides. All blood and life had fled from her face, but her long hair raged like a hell-born fire trailing in a blaze behind her.

She looked like the figurehead of the devil's own ship.

I pulled the knife and kicked with a flurry, swimming up and away. The manta's terrifying maw missed my legs but struck my ankles, pitching me sprawling up over its head. With its widespread body sliding underneath me, I slammed the knife down into its flesh. The blade pierced the leathery hide, and the knife ripped out of my hand. I turned and watched the black handle swiftly float away, protruding from the broad white back of the beast. The manta ray soared into the gloom.

I waited there a moment. Partly I waited out of shock and fear, and partly from the rush I felt, the odd exhilaration. Inhaling deeply to catch my breath, I watched to see if it would circle back again. The water's indiscernible edge seemed alive with indiscernible wings. Turning slowly, I scanned through the mist. *Mustn't let it sneak up from behind,* I thought—that's how it must have taken Candy. She had been swimming to reach the distant *Orchid.* The creature had risen up and caught her from behind. It crushed her in its mouth and plunged into the depths, drowning her in the darkness and the slowly building pressure. I wondered how long it had kept her down there. I wondered how deep it had gone. I wondered where it would take her now. There was no way that a manta ray could digest a human corpse. Would it dump her in the shallows, let her wash up onto shore? Another grisly gift for the merry village elders?

The manta appeared far off in the distance. Once again it was charging toward me, swiftly growing larger. It seemed to draw in all the light of the water, sucking it into its ghostly void like the swelling of a bloodless heart. The great beast was swimming directly toward me, its vast fins mightily swaying. Candy's face glared from the vastness of its maw.

I had no knife now, no way to fight it off. Impulsively, I grabbed the silver cross at my chest and ripped the leather strap from my neck. Clutching the cross tight in my fist, I held it up to pierce the White Devil's eye.

But the manta slowed as it saw my hand rise. It turned aside its massive mouth and idly floated past, its giant eye rolling by me. The cross caught a lick of light from the sun, flashing it into the eye. I could see the bright reflection shining back in the bottomless blackness.

The manta turned away.

It swam off unhurriedly into the distance. It did not turn around. It simply disappeared.

El Diablo Blanco was gone. Once again I'd been spared. The shimmering light in the water around me danced on the silvery cross. I clutched the magic trinket to my chest. *If somehow I manage to survive all this,* I thought, *I'm going to find that midget bead peddler in Boca and hand her a fat gold brick!*

I tied the precious cross around my neck and headed off swimming east. I had to get back to the *Obi-man.* The *Orchid* was about to blow.

◆ ◆ ◆

I never saw another glimpse of the manta the whole way back to the boat. By the time I surfaced, some twenty yards off the stern, I was convinced the creature had abandoned the area—or gone off to disgorge Candy.

I snorkeled to the back of the boat, grabbed the hanging ladder, and tossed my fins and mask on board. No one offered to help as I struggled up the steps. Eva looked relieved to see me but didn't say a word. Rock sat stone-faced, clutching his belly, and Bellocheque, still tied to his chair, couldn't turn around. José must have demanded that no one make a move. He peered over his shoulder at me as I crawled up dripping onto the deck. I peeled off my weight belt, and when he saw I carried no gold, his grin turned into a scowl.

"You a fucking *cabrón* like your brother."

"Don't worry," I said, though my heart was banging like a broken motor. "There's plenty of gold."

He wagged his gun. "Then why you no bring it?"

With water in my ears and blood pounding through my head, his voice sounded faint and far away. I pulled off my tank and unstrapped the depth gauge and compass from my wrist. With as much nonchalance as I could muster, I said, "I got a little distracted. In case you forgot, two people just lost their lives down there."

José continued glaring at me. His eyes reminded me of the eyes of the girl, permanently dilated from overdosing scag. Just above his shoulder I could see the waiting *Orchid*. I slid across the raised deck to be close enough to strike him. I was hoping, when the time came, that Rock would give me help.

"It was the White Devil," I said. "The manta ray." I dropped my legs over the rear seat of the cockpit. "I saw it with my own eyes. It killed them both. Swallowed them whole. Then it came after me."

José wasn't listening. He was staring at my leg.

I looked down. The sheath for the dive knife was strapped to my calf. I had forgotten to get rid of it.

Jose raised his gun. "Fucking *cabrón*."

My studied nonchalance quickly morphed into panic. "It's not what you think," I pleaded.

"You no take Gonzalo's knife?"

"No," I said. "I mean, yes, but—"

He pointed the gun at my head.

Rock stood up. "Hey—"

The cowboy's left hand flipped out the switchblade. Eva shouted. Rock stood still. It was déjà vu all over again.

"I didn't kill him," I said. My body was trembling.

He pressed the barrel up under my chin, his face only inches from mine. "You no kill him?"

"I swear I didn't."

Blood was dripping onto my lap.

"Then tell me, *gringo*—how you cut your nose?"

I touched it and found it was covered with blood. "The White Devil. I told you—"

"Lies!"

He pronounced it "lice," and for a second I thought I had worms in my hair. "No," I said. "It's true. No lice. I swear." I glanced nervously at the *Orchid*.

He lifted my chin with the gun. *"El Diablo Blanco."*

"Sí. The White Devil," I said.

"He kill Gonzalo."

"Sí, sí. Gonzalo."

"And the red hair woman?"

"It killed her, too."

"But he no kill you."

"No. He no kill me."

José shoved the gun and pushed up my chin. *"Why?"* he asked. *"Why* the Devil no kill you?"

The cowboy's eyes were as black as the manta's. They peered into mine with the same empty glare. Staring back into those black holes of nothing, I suddenly thought I should tell him the truth.

"The cross," I said.

"Cross?"

"*Sí.*" I reached up to my necklace and held the silver cross out to him.

He stared at it in mild confusion. Then he looked back at me and laughed in my face.

"It's true," I protested.

He laughed and laughed, gnawing the air with his broken teeth. He glanced at Rock, as if to share the joke. But Rock seemed to find it more peculiar than funny. He looked at me like I'd lost my mind.

"I swear to God it's true," I said.

"True, true, *verdad!*" With a quick jab José sliced the necklace from my throat. Laughing, he draped it up between his loaded hands—gun on one side, knife on the other. The silver cross dangled brightly between them, as if it had been looted from the wreckage of his smile. Responding to a sudden impulse, he tossed the necklace into the sea. The smile went with it. "You want to know the truth, *gringo*?" He thrust the gun barrel into my ear. "I show you the truth."

Death had come close in the last few days. Now it was staring me directly in the face. I wondered if I should shut my eyes—there was nothing else to hide behind, not half-assed jokes or half-baked lies, not even half-truths like my trinket cross from Boca. Looking into the cowboy's eyes, his simple-minded truth suddenly took me by surprise. Death, I realized, is easier than life. There was nothing I had to do. I didn't need to close my eyes. I didn't need to listen. I didn't need to plead for my life or to cry for help, or even to whisper a final prayer or to ask for God's forgiveness. I didn't even have to wait. Death is timeless. Even the longest finally occurs in a single, fleeting moment. A click of the clock, a turn of the page, a tug of the trigger. A so-called passing into the dark. All that moment asks is to allow it the freedom to happen. You only have to get out of its way, and that you do by staying exactly where you are.

So that's what I did. I didn't move. I didn't close my eyes. I stared straight ahead. All I could see was the blacks of José's eyes, dilated from drugs and the dark desire for death.

I could hear the hollow sound of his gun barrel in my ear, like the empty roar of a seashell, or the surf subsiding as you sail off into sleep. An ocean of blackness seemed to flow out around me, and I thought of the girl's blood oozing toward my feet, and the black Lab Gracchus with his endless bark, and Eva in the water with her tentacles of hair, and the skull-head scar in a sunglass lens, and the song of the black priest in Punta Perdida, and the branches that reached to a moonlit window, and the crone in her cloak with a knife held high, and a deep dark cavern with a flame-haired corpse and a gate that shut like the jaws of hell.

I didn't have to close my eyes; the darkness closed them for me.

The explosion hit as I fainted to the deck, the roar of it thundering around me. I heard Eva scream and the cowboy shout, and gun blasts shook my body. Debris rained down like confetti from the sky, and Rock appeared above me. He was holding his gut, and he spoke my name, and a black wind moved above him.

W hen I awoke, black smoke was billowing across the sky, blotting out the sun and blowing like a ragged fog over the deck. Out across the water, I could see the orange fire and burgeoning plume of the rapidly sinking *Orchid*. I had only been unconscious for a matter of seconds, but everything had changed. The cowboy lay sprawled across the raised rear deck, a bullet hole torn through the top of his throat. From the saturated look of his shirt I assumed that more bullets had opened his chest. On the deck above his head, his black felt hat sat upside down, blocking the stream of his flowing blood. His toupee had come loose and was lifting in the breeze. I had little reason to doubt the man was dead.

I was less certain about Rock. He was piled in a heap on the floor behind Bellocheque. Eva was frantically tugging at him, struggling to turn his big body over with José's revolver still in her hand. I crawled off the bench and went over to help her. We moved his arm out from under him, straightened his leg, and rolled him over onto his back. The switchblade had been jammed up under his ribs, and he seemed to be gurgling and drowning in blood. I tried to open his airway, but a lung had been punctured, and moving his head only brought up more blood. Eva quickly pulled the blade from his body and pressed her palm down tight against the wound. Both of us stared at his face. His eyes looked like they were halfway to hell, fixed on some horror that only he could see.

I didn't know what to do. Nothing seemed real, and at the same time it all seemed far too real. I'd like to claim that I was simply in shock, but that would be too easy, and probably not true. It felt more as though I had not fully awakened, as though in coming out of the darkness the darkness had come out with me, and now it engulfed us like the black smoke sweeping past that made it seem we were moving somewhere when we weren't really moving at all. We were all of us lost in this same dark fog, as bound and helpless as our tied-up captain, our ship drawn toward the accumulating night, and nothing but a halt in the turning of the earth could offer any hope of saving us. Eva turned to me and I could see it in her eyes. I had stared unblinking into the portal of Death, and now it was staring back at me, filling the eyes of all of us, making the frightful world the same from every point of view, like the ocean to drowning seamen, or fire to the wailing damned. It seemed that once you loosened your grip, once you allowed it to enter inside, then all you could do was to watch it take hold, watch your best friend die in front of you and not be able to stop it.

Eva placed my hand over the hole in Rock's chest. She took the switchblade, rose to her feet, and went to cut Bellocheque loose. For a moment I was alone with Rock.

"You're going to be all right," I told him.

His face turned toward me and he looked into my eyes. A sputter of blood came out of his mouth, and I realized he was trying to tell me something. I lowered my ear and listened. It was difficult to separate the words he spoke from the blood that seemed to encase them, but eventually I was able to pick out the sound of a single, startling utterance. It came in a guttering gurgle, a noise like the churning of molten rock and the sizzle of air in a cinder.

"Devils."

I raised my head and looked into his face, not quite understanding, or not quite wanting to understand. The word, the single word he spoke, had sent a terrible chill through me and filled my head with horrors. I wanted to deny it.

"No, Rock. You're going to be all right. Just hang on. We'll get you help. Rock—"

But it was too late for my friend. The heart beating beneath my hand came to a stuttering stop. Now his gaze drifted off into the smoky air, and I saw his eyes turn hard and still as the seething hell they fell upon annealed them into crystals. A final sigh broke through his lips, a hollow, horrid rattle. With that, the dreaded moment was over. My friend was gone forever.

I could not draw my eyes from his. Staring into their emptiness, I felt that I had been emptied, too. It seemed my heart had stopped as well, and now there was nothing left inside but a thready pulse of anger, a voiceless, helpless rage that left me paralyzed and numb. I turned to see Eva and Bellocheque behind me. They averted their eyes from the madness in mine and stared down grimly at the lifeless body. Hunched in his boxers, his sweaty face in a grimace, Bellocheque was rubbing his rope-burned wrists. Eva was still holding the switchblade in her hand. When she saw me eyeing it, she looked at it herself. Then, in disgust, she dropped it to the deck.

The cowboy moaned.

I rose to my feet, peering toward his body.

"Don't touch him," Bellocheque warned. He hurried down the gangway.

I picked up the switchblade.

"Jack—"

I looked at Eva and told her with my eyes there was nothing she could say. Rock had given his life for mine. The killer who had taken it might still be alive. I turned and moved toward José's body.

Eva stayed behind. "Jack—don't—"

The cowboy lay supine across the ledge of the deck, soaked in a growing pond of thick and inky blood. The blood was dripping down over the ledge, splashing into the cockpit, splattering the toe of his dangling boot. Much of the blood came from his chest and gut, but most of it flowed out from under his chin, where a bullet had opened a neat, round hole and apparently severed an artery. His head had been thrown back from the impact of the shot, knocking off his hat and loosening his rug, exposing a glimpse of his hairless skull.

I moved closer. Behind me, Eva called to Leo.

The nearness of death had turned the Mexican's gaunt face a ghastly white. His black eyes, like dying embers in a cold fire, still held some tiny glimmer of light. I couldn't tell if he was actually breathing, but I heard another meager moan, like the feeble pule of a distant horn, rising from the gutter of his ventilated throat. A repulsive odor hung about him, a smell of rot and bile, most likely carried out of his body in the copious discharge of blood. His total baldness intrigued me. Was it cancer? Chemo? AIDS? I could almost see the underlying bone of his skull. It brought to mind an image from Dan's notebook: the old crone obsessively picking through his hair. Had it only been lice she had been looking for?

What had Rock meant with the last word he spoke?

I swallowed the lump that had gathered in my throat. The cowboy's black eyes stared up blankly. Slowly reaching out with the switchblade, I slipped the tapered tip under his loosened toupee. Delicately, I lifted it, exposing the crescent shadow beneath to the smoky light of the sun. The scalp looked sallow and mottled and utterly devoid of hair. I proceeded to peel the wig completely off his head.

His scalp was bare as a cue ball. He had no devil's horns. What the hell had I been thinking?

Suddenly his bloody hands shot up, seizing hold of my

throat. I grabbed his wrist and raised the knife. His thumbs pressed into my trachea. I gasped; my vision blurred. Eva screamed behind me.

I slammed the knife down into his chest, cracking through bone and muscle. Still his thumbs squeezed into my throat, his long arms stiff as iron. I forced the blade deeper. His grip tightened, choking off my windpipe and filling my head with blood. The air appeared to darken. His grimacing face began to fade. All I could see was his bone-white teeth and the hollow holes of his eyes.

I was being strangled to death by a corpse.

"Heads up, Jack."

My eyes strained up to see bare-chested Bellocheque, blocking the sun, black smoke billowing past him. His voice was calm. He was holding a long-handled axe in his hands. "Careful now."

I wrenched my head back as far as I could, my throat still locked in the killer's grip. Bellocheque swung the axe up high.

The cowboy squealed. His eyes came alive.

The axe fell sweeping down.

With a splash of blood it split his neck and embedded itself in the deck. The cowboy's iron grip went slack. I broke free and stumbled back gasping, my face splattered with blood.

Bellocheque struggled to pull the axe loose—the cowboy's head, lying limp on its side, had not been completely detached. Abandoning the axe, Bellocheque bent over the corpse and extracted the knife from the dead man's chest. Then he slipped the blade under the stubborn braid of neck tissue and tendons and, with a vigorous upward sawing motion, severed them. He took the head in his hands and heaved it into the ocean. It sank at once.

"Jack?" Eva was beside me, staring in horror at the blood on my face. I nodded to her that I was all right.

Bellocheque picked the toupee off the deck and flung it into the water. He eyed me as I rubbed my swelling throat, then turned his gaze to Eva. "Lend me a hand, dear." He grabbed hold of the corpse's arms and gestured toward its feet. Eva stoically took hold of the fellow's ankles, and they swung the body overboard. It smacked the water and slowly disappeared.

Bellocheque found a beach towel on the floor and wiped the blood from his hands. When he looked up and saw me staring at him, he tossed the towel to me.

"Not to worry, my friend," he said. "Beheading does the trick."

THE SHANGO GOD

The *Orchid* had sunk—but not without a trace. The surface was littered with flotsam and painted with an iridescent sheen of oil. A glance over the water revealed an orange vinyl seat cushion, a bobbing bottle of Fiji water, a balled pair of silk socks, pieces of shattered wood planking, a white pier bumper with a gray tail of rope, a sealed carton of Marlboros, various scraps of paper and shreds of smaller debris, and—so close that for a moment I considered reaching out with the boat hook to grab it—the dead girl's red bikini top. Along with the rest of the trash on the water, that bright little reminder of murder would soon be washed ashore. The sight of it added to my anxiety, and I found myself scanning the waves for her body. If she hadn't been blown apart in the blast, her corpse, like José's, would have sunk to the bottom by now, but I couldn't help wondering: How long before she'd float back up?

"Not for a few days," Bellocheque said. He explained that it would take that long for the bacteria inside her to generate enough air bubbles to lift her corpse. "We should be long gone by then," he assured me.

I suppose I should have wondered how he knew of such things—bubbles in bodies buried at sea—but I didn't think to question it. Bellocheque had more secrets than I could ever hope to uncover. He would reveal what he knew when he decided I should know it, not a moment before. I had signed on for a go at the gold, but it was his ship, his command. I was nothing more than a member of his crew.

Floating corpses might be a problem somewhere down the line, but he had been more immediately concerned with the effect of the smoke from the fire. Although it had dissipated once the *Orchid* had sunk, while the vessel was burning the column of smoke had been a compelling distress signal. If any other boats had seen it on the horizon, they might have decided to check it out or to radio an alert to the Mexican coast guard. The possibility put a crush on our time. We had to bring up the gold, load it aboard the *Obiman,* and clear out of the area before anyone showed up. Bellocheque decided that he and Eva would make an immediate dive. They would send up lift bags filled with gold; I would empty the bags into the dinghy and send them down for more.

There was little time for talk, but I had a question that had to be answered. "What about the manta ray?" I asked. The ghostly image of Candy's face was branded on my brain.

Bellocheque was working loose the embedded axe. "Wariness is the best protection," he said. "But we'll also need to arm ourselves."

I wasn't sure what he had in mind, but the real gist of my question had not been addressed. "What do you know about it? Who told you?"

Bellocheque freed the axe and hefted it in his hands. "The elderly chap on the beach in Boca. I believe he was one of your disobliging boatmen."

The old man in the straw hat, the one with the nasty limp. I remembered seeing Bellocheque talking to him shortly before we left. He said he had consulted with the old man about the sail to Punta Perdida. He never mentioned discussing *el Diablo Blanco.*

I was incredulous. "Why didn't you tell us?" I asked. "You might have saved Duff's life. And Candy's." I looked down at Rock's livid corpse, already giving off the scent of death. "Even he might be alive now." Again I peered at Bellocheque. He was toweling blood off the edge of the axe. "Why didn't you warn us?"

He scrutinized Eva and me for a moment, as if trying to decide how honest he could be. His eyes betrayed a twinkle of daring. "It's simple, really. I needed your help."

The bluntness of his statement stunned me. Eva looked equally surprised. We stared at him numbly without reply.

It really was simple. If he had told us there was a man-eating manta below, who among us would have joined his effort to search for the gold? His deception had been a purely practical matter, and now he knew he no longer had anything to hide. Duff, Candy, and Rock were dead—not to mention my brother. Yet here were Eva and I, standing before him, asking him questions and awaiting his commands. Whatever anger we might feel toward him, however much we might hold him responsible, he knew that something larger had come into play. A kind of desperate mania had undermined our will. I could see it myself in Eva's face: the grim determination in the tightness of her mouth, the icy keenness in the green glint of her eyes. Perhaps it had always been there and I simply hadn't noticed; clearly she had been on this quest for a longer time than I. The same dark force infecting her was no doubt now infecting me. Bellocheque had seen it happen; he'd watched it taking hold. He knew I couldn't abandon him now. Not after having come so far and given up so much. The only thing left that held any meaning, that could give any purpose to the lives that had been lost, was the treasure waiting for us in the sea.

The gold was everything. I wanted it now as much as he did. Given that my friends had died to get it, maybe I wanted it more.

"You're not afraid of the manta?" I asked.

"On the contrary," he said. "I'd be a fool if I wasn't."

"Why is it hunting us?" Eva asked. "It's not . . . natural."

"I don't have an answer for that, I'm afraid." He turned and squinted toward the distant village. "Perhaps you should inquire of the obi-man," he said.

Eva and I glanced at one another. "Obi-man?" I asked.

"The tall black priest. The one you said wore glasses and a turban."

I remembered him leading the parade and the chanting.

Bellocheque peered at me. "That rattle you found on the street. It's called a 'shock-shock.' An obi-man uses it to summon their god."

I recalled the priest holding the rattle aloft, and the squat diamond shape with the long tail carved into the rounded end of the gourd. "You mean . . . the manta is a part of their religion—the Shango cult?"

Bellocheque lowered the axe head to the floor and rested his palms on the upturned handle. He looked at us a moment, as if he were again debating how much he could tell us, or how much we could believe.

"Shango," he explained, "was the god of thunder in Nigeria. He commanded the world with his blinding shafts of fire and his terrifying roar. Only one man in the tribe had the power to summon him: the *obeah,* the obi-man, a sort of shaman-priest."

Again I glanced at Eva. She looked as intrigued as I.

Bellocheque peered at the horizon. "When my ancestors were taken out of Africa in chains, the power of their god was not strong enough to save them. They say he fell out of the heavens into the sea and followed them over the ocean. On the way to Brazil, off the island of Tobago, their slave ship succumbed to a storm. The whole of the Spanish crew perished. Only a handful of Nigerians survived. The obi-man claimed he had summoned their god, who arose to annihilate their captors."

Bellocheque turned to look at us. "That obi-man was Hector's father," he said. "I christened this boat in his honor."

I stood there gaping at him. Then I turned to Eva. The question I had asked her days before had finally been answered: Why the odd name for the boat? She had thought she knew the answer then, but not in the way she knew it now. Her face looked as pale as the corpse at her feet. The boat wasn't named for some vague myth of black magic or Caribbean voodoo. It was named for Bellocheque's progenitor, and the mysterious faith that had sustained him. That faith had withstood iron chains and crossed a mighty ocean; we shouldn't have been surprised that it survived in his descendants.

I turned back to Bellocheque. "But you don't really . . . *believe* all this?"

He lifted the axe and set it to the side. "The story is only a legend," he said, fixing me with his eyes. "The fact is there's a creature down there intent upon destroying us. If I didn't know any better, I'd say the 'legend' is alive."

The two of us simply stared at him.

Seemingly unconcerned with the incredible statement he had just uttered, Bellocheque began pondering the problem of Rock's corpse. If a coast guard vessel should suddenly appear, he wanted no evidence to implicate us in the blowup of the *Orchid*. He turned to Eva. "There's a tarpaulin in the lower bin. Under the sail bags."

Eva hesitated, glancing at me briefly. We exchanged a look of confused resignation, a humbling acceptance of our selfish complicity in the mystery unfolding around us.

She went below. Moments later she emerged with the folded square of a blue vinyl tarp. Without speaking, she opened it, shook it out, and let it settle onto the deck. Then she grabbed hold of Rock's wrist, Bellocheque took hold of his ankles, and I found myself dazedly joining in, taking his other cold arm in my hands, the three of us now lifting the mass of his body and setting it down on the tarp. We wrapped the crinkling vinyl around him and tied it with a length of nylon rope. Bellocheque opened the large trapdoor built into the bloodstained aft deck, and with a strained and concerted effort the three of us lowered the blue-wrapped body down into the tomblike darkness of the hold.

After shutting the trapdoor, Bellocheque seemed satisfied. He lifted the axe to his shoulder like a lumberjack and went below deck to change into his suit. Eva and I filled pails with seawater and went to work mopping the blood off the decks. I tried not to contemplate the fact that Rock was dead, that his body lay rotting just beneath my shuffling feet. I tried to push it to the back of my mind, to stave off the burgeoning tide of emotion and get on with what had to be done. This actually proved easier than I might have expected. The whirl of work kept my thoughts in a spin, while beneath them, like the stillness beneath a stormy sea, a feeling of unreality and remoteness pervaded me, a sense of separation from my actions and my life. It was something even Rock's grisly death could not disturb. I had felt this odd detachment since my nightmare on the beach. Bellocheque's revelations had only made it stronger. His bizarre claims and the peril they implied seemed to amplify the strangeness of the world I was in.

We dropped down onto our knees to scrub the ruddy stains. Working with Eva, side by side, I realized it was the first time I had been this close to her and hadn't thought of sex. She seemed to be a different person to me now, a woman with a mind and a will of her own, separate from her beauty and devoted to her goal. The bite of death had frayed the fragile cord of our affection; where only a matter of hours before there had been a violent passion, now there was a coolness and a hardness of demeanor. We said nothing to one another, and our bodies never touched. We crawled across the killing floor scrubbing out the blood, like silent slaves in thrall to a diabolic master.

When our work was finished, Eva went below to change and to gather up her gear. Bellocheque, huffing and puffing, emerged with his tank and equipment—and a spear gun I had not seen before. The spear was long, with a hinge-barbed point, and a spare was fastened under the barrel. As he laid the gun down on the teak side bench, he noticed José's pistol, along with his knife and his blood-soaked hat. He checked the barrel of the revolver, saw there were two bullets left, and set the gun carefully back down on the bench.

I picked up the hat and examined its band of turquoise beads with the tiny, carved-bone ox skull in front. The pair of hellish horns on the skull made it a fitting emblem. "I guess in a way it's true," I said. "Some people do become devils."

"Indeed they do," said Bellocheque. "Particularly when there's gold in the bargain." He gingerly took the hat in his hands, avoiding the blood on the brim. "It appears that José had completely succumbed." He flung the hat over the water.

I watched it strike a foamless wave and linger at the surface. "The people of Punta Perdida," I said. "They thought I was a devil."

"So it seems."

"And Duff, on the beach—that's why they cut off his head?"

"It's possible, I should think."

He seemed uncertain. "Isn't that why you cut off the cowboy's head?"

Bellocheque looked surprised. "Sorry to disappoint you, Jack. I was simply making sure the bastard was dead."

He appeared to be telling the truth. I didn't know what to believe anymore. "I killed that girl on the *Orchid*," I said. "You killed José with an axe. How do we know what they say isn't true? How do we know we're not evil?"

Bellocheque turned and looked at me. "We have to be wary, Jack. All of us need to be wary."

I looked back at the water. The hat had sunk out of sight.

Eva emerged from the stairwell behind us, lugging her scuba gear onto the deck. As I turned and saw her across the cockpit, I was struck by how unusually fragile she looked, a quality I had not noticed before when scrubbing the deck beside her. Now she appeared rather drained and delicate, as if in a daze from all the killing. As she sat down on the bench and reached out to her tank, she glanced up at me with a wistful look that nearly broke my heart. I felt a wave of tenderness and pity for the woman, so caught up, as we all were, in the merciless machinery of fate.

Bellocheque lifted his tank onto the bench. "Lend me a hand here, would you please, Jack?" He sat down heavily in front of it, and I helped him loop his arms through the straps. "Diving no longer affords me the pleasure it once did. All this cumbersome apparatus." He threaded and locked the buckle at his waist. "We don't really belong in the ocean, you know."

I thought that had been proved abundantly clear. I handed him my weight belt and looked him in the eye. "All that stuff about the manta," I said. "I know you don't really believe it."

"It doesn't really matter what I believe, Jack. It only matters what you believe."

"Well, I don't believe in manta ray gods, I'll tell you that."

Bellocheque added a weight to the belt. "Then tell me what it is you do believe. That cross you were wearing today, for example—you believe that it saved your life?"

"Sure seemed that way," I said.

"Then I assume you believe in the Christian God, a God of mercy who intervenes to relieve the suffering of His children."

I paused. My belief had never been terribly precise. "Yeah. Sort of."

"Yet you've never actually seen this God, have you?"

Again I paused. "No, of course not."

"Then you believe in a God whom you've never seen, but refuse to believe in a god whom you have."

For a moment I was speechless. Then I grew annoyed. "That *creature* is not a god," I said. "There's got to be some kind of explanation."

Bellocheque buffed the glass of his mask. "I assume you mean a scientific explanation. That can only take us so far, I'm afraid, but I'd be glad to give it a try. Would you be so kind as to hand me those fins?"

I did what he asked, and glanced at Eva, who seemed to be equally curious.

Bellocheque began. "As I'm sure you're aware, there exists in nature the genetic potential for extreme variability. It's the basis of evolution. Chromosomal aberrations can produce, on occasion, aberrational traits or behaviors. In certain instances, such aberrations can lead to the development of creatures the likes of which have never been seen. Such anomalies are rare, of course, and in the vast expanse of the world's oceans, they mostly go undetected. Evidence of such unusual creatures is largely anecdotal, limited to incidental surface sightings. Reports are therefore scarce and often disbelieved, yet numerous records remain.

"In 1848, Captain Peter M'Quhae of HMS *Daedalus* reported to the British Admiralty a sixty-foot sea serpent off the Cape of Good Hope. A French naturalist in 1850 reported a giant octopus grappling a ship, pulling a sailor from the rigging. In 1861, the French warship *Alecton* battled a humongous flame-red squid. Captain H. L. Pearson of the royal yacht *Osborne* spotted an enormous unknown sea creature off the coast of Sicily in 1877. In 1880, Captain S. W. Hanna at New Harbor, Maine, captured dead a twenty-five-foot-long sharklike eel, a creature that has never been seen again since."

"Sea monsters," I said. "Legends. Creatures that supposedly lived a long time ago. People didn't have cameras then. Sailors made things up. There were no marine biologists around to verify the facts."

Bellocheque was undeterred. "The sightings have continued. Bernard Heuvelmans, the father of cryptozoology, compiled a list of 358 'significant' reports. As recently as 2003, a huge, gelatinous sea creature was found dead on the coast of Chile. The forty-foot-long mass of flesh was identified as invertebrate by the Center for Cetacean Conservation in Santiago. They suspect it may be a new, unidentified species.

"Such suspicions may be well founded. The fearsome *Megachasma pelagios,* one of the largest shark species in the world, was wholly unknown until a specimen was hauled up by accident in 1976. The Indo-Pacific beaked whale is known from a skull found on a beach in Australia and another found on the coast of Africa some thirty years later, but an actual specimen of the animal has never been sighted, alive or dead.

"The global Census of Marine Life has so far listed over twenty thousand fish species in its database, with an average of three new species added every week. On the deep ocean floor, more than eighty percent of the creatures being found are unknown. Scientists say that, in the ocean at large, more than five thousand species may as yet be undetected."

"How do you know all this?" I asked.

Bellocheque grew pensive. "All through my childhood the old men told us stories. Stories of the Shango god who had fallen into the sea. The fishermen on the island had a proverb: 'What is the most cunning creature in the ocean? That which has never been seen.' Like you, I wanted to know the truth. It appears we may at last have found it."

I stared at him a moment, then turned to look at Eva. She seemed to be as dumbstruck and skeptical as I was. "I still don't understand why it's trying to kill us," she said.

"Perhaps there are some things that cannot be understood. The mystery of *el Diablo Blanco* is the mystery of nature itself. You might as well ask why it is that we die."

"There's got to be a reason," I said.

"A reason for reasonable men." He squinted toward Punta Perdida. "Who can say it has not come to guard their cursed gold, to assure that it remains in the ocean forever?"

His gaze had lost focus and descended to the water. I glanced at Eva, but neither of us spoke. It was clear to us that Bellocheque had wandered off the map. He had entered the unknown, his *terra incognita*. Whether he had actually lost his mind I had no idea. The only thing I knew for sure was I didn't want to lose my own.

"Dragons only exist in fairy tales," I said.

Bellocheque looked at me a moment, then peered toward the horizon. "There are limits to our knowledge," he said, "and limits to our belief. In the end all we're left with is the stories we've been told."

The three of us sat in silence a moment. Then Bellocheque ended his reverie and resumed his preparations. He strapped the weight belt around his waist. He purged his regulator. Encumbered by the burdensome bulk of his gear, he struggled slowly to his feet.

"Remember to be wary, Jack, always to be wary." He

lifted his spear gun and inspected its barbed point. I had begun to wonder if he would still be willing to use it—given
what he had said about the creature being a "god"—but if I
thought he had developed any doubts, my suspicion was
speedily dispelled. He said, "If you happen to see the White
Devil wander by, do me a favor, would you?" He nodded
toward the Mexican's revolver on the bench. "Shoot the
bloody bastard in the head."

ABADDON

The first real evidence that they had made it safely to the wreck came when a lift bag burst through the surface. The bright yellow urethane-coated balloon, filled with air from the extra tank they had carried down below, appeared only a few yards off the port side of the Mexicans' Zodiac. The Zodiac was tied to the stern of the *Obi-man*'s dinghy, in which I'd been sitting for nearly half an hour, anchored directly above the sunken *Argonaut* and directly beneath a blistering sun. I loosened the anchor rope, paddled over to the bag, and reached out with the boat hook to snatch the booty up. The bag was incredibly heavy; trying to haul it toward me, I pulled the boat to it instead. Beneath the yellow dome of the balloon, I could just make out the black-strapped harness of the bag itself, and within it the muted glimmer of gold. Too heavy to haul up whole from the water; I would need to unload it bar by bar, but I quickly discovered there was no way to reach down into the bag from the lofty perch of the dinghy— not without tipping over. I'd have to climb into the water and unload it from there.

Realizing finally that I had no choice, I slipped over the stern. The water was cool and invigorating, and for a moment I lost my concern for the manta, taking pleasure in the sudden release from the sun. I swam to the yellow globe and reached down deep into the bag. Wrapping my fingers around one of the gold bars, I tried to lift it out. Instead, I was pulled under and came up spewing water. The single brick was heavier than a fully loaded weight belt. Eva had said the bars were four hundred ounces each—that's twenty-five pounds. To collect them all, Bellocheque had suggested we fill the Zodiac as well as the dinghy. The effort now appeared daunting.

Trying once again, I reached my right hand into the bag and took a firm grip on the brick, pressing the tips of my fingers into its backside indentation. Holding hard to the rim of the boat, I lifted the weight. I'd been hauling five-gallon paint pails all summer, so my arms were thickly muscled and my grip was solid and strong. Nevertheless, the effort to raise the single brick took everything I had. The boat tipped as I hauled out the bar and pushed it up strenuously over the gunwale. I heard it slide heavily down the inside wall of the dinghy and come to a sudden stop at the floor. Repeating the process, in little more than a couple of minutes, I had emptied the bag of twelve gold bars. One remained; I left it there as a weight. Then I opened the valve on the balloon to release the air and watched as it slowly began to sink, leaving behind a pearly trail of bright, babbling bubbles. In seconds it was gone.

Seeing how quickly it vanished sent a sudden shudder through me: The manta could be lurking beneath my feet. Clinging to the rim of the dinghy, I hurriedly maneuvered to its opposite side and, balanced by the counterweight of the gold, awkwardly hauled myself up.

I had made it—alive—and the first of many bags of gold had successfully been unloaded. Filled with excitement, I moved to grab a gold brick. The unbalanced boat tipped steeply, and I tumbled painfully onto the pile, smashing the top of my head on the dinghy. The impact made me dizzy. I crawled up smarting onto the seat, rubbing my scalp and straightening my battered knees. Drops of blood fell onto my thigh: The bite on my nose had reopened. I pinched it to stem the bleeding and cursed the dead girl under my breath. *That little bitch deserved to die. Fucking lunatic.*

I caught myself: What was I thinking? I had watched a girl younger than I bleed to death at my feet. Yet hardly an hour had passed since then, and here I was callously cursing her. Had all the blood drained from my heart?

I cautiously reached again toward the pile and picked up a bar of the gold. It brought to mind immediately Bellocheque's coin, the one that Dan had sent him. It gave off the same richly colored luster, a marvelous luminosity that under the blazing eye of the sun seemed blindingly brighter than ever. The oblong brick's bubble-marked backside sloped to a central indentation, an apparent by-product of the molding process that luckily made the bars easier to grip. The front face was smooth and flat, stamped with numbers for weight and purity and imprinted with a tiny, indecipherable name. Like all the other bricks, this one had a single chipped-off corner—the price, according to Bellocheque, of the ingot maker's assay.

I set the bar down on my lap and, with a beach towel, wiped off the water droplets and buffed its gleaming surface. The stamped numbers stood out sharply now: 399.96 OZ. 935 FINE. Fine indeed. The yellow gold glistened like a misty mirror; I could almost see my face in it. A drop of blood suddenly dripped from my nose and splashed on the imprinted name. As I thumbed it away, I saw that the blood had filled the recessed letters and brought them out more clearly.

ABADDON.

The word released a chill. I'd encountered it somewhere in one of my classes—a course on Milton, I think. "Abaddon" was another name for the bottomless pit of hell. I assumed it had been taken as the moniker of the mint or the brand of the ingot maker. An allusion to Hades, King of the Dead, the ancient god of precious metals hidden in the earth. As I stared at the name on its golden bed of fire, the fire seemed to eat it up and turn it into light. The chill I felt gradually transformed into elation, an intoxicating feeling of expansiveness and power. My hands began to tremble.

I had a quarter million dollars in my lap—and eleven more glistening bars at my feet. I was sitting on nearly three million dollars!

Barely had this realization dawned on me when, directly beside the dinghy, another yellow lift bag broke through the surface. This time I eagerly jumped into the water and immediately began unloading the cargo of gold.

Bellocheque had brought two lift bags to use in the operation. While I was unloading one at the surface, he and Eva would be filling the other below. The speed with which this could be accomplished depended on a couple of factors. One was access. The tool case in the wreck contained a short-bladed handsaw; they had hoped to be able to saw an opening in the hull, creating a direct exit from the chamber with the gold. Given how quickly the second bag had followed the first, it was likely that this had been accomplished. Now, aside from running out of air, the only real problem was the danger of the manta.

The plan had been for Bellocheque to stand guard with the spear gun while Eva—armed only with the Mexican's switchblade—swam out into the open water to retrieve the empty bag. The trickiest thing, of course, was the silt-blowing currents, which, if strong enough, might pull the falling, deflated balloon too far away from its mark. The real test of the system, then, would come with the bag I had sent back down. Would it land where Eva could find it? If she did, could she make it back to the wreck without encountering the manta?

Just thinking about it made me anxious. The second I finished unloading the bag, I popped open the balloon's release valve and hastily clambered aboard the dinghy. The bag dropped quickly; when I peered back over the side of the boat, all I could see was the bubbles. Except for the *Orchid*'s flotsam, the water itself looked clear and empty, devoid of any life. I scanned the ocean around me and considered what I'd do if I saw the White Devil. The revolver lay ready in the seat pocket beside me. Though I had never fired a gun in my life, I gladly would have tried it. Two bullets remained. Perhaps enough to kill the beast—and obliterate the memory of Candy's haunting face.

It happened that at the moment I was thinking of this image, I noticed some commotion at the shore. A group of men had gathered at the water's edge, and from what little I could tell from the distance of my boat, they were circled around a small, bent figure dressed in black—the crone, no doubt, the one I had seen during my night on the beach. I cursed myself for leaving the binoculars on the *Obi-man*; without them, the precise nature of what they were doing was impossible to discern. The crone seemed to be bent over something and was reaching down with her arms, while the men closed in around her, blocking out my view. After several moments, it appeared they were lifting something from the water. Moving en masse, they carried it away, shuffling down the beach like a funeral procession.

I thought at once of the scene I had witnessed: Duff's bloated body and the *bruja* with his head. No doubt the same thing had happened again—this time in broad daylight, and now with Candy's corpse. I couldn't be certain it was Candy, of course, but something told me it had to be her. Why else had these men gathered on shore, and the crone come limping such a long way up the beach? The same thing that had happened to Duff now must have happened to Candy. The manta had released her body in the shallows, and the waves had washed it to the beach. The creature's behavior could not be deliberate—fish do not fetch like a dog—but I had little doubt how the villagers would see it: Another devil had been devoured by their god and delivered to their ritual shore.

I was so absorbed in the action on the beach that I neglected to notice, behind me, a boat swiftly approaching. By the time I turned around at the sound of its motor, it was only a few hundred yards away. We had seen boats passing by on occasion, but they had all remained distant, having no reason, apparently, to enter the bay, and plenty of reason for staying away. This one, however, was heading directly toward me. I couldn't tell at first if it was a Mexican coast guard vessel or a police cruiser or a fishing boat; I wasn't sure I could even tell the difference. All I could see was its high white prow and the roof of its cabin and, as it came closer, a man standing out on the deck at the bow.

They must have seen the smoke, I thought, or somehow gotten word of it. I froze for a moment, uncertain what to do. Debris from the *Orchid* still littered the water. Rock's dead body lay rotting in the *Obi-man*. The Zodiac was conspicuously tied to my stern, and there was three million dollars in gold at my feet.

So what did I do? I did what any scared-as-shit, up-to-no-good *gringo* would do: I grabbed the gun.

It was an old-fashioned revolver with a rotating cylinder and a loose wooden grip that rattled in my hand. Placing it at my lower back, I carefully tucked it under the waistband of my suit. Then I spread a beach towel out over the gold. It barely covered the pile of bars, but unless you knew what lay beneath it, you probably wouldn't guess. I sat down and tried to think of what to tell them. My mind raced off in a dozen directions until it finally just locked up. Involuntarily, I rose to my feet. I stood there with my knees knocking as I watched the boat approach.

The Mexican on the deck wasn't a cop, and he didn't look like a member of the coast guard, either. He was a kid, not more than fifteen or sixteen years old; he wore a grimy baseball cap, with the visor turned to the back, and rubber-booted overalls smeared with guck. His acne-studded face was scrunched-up cockeyed with a lopsided grin, half of it a frown and the other half a smile. This mishmash gave him the lame-brained look of an escapee from an asylum for the criminally deranged. The boat was an old wooden trawler, in the same decrepit shape as the *Orchid,* only this was a functioning fishing vessel, with cranes and winches and ropes and rigging, and a slew of nets and rods in back. Nearly hidden in this jungle of paraphernalia was a gaunt, gray-bearded, frail old man, peering out at me with leery apprehension. He wore a frayed, wind-battered straw hat, and he held upright in his hand a tall, steel, fish-hook gaff that looked like a wizard's walking stick or a shepherd's herding staff. Mysteriously, he hung back behind the swaying nets, reluctant to expose himself to my view.

Through the flare of sunlight on the cabin window, I

could just make out the face of the pilot, who looked to be as young as the kid on the deck, with thicker black brows and squinting eyes, and a nose that seemed too big for his face. He called outside to the boy on deck. Recognizing a certain similarity between them, I assumed that the two of them were brothers.

The boy on deck turned and shouted back to the pilot, then called out something in Spanish, politely, to me.

"No comprendo," I replied.

The boat had come to a stop, close enough that its stench of dead fish saturated the air. The kid in the cabin stepped out on deck, and I could see now that he wore the same gut-smeared overalls as his younger brother, and that his nose looked big because it had been smashed into his face and never properly healed. It made him look uglier and meaner than the boy with the acne, who kept scratching his knee while looking away with that lopsided, lame-brained grin on his face. The one with the nose surveyed the debris and pointed out a gym shoe floating nearby. He mumbled something to his brother, then called out a question to me.

"No speak Spanish," I said with a shrug. *"Americano."*

He stared at me a moment without expression, then peered at the suspect towel at my feet. Behind him in the shadows, the old man grumbled. Being in the bay seemed to make him uneasy; it was obvious that he had not wanted to come.

Again, the Nose asked me a question in Spanish.

"Boat tipped over," I said. "But I'm okay. We're all okay."

He stared at me blankly, not comprehending or not believing—I wasn't sure which. I shrugged lightly, acting nonchalant. Just another *gringo* tourist fuckup. *"No problemo,"* I said.

Just then the huge yellow balloon broke the surface—directly between us, and closer to their boat, in fact, than mine. I cursed under my breath. Their eyes were glued to it. They could see beneath the water the dangling bag, and inside the bag the glimmer of gold.

"Oro!" the cockeyed brother shouted.

"Madre de Dios!" the Nose exclaimed.

From the curtain of dangling nets in back, the old man staggered out on deck, his face filled with dread, calling out with great alarm while hurriedly limping toward them. I couldn't understand a word he was saying, and the brothers, entranced by the gold, completely ignored him. Finally the lame-brained boy grabbed the gaff right out of the old man's hand. He ran with it to the edge of the bow and reached out to haul in the bag.

"Hey—leave that alone!" I yelled. The old man, still shouting, tried to pull the young man back. The kid shrugged him off and poked at the balloon.

I was afraid he'd puncture it. "Leave it alone!" I hollered. "It's mine!" Grabbing hold of my own boat hook, I swung it out over the water and tried to knock his gaff away.

The Nose, who had vanished, suddenly reappeared, wielding an even longer boat hook than mine. He shoved aside his brother, reached out with the long pole, and tried to hook the bag.

"It's mine!" I shouted, struggling to fend him off.

Our hooks entangled, and we pulled at one another. The gray-haired geezer was shouting at him, and I kept on yelling for the guy to let go, but he gave a sharp tug on his pole, yanking the boat hook out of my hands. It fell into the water where I couldn't reach it.

I yelled again and cursed him loudly, all to no avail. He snagged the bag and dragged it closer. Then he and his brother tried to pull it from the water. These kids were strong—it was clear they had been hauling up fish from the time they were toddlers—but the load in the lift bag proved too much.

Behind them the old man kept on pleading, *"Por favor! Por favor!"*

I pulled out my gun and pointed it at the sky. "Let it go!" I shouted. "Let it go or I'll shoot!"

Amazingly, they dismissed my threat, as if I wouldn't dare. The Nose continued hauling the pole while his brother, hanging off the edge of the boat, stretched his arm into the bag.

"No, por favor!" the old man cried.

I aimed at the boy with his hand in the bag. "I'll shoot!" I said. "I swear to God I'll shoot!"

The boy, his acned face red with the strain of his reaching, looked up at me with his sickly half-grin and glanced at the gun in my hand. His brother and the old man were staring at it, too.

My outstretched hand began to tremble. If I didn't pull the trigger now, our secret would be out, our fortune would be lost. Everything that had happened, everything that had brought me here, would all have been for naught. But could I pull the trigger? Could I kill this boy for a bucket of gold? If I killed him I would have to kill them all, then sink their boat as I had done with the *Orchid*.

The boy reached deeper into the bag, and my finger slowly tightened on the trigger. The movement of his hand and the movement of my finger seemed to be intertwined, like interlocking cogs in some cosmic apparatus. They were parts of the same machine that sent the sun across the sky, the black box of Fate that had brought me here, that had placed this grim gun in my hand and this boy at the end of my sight. Call me a devil if that's what I was, but I was a man with a fortune at his feet and the world in the grip of his finger, and if I didn't pull the trigger now, if I didn't pull the trigger—

The water beneath us turned white.

The kid withdrew his empty hand and scuttled back up the wall of the boat. The great white manta lunged from the surface, launching its massive form into the air. Its horns splayed out and its mouth yawned open, just missing the boy's frantic feet as they clambered up over the gunwale. Carrying with it a great rain of water, the creature arced smoothly above the waves, one wing wheeling into the sky, the other still touching the well of its wake. I raised my pistol, aiming at the moonlike wall of flesh, and shot a single bullet into the spray. The loud blast jarred my body back, and for a moment I couldn't hear a thing. Through an acrid cloud of smoke and mist, I saw the brothers scurrying like crabs across the deck while the old man kept up his raving rant, angrily shaking his gaff at the beast. With a mighty splash, the White Devil plunged back into the sea, deluging my tottering dinghy.

I held tight to the gunwale and peered down in fear at the foaming water. The cascade of bubbles gradually cleared. As quickly as the creature had risen, it had vanished into the depths. There was nothing now below me but the luminous sea.

Across from me, the brothers peered out over the bow of their boat, their mouths agape. A long-forgotten legend, a derided folktale sea monster, had burst into life before their unbelieving eyes. No longer could they disregard their granddad's exhortations. He poked his gaff at the boy with the nose, hollering at him to hasten them off. He continued his scold as the kid, in a stupor, staggered back to the wheelhouse and started up the boat. The other boy, oblivious, looked up to watch me as the boat pulled away. The grin, which had been gone for a while, came back slowly to his cockeyed face. This time it grew brighter, a full-out smile of wonder. It would still be there, I imagined, a long while after they had fled from the bay.

DANCE WITH THE DEVIL

T he second lift bag broke through the surface. Only a
few feet away from the other.

I paddled the dinghy closer and considered the
risk of entering the water. The manta was nowhere to be
seen, which made me wonder if the gun had scared it off. It
seemed unlikely. The shot had surely missed its head, and if
a knife in its back had not discouraged it from returning,
what possible effect could a tiny bullet have? Little more
than an annoying irritation, I thought. But the idea of the
creature roaming angrily below aroused my concern for Bellocheque and Eva: Any minute now they'd be running out of
air and would have to make their ascent.

We didn't have much time. The fishing boat had vanished
around the north arm of the bay, heading back to Yalapa or
Boca, or maybe all the way up the coast to PV. Wherever
they were going, I knew it wouldn't be long before news of
the gold and its guardian got out. The old man might have
kept it quiet, but the boys were sure to be buzzing. We were
bound to be having more visitors, and sooner rather than
later, I feared.

I rose to my feet and peered into the water beneath the
balloons. The glare of the sun on the surface mingled with
the glimmer of gold in the bags. I rubbed my eyes. The
headache I'd had since cracking my scalp was getting worse
by the minute. I pressed my thumbs into my temples and felt
the smarting lump on my head. It had left a wet trickle of

blood in my hair. It seemed that over the last few days my blood had wanted nothing more than to find a way out of my body. Through cuts and punctures, scrapes and bumps, it kept spouting out of my skin, as if something outside me wanted it out and something inside me was helping. My heart, I suppose, that mindless pump, as anxious to kill me as keep me.

My heart seemed to hold a similar yearning for the gold: a contradictory, double desire to fulfill my life and end it, too. Staring at the golden glow in the bags, I found myself gradually climbing into the water. Maybe the creature would come back to kill me; maybe it wouldn't be bothered. Either way, I wanted the gold. Wanted it more than my life, it seemed. I didn't admit that fact to myself. I didn't even think it. I just saw the gold glinting there and did what it demanded. *Free me from this watery world; deliver me to your dinghy. Turn a blind eye to your dangling legs and the darkness that lies beneath them. Spit the seawater out of your mouth; fill your lungs with air. Lift me up to the shining sun and release me like a roll of thunder.*

Plunging my hand down into the bag, I hauled up one bar after another and dumped them rumbling into the boat. There was something utterly thrilling in the act. A conquering of nature, a triumph of the will. I had overcome my fear and given reign to my obsession. I felt like a god in the guise of a man gloriously invincible and unafraid of death.

It lasted for all of a minute.

The exhaustion of the effort had something to do with it. These gold bricks were more than heavy; they seemed to contain all the mass of the earth. By the time I had finished the first bag and begun to empty the second, my hands and arms were shaking and couldn't seem to stop. I lost my grip on the rim of the boat and sputtered into the water. The brick in my hand, its dead weight like a drowning man's grasp, pulled me even deeper. I thrashed about, holding my breath and reaching out wildly for the lift-bag balloon. I missed it and began to plummet. A terror spread quickly through my body, tightening around my chest and knotting up my gut.

All I had to do was let go of the brick, but that was an awful lot of money in my hand. I plunged deeper. A tickle of panic rippled through me. My eyes burned in the briny water. *Let go of the fucking brick,* I thought, but my hand would not obey me. I kicked my legs and flayed my arm but could not stop sinking. I was rapidly descending and running out of breath. If I didn't stop—

The water around me went dark. I dropped the brick in fright. The White Devil's horn-fin was sliding past my face. In a second the manta engulfed me. A powerful current of water propelled me deeper into its throat. I grasped about in panic. The walls of its gullet felt hard but alive, like the stony skin of a starfish or the crust of a living coral. I reached to grab the rows of gills and cut my hands on thornlike teeth. The current swept me back as the creature soared through the water, and I glimpsed two gold bricks caught inside its gills. They looked like filtered crumbs. Finally I crashed into a solid knot of flesh. I feared that any second the manta would close its stony throat and crush me like a crab. My lungs were burning. I started to push off toward the light of its open mouth—and my hand fell on a diver's mask. Wide-eyed, I turned and looked at the blurry form behind me.

. It was Bellocheque. The mask had been knocked loose from his face, along with his tangled regulator; its hose was curled around his throat like a strangulating necklace. His bloated head lolled about as if his neck were broken, and his eyes bulged out like a pair of billiard balls.

I was too desperate for air to be shocked. I shoved his regulator into my mouth, purged it of water, and sucked in a series of frantic breaths.

The manta began to descend. I had to get out fast or I'd be drowned in the deep.

Still sucking on his regulator, I tried to haul out Bellocheque with me, but his body was caught in the narrow gullet, and I couldn't seem to break it loose. Then I saw why: A metal spear had pierced his back and come out through his shoulder. The spear had become lodged in the manta's gullet, propping it open while holding Bellocheque firmly in place. This steel bone caught in its throat was what kept the creature from chomping down on me.

The hell with Bellocheque—I had to get out. I took in one final deep breath of air, then yanked the regulator out of my mouth and started climbing forward. The shriek and roar of rushing current filled the fleshy vault. The manta was diving fast, and water streaming into its mouth tumbled through its gullet and poured out through its gills. Fighting the current, I tried to avoid these toothy vents and grabbed at the rock-flesh walls around me, but my foot slipped through a gill slot and my ankle snared in the sharp little teeth. I ripped it free, tearing off bloody lines of skin. Twisting over, I climbed forward on the inside roof of its mouth. Ahead of me, the mouth appeared to be straining shut, the uncurled horn fins closing in. I reached out, grabbed hold of the upper jaw, and pulled myself through the converging horns. Now I could see out over the broad back of the creature, but my waist was caught between the horns, and my legs were still in its mouth. The manta lurched abruptly upward, trying to suck me back inside. Groping out over its leathery hide, my hands sought vainly for something to hold, while the beast continued somersaulting back in a perfect, barnstorming loop.

I didn't know up from down, and was slipping feet first back into its mouth. Then, in front of me, I spotted the protruding handle of the dive knife in its back. Reaching out, I grabbed hold of it. I hauled myself out onto the broad lunar surface, then ripped the knife loose and pushed off tumbling into watery space.

Before I could even find my bearings, I saw the White Devil's blurry form slowly turning back toward me. Dark blood flowed from the wound in its back, and the cavern of its mouth was swiftly growing larger. I found myself floating toward it and realized that far beyond the beast was the shimmering light of the surface. I had to be nearly forty feet down, and the ray was descending on me. I gripped my knife, gritted my teeth, and swam up to face it head on.

The creature fell on me like sudden darkness. I tore at its jaw with a slash of my knife. My legs were sucked into its gaping mouth, and when I struck at the leathery lip, the knife slipped out of my hand and gently flickered away. I reached out around the manta's curled horn and held on for my life. Then I tried to crawl out around it. I saw, staring back at me, the great black orb of the creature's eye. Even without a mask, in the blur of stinging water, I could see in it the reflection of my horror-stricken face.

The creature looped back through the water, trying to suck me into its mouth, but I clung to the muscled horn and pulled myself away. Then, as we arced back, the horn began to bend, to close toward its sweeping twin and feed me into its maw. The massive eye slipped out of view, and I started to lose my grip. The current was pulling me into the dark.

Then, through the gap between the swiftly closing horns, I glimpsed a swimming figure and the silver glint of steel. The horns flew suddenly open, and I slipped out under the creature's jaw. I rolled across its underside, bouncing over rows of gills, until a great swell of water from the sweep of its wings blew me out past the rodlike tail, into the open water.

I twisted around, searching for the surface. My lungs were on fire, and my vision was fading from the long lack of air. I saw the empty spear gun slowly falling past me. Then, upside down, like a dreamy apparition, the scuba-clad face of Eva descended into view. She reached out and pressed her bubbling regulator into my mouth. I sucked in cold gasps of life-giving air. My scalp tingled and my body went numb.

Eva guided me up toward the surface. I handed back the regulator, and as she took a breath, I saw her peer down into the depths. The White Devil, trailing blood, was heading off into the dark, the pin of a spear tucked into its back. It hung like a matador's lance in a bull: cruel and debilitating but scarcely lethal. If the creature could expel the corpse in its throat, I felt certain it would come back to hunt us again.

I looked at Eva's face as she handed me the air. Her green eyes, usually such a pleasure to behold, were a dark and empty blur behind the foggy glass of her mask.

It bothered me that I could not read them.

✦ ✦ ✦

It was an accident," she told me as we climbed aboard the *Obi-man.* "You have to believe me, Jack—I didn't mean it to happen."

She was panicky and frantic. She began nervously tearing off her gear, dropping it pell-mell onto the deck.

I sat down on the teak side bench. "Slow down," I said. "Tell me what happened." The least I could do was to hear her out; the woman had just saved my life.

"We were running low on air," she said. "We had to make our ascent. Leo had found two more bars in the debris and wanted to carry them up with him. So he dropped his weight belt, gathered up the bars, and left the spear gun to me. I tried to refuse, but he was insistent." She sat down beside me, pulled her hair back from her face and looked into my eyes. "I've never in my life shot a spear gun before. I swear to God, Jack. Never."

The sun threw shadows on her troubled face. Her lips trembled; her eyes filled with tears. It seemed to me she was telling the truth, but I wondered if I only felt that way because I wanted so badly to believe her. "Go on," I said. "What happened?"

She shifted her gaze out over the water, and a stillness came upon her. "The manta ray," she said. She seemed to be seeing it out in the air. "It came out of nowhere. We tried to swim away, but . . . Leo . . . with the gold . . ." She looked at me again, her shining eyes like wet green glass. "I tried to kill it, Jack. I aimed for its head. You've got to believe me."

Staring into those glistening eyes, I saw it was no use, that I had no choice in the matter. "I believe you," I said. I took her hand in mine. "I saw the gold he carried. It was caught in the manta's gills."

Her voice cracked. "It was horrible, Jack. Horrible." Tears crawled down her cheeks, joining drops of seawater still dripping from her hair.

I pulled her close and held her in my arms, and she clung to me like a child. She seemed smaller than she'd been before, weaker and more vulnerable, as if the weight of all the deaths had deflated and diminished her. Days before, out on this deck, we had danced together under a dome of stars. I had been contemplating Beauty and Death, as if I could unravel the puzzle they posed. Now, under the glare of the sun, we seemed to be the final remnant of that puzzle, the last entangled pieces still floating on the sea.

I wanted to protect her. I felt responsible, even guilty, as if I had shot the spear myself. The truth was, deep down, I felt relieved that Bellocheque was dead. There was something profoundly disturbing about him. Island myth had mixed up with his Oxford education, like the splash of Barbados rum he poured in his cup of British tea. This had allowed him access to an eerie sort of logic, a curious blending or bridging of worlds. He had lifted the rules of ordinary life and engaged us in something stranger and deeper. With Bellocheque at the helm of the ship, superstition and legend had a way of coming true.

"Jack?"

I looked at Eva's face. The tears were gone; she had made up her mind. "We have to leave," she said calmly. "Take the gold we have and go."

I gazed out over the water. The horizon was clear, the sky devoid of clouds, and the sun, though descending, still offered hours of light. The shoreline, too, was empty: No villagers had gathered to collect their bag of bones. It occurred to me that if the injured manta failed to disgorge the speared body, perhaps it would remain below, to linger and slowly die in the depths.

"No," I said. "We can't leave yet."

Eva pulled gently from my arms and looked into my face. "Jack—"

"We've got less than half the gold, Eva. We can't just leave it down there for someone else to take."

She looked at me as if she feared I might be losing my mind. "People have *died*, Jack. Leo. Candy. Your friends. That *monster* down there—"

"—is badly wounded," I said. "The spear that killed Leo is stuck in its throat. You've put another one into its back. I shot it once, and it's still bleeding from the knife wound—"

"You shot the manta ray?"

"Yeah," I said. "I think I nailed it in the head." I knew very likely this wasn't true, but having had the aplomb to even get off the shot, I felt a touch of pride about it and thought it might help my case. I told her about the fishing boat and the boys who had tried to take the gold. "Now everyone's going to know about it," I said. "They'll be coming here in droves."

"All the more reason to leave while we can."

"No," I said. "The gold is ours. My brother found it. Our friends have died for it. I'm not going to leave it for somebody else."

"But you admit it yourself—there isn't time!"

"There is if we hurry," I said. "I'm going back down there, Eva. I'll send the gold up to you. All we've got to do is figure out how to get the bags out of the water—"

"But there were only two spears—you've nothing left to defend yourself with!"

"There's this." I picked up the cowboy's switchblade, which she had discarded with her gear. I popped out the blade and held it up to the sun. Its tapered tip still held the dried stain of the cowboy's blood—but in truth, the six-inch blade that had once appeared so menacing now looked merely pathetic.

Eva leveled her gaze at me. "It's not enough. You know it's not." She squinted at me. "Jack . . ." She reached out and touched my forehead. The skin was damp with blood.

"It's all right," I said, grabbing a towel to wipe it away. "I banged my head in the boat. Still got a hell of a headache from it."

"You might have a concussion," she said.

"Don't worry," I told her. "It's nothing."

Eva remained uneasy. "You're sure . . . you're sure you're all right?"

"I'm fine," I insisted, and tossed away the towel.

"We should really do something about it." She reached to move my hair aside. "It might keep bleeding if—"

I knocked her hand away. "I said I'm all right!"

Eva drew back, frightened.

I didn't know what had come over me. "I'm sorry," I told her, and took her hands in mine. "It's all right, Eva. I'm sorry I shouted. I swear to God I'm okay."

"Jack . . . I'm scared."

I pulled her into my arms and lightly kissed her face. "I won't let anything happen to you," I said. "I promise I won't let anything happen."

For a long moment we held each other, silently under the sun, until the distance we had felt between us finally faded away. For the first time since our voyage had begun, I felt a real bond with Eva, a sense that we belonged with each other, that after our having been through so much together, nothing could pull us apart. "We're going to do this," I told her. "We're going to do it together. We're going to finish what we started." I lifted her chin and looked into her eyes— those beautiful, sparkling emerald eyes. "Then we'll go away together, as far away from here as we can."

She looked at me and touched my cheek, and a tentative smile came into her eyes.

"I promise," I said.

Then I kissed her. Her mouth was delightfully fresh and familiar; I realized at once I'd been away from it too long. The taste of her triggered memories of the intimacy we had shared, our blind night of lovemaking and the fierce indulgence of our pleasure. I wondered now if I could ever be without her. The truth of it was, I knew that I couldn't; I had fallen for her completely. If anything had come between us, if any doubts had arisen, they were lost in this long, lingering kiss.

"Okay," she said when our lips finally parted. "I love you, Jack. I'll do whatever you say."

I didn't want to ask her to go in the water. We had to find another way to unload the bags. I asked about the sail winches, but she said they wouldn't handle the enormous weight of the gold. "We might try using the windlass," she said. "Hook the bags to the anchor chain. The power's out in the boat, but we could use the manual crank."

In the sail storage bin, she found a nylon cinch strap with a steel S-hook looped in each end. I took it with me in the dinghy, motored out to the nearest lift bag, and hooked it into the sling. Then I dragged the bag slowly across the water to the anchor chain, hooked the other end into a link, and gave Eva the thumbs-up. She cranked the windlass, and the chain gradually tightened. The bow of the *Obi-man* inched its way in the direction of the anchor, until finally the chain grew taut and the bag began to rise out of the water. When it reached the rim of the dinghy, I called for her to stop. "If you go any higher," I told her, "you'll pull the anchor loose." I reached into the dripping bag.

"Be careful, Jack."

I remembered the boy reaching into the bag and was glad I was out of the water. Lifting out a bright gold brick, I held it up for Eva. "Piece of cake!" I shouted.

She smiled uneasily. I might have been enthusiastic, but she remained in doubt. At any moment a boat might appear, or the manta come leaping to grab me. She knew it was only a kind of madness that kept me after the gold. I had appointed myself the captain and taken over the ship.

I added the brick to the pile in my boat and continued to empty the bag. Twenty minutes later, the second bag had been emptied as well, and I was aboard the *Obi-man,* pulling a scuba tank onto my back. "You'll have to start filling the Zodiac next," I said. "The dinghy's getting low in the water."

Eva handed me a weight belt. "It'll take time, you know. Climbing aboard the *Obi-man* to operate the windlass, then back in the tender to unload the bag."

"It's all right," I said. "I'm going to try to conserve my air."

Loading the gold from the boats to the *Obi-man* would have to wait until I returned to the surface. There was only an hour of good sunlight left, and the last thing I wanted was to dive in the dark. With any luck, we could finish loading the gold by nightfall—assuming we had no disruptions.

I tucked the closed switchblade into the Velcro pocket of

my suit and handed the pistol to Eva. "There's only one bullet left," I said.

Eva looked at the gun in her hand. "I hope I won't have to use it."

"You won't," I said.

She lifted her emerald eyes. Despite the worry that haunted them, they gleamed with a gemlike beauty, and for a moment her hair and her lips and her cheeks seemed so utterly perfect, so completely made to please me, that I reached out to touch her beautiful face to assure myself she was real. She took my hand and kissed it softly, and then she put her mouth to mine. *It won't be the last time,* I told myself. *It won't be the last time I taste these lips.* I savored the taste as I stepped to the ledge and stared down into the water. It suddenly occurred to me I might just be insane.

"Jack—look!" Eva was shielding her eyes, peering out toward shore.

At the water's edge, the village pilgrims were assembling again like a congregation of cockroaches. We couldn't see what it was they were doing, but it wasn't hard to guess.

Eva turned to me. "Jack. Please. Don't go."

As I looked back down at the water, I felt myself again in one of those moments, moments that had come too frequently of late. Life or death? Folly or fortune? Perhaps we have only the illusion of choice. I had imagined myself the captain of the ship, but in fact I was the sword point of mutiny as well, and my fate, like the doomed sailor's walk to the end of the plank, would only be completed with a step into the air.

THE GUARDIAN

If the manta ray had disgorged our captain near the beach, it hadn't made the mile-long journey back for more. Not yet, anyway. Clutching my knife and spiraling through the water, I never saw a glimpse of it all the way down, and all the way down was a long way to go. I barely dared to breathe.

The *Argonaut* appeared as it always had, emerging like a remnant of some long-forgotten dream. There was still a good deal of silt in the current, flowing past like a mist, but the water seemed clearer than after the storm—clearer, in fact, than I had ever seen it. It made the ship look different. Its pale cloak of silt and sand gave off an unearthly shimmer, as if it contained its own source of light, like the bloom of a cloud enshrouding the moon. It brought to mind the thrilling glow of gold in the water, and the phantom light of the manta ray, rising in the dark.

Now something else made it appear to come alive: The *Argonaut* had an eye. It was the porthole cut by Bellocheque and Eva to speed our access to and recovery of the gold. Carved into the slope of the stern, the hole seemed to swallow the sand on the hull and suck the mysterious light in with it. I swam into it like a frightened fish and was suddenly engulfed in blackness. For the first time I felt safe since entering the water. This hole was my refuge now. Darkness was my ally.

My eyes grew quickly accustomed to the dimness, and I

discerned on the rear wall the ladder leading to the captain's quarters and below me, in the jumble of debris, the encrusted shapes of the iron chests. Bellocheque and Eva had chiseled them open. I unhooked my dive light and turned its beam on the floor of the room. The scattered bars from the small chest had all been collected and taken away, and one of the large chests had been emptied completely, but two more chests were full of bars, and another was only half depleted. Sediment falling from the opening above had drifted down into the trunks, coating the golden bars in dust, disguising them as ordinary bricks.

I dropped the lift bags and ventured toward the open door to the food locker. Gonzalo's body no longer lay where it had fallen; Eva and Bellocheque must have hauled it away. With morbid curiosity, I aimed my flashlight through the door and scanned the room beyond. Silver fish fled my light. Then, below me, amid a field of silted jars, I spotted the gray lump of the Mexican's corpse. It, too, had been coated with dust; the half-eaten face looked like a half-melted mask.

I beamed my light around the room. No moray eel in sight.

Back in the treasure chamber, I found the scuba tank for filling the lift bags lying behind the half-emptied chest. I set to work at once, loading up a bag. There were two dozen bars to each chest, and the bags could only lift twelve at a time—plus one to bring it down again. It would take at least five "shipments" to collect the remaining gold.

The bricks didn't feel any lighter in the water, though I suppose they probably were. I lifted them one at a time with both hands and lowered them into the bag. It was certainly easier than it had been at the surface, unloading them while clinging to the dinghy, and I filled the bag in only a couple of minutes. Then I eased open the valve on the extra scuba tank and slowly filled the balloon with air, sending up bubbles through its open bottom. The whole rig resembled a hot-air balloon, with the bag in the place of a basket, and parachute straps to the balloon above.

When the balloon grew large enough to begin lifting the bag from the floor, I maneuvered it into position under the portal in the hull. The portal was barely large enough to fit the swollen bulb through, but when I pulled my regulator out of my mouth and gave the balloon a final blast of air, it popped out of the wreck like a cork from champagne. I watched it soar up through the mist, seeming to gather speed as it went, until it finally vanished.

The entire effort had taken me less than five minutes. I quickly filled the other bag and sent that one up, too.

Clearly, the time problem wouldn't be on my end. Assuming I could recover the bags—and make it back to the wreck without encountering the manta—each load could be accomplished in just a few minutes. Eva's task, however, was far more arduous. Hooking the bag to the anchor chain, climbing aboard the *Obi-man* to operate the windlass, then going back out to load up the boat—all this would likely take a good deal more time.

There was nothing for me to do but wait.

I settled down inside the chamber and tried to breathe as little as I could. It occurred to me that the amount of air I used could well determine the amount of gold I retrieved. The longer I stayed, the more I would get. How much was a single breath of air worth, I wondered. One gold bar? Twelve? If I left behind a single shipment of twelve gold bars, that was three million dollars. More money than I had ever hoped to see in my life.

I filled my lungs and held my breath. Then I aimed the light at my wristwatch and set the rotating bezel. The watch was a Hamilton, a beauty, waterproof to 660 feet. It had belonged to my father, who never dived in his life. He had used the bezel to clock his commute into the city and to time the cooking of steaks on the grill—both of which he tended to be a little obsessive about. The watch had been an anniversary present from my mother and was less than a year old when the accident occurred. It was ticking away on my father's wrist when they extracted him from the wreckage. Dan said he had been timing their ride home from campus. The bezel was probably the last thing he touched.

Life, as Bellocheque had said, is lived in the moment.

One after another after another. How much would a dead man give for a single one of those moments? All the gold in the world, I imagined.

I continued to hold my breath. Barely thirty seconds had passed, and already it felt like my lungs were on fire. My headache had grown worse with the pressure of the depth, and depriving my brain of oxygen didn't seem to help. I focused on the pain now, as if it might distract me from the burning in my lungs.

It didn't.

The air burst out of my mouth all at once, sending up a swell of black bubbles through the portal.

I sucked in a hefty refill. Then another. And another.

Forget about holding your breath, I thought. *Just try to slow it down.* I remembered Dan's meditation phase, his stint with Zen and yoga, and his purchase of a nineteenth-century bronze of the Hindu god Shiva. He had pasted on it a scribbled quote from a poem by Wallace Stevens: *And, nothing himself, beholds nothing that is not there and the nothing that is.* It had all been a lot of nothing to me, but as I settled down now on the edge of the chest and tried to calm my breathing, I repeated the quotation silently to myself, to still my beating heart.

I closed my eyes, and indeed a calmness did come over me, a sense of stillness, of clarity and detachment. Gradually the awareness of my body dissolved. I still had the devil dancing in my head, but the pain seemed to somehow separate itself, to become the torment of another man's brain. My finger flicked the flashlight off. My eyes cracked slowly open. Dim light falling from the portal above cast the room in shadows, and the iron chests around me had the look of open graves. Staring into their darkness, I felt as if I were buried, lost forever beneath obliterating sands. Never had I felt so utterly alone.

Was this, I wondered, what it was like to die?

I had had my share of the taste of death. My father was gone. My brother was gone. Duff had been dead for a couple of days, Rock for only a couple of hours. Bellocheque and

Candy had been taken as well. I had nearly been killed myself more than once.

Still, I didn't really know what it meant—to leave this life forever.

I thought of my mother, alone in her house, fallen asleep at the rolltop desk in a night-bound island of lamplight. I hadn't written a postcard, hadn't even called. If I died now, she might never know what happened. Never know about Dan or me, lost to her forever. She'd have nothing left of her family but postcards and a rolltop desk and a little brass monkey with his hands over his eyes. I thought of that look I had seen in her face, the one that had driven me off to Mexico, the one that had driven off Dan. Her eyes had held the glint of some terrible truth. A truth that I myself had been unwilling to admit. The cowboy's truth. *Verdad.* The truth it seemed that somehow she had always known about.

I couldn't stand the thought of it. I turned on the flashlight and set it upright on the floor. A feeble beacon in the beleaguered night.

I swam up through the chamber and stuck my head out the exit hole as if to get some air. I felt like one of those ugly-mug rockfish, peering out from its makeshift abode like some paranoid bottom-feeding vagrant. Silt was drifting through the portal like sand through an hourglass, while outside, the covering on the hull seemed to shift and shimmer, like the dust of dead cells on a dune of skin. I peered through the misty current, scanning for the descending lift bag, all the while wondering when the manta would appear. It could be circling now, I thought, just beyond my range of sight, waiting for the rockfish to venture from its lair.

I saw nothing for several minutes, and was beginning to convince myself that something had gone wrong, when I glimpsed from the corner of my eye a sudden streak of yellow. The lift bag plummeted into the current and then vanished, landing somewhere amid the boulders on the ledge. I steeled myself to go after it. I pulled the cowboy's knife from my belt and opened the six-inch blade. Somehow it looked even more pathetic in the water. It was a weapon designed to impress Mexican gangbangers, not to do battle with colossal sea monsters. I took one last careful look around the wreck, then popped through the portal and swam for the bag.

My heart raced, and I lapped up more air in those first few seconds than I had breathed in the last few minutes, but I quickly spotted the bag amid the boulders. I snatched it up with its heavy gold weight and headed back to the wreck.

Halfway back I noticed something, a dull glint of metal in the rocks below. At first, from the size of it, I thought it might be a coin, but as I drew closer I was treated to a happy shock. Lying on the slanted face of a boulder, and dusted with a fine layer of silt, was an object I had been certain I would never see again: my silver cross necklace. It had only been lying there for a couple of hours, ever since the cowboy had cut it from my throat. The idea that I could have stumbled upon it, sixty feet below the place where he had tossed it into the water, seemed like a kind of miracle to me. Taking it into my hand, I felt a surge of joy, a sense of inevitability, as if my golden destiny had somehow been confirmed.

Devil be damned, I thought to myself as I swam back into the hole. *I have the blessing of the sweet Almighty.* Even my headache was fading.

I quickly emptied the fourth chest, filling the lift bag with twelve gold bars. As I watched the bag float up toward the surface, I thought how easy this whole thing could be. The manta seemed to have disappeared. Our plan was going like clockwork. One more chest left, two more shipments. Eva had unloaded the first bag quickly; the second might come even faster. *What a remarkable woman,* I thought. Not just strikingly beautiful and sexy but amazingly strong and agile and smart. With such a pleasing, capable partner, what could possibly go wrong?

I pulled the necklace from my swimsuit pocket and tied its strap around my neck. I felt again what I'd felt before when I'd worn the cross in the water: a sense that it made me invulnerable. It could have all been in my head, I suppose; a double martini might have had the same effect. What was courage, after all, but a kind of willful blindness? Yet the cross had saved my life before, in my first encounter with the manta—how else to explain why the beast had turned away? I understood all too clearly now why the knights of old painted crosses on their shields, why ships like Braga's *Argonaut* had them sewn onto their sails. There were forces of good and evil in the world, and you had to learn to heed them. The shiny cross necklace, laughingly dismissed by the cowboy (now dead), seemed to have something truly magical about it. *Hueso colorado*—blood of the bone. Obviously, I was no fervent believer; it was more that I simply had the need to believe. I needed to believe the forces at work were working in my favor. You could call it the grace of God, the luck of the devil, or the whim of fickle Fortune. The only thing I knew for certain was you couldn't call it your own. Like the flying arrow that falls on the shield, or the storm that blasts the sail, it comes from a place untouched by your will; it comes from completely outside you. All you can do is pray for mercy and hope that it doesn't kill you.

As if on cue, a sign appeared, a sign of Fortune smiling: The second lift bag fell out of the sky.

Yes! Thank You!

I flew out of the hole. With the cross on my chest and the switchblade in my hand, I felt like a one-man army of God. Nothing was going to stop me now. The bag had fallen farther out and a little more down current, but still in range of sight. I found it lying among the rocks, grabbed it up, and started back.

Once again I spotted something glimmering nearby. A lone, gold brick. How had it found its way out here? I wondered. Judging from the scant bit of silt on its back, it hadn't been out for long. Had Bellocheque dropped it? I had seen his two bricks in the gills of the manta—could it be he had tried to carry *three* up with him? It seemed unlikely, if not impossible; how could he manage to hold them?

Wherever the bar had come from, I wasn't about to leave it there—not I, the guy who picks up pennies on the street. I set down the lift bag, took up the bar with both hands, and dropped it into the sack. Now there were two weights to haul back with me. Clutching the heavy sack to my chest, I swam off toward the portal, eyes straight ahead, the deflated balloon like a trailing tail. From the weight of the bricks, I decided for certain that Bellocheque—without a bag—could definitely only have carried two, and if that were true, then what about—

A shadow passed over me, like the shadow of an airplane crossing the sun. I turned to look above me, saw nothing in the mist, and crashed headlong into the side of the hull. For an excruciating moment—I had smashed the bump on my head again—I was lost in a spinning field of stars and, fumbling, let the heavy lift bag slip out of my grip. I watched it slide down the slope of the hull, wiping a path through the blanket of silt, stirring up a fabulous sea cloud. The cloud billowed toward me.

For a moment I didn't know what I should do—swim for the hole or go for the bag. Had it really been the shadow of the manta I had seen? How had it vanished so quickly?

Silt filled the water around me; I was suddenly engulfed in a fog. I started up toward the portal, then abruptly decided to go down for the gold. My old rule had come into play: If the prey was blind to the predator, then maybe the predator was blind to the prey. I followed the path the bag had left, feeling my way down the curve of the hull. Finally the deflated balloon appeared, waving in the water like a flag. I lifted the bag into my arms and started back up toward the portal.

My heart was banging wildly again, my tender scalp was throbbing, and my vaunted shallow breathing was entirely out of control. Never had the ship seemed so massive to me; I felt like a snail on the corpse of a whale. In one fell swoop, the manta could pick me off. I peered ahead, steeled myself, and pushed up slowly through the silty murk. When the lift bag's rutted pathway ended, the blanket of silt became a velvety dune, and I started to lose my way. Then I suddenly emerged from the fog and spotted the eye of the portal.

I dropped the lift bag through it and dove inside. In the

darkness I felt a rush of relief—the relief of the rockfish back in its hole. I poked my head out cautiously and took a look around. There was nothing but the dissipating fog of silt and the shimmer of empty water. *White Devil indeed,* I thought. I wondered if the shadow that had frightened me to death had been thrown by the dinghy or a fast-moving cloud.

Never mind, I told myself. *Just hurry up and fill the bag.*

Three minutes later it was loaded with gold and bursting through the portal. I watched it vanish into the mist.

Four down, one to go. I checked my pressure gauge and figured I had maybe ten minutes left.

Once again I had to wait. I set my dying flashlight down and rested a moment on the edge of a trunk. I tried to calm my breathing down. Easy in. Easy out. Easy in—

My body refused to cooperate. My headache was in full force again, and my heart would not stop racing. Watching the minute hand sweep the dial was starting to make me crazy.

Something was bothering me.

I peered into the last unemptied chest, sitting open in front of me: thirteen bars waiting to go. The extra one I had found outside had thrown my careful planning off. The lift bags were designed to carry 300 pounds of weight. With thirteen bars, we had pushed it to 325 and gotten away with it. But another twenty-five pounds? I couldn't be sure it would lift off the bottom.

Again I wondered where the extra brick had come from. If it hadn't fallen from Bellocheque, perhaps it was from Eva. Had she also tried to carry one up with her? How—if she was carrying the spear gun in her hands? She couldn't. Maybe something else had happened. Maybe Bellocheque had gone out to retrieve the bag and . . . Maybe the story Eva had told me wasn't true.

Sitting in the dark at the bottom of the ocean wasn't a good place for a thought like this. I swam up to the portal and watched for the final lift bag to fall. I watched for seven long minutes. *It's coming,* I told myself. *It's got to be coming. She wouldn't just take off and leave me like this. She wouldn't do that. Not Eva.*

My heart continued pounding out its manic drumbeat, banging blood to my throbbing head. I was breathing too much air; I needed to calm down. But staring out at empty water only made it worse.

She could have made up her story. Told me anything. Killed the greedy captain, kept the gold herself. All of it to herself. Why, after all, did she really need me? Only to send her the rest of the gold.

Another minute slowly passed. I thought of the spear through Bellocheque's back.

What did I really know about Eva? What made me think I could trust her?

From the first time I laid eyes on her, sauntering down the shore, I could see that beyond the dazzling flesh and curled locks of raven hair there was something mysterious about her, something hidden and wild. I had thought that by my touching her, by taking her to bed, by forcing myself inside her, I would somehow be able to solve that mystery, to tame her wildness and make it my own, but this hidden part of her could never be touched; it was, I now realized, the essence of her being. Inaccessible even through love, this vital core of mystery was the wellspring of her power, the source of her bewitching allure. Her lofty class and breeding, her natural grace and strength, her bristling intelligence and eclectic expertise—all of these were servants to this deeper, darker master; this feral, half-hidden secret, betrayed by the untamed light in her eyes.

I heard the echo of Bellocheque's voice booming through my head: *Remember to be wary, Jack, always to be wary.*

Eight minutes had passed; I'd be running out of air in two. I had no question now about what had happened. I'd been played for a sucker. Eva had left me and taken all the gold. All but the one brick I could carry up with me.

One lousy gold brick. Hardly worth risking your life—

Wait a minute, I thought—*I know where that bar came from.* How could I have forgotten? It had nearly cost my life.

It was the bar I had tried to hold on to when I slipped while loading the dinghy. I had finally been forced to let go of it when the manta ray attacked.

At the very moment of this realization, like a signal sent from heaven, the yellow streak of the deflated balloon came streaming down through the water. With the ball of the weighted bag beneath it, it looked like an exclamation point.

Yes, Eva!

A great relief washed over me. What had I been thinking? Eva, after all, had saved my life, rescued me from the manta. She had wanted us to leave the gold; I talked her into staying. Now she was working her tail off while I filled my head with suspicion.

I swam out into the water after the bag. Why had I been getting so paranoid about her? Why had I yelled at her before? Was it all from this raging headache? Or was it from something deeper? That emptiness inside me. That coldness in my heart.

I had been warned to be wary.

The bag had landed closer than the last one, only a few yards up current from the wreck. I snatched it up like a dog with a bone and shot back toward the portal.

Halfway there, I froze. My heart slammed to a stop.

El Diablo Blanco.

From behind the wreck the manta rose like a mother ship in liftoff. I gaped at it in awe. It had a terrifying stillness about it. Its wide mouth was closed in what looked like a frown; its horn fins were neatly furled and pointed. It hung there magically just beyond the wreck, its vast wings barely moving, while it peered with its great black eyes through the water, fixing me with an unblinking, deathlike stare.

My breathing went frantic. My heart pounded painful blasts of blood through my head; I felt like my skull would explode. I couldn't move my body.

Then, to my surprise, the creature did not attack.

I waited. My breathing slowed. A creeping curiosity came over me. Didn't manta rays—like sharks—have to move to stay afloat? How was it effortlessly hovering there? Why was it not attacking?

I found myself drifting slowly toward it, nudged by the coursing current. Suddenly I realized it was this very current that was holding the creature aloft. Like an eagle floating still against an oncoming wind, the manta ray hovered with an effortless ease as the streaming water flowed beneath its outstretched wings. The effect was uncanny.

The creature was ethereally beautiful, yet utterly real and frightening. Its leathery, scarred, moonlike flesh shone with a haunting glow, while the deep blackness of its staring eyes seemed to lure me in like the current. I felt again the presence of an ancient intelligence. It seemed to reach deep inside me and far out into the cosmos, as if it held the vastness of Creation in its thought. I saw in its eyes the source of life and the doom of death as well, and I saw in the light of its naked hide the naked light of truth: The frightful beast of this world may indeed have been the god of another. A Zeus-like god of lightning bolts with a voice of roaring thunder. A god of glory who had failed his people and given himself to the sea. Once worshipped by the tribesmen of the Ivory Coast, and exalted in the ecstasy of Caribbean slaves, this stunning god of thunder, this brilliant angel of light, had become a demon guardian who ferried souls to hell.

I swallowed a dried-up gulp of fear. Shifting the lift bag to my left arm, I slipped the switchblade out of my pocket. I popped it open, held out the blade, and swam with the current toward the open portal.

Still the manta did not move.

Why was it not attacking me? The big silver cross dangled brightly from my neck—could it be this simple peasant's charm was working holy magic? Or was the threat of the switchblade keeping it at bay? I could see the spear hanging like a needle in its flesh. Perhaps the piercing sting of steel had given it some pause. I didn't really think so. It seemed to me the manta was merely biding its abundant time, waiting to catch me fleeing with the treasure in my hands.

All that mattered at the moment was that I make it into the hole. I drifted slowly over the dune of the wreck, moving ever closer toward the pair of glassy eyes. They watched me without moving, great black vacancies like windows onto

night. The mouth opened slightly, revealing its own darkness; then, as if reluctant to speak, it slowly closed again.

I dropped the bag through the hole and ducked in after it.

This time I didn't have the luxury of relief. The beast was
waiting at my very door, and soon I'd be running out of air. I
swam down to the open trunk and the upright, burning flashlight. It cast my shadow so large against the hull it seemed
like the manta's dark double. I tore open the lift bag with its
gold-bar weight and began to add in more. Two. Three. Four.
Five. The beam from the flashlight was weakening, and the
darkness in the chamber seemed to press into the trunk.
Eight. Nine. Ten—

Clumsily I dropped a bar—it landed in the silt with a
muffled crack. My hands groped through the rising cloud
and into jagged glass. Filmy red streamers flowed from my
fingers—once again the hungry devil siphoning my blood.
Finally I found the brick and thrust it into the bag. Eleven.
Twelve. Thirteen.

Fourteen. I hesitated. This extra brick I'd probably have
to carry in my hands. How could I do that and defend myself? I wasn't going to end up like Bellocheque.

I left it in the chest.

I grabbed the air tank, opened the valve, and began to fill
the yellow balloon. An increasing sense of panic was quickly
taking hold; I seemed unable to focus. What could I do with
the manta there, lurking outside the portal? All I had was the
six-inch blade—that and my faltering faith in a trinket.

I sucked in another paltry breath, the air in my tank growing thinner.

Now another problem emerged. Unanticipated. The air
tank filling the giant balloon. The bubbles dwindled to a tiny
trickle and then went down to nothing. I toyed with the
valve, but the tank was empty. All those massive balloon fills
had used up all the air.

I tugged on the lift bag to check its weight. The balloon was
still not inflated enough. Without more air—or less gold—it
would never get off the bottom. I could use what little air was
left in my tank, but I'd have nothing left for my ascent.

A sudden realization struck me like a thunderbolt: I could solve both my problems at once! The balloon was filled with breathable air—and offered a camouflaged means of escape. If I climbed inside, and added the remainder of my own tank's air, I should have more than enough to lift the balloon and breathe all the way to the surface!

I set to work at once. While carefully exhaling each breath into the balloon, I tugged the bag across the floor to position it under the portal. This stirred up a massive cloud of silt. Soon the hole of daylight above appeared as a shrouded moon, while the dying flashlight beam by the chest faded completely from view. Repeatedly I sucked in breaths, blew them into the balloon, and dragged the lift bag across the floor. The bag was growing lighter, but my hands continued bleeding, and my head was throbbing wildly. By the time I had pulled the bag under the portal, I was perilously close to fainting.

I stopped and breathed to calm myself, exhaling into the balloon. Watching the bubbles rise up inside, a thought began to tempt me: Why not add in the extra gold brick? It might just be able to take it. I had watched the balloon easily fly up before, gathering speed as it went. The fact was, if it rose too quickly, I might risk an air embolism. I could use the extra brick as a kind of brake to help slow down the ascent. Keep it if I lifted off, dump it if I couldn't.

Besides—how could I leave that beauty behind?

I groped back through the cloudy water, peering into the dark. Only the dull eye of daylight above lit the murky chamber. Picking my way through the field of debris, I finally spotted the dying beam of the flashlight and found beside it the open chest. Stretching out my blood-streaming hands, I reached into its darkness. My fingers fell on the cold, heavy bar, and I pulled it out before me. Even in the gloomy twilight of the chamber, with my bloody hands trembling and my heart full of fear, I could marvel at the gold bar's luminous glow, its brimming cauldron of color.

My fate. My destiny.

A spasm of shadow shot out from the dark, knocking the brick right out of my hands and latching on to my arm. The moray eel had smelled my blood. Now its teeth clamped into my wrist, bursting veins and arteries. I wanted to scream but couldn't. All I could see was its beady red eyes, angry sparks of firelight. I waved my arm to shake it loose. The serpent held tight, thrashing wildly, thumping the open chest like a drum.

The water grew black with the ink of my blood. The pain became intolerable. I reached with my free hand into my pocket, found the knife, and popped the blade. I pushed my forearm down in the silt, pressing the eel's head against the fallen gold brick. Its frantic tail raised holy hell, flogging silt and debris. I raised the blade and came down hard, plunging it into its flesh.

The serpent vanished like a shadow into empty air, taking the switchblade with it.

I raised my wrist. Blood flowed freely from the punctures. This was the same wrist the dog had bitten. In the silt below lay the golden brick, scarred from the thrust of the knife.

I now had no way to defend myself. My wrist was bleeding badly, and I seemed unable to breathe. Was I out of air? No. I was in a state of shock. Any moment I could pass out.

Deliberately, willfully, I sucked in a full breath of air. I exhaled slowly and took in another. Then I dazedly picked up the brick and headed back to the bag.

At the balloon I took one final look to check on its position. It lay directly under the portal. I unfastened my weight belt, let it fall to the floor. Then, clutching the gold bar, I squeezed through the parachute straps stretched between the bag below and the open mouth of the balloon above. Dropping the gold brick into the bag made me suddenly buoyant, and I floated up through the opening, surfacing inside the balloon's vast bubble.

The interior was completely enshrouded in darkness. The strangeness of it unnerved me. I pulled the regulator out of my mouth and cautiously inhaled the air. The air had a rubbery taste, like water from a garden hose, but it seemed perfectly breathable, and I tried to calm my nerves. The slap of sloshing water echoed around me, and the sound of my breathing seemed to roar in my ears. I pressed the release valve on my regulator, and a steady hiss of air flowed out into the open space.

Apparently I had used less of the tank than I thought: It bled out for over a minute. The balloon refused to rise, however, and I thought for sure I'd have to lighten the load. Then, just as the air was reaching the brim of the balloon and the hiss from the tank was fading, I heard the gold bricks jostle below me. Seconds later, as the tank gave out its final gasps, the bag miraculously rose off the bottom.

For a moment there was silence. Then a jarring squeak as the balloon scraped through the portal. Light quickly spread through the water below me. Swinging up my legs, I crouched like a spider inside the rim of the balloon and poked my mask in the water. The manta was nowhere in sight, but I couldn't see above me, and only partly to the side. I imagined it carving the water overhead, an eagle circling its prey.

Beyond the hanging bundle below, I could see the pale hump of the *Argonaut* receding. I stared down pensively at the empty black hole, from which I had emerged like a thief, and the gaping mouth of the prow on the ledge, and the dark abyss beyond it. I knew it was the last time I would ever see the wreck, and despite the heart-thumping tension that filled me, I felt a peculiar sadness: pity for the souls who had perished below, and guilt for absconding with their treasure.

I lifted my head to take in some air, then pressed my face back in the water. The *Argonaut* was gone. All that was left was the wavering half-light of late afternoon, filtering through empty water. It looked like I might not be moving at all, like the balloon had come to a standstill. I stared at length at this empty nothing, scanning its nebulous boundary, until I noticed a trail of blood in the water, dreamily streaming away. It was flowing out freely from the wound on my wrist, a silky ribbon of blood, and seemed to be drawn down into the dark as if pulled by the ghosts of the dead.

I was growing faint again and lifted my head up to take another breath. The air inside was a rubbery fug, a clammy, unnerving blackness. I plunged my face back in the water.

The sea appeared to have darkened. Then I saw the shadow pass and the water abruptly brighten. Several seconds later the manta ray appeared.

The colossal size of it once again stunned me. It seemed as if the ocean itself had come alive, the water taken on form. Somewhere at its outer edge I thought I glimpsed an eye, but then its broad back was sliding silently beneath me, as though I were passing over a continent of flesh. I watched the silver spear drift by, then the endless tail. The great wings swept the invisible water, moving with a leisurely grace. It seemed as though the beast had all the time in the world, as if it were in no hurry to destroy me.

I came up gasping for air in the balloon. Certainly the creature must have seen me. I thought I might be safer in this rubber shell of air, but the dripping, inky confinement and the close reverberation of my breathing gave rise to unbearable anxiety. It was all too similar to the inside of the manta. I took in a few more anxious breaths and again pressed my face in the water.

For a long moment I saw nothing, just the gradually brightening blue of the sea, but I felt the creature's circling presence. I knew it was still out there.

When finally it appeared again, soaring out of nowhere, I did not move to hide myself but stared at it, transfixed. Everything was silent but the pounding of my pulse. The White Devil angled majestically upward, twisting past the bag of gold, the great black eye on the side of its head slowly drifting toward me. I saw in it my body afloat in the balloon, my masked face peering outward, and the bright silver cross hanging down from my neck, brandishing its light in the water. The light lent a silvery glint to the eye, like a glimmer of life, or of wisdom. Then it bloomed into whiteness with a flare from the sun, and the creature turned sharply away.

My heart continued pounding as the manta journeyed off, its majestic wings sweeping through the water. I held my breath and watched until it slowly disappeared.

Seconds later, the balloon broke the surface.

PARADISE

Eva cried out my name. She reached out her hand. She helped me into the Zodiac and laid me down on the seat. There was a graceful perfection in her manner and her movements, as if she had spent her life pulling sailors from the sea.

"I love you," I told her.

She wrapped her arms around me and covered me with kisses. "I love you, too," she whispered. Then she saw how badly my wrist was bleeding. "The manta ray?" she asked.

"The eel," I said.

She tore a strip from the open blouse she was wearing over her swimsuit and wound it tightly around the wound. "We'll have to dress it properly on the boat," she said.

I was staring lovingly at the gorgeous pile of gold. "Later," I said. "We've got to load all these bricks before dark."

The sun lay on the horizon, and the last bag of gold was still in the water. Eva hooked it to the Zodiac and towed it to the anchor chain. In the boat I noticed the Mexican's pistol, lying on an orange life vest. I picked it up and popped out the barrel. The single bullet was left.

"You never had to use it?" I asked.

"I never saw the manta," she said. "How about you?"

"I saw it, all right, but it left me alone." I told her how I had stumbled on the discarded silver cross, and that it seemed once again to have saved me.

"*Hueso colorado,*" she said with a smile. "You're turning into a real Mexican, Jack."

We unloaded the bag of gold together, adding the bricks to the pile in the boat. Clouds gathered loosely on the western horizon, and the sun, quickly falling from the indigo sky, lit them with a final gasp of glorious color. Despite my growing weakness from exhaustion and loss of blood, despite the awful headache still pressing at my skull, I lost myself in the beauty of the world in that moment. The luscious bars of gold, the matching splendor of sea and sky, the presence of this magnificent woman—all contributed to an intoxicating happiness, a heavenly, transcendent state of all-consuming bliss.

The feeling stayed with me. By the time we began loading gold on the *Obi-man,* the moment I had experienced had become another moment, and that became another and another and another, all of them blending seamlessly together until I lost all sense of the passing of time, or of the passing of gold from hand to hand, or of the distance it traveled when crossing between us, or of giving or taking, which both seemed the same. It all became a marvelous, multifarious movement, a Shiva-like dance on floating water lilies, wrestling an endless chain of gold from the sea.

That moment, that hour, that twilight time with Eva, was the most complete and perfect of my short-lived life. It may have only been the result of a delirium, triggered by my concussion and the drastic loss of blood, or perhaps by the debilitating fatigue that I was in. Whatever it was that had brought it about, I'm convinced that I became in that moment—to paraphrase Mr. Stevens—nothing: *beholding nothing that was not there and the nothing that is.* I was in a state of pure awareness, riding a wave on the ocean of Being, one foot planted firmly on deck, the other stepping lightly into heaven.

Dan would have been proud of me. I don't know that he had ever managed to reach the state himself. I'm sure that he had always been trying.

I wanted the bliss to carry on forever. I wanted to sail the seven seas with Eva, the ship laden down with our limitless treasure, winging through this dream of a golden paradise.

But it was not to be.

The blind desire that begot the dream was blind to the guile of the devil. Treachery turned my golden heaven into holy hell.

This is how it happened:

We were just finishing up the loading of the gold. It had all been stacked in the locker below, alongside Rock's dead body. Just one bright bar remained on deck. I was wrapping my fingers around this bar in my state of exuberant bliss when I realized that Eva was speaking my name, that she had spoken it aloud more than once, and that only now had I finally heard her. I looked up.

It was dark but not completely dark; we were in that last subtle moment of twilight, the time that seems so infinite but passes in a twinkling. A cool breeze was stirring, and the clouds that had looked so far away were now blowing by overhead. They seemed to contain the only light in the sky, as if they had absorbed it from the setting sun and were carrying it eastward on their journey into night. Eva was standing on the deck before me, and the luminous clouds were moving above her, casting her face in lambent shadow and her body into bold silhouette.

It took me a while to notice something was amiss. It had to do with the unfamiliar hunch of her shoulders and the peculiar, lightless gleam in her eyes. She seemed to be looming above me, with a menacing power I'd never seen in her before. Then I perceived that this power of hers was focused on a single point: her hand, which she held very steady at her hip. It was whipped by the tail of her torn white blouse, and it took me a moment to discern in all the flapping that the object she was bearing in her hand was a gun. It was the Mexican's pistol with the single bullet left. She was pointing the barrel at me.

I laughed. More like a cackle, really. I don't know where it came from. Maybe from the source of the dusky light that seemed to fall on her face like a shadow. Or maybe it erupted out of simple disbelief; I may have thought the gun was just a joke. That was exactly the problem I had: I wasn't able to think. My mind had spiraled out of control into a giddy vertigo. Eva appeared to be floating around me, an illusion produced by the movement of the clouds. Bellocheque? Braga? Did she say "Captain Braga"? Her mouth was forming words that I couldn't understand. My headache, which I had all but forgotten, had taken on the sound of a wailing voice, a cry with a never-ending echo. The cry soon resembled the high-pitched chant I had heard in Punta Perdida. I thought it must have come from the red-turbaned priest, but he turned out to be nothing more than a growing stain of blood. The blood had soaked the bandage that was slipping from my wrist. Now it was leaking profusely from the wound, running in rivulets down my hand, dripping over the gold brick and forming a crimson puddle.

I rose, reeling, to my feet, clutching the dripping brick in my hands.

Eva said she was sorry. I watched her raise the pistol from her fluttering shirt. I saw her finger squeezing on the trigger.

The crystal clarity of certain death finally broke my spell. I went at her like a madman with the brick.

PARADISE LOST

I don't know how much later it was. The clouds, having lost their light, were sweeping darkly past the moon. The moonlight's intermittent glare roused me from my sleep, a sleep that had been like a waking death. My eyes had never closed.

I sat up and felt a surge of pain. I had another massive lump on my head. This one was a bleeder, too, just above my ear. Amazing I still had any blood left after all the bleeding I had done. It was on my body and all around me on the deck. Then I saw that it wasn't all mine—much of it had come from Eva.

She was lying in her swimsuit at the edge of the deck with an arm dangling over the water. Her open white blouse was stained with blood, and blood was still dripping from the blow to her head. I turned her face toward me and saw with some relief that her features were intact. Her eyes were frozen open; it looked like she was dead. I tried and failed to find a pulse in her throat. I pressed my ear to her chest and listened for her heart. There was nothing but a lifeless silence. She was still holding the pistol in her hand. I pried her fingers off the handle and took a look at the gun. There was glistening blood on the butt of the handle. I realized she must have struck me with it. How had the bullet missed?

I opened the barrel. The single bullet was still there—two chambers away from the trigger.

I suddenly realized what had happened. When I had

checked the bullet earlier, in the Zodiac, I must have inad-
vertently rotated the barrel when I shoved it back in the gun.
Eva had squeezed off a "shot," but no bullet had come out.
When I attacked her, she resorted to whacking me with the
handle. Just before I landed the brick to her skull.

I looked at the loaded pistol in my hand. Why had she
wanted to kill me? Was it nothing more than greed? With a
sudden upwelling of disgust, I pitched the gun overboard.

Watching it soundlessly splash into the sea, I lifted my
gaze to the Stygian shore and saw a bonfire burning. Bellocheque, I thought. The townies were roasting up the big
black devil. I looked back down at Eva, murdered by my
hand. This paragon of beauty had been my lofty love. Now
she lay dead and bleeding at my feet. I felt the same emptiness I had felt before, as if with every death I caused, the
grave of my heart grew deeper.

My head spun. Blood was dripping from my hand. If I
didn't stop the flow from my wrist, I might not last a minute.
Staggering across the deck, I headed for the gangway.

The cabin below was dark and airless and smelled of rotten food. I flipped the light switch, but the lights were still
out from the storm. The battery-powered emergency light,
left on all day, had dwindled down to nothing. I climbed
back out on deck and found Eva's underwater flashlight in
the pile of diving gear. I turned it on, went back below, and
scanned the beam through the room.

The saloon and the galley were in chaos. The cabinet
doors had all been opened, their contents scattered about.
Pots, pans, provisions, bottles, maps, books, life jackets,
slickers—all still lay where the cowboy had tossed them in
his ruthless search for the gold. Even the fridge had been rifled through; a carton of milk lay spilled on the floor, and
food was strewn about.

The place reeked of rot.

The bandages were in Eva's bathroom; I went directly
there. Like the rest of the ship, her bedroom was a mess.
The drawers and closets had been emptied, and her clothes
lay strewn over the bed and the floor. I stepped over them

into the bathroom and saw that her bag of toiletries had been emptied into the sink. Above the sink, the medicine cabinet door hung open. I found a roll of gauze inside. I set down my flashlight and wrapped the bandage around my wrist. It seemed to stem the bleeding. I cut and tied the bandage using a pair of hair-trimming scissors I found lying in the sink. As I put the roll of gauze back and closed the cabinet door, I suddenly encountered a devil staring back at me in the mirror.

I was horrified.

I looked haggard and hollow-eyed, as if I hadn't slept or eaten in days. I was still wearing only my swimsuit, and my bare chest was swollen with the *beso del diablo*, and with bright red streaks from fingernail scratches, and with the horrible contusion on my ribs. My throat was black and blue from the strangulation, and my face, largely drained of blood, had a sallow, almost greenish hue. My eyes looked empty and haunted, the irises seemingly drained of color. The bridge of my nose was punctured with teeth marks. My hair was clumped and stiff with blood, some of it stuck to my forehead. I had a large, swollen bruise at my temple, with glistening blood where the skin had broken, at the place where Eva had struck me.

I took a step back in repugnance—and nearly tripped on a pile of clothes. The pair of cut-offs and tangled T-shirt were spattered with blotches of blood. Eva had thrown them on that morning, after the cowboy had discovered us in bed. She had discarded them here later, after all the killing, when she had changed into her swimsuit to make the dive with Bellocheque. I noticed something now at the pocket of her pants: a tiny gold chain trailing out onto the floor. I reached down and pulled on the chain, and out came the antique gold pocket watch, the one José had lifted from her room.

Examining it under the light, I saw at once why the cowboy had coveted it, and why Eva had made certain that she had gotten it back. The lustrous gold case was as ancient and entrancing as Bellocheque's original gold piece, the one that had so enthralled us all and lured us to this bay. Unlike the

coin, however, this watch was not emblazoned with the im-
perial image of a bald eagle or a lofty Lady Liberty but was
instead covered with a more intimate and intricate foliage
engraving. The elaborate design of lushly interweaving
leaves and vines wrapped seamlessly around the entire case,
front to back, as if it were a sealed and complete work of art,
never meant to be opened, and certainly not for something
so mundane as the time.

Nevertheless, open it I did, forcing my thumbnail under
the lid and gently prying it loose. The ivory-colored face of
the watch emerged like a hidden treasure. It was circled with
cursive golden numerals, flaunting delicate serifs, and the
hands were slender arrows of gold, flaring in the beam of my
light. The name of the watchmaker was too tiny to read, but
across from the dial, on the burnished inner face of the lid,
were words of dedication engraved in an elegant script. This,
too, was difficult to read. The lettering, though large enough,
was so wispy and ornate, and the words so elaborately intertwined, that it took me nearly a minute of study to discern
that the language wasn't mine.

I decided it must be Portuguese. This was Eva's native
tongue, and presumably that of her mother, the one who
had passed the heirloom on. I recognized a single word:
amor. Other words seemed to be words of love as well:
Mina. Promessa. Eternamente. Words of love or the promise of love. This had undoubtedly been a gift of passion—
but from whom?

I studied the extravagant signature, flamboyantly in-
scribed at the bottom. I had to extract each letter from its
own elaborations and from the vinelike entwining of the letters fore and aft. Finally it resolved itself into three distinct
names: *Cesar. Luiz. Braga.*

Captain Braga.

The slave trader. The gold swindler. The very devil himself.

Gently, I lowered the watch, setting it down beside the
scissors on the sink. I looked at my reflection for a moment
in the mirror. Then I grabbed my flashlight and hurried from
the room.

Outside, a gust of wind caressed me like a hand. The clouds were rolling swiftly now, filling up the sky. The sea had begun to move. I crossed the cockpit toward Eva, still lying on her back on the edge of the deck. Her torn white blouse fluttered in the wind, and the full moon lit her face and flesh with the same silver bluish light that stirred like a mist on the water. She was lying still as stone, but her hair was blowing wildly. I knelt down beside her and lifted from her eyes the flowing tresses, those long black locks that had so thoroughly beguiled me. Her eyes remained open and lifeless, their emerald color faded to gray. When a cloud passed beneath the moon, even the gray was taken away and the eyes turned a bottomless black.

I shuddered.

Lifting my flashlight, I turned its blinding beam on her face. As it fell across her eyes, I thought I glimpsed a tiny movement and a sudden glint of green. I pointed the light directly into the blackness of her eye. The pupil tightened.

I drew back, gasping.

The eyes stirred. Her lungs took in air. She choked.

I rose to my feet in a panic. Eva was coming alive.

Immediately I thought of José, and the way that Bellocheque had finally dispatched him. Suddenly I was hurtling down the steps to the saloon. I tripped on a life jacket and crashed through debris on the floor. The flashlight went dead. Cursing, I smacked it in my hand. The light flickered and came back on. I scrambled to the closet where the axe had been kept. The closet had been ransacked by José and was empty except for a pair of rubber boots and a folded canvas deck chair. I turned, scanning my beam across the mess in the saloon. I checked under the table and into the galley. The axe was nowhere.

The last time I had seen it was in Bellocheque's hands. Perhaps for safekeeping he had put it in his cabin. I hurried out of the galley and around the stairs and down the short corridor to the master suite. The door was open, the cabin in chaos. Drawers had been left out and cabinets left open. Clothes and books and shoes lay strewn about everywhere. I searched through them, moving my light beam over the debris as if I were back in the *Argonaut*. I checked around the bed, even into the bathroom.

Nothing.

I headed for the door. That's when I noticed that the wall beside the door was actually a narrow closet. It was the only storage space in the ransacked room whose door had been shut again. I yanked it open, aimed my light, and saw at once the long, shapely axe handle leaning against the interior wall, its bloodstained iron head resting on the floor. I reached for it.

At that instant I heard a noise on the boat.

I stopped and listened. Could it have been Eva moving about? Instantly I shut off my light. *She doesn't know I'm here,* I thought. *Doesn't know what I'm up to.* Darkness again was my ally. I set the flashlight down quietly on the carpeted floor. Then, careful not to make a sound, I reached back into the closet and lifted out the axe. I hefted it in both hands. Then I moved silently out into the hall. My eyes were still adjusting to the dark as I slowly began creeping forward. Moonlight showed through the curtained windows, casting dim shadows on the walls and floor, but the light was unreliable, fading abruptly into darkness when a cloud passed under the moon. One moment the hall was bathed in blue, the next in total blackness.

At the end of the corridor, I stopped again and listened, peering into the darkness of the shadowy saloon. All I heard was the muffled slap of water against the hull. Not a sound from the deck above, and nothing from inside. Perhaps it had only been the rigging, I thought, flapping in the growing wind. I turned and crept up the steps of the gangway.

The wind was indeed blowing harder, and threatening clouds crowded the sky. I peered across the deck toward Eva, and my heart came to a stop. She was gone. I stepped out into the cockpit and twisted around, scanning the roof of the cabin and the outer decks. She was nowhere to be seen. The spot where she had been lying was a smeared pool of blood. Beside it lay the last gold bar, the one I had used to strike her. I looked for footprints or a trail away but could see no trace in the dark. It was as if she had vanished, or tumbled over the side. I climbed out onto the rear deck and peered down into the open locker. Rock's corpse was wrapped up like a mummy. The gold bricks lay piled in a large stack beside him; there was no room for Eva to hide. I checked the access ladder at the stern and looked up along either side of the boat. She wasn't in the water; she wasn't clinging on. She was gone.

For several moments I stood there in the wind, stupidly clutching the axe in my hands, scanning out over the water. The waves were welling deeper, and the boat had begun to sway. She would not have gone overboard, I thought, not at night, not in this water, and certainly not in the condition she was in. Twin bolts of lightning flared on the horizon, followed by a double roll of thunder. I thought of the manta and realized that neither of us could escape the boat alive.

The clouds above cracked open briefly, and the moon shone brightly down. I peered into the gaping hold at my feet, at Rock's mummied corpse wrapped in blue, at the gold bricks gleaming beside him. Beauty and Death, the great mysteries. The moon slid behind the clouds, and again the ship went dark. My eyes came to rest on the mouth of the gangway. That's what she had vanished through. She had slipped down there while I was busy searching through Bellocheque's room. It was probably the noise I had heard.

I slipped down into the cockpit and listened for a moment at the gangway steps. There wasn't a sound from down below. Just an empty, tomblike darkness. I moved stealthily down the narrow steps. Before I could even see it, my feet found the floor. Across the room I saw the faint trace of the curtained windows. The dining table was a shadowy blur, and the windowless galley lay in darkness, its skylight barely visible.

For a long moment I stood there and listened. The boat was rocking; my hands were trembling. I realized I was clenching the axe, hugging it close to my chest. I relaxed my grip, took in a long, deliberate breath, and tried to calm my heartbeat. I had thrown the gun overboard, I reminded my-self, and the switchblade was stuck in the moray eel. No gun, no switchblade, no spear. What could she use to kill me? Bare hands?

The kitchen knives in the galley. I thought of the girl who had attacked me on the *Orchid* with a slender fillet knife clutched in her hand. If she had been as strong and agile as Eva, she might very easily have killed me. Now, with all my loss of blood, it wouldn't take much to finish me off. One lit-tle slice at my throat. I remembered there were three cutting knives in the galley—all of them stored in the same top drawer. I had used two of them myself. One was a short-bladed paring knife; another was long-bladed, for boning fish, and the third was a heavy butcher's knife, with a broad blade designed for chopping. Any one of them could easily kill me.

Had the noise I had heard before been the sound of the drawer opening? Had she taken out a knife and fled into the ship?

I pulled myself away from the stairs and moved un-steadily out into the dark. The room was rolling, and the air was ripe with the stench of rot. I seemed to sense something in the dimness before me. Was it only the wind in the win-dows or the spray of water striking the hull? Or was it the sound of Eva's breathing? I began to feel her pulsing pres-ence. Had she only just come into the galley when I came down the stairs? Was she hiding in here now, waiting for me?

I stopped where I stood and whispered into the dark. "Eva. Please. Listen to me. I don't want to kill you. Really I don't. And I really don't think you want to kill me."

I listened but heard only the sound of the wind. I took an-other careful step into the dark. "All I'm asking is to talk to you. Maybe we can come to some kind of arrangement. There's plenty of gold for the both of us."

She answered with more silence.

"I know about Captain Braga," I said.

Even this brought nothing.

"Who was he to you, Eva? Did he marry your great-great-grandmother? Or did he only promise to marry her? Promise to return to Rio with a ship full of gold?"

Not a breath of sound came out of the dark. I began to think that she might be dead, that perhaps it was only her ghost in the room, watching me silently and waiting. Or perhaps the living Eva herself had been conjured out of darkness. A trick of the devil inside me.

I reached out along the counter, feeling blindly for the handle of the drawer. All the while I prayed to my childhood God, the God of the shining cross on my chest. Wake me from this awful dream. Show me she's not here. Rouse me from my drunken sleep, back on the beach in Boca. Open my eyes to the stunning woman strutting through the surf. The one with the silver bracelets, the baby blue bandanna, the long black tresses trickling softly down her back. The one with the eyes I could never forget.

The one now trying to kill me.

A flash of lightning blazed through the skylight. I saw the drawer. I opened it. All three knives were there.

"Eva . . ."

The light vanished. The thunder howled. It sounded like my name.

I turned and discerned her form in the dark. "Eva," I whispered. "I love you."

A glaring flashlight beam struck my eyes. I raised a hand to shield them.

The scissors slammed into my chest. Inches from the heart that had only beat for her. The axe fell limp and thudded to the floor. The last thing I saw before I collapsed was the pair of eyes that had once been so bright and were now as black and fathomless as the beckoning abyss.

HELL

L ying lifeless on my back, I roused to the clicking crank of the windlass and the grind of the anchor chain. The boat had descended into a tempest; my killer was cutting us loose.

A wailing gale swept the deck, the sky boiled with inky clouds, and bolts of lightning cracked the air like veins in cracking glass. Eva's face came into view, her eyes carved out of night, tendrils of her long black hair lashing her like whips. She swooped down like a succubus to plant the kiss of death. Then the black whips dragged across my face and the dark eyes drifted by me, and I heard her whisper in the shell of my ear with a voice like the whispering sea.

"Adeus, meu amor."

A sucking spike of pain brought me gasping back to consciousness. Eva, kneeling beside me on the deck, had wrenched the pair of blood-tinged scissors from my chest. She cut the leather necklace that hung from my throat and scowled at the glare of the silver cross as a bolt of lightning flashed. Then she hurled the cross out over the water into the rebounding darkness.

She grabbed my wrists and dragged me across to the rising rim of the ship. I left a trail of blood behind, washed by rain and pounding sea, and saw beyond it, alone on the deck, the last remaining brick. How much was that bar worth now? One more moment? One more breath? My life was to be thrown away for these cursed lumps of ore.

Eva released my wrists, then slipped her hands under my body and rolled me onto the rim. I looked down at the black water, heaping itself against the ship, and saw what looked like the glow of a ghost. It may have only been a glimpse of the moon caught in the gloss of the water, or it may have been the moonlike light of the White Devil, rising from the darkness below. But whether it was a ghost or the moon or the Devil, it wore the same face I had seen in the mirror, the face of the *terra incognita,* the face of impending Death.

I tried to turn my eyes away. I tried to keep from falling. I grabbed hold of Eva's arm even as she pushed me. Hanging over the black water, clutching to her wrist, I locked on like the cowboy who had locked on to my throat. A bolt of lightning flared above us. Eva's face went still. She stared at something just beyond me, floating in the water. I turned and caught a glimpse of it before the lightning faded. The ghost that I had seen before, the face I thought was Death, was not my face, not a ghost, and not the White Devil either. It was an empty white rowboat, rocking on the water. I had seen this whitewashed hull before, while spying on the bonfire at the Playa de los Muertos. Who had rowed it out here now? The obi-man? The *bruja*? The witches come to kill us?

I looked back at Eva as again the sky turned white. Behind her in the shock of light, a hoary, bearded man loomed up, broad-shouldered, bare-chested, his mouth stretched wide in fury, his eyes fierce as the sea—the figurehead of the sunken *Argonaut* suddenly sprung to life!

The man reached down for Eva. She turned to him in fright. Then the sky fell back to blackness and their bodies disappeared. A massive wave struck the ship and thundered down around me. I lost my grip on Eva's arm. Sliding off the deck in the wash of the wave, I latched on to a stanchion post that held the handrail rope. The post broke as the deck rose up. I fell but clung to the nylon rope, which stretched like the string of a bow. Dangling down against the hull, I twisted toward the water.

The stormy sea and sky were black. Out of this blackness a lightning bolt ignited. Out of this daylight came the progeny of night—the manta ray soaring from the water. It wheeled on its wing above a mountainous wave, gathering the force of its orbit in the air, then abandoned that force as the lightning abated, and descended with the tumbling darkness.

I plunged as the deck dipped back to the water and clung to the bowstrung rope. The roar of the storm seemed to follow me under with the riotous roar of the sea. My eyes burned in the briny blackness. I swallowed what tasted like a mouthful of tears. Somewhere deep in that undersea night, I glimpsed the glow of the manta ray moon.

As the boat tilted back, the rope hauled me with it, lashed like a buoy to the hull. I gasped for a breath, shook the brine from my eyes, and peered back down at the darkness. Deep under the wave-hollowed well of water, the rising specter of the manta ray appeared. It looked like a watery reflection of the moon falling from the sky to the sea, as if it were descending to its double down below, a merging of the luminous and the lowly.

A splinter of darkness severed the moon as the creature's maw cracked open. I stared down in utter terror. The gaping darkness deepened.

I had no strength to save myself. I had no means of escape. I hung there staring down at my fate in the spiraling eye of the storm, mesmerized by the gravity of it, the awe-inspiring horror. Life and death seemed to merge in that moment, like the blur of a spinning coin, each side no longer blind to the other, together begetting a world. That world shone with a clarity now I had not seen before, revealing vast, unknown realms that lay beyond mere sight. The dark rising up from the water below arose from a deeper darkness. The bolt that bore through the air overhead leaked from a crack in the sky. The man I had seen emerge from that crack had come from some other bright world, perhaps from the place where all brightness is born and darkness is banished forever. I thought I had glimpsed in the seaborne stranger another bright beam from that heaven, like the glint of my cross at the bottom of the sea, or the promise of light at the surface.

I held to that promise of light now; it was all the light that I had. The darkness I was staring into was all that I could see.

The White Devil burst through the surface, launching itself at my feet.

I suddenly lifted up into the air. The stranger's strong arms had reached from above and raised me out of the rope. My dangling feet just missed the Devil's darkly gaping maw. The white beast soared above the rim as lightning lit the sky. I heard Eva's frenzied shriek, and the arms that had been hauling me back dropped me onto the deck. The monster turned its monstrous arc and fell back into the sea. Then a massive wave crashed over the gunwale and buried the boat in water.

I clung to a skylight on the deck. The yellow Zodiac tumbled past. A cable snapped and whistled. I held to the skylight as the water receded, and I thought I glimpsed, in the cabin below, Eva with the axe in her hands.

A bolt of lightning flared on the deck and shook the boat with thunder. I turned to see the bearded man rising to his knees. He leaned his hairy head aside and reached to pull the scissors from the lower back of his neck. Another streak of lightning saw blood run down his back.

The man collapsed.

I struggled feebly to my feet. I saw the Zodiac incongruously caught upright in the cockpit. The boat listed steeply, and the steel mast whined. A sudden smack across my face knocked me back to the deck. I lay there stunned and dizzy, awaiting the fall of Eva's axe. Then another flash of light revealed the swaying cable. The cable hung from the top of the mast and tossed in the wind like a whip. The bracket on the end had struck my cheekbone, tearing open a gash. Now it dangled tauntingly above me, as if savoring its devilish deed.

I reached and grabbed hold of it and attempted to pull myself up. Blood spouted from the wound in my chest, which flared with a staggering pain. Another crashing wave rained down. I wiped the spray from my eyes, and across the deck I spotted Eva moving through the dark. She rose out of the cockpit and approached the fallen man.

I tried to yell a warning, but my voice was too weak. I seemed unable to stand or move. The deck tilted, or seemed to tilt in the blur of my fading vision—the dark returning to cloak my eyes. I clung like a drunk to the steel cable, trying to keep from blacking out. The cable tingled strangely in my hands, and with a sudden blinding flash a forked bolt of double lightning tore across the sky.

Over the man at the edge of the deck, Eva raised the axe. I saw its glinting iron head reach into the air. Its hefted weight gathered like the orbit of the ray, wheeling into space, rising like a rage. As it found its apogee, the rest before release, I saw behind it the great White Devil, soaring up out of the sea, while high above, in mirrored motion, a jagged root of lightning reached to touch the metal mast.

I flung the steel cable. It lit up bright as fire as it flew across the deck. It whipped around the plummeting axe and caught the iron blade—and formed a perfect conduit.

Eva's face burst into sun, a blazing skull of whiteness. Her body radiated light; her bones turned incandescent. Tentacles of lightning flared out from her hair. Ablaze, she toppled off the deck as the manta ray descended. It scooped her neatly into its maw like a feral tongue of fire, swallowing her in a darkness that was swallowed by the sea.

I stared stunned at the heaving water. The deck dipped low, then rose again. The fallen man struggled slowly to his feet. Another wave crashed and knocked him over, and then it came for me. As I wrestled through the rolling torrent, I heard a horrid scraping sound rumble from below. With a loud boom, the boat lurched and tossed me down the deck. At the stern I caught the railing. Another bright streak of lightning stretched across the sky, and I saw in the crashing water below, dark, brooding shoulders of rock pushing up out of the waves.

These were the rocks that had brought down the *Argonaut,* the rocks that had drowned Captain Braga and his crew.

Another foul scraping groaned deep across the hull. The ship quailed and shivered. I clung in terror to a post of the rail. The sweeping keel struck a rock, and the tall mast pitched steeply. A wave like a mountain fell over the deck, and I held to the rail underwater. The raging torrent tugged my limbs and bore its way into my throat. For a moment I heard a terrible silence, then a sudden turbulence as the boat bobbed back to the surface. The water quickly crawled away, but my throat was still clogged with the gagging sea, and I found it impossible to breathe. I rolled onto my back, my mouth locked in a suffocated scream.

The sea rose up around me. There was nothing I could do. I stared in horror at the merciless sky. Soon the cracks of lightning no longer seemed bright but only faint fissures in a deepening dark, as if I were dying in a half-hatched egg, or coming back to life in a coffin.

THE OTHER SIDE

When the lights go out, the rules give way. Darkness discombobulates. It brings your demons out. So when the terrors finally came, they were not unexpected.

I'd had a hint of this with Eva, the lightless night spent in her room. It wasn't love I'd found in there; she'd had no soul to meet. What I had found lay in myself, my double-sided nature, half of which I had known about, half of which I hadn't. My greed for gold had made me blind, as had my lust for her. With that blindness came the dark, and with the darkness, evil.

That was all that I was left with now. My soul had fled away. An emptiness remained behind, a void of sleep that was not sleep, and dreams that were not dreams. They seemed to form from nothing, to take their shape from air. What were these ghastly creatures, emerging like a vapor? Horrid faces drawn and pale, bodies lean and beastly. I saw the gleam of horns and fangs, and mouths that ran from ear to ear, and white skull faces, eyes unblinking, bone teeth locked in grim-faced grins. Sinewy, catlike figures crept through fiery, flickering shadows, an infernal bestiary, a grotto of grotesqueries.

One of these skull-faced ghosts approached and stood there staring down at me. I detected within him some vestige of life, defying his cadaverous condition, and I thought of the revelers in Punta Perdida: skull-headed altar boys dancing in the street; bone-faced women bravely baring their breasts; devil-masked, painted men whirling their machetes. They had not strapped on blindfolds or lulled themselves to sleep. These celebrants who laughed at death wore it like a carapace; their shield of protection was the very fear itself.

The demon lowered himself beside me, and now I had a closer look at his face. I saw that beneath his bony brow, his lidless eyes were moist with life, while the back half of his cranium seemed to vanish into the dark. I thought of the skull that Duff had found half buried in the *Argonaut,* its cranial dome oddly half corroded. Had it been the skull of the notorious Captain Braga? Was this skull before me now the remnant of his face? Or was it the ghost of Hector Bellocheque, the man whose golden stroke of luck brought tragedy and death?

One man was a sinner, the other a saint. Was this a halfway house to heaven or a corridor to hell?

I reached my hand out toward him. I tried to touch his face. Was it bone? Was it air? Was it only darkness?

The demon reached his hand up and pulled his mask away. Behind it was the man from the white rowboat, the stranger who had saved me from Eva.

He took my hand. He spoke my name. The sound of his voice brought me rushing back to life.

The stranger, I realized at last, was my brother.

His hair and beard that had looked so white in the blinding light of the storm now looked merely long and filthy. His fingernails were chewed to stubs, just as they had always been. Barefoot, shirtless, in a ragged pair of cargo shorts, he looked like a derelict beach bum. Apparently he had gone for months without a single shave or shower. Yet he appeared to be as strong and fit as ever—if a little the worse for wear. A bloody bandage covered the wound at the lower back of his neck. Another nasty cut had been slashed across his forehead. His chest had been badly scraped, and his knees were bruised and raw. He had barely come out of the storm alive, yet somehow had managed to save me.

I was lying flat on a reclining deckchair beneath a turquoise Mexican blanket. The chair was set behind rows of seats on the lower deck of a boat. An engine rumbled below us; we were cruising over the ocean. The music of a mariachi band floated through the air. The setting sun cast fiery beams through gaping, glassless windows. Outside them on the deck, passengers were strolling by, wearing gaudy plastic masks, laughing drunkenly with sloshing margaritas.

My hellish bestiary was a boozy tour-boat bash.

"El Día de los Muertos," Dan said, setting down his mask. "Know what that is?"

"Do I ever," I said groggily.

"You've been drifting in and out all day. You nearly drowned last night."

I remembered the rising water. The terrifying feeling of helplessness. I lifted the blanket and saw that my chest had been thickly wrapped in gauze, with a pink bloodstain over the wound where the scissors had miraculously missed my heart. Around us, I noticed the seats were mostly empty, just a few sleepy Mexicans, and a family of obese Germans devouring a platter of enchiladas. At the front of the cabin, a cripple in a straw hat was picking up trash. The Halloween party was out on the deck. Just beyond a throng of death-masked drunks, I spotted the yellow Zodiac stacked against the rail.

"That's what saved our lives," Dan said. "The yacht went down in the rocks, but the Zodiac's unsinkable. I had to strap you into it."

I started feeling dizzy again, my thoughts in a spin. "But . . . how did we . . . ?"

"The storm passed during the night. At dawn, I headed north for Yelapa. We ran out of gas, but late this afternoon, this charter boat spotted us. They're on their way back to Puerto Vallarta."

"The gold . . ." I said.

"Went down with the ship."

This came as a kind of relief.

I tried to sit up but felt a sudden stab of pain in my chest and a sickening wave of nausea. Dan must have noticed; he quickly moved closer and guided my head back down on the deckchair. "Easy, little brother. You've lost a shitload of blood." He looked me over, then looked in my eyes again. "We'll be there in less than an hour. The captain said he'd radio ahead to have an ambulance waiting."

I closed my eyes for a moment, then opened them again. I couldn't believe I wasn't dreaming. Through the wilderness of Dan's beard, I detected a familiar grin. "You're going to make it," he said.

I looked into his crinkling eyes. They were blue, like my father's, and seeing them made me incredibly happy—I almost started to cry. "I thought . . . I thought you were dead, Daniel. I really thought you were dead."

Tears welled in his eyes. He took my hand in his and pulled it to his chest. "I'm sorry, Johnny. I didn't mean for this . . . I didn't have any idea . . ."

As he continued talking, I closed my eyes again and began at once to drift away. The darkness was seductive; it gently lured me back. Beneath its occasional terrors lay a profound tranquility, a still and lulling silence. No more the whirling coin of life, the perilous spin and fall of fate. Nothing bad could befall me now. Nothing but this happy end— my brother's resurrection, my promise made complete. *I'll just leave it at that,* I thought. *I'll just leave it at . . .*

"Wake up, Jack. Wake up." Dan was shaking my shoulders. I cracked my eyes and mumbled something.

Dan spoke sternly now. "Stay with me, goddamn it. Don't go drifting off again. Keep your eyes open. Stay focused. Don't let it pull you down, you hear?"

The death pull. For some reason I thought of a black umbrella splashed by teeming rain. Then I thought of Rock and the final word he whispered. And Duff in the child's casket burning on the pyre.

"They're dead," I murmured.

"Who?"

"Rock. And Duff."

Dan shook his head in disbelief.

"They were killed," I said.

He looked stricken. He stared at me intently before he finally spoke. "Tell me what happened, Jack. Tell me everything."

I didn't want to tell him. I didn't want to remember. The story was incredible. Who would ever believe it? I wanted to forget it all, but I knew that in forgetting I would lose myself again. I'd fade into the darkness that was luring me to sleep. So I did what he asked; I told him what had happened. Who had died, when they died, how they died, and why. I let all the darkness out; I didn't spare a thing. Nothing was forgotten or avoided or denied. I told my terrible tale of death to keep myself alive.

By the time I was through, night had fallen. Recounting the story had exhausted me, but somehow I felt more conscious and alert. Dan had listened without saying a word. Now he finally responded. "If it wasn't you telling the story . . . if I'd never been to that godforsaken place . . . if I hadn't seen the manta with my own two eyes . . . I wouldn't have believed a word of it." Then he fell silent.

We had come within sight of Puerto Vallarta, which glittered along the distant shore like the glittering stars in the sky. The band struck up a ballad, a slow and soulful tune, and the party hounds aboard the boat began to settle down. They dropped their masks and finished their drinks and fell out of their conversations, wandering now to the rails of the ship to behold their return to the world. Like diamonds around a woman's throat, the arc of glitter around the bay seemed to draw their eyes and entrance them. Daniel, too, stared out with a spellbound look of longing. I asked how long he had been away, where he had been, and why.

"I was hiding in the mountains," he told me. "I was staying at the rancho of my Huichol friend, Sebastián."

He explained that, after finding the wreck of the *Argonaut*, he had gone to Puerto Vallarta to send the letter with the coin to Bellocheque and to refill his scuba tanks. When

José found out—through Gonzalo again—that Dan was back in town, he ordered his goons to grab him.

"A deal had gone bad," Dan said. "I owed José money. A lot of money. It's why I'd run off to the mountains the first time. This time he wanted his pound of flesh. He wouldn't take any excuses. You know what he was like."

I did indeed. Apparently Dan had also come under the threat of his twirling knife.

"The only way I could think to save myself was to tell him about the gold. I didn't tell him I'd already found it, just told him I thought that I could."

He gave the cowboy enough detail to make his story convincing—the gold rush, the slave trader, the steamer's report of a storm—but he told him he thought the ship went down a whole lot closer to shore, far from its real location. "José ordered Gonzalo and his two goons to take me to Punta Perdida. Gonzalo didn't want to do it—he thought for sure I was lying—but José was a greedy bastard. He couldn't pass up the chance I was telling the truth, and he persuaded Gonzalo to take me."

Dan was stroking his beard as he spoke. For a second I flashed on Gonzalo's bearded face, gouged by the moray eel.

"We cruised down to Punta Perdida on the *Orchid* and anchored in close over the rocky point. It was late in the day, but I told them I thought we could squeeze in a dive. I went down with Gonzalo and slipped away when he wasn't watching. I swam underwater all the way in to shore and hid in the rocks until nightfall. Then I scratched up my tank and cut the harness to make it look like a shark attack. I doubted Gonzalo would buy it, but at least it would give him an excuse with José. I left the tank at the edge of the surf and snuck back into the town."

I told him his ruse might very well have worked. "I came across the same tank out about where you were anchored. I bet his goons found it on shore and brought it back to show him. Gonzalo must have taken one look and tossed it overboard."

Dan, meantime, had gone straight to his friend, Padre Ramón. "I told him what happened and said these men would come looking for me, that I had to leave immediately to hide out in the mountains."

"What about the wreck?" I asked. "What about the gold?"

"I figured José would give up on it. Like Gonzalo, he'd assume I just made the whole thing up. But I knew Bellocheque would never relent—he'd eventually find his way to Punta Perdida. So I asked the padre to come and get me the moment the old man arrived."

"But the padre . . ."

"Yeah." Dan turned suddenly pale. The thought of the padre's maiming seemed to make him physically ill. "The village of Punta Perdida is incredibly xenophobic. They don't like their citizens consorting with outsiders. They believe the sunken gold is cursed and should never be retrieved. Apparently they didn't like my returning to recover it with a boatload of thugs. They must have decided to teach the padre a lesson."

I told him that my visit with the priest must have led to his blinding.

"Padre Ramón had been sent out by the bishop in Guadalajara. Apparently, every decade or so, the diocese makes some effort to bring this wayward flock into the fold. Ramón had only been there a year or so. I don't think he was ever accepted."

I didn't understand how such cruelty was possible.

"The old priest is behind it," Dan said. "Father Four-Eyes—the one you said you saw in the parade."

"Bellocheque thought that guy was an obi-man. Direct descendant of the African slaves."

"I believe it," Dan said. "I saw him in action last night."

After hiding out for weeks in the mountains, Dan had intuited something was wrong and decided to return to the town. When he arrived, he found the padre blinded and deaf, and Bellocheque's sailboat anchored in the bay. He waited until dark, then snuck down to shore to steal a boat and investigate.

"The old priest was standing at the end of the pier with a convocation of his followers. He was chanting some Shango incantation and shaking a rattle at the air. In a matter of minutes, the wind picked up. Soon a gale was blowing. If I didn't know better, I'd say his little magic act conjured up the storm."

I had to wonder if it wasn't true. Bellocheque had suggested as much. Perhaps his great-great-grandfather, locked in shackles in the darkness of the hold, had chanted this very same supplication and brought about the *Argonaut*'s demise.

Dan had waited until the congregants dispersed, then dragged the rowboat into the water and headed out for the *Obi-man*. By the time he reached it, the storm was blasting. He climbed on board and spotted Eva bent over a body at the edge of the boat. "The last thing I expected," he said, "was to find out the body was yours."

He'd had no idea that I had come to Mexico looking for him. He had expected to find Bellocheque on the boat—not a woman committing a murder.

Eva, my killer. Seed of Captain Braga. It seemed even my lust for her had been a kind of greed.

"What about the manta ray?" I asked. "How did you avoid it when you were searching for the wreck?"

"Never crossed my path," he said.

"Never?"

"Last night was the first time I ever laid eyes on it."

I found this astonishing. All those weeks of searching and never saw it once? Of course, he had only discovered the wreck at the end of his last tank of air. He had never entered its sacrosanct darkness, broken its fatal taboo. This might have saved his life, I suppose, but for some reason I felt disappointed. It seemed to me that Dan had missed something vital, something life-giving and true. To have entered the darkness, to have found the gold, to have faced the White Devil alone—these were themselves a kind of dark treasure, a treasure far greater than glittering ore. Even now I shuddered with an exhilarating thrill.

Instinctively I reached for the cross on my neck, then remembered how Eva had thrown it into the sea. "I'd like to find the woman who gave me that cross," I said. "I think I owe her my life."

Dan shrugged. "Might have just been the reflected light," he said.

"How do you mean?"

"That manta ray was completely white—some form of albinism. Albinos lack pigment in their eyes and can be highly sensitive to light. It's called 'photophobia.' It's probably what made it so crazed by the lightning."

Dan was suspicious of anything religious. He had deliberately expunged any belief he had in God while retaining what he claimed was a purely scientific interest in "metaphysical research." He called himself a "spiritual atheist." I should not have been surprised by his albino explanation, but it was all that was needed to revive my sense of doubt, that ever-present, ever-smirking sidekick of faith.

I fell back into silence. Dan immediately sensed my gloom. He knew he had to keep my spirits up in order to keep me alive. "It'll be good to get back home," he offered cheerily.

I stirred and found his sparkling eyes. I thought of the promise I had made to my mother. "Mom will be happy to see you," I said. "She's always been worried about you." This made the two of us thoughtful. I asked him, "Why were you gone so long?"

Dan shrugged, then answered: "I was looking for something, I guess. Something . . . extraordinary."

"That's what Mom said: You were looking for something— she didn't know what. She said you didn't know, either."

Dan nodded. Then he stared at me a moment, as if he were arriving at some kind of a decision. He glanced around to make sure no one was watching, then reached down under my deckchair. He pulled out his shirt, wrapped in a bundle. "I got her a little present," he said. Again he glanced around the boat, then carefully unwrapped the shirt. Inside was a gleaming gold bar.

I sat up, astonished. "I thought we lost it all," I said.

"We haven't 'lost' anything, Jack. All that gold's still down there. It'll only be lost when it's spent."

I didn't like the sound of that. "Where did you get the bar?" I asked.

"I caught it sliding across the deck. Practically flew into my hands."

I remembered seeing the brick in the storm as Eva dragged me away. I had thought it might be the last thing I'd see, like my father with his ticking wristwatch.

Dan set the bar on my lap. I noticed at once that half of it was dark. Blood had seeped into the pores on the rough side and turned its gold sheen a burgundy black. This was the brick I had struck Eva with, the brick that had nearly killed her. Remembering that savage moment, the sudden urge to self-defense—a rage arising like a storm inside me—I felt a chill run down my spine, the freeze of recognition. This was me, this bloody bar, this face my dark reflection.

I turned it over. The bar felt enormously heavy, as if it contained some unseen weight. Its polished side, stamped with numbers, shone with a glossy golden hue, and I saw in its light my ghostly face, filled with a childlike awe. I was staring at a gash in the center of the bar, near the tiny imprint, ABADDON. I had put that gash in the bar myself, when I stabbed the eel with the switchblade. This was the bar that had dragged me underwater, the bar I'd been unwilling to release. It had dropped to the bottom when the manta engulfed me; later I recovered it and brought it to the wreck. It had raised dark suspicions of Eva, even as it shone with a pristine light. This was the very last brick from the wreck, a brick that had nearly drowned me, a brick I had used to kill. It had been a treasure and a weight and a weapon, and now it was a double-sided mirror into my soul.

How much was this bar worth now—how many breaths? How many moments? How many lives?

I looked at Dan directly. "This belongs to me," I said.

Dan expelled a quick breath in surprise. "What—?"

"You heard what I said." I didn't want to argue. I didn't want to lie. I didn't want to tell him what it was I had to do.

"Look . . . Jack. I understand, okay. What you've gone

through. My God, you nearly *died*. But . . . you've got to re-alize . . . I mean . . . I'm the one who found the wreck. I'm the one who dreamed about it. For *years*. I didn't ask you to get involved. I didn't ask your friends."

"It's mine, Dan."

"C'mon, Jack. I don't even want it for *myself*. I want to give it to Mom."

I studied him a moment. I had no doubt he was telling the truth, but he knew my mom had plenty of money. The life insurance had paid her well. "For what?" I asked.

Dan shrugged. "For . . . I don't know . . . For everything."

"For what, Dan?"

His eyes darted about. He couldn't seem to find an answer he liked.

"I know why you've been gone," I said. "I know what you've been looking for."

He stared at me without blinking.

"He's not going to come back, Dan. And you can't buy him back. Not with all the gold in the world."

He continued to stare at me a moment. All trace of expression drained out of his face. Then he lowered his gaze to the brick on my lap. The sparkle I had seen in his eyes had faded, leaving only an icy glimmer behind, a cold, intractable need. I knew it was the need to redeem himself, to expiate his guilt for our father's untimely death, but I suspected there was also something darker in the mix—the lure of the cursed gold itself, worming its way into him, planting its demon seed of greed.

It'll only be lost when it's spent, he had said. I knew another way to lose it. "I'll tell you what," I said, reaching into the Velcro pocket of my suit. "You used to say 'God' was another name for chance. Let's leave it up to God, then." I pulled out my hand and opened my palm. On it was Bellocheque's gold piece.

He recognized it the moment he took it in his hand. "Sebastián gave me this coin. Said he stole it from the church in Punta Perdida when he was just a boy." He held it up in his fingers, admiring its age and weather-beaten beauty. "This is what got the whole thing started."

"If he gave it to you, it's yours, then. Spin it on the floor. If it comes up tails, the brick is yours, too. If it comes up heads, the brick is mine."

Dan looked between the coin and me, carefully considering my offer.

I waited.

"Okay," he said at last.

He bent down and spun the coin, and I leaned from my deckchair to watch it. This time its blurring world looked different—neither a pit of darkness nor a golden ball of light. The coin was in the moment, and the moment was mine. I had made myself a part of it. Now I watched it whirl through its precarious balancing act. A temporary triumph of faith over fate.

The coin fell flat. Liberty showed her ghostly face. I thought she might be smiling.

For a long moment, Dan stared at the coin on the floor. Then he picked it up, looked it over again, and stuffed it into his pocket as he rose to his feet. He leaned over and carefully covered the brick on my lap with his shirt. "I hope you know how to get it over the border," he said.

"No problemo," I assured him.

Dan rolled his eyes despairingly. *"No hay problema,"* he corrected.

"I better let you do the talking."

He allowed a tiny grin. "I guess you are going to make it," he said. "I'm almost sorry to see it."

I laughed. It hurt to laugh. It felt like I hadn't laughed in years.

Dan leaned out through a window and peered at the distant shore. He came back and looked me over again. "I'm going to check with the captain," he said. "See if they got hold of that ambulance. They said I need to fill out a form." He nodded toward the brick, still covered by his shirt. "Make sure you keep that out of sight."

"Don't worry," I said. "I will."

He headed off.

Few people were left in the cabin. The German family had gone outside; only a few old-timers remained, slumped and snoozing obliviously, and a Mexican girl, lost in a book, in a row of seats up front. The music had stopped, and everyone else was standing outside, watching the lights of the city draw closer. No one took notice when I sat up in the chair and dropped my feet to the floor. My feet were bare, and the floor felt warm, as if it were heated by the rumbling below. I pulled the blanket over my shoulders and gathered it around me like a cape. Then, using all the strength I could muster, I took hold of the brick in my lap and slowly struggled to my feet.

The pain in my chest was excruciating. I teetered at the bedside for a dizzy moment and glanced around the room. Again it appeared that no one had noticed my arduous rise from the dead. But as I turned and started toward the exit at the rear, holding the weight of the brick in my arms, I felt a light touch on my shoulder.

"Señor?"

It was the young Mexican woman, the one who'd been reading a book. "Would you like for me to bring you something?"

I had not seen her face before and found it rather striking. It took me a moment to respond. "No. *Gracias*. I'm just . . . getting some air."

"You are okay?"

She was wearing a sleeveless ivory dress with a square-cut neckline, and my eyes were drawn to the tiny silver cross that lay below the hollow of her throat. It hung from a slender silver chain and barely reflected the lamplight. Unlike my gaudy, guardian bling, this delicate cross was unimposing, a modest affirmation of an intimate faith. It reminded me of the one I had seen on the girl I passed on the Malecón, what seemed like a lifetime ago. In that weary hotel worker's glance I had caught a hint of the darkness to come, a glimpse into the mystery of death itself. This girl's eyes gave no such hint. They were fully alive and engaging, bright and disarmingly beautiful. Honey-colored irises afloat in a pearly white; attentive pupils following my every move and thought. She was smiling slightly, hesitantly, waiting for my answer, which creased the corners of the eyes and lent them a generous warmth.

Another kind of guardian altogether, I thought. Hunched and sweating, concealing the shrouded brick, I found myself smiling back at her. "Yes. I'm okay. Thank you." I noticed the worn cloth book in her hand, her index finger inserted to hold the page where she had left off.

She saw me looking and showed the cover: *Huckleberry Finn,* in English. "I am trying to better my speaking," she said.

"Good place to start," I told her. "But your English is already better than Huck's."

She smiled shyly, then eyed me again. She still seemed uncertain I could make it on my own. I grinned in assurance, then waited until she turned away and headed back up the aisle. She glanced at me and smiled again before turning to take her seat. I noticed that her hair was braided and pinned in a whorl at the back of her head. It was elegant yet ordinary, and somehow curiously charming.

I wanted to ask her name.

The effort to stand was tiring; the brick was dragging me down. I renewed my grip on the bundle, then turned and started again toward the rear. A breeze was blowing in through the door, carrying a mix of diesel fumes and the charred scent of fajitas. I shuffled down the trembling aisle and stepped out through the exit. The low rumble of the motor gave way to the muffled drone of propellers. This dim lower deck at the stern of the boat seemed to ride just over the water, where a tumbling wake of widening waves reached out to embrace the darkness. Except for the old man bundling trash, no one occupied the stern; all were gathered at the prow and the top deck to watch the approach to the shore.

I was shaking as I slowly crossed toward the rail. The weight of the brick seemed to grow with each step, and my rubbery legs went wobbly. My heart seemed to thump against the hole in my chest, angrily pounding at the wound from within. A rivulet of blood had escaped from the bandage and was trickling its way down my ribs. Little drops fell like tears to my feet. I looked out into the black sky and searched for the black horizon, but the sea and the sky had merged with each other, and the boat itself seemed to merge in with it, and suddenly I found there was nothing to hold me, nothing to keep me from falling.

I heard the wrapped brick thud to the deck. Then everything went silent as I crumpled.

For a while I remained exactly as I fell, lying with my cheek to the floor. The pain was so great that my mind seemed to leave it, to depart from my body altogether. Soon I felt the heat of the sun on my back, and lifting my head I realized I was lying on Sand Fly Beach. I saw my father rise out of the water, tanned and strong and smiling. I saw Rock with his stick and Duff with his camera, chasing their way down the beach. Sunning herself on a blanket nearby was the Mexican girl with her book. She beckoned for me to join her. I started crawling toward her across the scorching sand, but something was pulling me, tugging me back. Something unfinished was nagging.

I woke up. The man with the sack of garbage had crouched beside me and taken my arm in his grip. The elderly Mexican was surprisingly strong; he practically lifted me up. I knelt on the deck for a moment. My head began to clear. Though I couldn't see his eyes beneath the shadow of his hat, I thought somehow the man looked familiar. He helped me back up to my feet. The two of us spotted the wrapped bundle lying on the floor between us. Before I could move to retrieve it, the old man was bending down.

"Please—"

He stopped when he felt its massive weight. I stared at the man's bent back.

"Just leave it. Please."

He ignored me and picked it up and held it in his hands. The weight seemed to drag down the angle of his shoulders, as if he could barely support it. The bar was still wrapped tight in the shirt, and nothing of it was showing, but I sensed that the man knew exactly what it was, and the look on his face confirmed it. The straw brim tilted to reveal his eyes. They were filled with grave suspicion.

"*Gracias,*" I said, and held out my hands.

The man now seemed to recognize me. He looked again at the bundle, then turned to peer at the water off the stern. When his gaze finally returned to me, his eyes appeared less wary.

He handed me the bundle.

"*Gracias,*" I said.

His eyes held mine. He reached to tip his tattered hat. "*Señor,*" he said, nodding.

It wasn't until he turned and hobbled off with his sack that I recalled where it was I had seen him. He had been the oldest of the boatmen in Boca, the one who had told Bellocheque about *el Diablo Blanco,* the one who had so adamantly refused all my offers.

We no take you to Punta Perdida, he had said. *Not for any kind of money.*

I was alone now in the dim light of the stern, with only the cool shimmer of the stars overhead. I tightened the blanket around my shoulders and continued my march to the rail. Bent and shuffling beneath my shroud, cradling the swaddled gold, I felt like a pilgrim partaking in some arcane religious rite, with the droning engine my crooning choir and the gazing stars my witness. My pilgrimage would end here at this altar on the sea. Pallbearer of a bloody brick, a bitter gift to Hades.

Below, the tumbling water opened in welcoming profusion. The deepest grave on earth, I thought. A fitting tomb for a cursed stone.

Dan, I knew, would never understand. He would tell me it was worth far more than I had thought. He would tell me how they lied. Underestimated. That brick, he'd say, would bring a million. Maybe two or three.

And it will not end there, of course. He'll want to take another chance, spin the coin again. He'll tell me we can find the ship just like we found the *Argonaut*. No reason not to try it. All that gold is out there, Jack. All that gold just waiting.

He'll never understand.

I had reached the heights of heaven, plumbed the depths of hell. I had lost my soul and broken my heart and passed through the portal of death. My dearest friends had given their lives—how many more would follow? If a coin had been the start of it, this brick must be its end. Sometimes it takes a devil's trick to do an angel's work.

I set my bundle atop the rail and stared into the dreamlike tumult of the wake. The muscled waves and boiling foam seemed the work of a cosmic compulsion, extracting the starry light from the sky and folding it endlessly into the dark. This was the matter and the method of Creation, the alchemy of life and death, turning stardust into gold, and gold back into night.

All our lives are in the end a kind of sacrifice. A story tendered to the night. A treasure to be lost.

I unwrapped the glowing bar and held it over the water. It lay in my open hands like a prayer. Let this be my offering, my requiem, my story. A debt paid to those who died. A lease to go on living. A bit of gold ripped from my heart to give back to the stars.

I looked at those stars now, dazzling in the sky, and felt a kind of clarity I had never known before. The unknown dark, I realized, abounds with unseen light. I thought of my father, and of Rock and Duff, and knew I would one day join them.

One day. One moment.

I inhaled a precious breath of air, and gave it back again. A girl was waiting for me. Time was passing by.

"I am alive," I whispered, and gave my gold to the sea.